S0-AYX-793

Conviction of Innocence

Conviction of Innocence

by

Chet Pleban

Gypsy Shadow Publishing

Conviction of Innocence
by
Chet Pleban

All rights reserved
Copyright © October 13, 2014, Chet Pleban
Cover Art Copyright © 2014, Charlotte Holley
Cover Photo and Author picture by Bill Streeter, www.
HydraulicPictures.com

Gypsy Shadow Publishing, LLC.
Lockhart, TX
www.gypsyshadow.com

Names, characters and incidents depicted in this book are products of the author's imagination, or are used fictitiously. Any resemblance to actual events, locales, organizations, or persons, living or dead, is entirely coincidental and beyond the intent of the author or the publisher.

No part of this book may be reproduced or shared by any electronic or mechanical means, including but not limited to printing, file sharing, and email, without prior written permission from Gypsy Shadow Publishing, LLC.

Library of Congress Control Number: 201

eBook ISBN: 978-1-61950--235-2
Print ISBN: 978-1-61950-236-9

Published in the United States of America

First eBook Edition: November 1, 2014
First Print Edition: November 25, 2014

Dedication

To all who have been the victims of injustice.

Chapter One

The 11 p.m. to 7 a.m. shift on April 23rd began like any night in the 7th district of the St. Louis Police Department: several peace disturbances, a traffic stop but mostly routine patrol for ten-year Patrolman Robert Decker and his inexperienced young partner, David Dombrowski.

Decker was grateful for the calm. Night watch in the 7th could bring anything from premeditated homicide to a drug deal gone bad, a random knife fight when the bars closed, a domestic dispute that turned ugly. Summer was the worst time of year. In the swelter of July and August, violence flared fast. But this was a damp spring night, the air cool against his skin. He was already looking forward to going home.

There'd been a time—five maybe six years ago—when Decker craved action. He used to *volunteer* for the 11-to-7, knowing that's when he'd find the most crime. "That's who I'm," he'd tease his worried mother. "I'm a crime fighter." The bravado was only half joke.

But now he was getting older—calmer, more mature, more resigned. And a whole lot less idealistic than Dombrowski, who'd only been on the job two years. Decker had to hide a grin every time Dombrowski blurted, "You're never gonna believe this one." Decker would. He'd seen it all. A guy's leg shot off. A decapitation. He'd held rape victims in his arms until their sobs quieted. He'd tried to comfort a mother who'd just lost her 10-year-old son to a stray bullet. Bobby Decker had seen it all.

Comfort wasn't always possible. He coped by making arrests, nailing the bastards who were responsible. Decker felt a weird thrill when he looked straight into the eyes of people who'd committed heinous acts of cruelty without a flicker of remorse. The worst of them, he thought of as something less than human—as animals that should be kept in cages, or better yet, in graves.

Sometimes those thoughts worried him. He could still hear the Jesuit priests who'd taught him in high school, talking about *the dignity of every human person.* Was he becoming just like those he hunted?

The worry passed fast; all he had to do was summon the memory of a rape victim trembling convulsively, or a three-year-old whose face was bruised and swollen from repeated beatings, or any one of the cops, three of them, men he'd known and joked with, who'd fallen victim while trying to stop these animals.

Tonight, though, Decker's mind was as quiet as the streets. This would be an easy night.

At 11:40 p.m., Decker and Dombrowski heard a call come over the radio for Officer Jake Corbett, a 12-year veteran, and his partner, Art Roughland, a rookie still on probation. A burglary alarm at a pawn shop, 2540 Chippewa on the south side of the city. Decker knew the building. It took up half the block. Sighing, he radioed in that they'd assist.

"Thought we were going to make it through the night without any bullshit," he grumbled, making a U-turn on Kingshighway and heading for Chippewa. "What kind of idiot would rob a pawn shop in the middle of the night?" He answered his own question: "Probably some doper, too strung out to realize pawn brokers lock up the gold chains when they close."

"Maybe the alarm's just not working," Dombrowski said.

"That's what we're hoping for."

They parked next to Corbett's marked car. He and Roughland had just arrived.

"I asked if they knew anything else," Corbett told them, keeping his voice low. "The dispatcher said the alarm was activated by a motion detector in the office, which is up on the second floor."

"Why didn't she say so earlier?" Decker asked. "The security company ought to be the one showing up. It's their system that's defective, my guess."

False alarms happened so often his captain had once suggested, only half joking, that they charge to answer the calls. It really was a poor use of police time, especially on nights when all hell was breaking loose in a different part of town.

Decker turned back to the car and grabbed his portable radio and flashlight. It was starting to rain and, mumbling, he threw on a police jacket. He didn't bother with a hat. He joined Corbett, who was dressed the same way and carrying his own flashlight. They told their partners to stand guard and started searching the premises, looking for any sign of activity that would have triggered the alarm system's motion sensor.

While Corbett checked the front door to see if it was secure, Decker looked in the pawn shop's display window. He saw only a dark blur of shelves and TV sets and a slant of light, a streetlight reflected in the front of a glass case. "The door's secure," Corbett called. They listened for half a minute. No alarm was sounding now. An engine turned over and roared, without benefit of a muffler, a few blocks away. Silence fell again.

Decker gestured with his head, and they walked to the rear of the building to check the back door and the alley. The door was secure; the alley was quiet. They returned to the front of the shop. As Corbett reached for his portable radio to contact the dispatcher, intending to clear the call and report that the building was secure, he saw what looked like a young, thin black male silhouetted on the roof of the building. He slashed his arm upward, shining his flashlight across the roof, and saw a figure duck behind a five-foot wall that appeared to separate the pawn shop roof from the roof of the company next door. Corbett told the dispatcher and Decker what he'd seen. "How the hell did they get up there?"

"Stay here," Decker said. "Let me look in back again. We need to make sure they have no way off that roof."

Three minutes later, Decker was back. "There's no way up—no ladder, no fire escape—and the pawn shop windows and door are all locked. I don't get it."

"We've got to go up there," Corbett said, wiping rain from his forehead. "We're gonna need some assistance." He called the dispatcher again. "Get us a fire truck with an extension ladder."

Decker could still see one of the figures on the roof. "Get down here!" he yelled. *"Police!"*

He expected no response, and he got none. The figure stepped back, out of his sightline. "Hey Dombrowski," he called. "You two secure the back of the building. We'll stay out here." Nobody was leaving.

As he stood in the light rain, squinting up at the roof, Decker wondered what they'd find up there. How many perps? Were they armed? Would they fire? They would if they were strung out on drugs or booze, fearless. A cop's worst nightmare.

"We've got to find a way to get up there without getting ambushed," he told Corbett, who just nodded. They waited, not speaking.

Finally the ladder truck pulled up. The fire department took its sweet time responding to calls for assistance; there was no love lost between firefighters and cops. The delay had bought Decker time to plan, though. He had a terse conversation with the driver, pointing to the exact place where he wanted to enter the roof.

When the ladder was in place, Decker started up, flashlight in hand. Corbett stayed close, less than a foot behind him. Just below the roofline, they paused and drew their service revolvers. Decker took the next step and slowly, carefully, raised his head above the wall.

Quickly scanning the entire roof, he saw a large structure jutting out of the roof. Turning and talking to the man who stood a few rungs below him, Decker told Corbett, "It looks like a skylight about 50 yards away that we can use for a little cover. It's not much, but it's all we have. We need to move quickly." Both stepped onto the roof, hearts pounding, and ran to the skylight, watching for any activity on the upper roof.

A section of the glass had been smashed. Corbett shone his flashlight through the broken window as Decker continued to watch the upper roof. "Here's how they got on the roof. There is an extension ladder they hooked onto this skylight," Corbett reported.

"Does this go into the pawn shop?" Decker asked in a low voice. "Is that how they got in?"

"No, I don't think so. Looks like some kind of garage storage area for the welding shop."

4

Corbett called for an assist. He gave the dispatcher the information about the ladder and storage area and asked for the location to be secured. Now they had to figure out a way to get the suspect off of the upper roof and into handcuffs.

The building was occupied by three businesses: a muffler shop, a welding company and the pawn shop. Each had its own skylight. The higher roof belonged to the pawn shop. Decker looked beyond it. To the south of the pawn shop, east of the welding company, there was a two-story building with a second story-porch. It wasn't connected to either building, but it stood less than five feet from both.

"Police! We know you are on the upper roof. Show yourself with your hands in the air," Decker yelled from his position behind the skylight now some 25 yards away. No response. He waited a few beats, then said, "There is no way out. Make this easy on yourself. Stand up with your hands in the air." Still no response. "*Comeoutnow.*" After the third command, a head rose above the wall dividing the roofs. Decker held his breath until he saw the top of the suspect's body emerge, hands out to his sides. The guy turned to his left and started talking to someone. Great—somebody else was with him. Decker craned, but couldn't see the other figure. "Remember what I said," the guy told his companion. "Come on. It's okay."

A second man stood up. He began to back away from the officers, moving closer to the north edge of the upper roof. Decker saw him look over the edge at the ground below. "Back away from the edge!" Decker yelled. "Walk toward us."

He hesitated, then came toward them, moving slowly.

"Get your ass down here!" Decker yelled. "I'm tired of standing in the rain, and I'm not fucking around with you. Right now!" Without looking at Corbett, he said in a low voice, "You take the one on the left, and I'll take the one on the right." Then he yelled again: "How many are up there with you?"

No answer. Both men stood on the upper roof with their arms in the air and their eyes fixed on the officers.

"I said is there anyone else with you? *Answer* me!"

"No," Corbett's suspect replied.

As Decker and Corbett moved toward the upper roof, weapons pointed at the suspects, Decker saw them more clearly. Both were black males, short, 5-foot-8 or less; thin, no more than 150 pounds; young, in their late teens or early twenties and dressed in dark clothing, no hats. "Slowly, v-e-r-y slowly, both of you climb down from there and keep your hands where we can see them," he directed, shining his flashlight into the eyes of his suspect. They shone, fierce and feral. *He's high; maybe crazy, too,* Decker thought. *Expect anything.*

The two suspects hoisted themselves up, so they could climb over the wall and lower themselves to the roof below. Decker holstered his weapon, preparing to grab and handcuff the suspect when his feet hit the ground. But the minute their feet hit the lower roof, the two bolted in opposite directions, separating Corbett and Decker as they gave chase. Decker's suspect headed for the second-story porch. *I've got to catch him before he hits that porch,* Decker thought. With just a few feet to spare and flashlight still in hand, he grabbed the suspect, pushed him into the south end of the wall, then threw him to the ground.

Corbett was still chasing his guy, who'd headed for the skylight and the ladder they'd left there. Realizing he was going to lose the foot race, Corbett shouted, "Stop or I'll shoot!" The suspect froze. "Get down on the ground and put your hands behind your back." He slowly went to his knees—and stayed there.

"I told you to get down on the ground and put your hands behind your back," Corbett yelled.

"I'm goin', man. Don't shoot. I don't have no gun." The suspect lowered himself, face down, onto the shingles.

As he approached, Corbett holstered his gun, took out his handcuffs and snapped them around the man's wrists. He pulled the man to his feet and walked him toward Decker, whose suspect was still lying on the roof. It was raining harder now, and Corbett could barely make out the figure's outline. He heard Decker telling the dispatcher, "We're gonna need an ambulance."

"What happened?" Corbett asked. Decker's suspect was lying on his back, eyes closed, his breath shallow.

"I don't know," Decker said, his voice shaking. "I don't *know.*"

Chapter Two

Bobby Decker started dreaming of life as a big-city police officer when he was five. Playing cops and robbers, he had to be the one who made the arrest. Through high school and college, the dream never wavered. He earned a bachelor's in criminal justice at Villanova University. The day after graduation, he applied for a position with the St. Louis Police Department.

His father, Ralph, a CPA who did the books for all the big shots in St. Louis, voted for liberal Democrats and socialized in the west county suburbs. He was not thrilled with his son's career plans. Decker's mother, Barbara, a teacher by trade and now a homemaker, who'd been a concert pianist, had just breathed a sigh of relief that her two boys' Prom-drunk, car-wrecking, football-concussion days were over. Now, something new to worry her. She feared the worst.

"Why do you want to risk your life every day you leave your house?" she demanded.

His father was a bit more direct. "Bobby, I *really* don't want you to be a police officer. The pay's low, the job's dangerous, and nobody appreciates what you do for them. You're interested in justice, and I admire that. So we'll pay for you to go to law school, just like we did for Jeff."

Decker's older brother had graduated from Georgetown University's law school. He did a lot of the pro bono work for one of the big downtown law firms, representing arts organizations and churches and people who'd grown up near Superfund sites and now had cancer.

Decker took a deep breath. "Jeff's great at what he does. But we're very different."

His parents were wasting their breath; his mind was made up. It had always been made up. He didn't know quite how to put this respectfully, but his parents' comfortable life in the suburbs wasn't enough of a dream for him. And God knows, the world didn't need another lawyer.

He got his acceptance letter two weeks after he applied. He'd start his seven months at the police academy in September, and he'd spend the first six weeks in the classroom.

Decker groaned. He'd seen enough classrooms. He'd just spent four years learning, analyzing, and dissecting theory; now he wanted reality. He wanted to be on the street, where the action was.

But the six weeks were non-negotiable.

Classes started with patrol, juvenile procedures, and report writing. Decker's brain went numb. He started making up scenarios in his head, imagining himself rounding up a juvenile gang or finding a killer during a routine traffic stop. He loved pulling the regulation blue T-shirt over his head, tucking it into his cargo pants, and walking into the classroom. But he still wasn't wild about sitting on his butt for the next eight hours.

It got better with the class on interrogation techniques. They learned a long list of gestures, eye movements, and verbal tics—like repeating the question or prefacing their answer with *honestly*—which could tip them off that a suspect was bullshitting. The firearms class was even cooler. He developed a healthy respect for the Glock he'd been issued and learned to control his breathing and use only the pad of his index finger on the trigger. He qualified to carry an ASP baton, a lethal little telescoping metal stick that could easily kill or seriously injure someone. He learned how to subdue and restrain his classmates, who stood in for suspects in hand-to-hand combat training.

Their instructors devoted quite a few hours to the legal aspects of policing, lecturing about the legal restrictions for probable cause; search and seizure; stop and frisk; inventory searches; Miranda warnings; arrest with and without a warrant; use of force, both deadly and otherwise; and pursuits, foot and vehicle. Bored and worried at the same time, Decker asked no questions, just wrote down everything they said. He wanted to get it right. He wanted to make sure he didn't screw up. But most of all, he didn't want a bad guy to walk, as the defense lawyers put it, just because Bobby Decker didn't know the rules of the game.

They took weekly exams and daily quizzes. Getting hired as a St. Louis police officer didn't mean you'd automatically wear the badge. You had to earn it. And here in the classroom, right and wrong answers were easy to distinguish.

Just over half of Decker's classmates were white guys, a third were black, maybe 15 percent were women. At 6-foot-3 and 226 muscular pounds, he fit in easily; nobody hazed him or worried he couldn't handle the toughest parts of the job. He tried to show the same confidence in the female students, just on principle. Then Jenny Garcia, 5-foot-2 with soft, curly hair, beat him at handball, and he realized he'd been patronizing them.

Race came up only once, when Sgt. James Morton, a tall, lean black man with the raw eloquence of an untrained poet, warned them about the hostility between the police department and the black community. "That is the phrase I'll use. Mind you, there is no actual *black community* in St. Louis. There are black folks of every class and kind. But St. Louis is still one of the most segregated cities in the nation, and when class and race come together, on the North Side and the Near West Side, you have what is politely called *the black community.* It's poor, uneducated, drug-ridden, gang-ridden, and wary of any outsider. Especially the po-lice." He hit the first syllable hard, driving home his point. "Every action you take, every word you speak, has to be carefully chosen with that tension in mind. Or you'll make it even worse for all of us."

The next session was on crowd control—specifically, how to handle spontaneous, explosive violence. How to quell a riot. How to calm an angry group feeding off each other's paranoia. The black and white students each kept their eyes on the instructor, instead of trading looks and cracking jokes under their breath as they usually did. The class ended with some sobering statistics about fatalities—police and civilian—in mob incidents.

This was exactly what Bobby's parents were talking about. They knew St. Louis wasn't just a baseball-crazed, wholesome Midwestern city with almost 250 years of history behind its red brick homes and Victorian parks. A lot of hatred was still pent up in this half-Northern, half-South-ern city, and they didn't want their son even to have to see, let alone experience, its increasingly frequent, increasingly violent eruptions.

What they didn't realize, safe in their suburban ranch home, was that the threat of danger *drove* their son. He wanted to prevent violence whenever he could. But above all, he wanted justice for every victim. And he didn't care what race they were.

Chapter Three

Graduation day finally arrived. Decker had passed every class, shot 12 bull's eyes, memorized the laws and procedures he'd need. His real life was about to begin. He sat with the rest of his class, listening to the preliminary speeches while his heart raced to different thoughts entirely. What if he failed? He didn't care if he got shot—not unless the bullet left him paralyzed. The possibility of dying didn't even occur to him. But he didn't want to screw up, make some bone ass mistake that cancelled any chance of justice. And he didn't want to shame his fellow officers.

The music started, and he saw Garcia, three seats away, tugging sharply on the sleeves of her light-blue uniform shirt, smoothing the wrinkles. The row rose and formed a line to the side of the stage. Gary Appelbaum was the first to climb the stairs. He crossed the stage, and accepted what they'd all been waiting for: the shiny silver badge.

Two more people, and then it was Decker's turn. The Chief smiled, eyes crinkling, as he handed over the badge. Decker glanced down fast—he'd study it later, feel the seal and inscription, let it flash in the light. For now, he just wanted to reassure himself it was solid and real. This small object gave him full authority to question, arrest, and charge.

After the last person crossed the stage, they stood together and took their oath. They swore to uphold the constitutions of both the United States and the great State of Missouri. They swore to protect those who needed protection without limitation, equally and fairly. Privately, they swore loyalty to each other, and to the job. They were a family, a police family, a brotherhood.

Decker looked into the crowd, wondering where his family was. During the weeks of his academy training, his relationship with his father had been strained at best. He knew his dad loved him and wanted nothing but the best for him. He just couldn't understand why his father refused to accept his career choice. It was more than the dangers of the job, had to be.

Didn't matter. He'd make his dad proud. Show him police officers dedicated their lives to helping people, often those who could not help themselves. Life behind the badge was honorable. More honorable than accounting, he'd bet—but he wouldn't press it that far. No criticism. He just wanted to save his piece of the world.

When the ceremony ended and the crowd made their way to the exits, Decker scanned the crowd more carefully. Was that his mother's blue blazer? She'd bought it in his honor, she'd told him that morning. She hugged him hard, her Shalimar wafting over him, and whispered, "I'm so proud of you." But her eyes were unable to shield the fear she felt inside.

"Nice ceremony," Jeff said. "Could've used an intermission."

"Right," Decker said absently. "Where's Dad?"

"He couldn't make it," Decker's mother said. She started to add something, but stopped. Jeff looked away.

So my father was that disappointed, Decker thought. He swallowed hard.

"I think champagne's in order," Jeff said. "How about brunch at Balaban's? I'm buying."

Jeff just grinned and suggested they all ride together to the restaurant. As he slid his Prius into an improbably narrow slot along the curb, he asked, "Where will you be assigned?"

"Fourth district," Decker replied.

"Where's that?" Jeff asked.

"Downtown." He saw his mother shut her eyes. "Don't worry, Mom. The down side is that it's *not* dangerous. We're talking City Hall, Busch Stadium, all the business execs in the high rises, all the hipsters in the loft district."

"Actually, that's great," Jeff said. "You'll get to know the business leaders. And if they like you, it will help you get a promotion when the time comes."

"Right," Decker said, uninterested. "The way I look at it, I'm in this job to reduce crime. That means going where the crime is—which is not in the polished streets of downtown St. Louis. It's a good place to get my feet wet, but I'll be hoping for a transfer."

"Do me a favor, Bobby," Jeff said. "Don't say that to Dad. It'll only make things worse—for all of us." Their mother was nodding fast.

Decker walked ahead of them into the restaurant, not ready to answer. When they were seated, Jeff went back to his earlier, casual interest: "When do you start?"

"Seven tomorrow morning."

"Have you got a partner? Surely they won't let you run wild in the streets of St. Louis alone."

"Very funny. I'm sure I'll be riding with somebody; I just don't know who yet."

"What about job security?" Jeff was the lawyer of the family for good reason. "What happens if you screw up?"

"Jeffrey, your language," their mother injected. Barbara was forever correcting both the language and the conduct of her boys. She considered it her full time job.

"I'm not planning to screw up," Decker replied. "Apparently, I have the right to some kind of public trial before they can fire me or discipline me. The department has to prove I screwed up. But frankly, I didn't pay a lot of attention to that when we covered it."

"Never hurts to know your options," Jeff said with a shrug, shoving a menu in the direction of his younger brother and ending all job-related conversation.

Chapter Four

The rain continued to fall as Jake Corbett and Bobby Decker stood on the roof with their suspects, handcuffed and in custody. As Bobby stared at his suspect lying motionless on his back, Jake contacted the dispatcher requesting a bucket lift from the fire department to remove the handcuffed suspects from the roof.

Meanwhile, Corbett's suspect, also lying on his back next to his accomplice, raised his head and said to Decker, "You shouldn't have hit him like that; he's not moving. You really hurt him. You didn't have to do that. We weren't doin' nothin'."

"Shut the fuck up or you'll get some of the same," Bobby shouted.

"Relax," Jake said, trying to calm the situation. "Let's just get these shitheads off this roof," he added.

Grabbing Bobby's arm and stepping away from the suspects, Jake again asked, "What happened? Why do we need an ambulance for this guy? He doesn't look like he is injured."

"I don't know. He was moving and jerking all around after I subdued him. He threw up a little, but I just figured it was from the dope he probably took, because I didn't smell any alcohol. Now he is just lying there and it looks like he is unconscious," Bobby said.

Decker's conversation with Corbett was interrupted by a radio call from one of the officers who'd come to assist. John Gleason and his partner, Derrick Johnson, were assigned to secure the scene below. They reported the suspects had broken into the garage where the welding company stored their tools. No alarm secured those premises. Access to the roof was gained through the broken skylight and the ladder that Corbett saw. The pawn shop was entered through a skylight above their second floor offices. No alarm sounded when that glass was broken. *A very elabo-*

rate scheme to avoid detection, Corbett thought. He told the officers on the ground he had two in custody on the roof awaiting a ride to the bottom. He didn't mention they also awaited the arrival of an ambulance. He thought that might be a conversation better reserved for a different time and place.

"What's your name?" Corbett asked the suspect he had arrested.

"Why? We didn't do nothin'. Why are we handcuffed? These things are hurting me," the unidentified suspect added.

"Let's start with who you are and then we can get to why you're cuffed," Corbett said.

"Jones, Daniels Jones."

"Daniels with an *s?* You have two last names?" Corbett asked.

"Why, are you making fun of my name?"

"I'm not making fun of anything. I'm trying to figure out whether you are feeding me a line of shit or whether your name is really Daniels Jones."

"That's really my name," Jones replied.

"Yeah, I guess that would be a hard thing to make up. What were you and your buddy doing up here?" Corbett asked.

"We were trying to find our way home and got lost," Jones said sarcastically.

"See, that's the kind of shit that really pisses me off, Daniels. A guy in your situation can't afford to be a comedian. What do you have in your pockets?" Corbett asked as he knelt beside him and put his hand in one of the oversized pockets of the suspect's cargo pants.

"Get your fuckin' hand out of my pocket!" Jones demanded.

"Well, what do we have here?" Corbett asked rhetorically as he removed a handful of items. "Let's see. Looks like we have some jewelry: rings, wedding bands; looks like women's rings," Corbett said as he counted the items in his hand. "Looks like we have 24 rings, 12 wedding bands, and 12 fancy women's rings with some kind of stones in them. Planning on marrying 12 different women, Daniels?" Corbett asked with equal sarcasm. "Do you want to tell me where you got this stuff, Daniels?"

15

"Like you said, I'm getting married. A guy like me satisfies a lot of women," Daniels said, trading sarcasm with the officer.

"You won't have to worry about satisfying women where you're going, Daniels. It's the boys you're going to have to worry about," Corbett said as he searched another pocket. "Well, look at this, more jewelry. Looks like necklaces and earrings. Wow! The boys are going to love you, Daniels. Maybe you can model this stuff for the gang in your cell block," Corbett said with a smile. "I'm going to ask you one more time, where did you get this stuff? You could do yourself some good and tell me the whole story. You would also be helping your buddy over there."

"Fuck you, I'm done talkin' to you. Besides, you haven't read me my rights," Jones said, this time without sarcasm.

"Suit yourself. We're not going to need any help from you. We like it when dumb shits like you get caught with their hand in the cookie jar. You do know we will be able to prove this stuff came from the pawn shop."

"I told you, I'm not talking to you, man. I want a lawyer."

"I doubt any lawyer is going to help you, Daniels, my man," Corbett said shaking his head.

"Jake, I think our ride is here," Bobby said, looking over the edge of the roof.

Chapter Five

The *St. Louis Post-Dispatch* already had a short article about the pawn shop burglary, and it was not police friendly. The headline read, "Suspect in Pawn Shop Burglary in Intensive Care." The story said that Jordon Mitchell, a 19 year-old black male, was in the intensive care unit of St. Louis University Hospital in critical condition after suffering a massive skull fracture. Mitchell and Daniels Jones were arrested by police officers Robert Decker and Jake Corbett on suspicion of the burglary of the JC Pawn Shop at 2540 Chippewa in the city of St. Louis. Physicians responsible for the care of Mitchell explained they were attempting to control brain swelling and the next 48 to 72 hours would be critical. The public relations officer for the Department indicated both suspects were apprehended on the roof of the pawn shop after an attempted burglary of that establishment. No additional details were known, but the article indicated the investigation of the incident would continue.

Mitchell's mother, Vera Mitchell, was already publically condemning the actions of the police officers. She appeared that morning on a radio talk show hosted by a black civil rights activist, Liz Barron, who made no secret of her complete disdain for the St. Louis Police Department and everyone in it.

It was 10 in the morning and Bobby had been to sleep for less than an hour when his phone rang. "Did you see the paper this morning?" Bobby heard an unidentified voice ask.

"What?" Bobby replied, still half asleep.

"Did you see the paper this morning?" the voice repeated.

"No. Why?" Bobby replied, recognizing the voice of his lawyer brother, Jeff, and pretending he had no idea of what could be in the paper.

"It's not good," Jeff said, trying to hide the concern in his voice. "According to the article, you and Officer Jake Corbett arrested some guys who were burglarizing a pawn shop someplace in the City and one of the guys wound up in the hospital. In fact, he is in intensive care and it doesn't look good. What the hell is going on?"

But before Bobby could answer, Jeff went on. "If that is not enough, some of the lawyers in my office said they were talking about you on some radio show. Apparently, Liz Barron was excoriating you on her show, claiming you violated the civil rights of this guy in the hospital; smashed his skull for no reason, and solely because he was black. The guy's mother was also on and she had nothing good to say about you. What's going on, Bobby? How did this guy get his skull cracked to the point where he might die?"

"I don't know," Bobby replied slowly and quietly.

"What do you mean you don't know?" Jeff pressed. "You were there, weren't you?"

"Yes, but I don't know."

"What is the police department doing? They said they were continuing the investigation," Jeff continued. "What does that mean?" he asked.

"I don't know," Bobby answered.

Not satisfied with the response, Jeff pressed again. "This sounds serious, Bobby, and you have got to treat it seriously. Let me ask again. How did this guy get a massive skull fracture that you wouldn't know about?"

"I don't know," Bobby repeated. "I have to go." With those words, Bobby ended the call with his concerned brother. He didn't go back to sleep.

Chapter Six

Whenever a city police officer makes an arrest, a report detailing the activities of that arrest must be prepared by the arresting officer. This case was no different. Bobby Decker and Jake Corbett would be the officers responsible. Because other duties and responsibilities prevented the preparation of this report the night of the arrest, Decker and Corbett decided to come to the station before the start of their next shift to begin the preparation process. Police reports generally are important because they serve to refresh recollections when the case comes to court, which sometimes can be years later.

The reports are also disclosed to the lawyers who represent the criminal defendants and can be used to cross examine the arresting officers during the trial. Testimony that differs from the report will be used by defense attorneys to suggest the police officers are mistaken, not worthy of belief, or worse, liars. The report detailing the arrests of Jordon Mitchell and Daniels Jones would be like no other Bobby Decker had ever written. Unknown at the time, this document would change Bobby Decker's life forever.

After reading the *Post* article, additional sleep was not going to happen. He decided to go to the station, arriving several hours earlier than he and Corbett had planned. With a limited amount of sleep, Bobby opened the computer to begin the process of describing the details of the arrests that had happened just a few short hours before.

Although his mind said he needed to prepare this report, his fingers were not cooperating. He sat, silently staring at a blank screen for more than an hour. Jake was not there yet. He wondered whether he'd read the *Post* article, as his mind continued to ramble. Fellow officers inquiring about the article in the morning paper didn't help matters.

The pressure mounted like a freight train running out of control.

Bobby's mind wandered. *What is the prognosis for Mitchell? When will I know? Will his injury be fatal? Will I be blamed?* The news media, the Mitchell family and the black community were already suggesting if young Jordon died, it was murder. *Could I be charged with manslaughter or worse, murder?* With all of these questions swirling through his head, the most important question of the hour was how he was going to explain in a police report precisely how this unarmed young black male sustained a massive skull fracture while in his custody and care.

Bobby's thoughts were interrupted by the sound of a familiar voice. Jake Corbett had arrived, also earlier than expected. "I assume you saw the paper this morning," Jake said as he pulled up a chair next to Bobby.

"Yes," was Bobby's only response.

"We need to prepare this report like our life depends on it," Corbett commented.

"Do you fuckin' think I don't know that?" Bobby snapped.

"Easy, easy. We'll get this done. We'll just write it like it happened."

"That's the problem. I don't know how it happened," Bobby replied, still staring at the blank computer screen.

"What do you mean? You don't know how what happened?"

"I don't know how this fucking little burglar wound up with a massive skull fracture," was the instant response.

"You mean you didn't whack him in the head?"

Bobby made no response to this question, but instead continued to stare at the blank screen.

"Bobby, this kid has a massive skull fracture. Somebody had to hit him in the head, and we were the only two on that roof who were anywhere near these two assholes. And I know I didn't hit him, which leaves only you."

"Thanks. I can see you are going to be a big help when they drop the net on me."

"Well, I guess we are going to have to write it in to write it out," Corbett said, suggesting the report be falsified to include a reason the suspect had to be struck in the head.

"Great idea, Jake. I had to use force, possibly lethal force, to subdue some kid who is a third of my size. I can't wait to see that headline."

"Do you have a better idea?" Jake asked.

"I don't have a fuckin' clue about anything right now," Bobby responded, putting his head in his hands and turning away from the computer screen, which was still blank.

As Decker began the process of writing this high profile report, his thoughts turned to another recent high profile case. St. Louis Police Sergeant Tom Cannon had been charged with the felony assault of a mentally-challenged black man, and lying on the police report. Now, another black individual was involved in an incident with a white police officer.

Today's news coverage, albeit brief, suggested this was yet another case in the city of St. Louis involving white police officers brutalizing black people. And this time, the target of police hostility might die. How would a political prosecutor who had her sights set on greater political office or even a judgeship react to this case? Everyone knew this prosecutor was embarrassed by the Cannon case. Her misfeasance had allowed an all-white Kansas City jury, outside the city of St. Louis and on the other side of the state, to decide a white St. Louis police officer was not guilty of assaulting a mentally-challenged black man and didn't lie in his police report.

After several hours and several rough drafts prepared separately by both Bobby and Jake, the final report detailing the arrests of Jordon Mitchell and Daniels Jones was complete, for better or worse. It didn't contain any portion of Corbett's rough draft justifying the massive skull fracture sustained by Jordon Mitchell. In fact, the report didn't even mention that injury. Bobby read it one more time and then pushed the computer key to file it for the world to see and perhaps eventually criticize.

Chapter Seven

The April 25th edition of the *Post-Dispatch* contained a front page picture of Jordon Mitchell in the intensive care unit of St. Louis University Hospital. The photograph graphically displayed Mitchell, eyes closed, head bandaged, with several tubes protruding from his nose and mouth and connected to machinery. The headline on this day read: "Suspect Remains Critical, Police Investigating." The physician responsible for his care was quoted as saying the massive skull fracture Jordon Mitchell sustained to the back of his head had resulted in a brain swell. He didn't speculate on Mitchell's medical future, but did indicate the doctors were working to control the swelling. The next 48 hours would be critical.

The article made only a passing reference to the pawn shop burglary. Instead, the focus was on those critical of the actions of the police officers involved in this case and the Department that employed them. That criticism continued to escalate in the black community.

Contributing to that criticism and the animosity between the black community and the police department was the recent acquittal of a white police sergeant who was charged with beating a mentally-challenged young black man. The *Post-Dispatch* story gratuitously refreshed the recollections of those who had forgotten about this emotionally charged case by recounting in detail the circumstances of that matter, including the mistakes made by the prosecutors.

Tom Cannon was a 22 year veteran with the Department at the time of the incident. He had been a sergeant for nine of his 22 years. His father had risen to the rank of Lieutenant Colonel, serving as the assistant chief of police for three of his 30 years. The Cannons were shining stars of the St. Louis Police Department, until that fateful day when a mentally-challenged black man was mistaken for a burglar.

On that day, Sgt. Cannon responded to a residential burglary in progress call in the 7th district, where he had been assigned for three years. When he arrived, he smelled an overwhelming odor of mace and observed the apartment in a total state of disarray—furniture broken and over-turned, and debris scattered throughout. He was met at the front door by a uniformed officer, who was one of the first to arrive on the scene. That officer explained when they arrived, the burglar alarm was sounding. As they entered the apartment, they were met by a large, 6-foot, 225 pound black male standing in the kitchen. That individual refused to identify himself and was immediately placed in custody. After placing one handcuff on the suspect's wrist, he de-cided he didn't want any part of that. He began to swing the cuffed hand as the officers attempted to subdue him. Force was then used and a fight ensued—arms, elbows and fists flying, mace sprayed like water spilling from a garden hose, and nightsticks swung like it was the bottom of the ninth and a homerun was necessary to win the game.

Sgt. Cannon, his eyes watering and throat irritated from the mace, left in the room and found the suspect in one of the bedrooms. He was seated on the floor, hand-cuffed behind his back, and bleeding from the area of his head. An officer explained when the mace had no effect, night sticks had to be used to subdue this incredibly strong individual. The struggle progressed to the bedroom area, leaving a wake of damaged items in its path. An ambulance was en route.

As it turned out, the individual the police encountered in the apartment actually lived there. Derron Harris, 24 years old, resided in the apartment with his mother. Un-beknown to the officers who were the first to arrive on the scene, Harris was mentally-challenged and unable to iden-tify himself or explain to the officers he was not a burglar, but rather a resident. Apparently, his mother routinely used the security system as a baby sitter to ensure Derron didn't wander off while she was at work. Believing him to be a burglar, and without any other explanation for his pres-ence in the apartment, the officers attempted to make an arrest with the ensuing consequences.

But the consequences didn't end in the apartment that day. The vocal critics of the police department immediately began to chant *police brutality.* The civil libertarians and activists in the black community began to demand an accounting from the police department as to why this young man was *beaten* in his own home. Eventually, criminal prosecutions would be demanded. The situation was developing into another chapter in the extensive history of distrust between the St. Louis Police Department and the African American community.

Within 24 hours of the incident, and before the investigation was completed, the Chief of the St. Louis Police Department, in an apparent effort to calm the storm and silence the voice of his critics, decided to emerge with a public statement. The Chief, himself an African American, announced to all media outlets, "Heads will roll." Rather than calm, his statement gave birth to chaos and internal paranoia among all involved. Clearly, the message implied one or more police officers would be fired or worse, indicted. Now it was everyone for himself; protect your ass at any price.

To further complicate matters, the Chief decided to participate in the IAD investigation, summoning certain of the involved officers to his office for personal chats. Eventually, the stories of the officers who were the first to arrive on the scene would change. Amidst the threats, both internal and criminal, one of the officers on the scene would claim he observed Sgt. Cannon, without cause or justification, strike Harris on the head with a night stick after he had been handcuffed and while seated on the bedroom floor.

The *Post* article, on this day when Jordon Mitchell lay in a bed in the intensive care unit of the hospital fighting for his life, recounted Sgt. Thomas Cannon was indicted, charged with felony assault, which could have resulted in a seven year prison sentence. The article also mentioned Cannon was accused of lying on the police report he authored, an equally serious criminal offense, particularly for a police officer. Readers were also reminded the case was eventually tried in a court room outside the city of St. Louis. Because of the extensive pre-trial publicity, Cannon's attorneys filed a motion for change of venue, claiming the inhabitants were biased and prejudiced against their client.

As a result, they argued that Sgt. Cannon could not receive a fair trial in the city of St. Louis.

When a motion for change of venue is filed in any criminal case, the party filing the motion, usually the defense, bears the burden of proof. Meeting that burden is difficult, if not impossible. Essentially, substantial evidence must be presented to demonstrate the inhabitants of that particular venue are biased and prejudiced such that the party filing the motion cannot receive a fair trial. Most experienced trial judges will deny the motion and proceed to trial in an effort to find a fair and impartial jury to hear the case.

The process used to make that determination is called *voir dire*, a Latin phrase meaning to *speak the truth*. During this process the lawyers are allowed to question the prospective jurors about a variety of issues including their likes and dislikes, life experiences, relationships, prior jury service, if any, what they have heard and read about the pending case and any opinions they have formed. Most lawyers don't favor jurors who have never heard of a pending high profile case. But the final test used by both the court and attorneys is whether the potential jurors can set aside any preconceived ideas and decide the case based upon the law given to them by the judge and the facts presented in the courtroom. If they say they can, they are eligible to be selected to be on the jury. If they indicate they cannot disregard any previously formed opinions, for whatever reason, they will be stricken from the panel.

The difficulty in supporting a venue challenge was never faced by the defense in *State of Missouri v. Thomas Cannon,* because the prosecutor failed to file a timely objection to the motion. As a result, Cannon's attorneys argued and the court agreed this failure had the legal effect of waiving any disagreement the prosecutor may have had to the requested change. The only question remaining was where to send the case for trial. The court decided on Kansas City, in the westernmost part of the state, far from St. Louis, the easternmost city. There the case was heard by an all-white jury who found Cannon, a white St. Louis police sergeant, *not guilty* of the felony assault of a mentally-challenged young black man, Derron Harris, and not guilty of preparing a false police report to conceal his alleged criminal behavior.

25

The black community was not happy with this prosecutorial misfeasance. Outraged would probably be a better description of the mood at the time. Resurrecting the Cannon case, in the wake of the current Mitchell arrest, had the inevitable effect of inflaming an already potentially volatile situation. At the time of Cannon's acquittal, both activist and non-activist members of the black community were relentless in their criticism of the elected prosecutor, Circuit Attorney Joan Cardwell. They blamed her for allowing the case to be tried by an all-white jury outside of St. Louis. Nonetheless, Cardwell continued to serve the city in that role, hoping to put the Cannon acquittal behind her.

Not unexpectedly, opinions were formed and sides taken in the Cannon case. The same was expected with the latest clash between the black community and the police. Jordon Mitchell was beaten mercilessly by a white, racist cop. The flip side of this war of words included those who suggested that Mitchell deserved what he got. Black, white or green, criminals who get caught burglarizing pawn shops in the middle of the night should expect an ass kicking. This debate, fueled by the news media, would eventually change the life of Bobby Decker forever.

Chapter Eight

When Bobby Decker arrived at the station to begin his overnight shift on April 25th, he was met by his sergeant. John Spicer was a veteran police officer who was nearing retirement. During his 29 years with the Department, he had seen it all. Police officers under attack by the news media were nothing new for Sgt. Spicer. He'd had assignments that included homicide, undercover drug task force and the intelligence division. But the majority of his career was spent in uniform on the street. His experiences made him sensitive to the everyday problems and crises of the men and women under his command. After reading the newspaper for the last two days, he knew Bobby Decker needed some counseling and comforting.

"How are you doing?" Spicer asked in a casual tone.

"Fine," was the one syllable response.

"I didn't see you last night after your shift ended. Was everything okay?" Spicer inquired, again as casually as possible.

"Yes," another one syllable reply.

"Do you think you could answer me with more than one word?"

"Yes."

"Oh, brother. Let's have a serious conversation, my friend. Frankly, I'm concerned about you. I also need to make a determination of whether I need to put you on the desk. At the end of the day, I'm responsible for what happens to you, in case you haven't noticed.

"Let me begin," Sergeant Spicer continued, as he attempted to make eye contact with Bobby Decker. "Look at me, Bobby. I feel your pain, man. I know what you are going through. You are worried about this Mitchell kid. Concerned he may die. Concerned the media influence may get you indicted. Concerned our asshole circuit attorney may charge you for her own political gain, and to avoid additional embarrassment after the Cannon fiasco. I get that. But listen, man. Right now there is nothing you can do about any of that. So don't worry about things over which you have no control. I looked at your report, but haven't approved it yet. Is there anything you need to add?"

"Nothing I can think of right now."

"You didn't address the fractured skull."

"I know."

"Is there a particular reason for that?" Spicer asked in a fatherly tone.

"Yes," Bobby replied without further elaboration.

"Okay. I won't ask any other questions. You were there, I wasn't, and you know the importance of these reports. Just remember what happened to Tom Cannon. Not only did that fucking circuit attorney charge him with felony assault, but she also accused him of a cover up by lying in his police report. I'll go ahead and approve the report for filing, if it's what you want."

"Thanks, I appreciate your confidence in me and your concern," Bobby said, looking directly into the eyes of his sergeant.

"How are things on the home front?" Spicer asked, moving into Decker's personal life.

"Not so good. Kathy doesn't like the publicity. As if I do. But she is concerned about her position with the circuit attorney's office, given the way the media is handling this and the way the black community is responding."

Kathy Adams and Bobby Decker had met when he was a rookie. She was a beautiful woman, tall, blonde, model material and a lawyer who also happened to be a prosecutor in the circuit attorney's office. Her boss, Joan Cardwell, was the very same person who had prosecuted Sgt. Cannon and might end up prosecuting Bobby Decker.

They'd met at a bar called Humphrey's on the campus of St. Louis University during a happy hour after Bobby finished his first day on the job. They shared a drink, family stories, and common interests which obviously included catching and prosecuting bad guys. That was their common thread. Now that thread might be stretched to the breaking point because Bobby Decker might be the unwelcome recipient of a new title: defendant.

After their first casual meeting, they began to date. When the dating became more serious, they decided to live together while they contemplated marriage. That was six years before. At first, they'd had some concerns. How would their serious relationship be viewed by both employers? Although they were on the same side of the fence, there was no love lost between the prosecuting attorneys and the police officers.

Repeatedly, the officers would complain the prosecutors rejected perfectly good cases that the officers busted their asses to make. When a case went south and an acquittal resulted, the police blamed the prosecutors and the prosecutors blamed the police. Neither engaged in any introspection. That animosity had reached epidemic proportions when Tom Cannon had been charged criminally. That hostility had put a strain on the relationship between Bobby and Kathy, as each felt an obligation to protect their respective interests. Now their relationship was being threatened by a burglar arrested on a rooftop in the middle of a rainy night who might die with an unexplained massive skull fracture.

"I'm sorry to hear that, Bobby. You two make a great couple, even though Kathy is hooked up with that incompetent political hack who parades as a prosecutor." *An obvious reference to Cardwell.* "But I'm sure this will all work out, and you'll work it out with her. But, in the meantime, Bobby, I think it would be a good idea to have you stay inside tonight on the desk. I hope you understand. I believe it is in your best interests for the moment. When this passes, which it will, you'll be back on the street."

Ordinarily, Bobby would have put up a fight, but on this day and under these circumstances, he offered no resistance and accepted Spicer's decision, realizing his sergeant was doing what he thought was best. The last thing any good police officer wanted was to be taken away from the action and chained to a desk. At the moment, Bobby was not feeling like a good police officer.

Chapter Nine

After finishing his shift on the desk without incident, Bobby left the station shortly after 7 o'clock, heading home to try to get some sleep. For the past several days, sleep had been at a premium—a few hours here and there. Thinking sheer exhaustion would allow this day to be different, he went to bed just before 8. Fortunately, Kathy had already left for work, so he didn't have to engage in Mitchell-type conversation and endure the cross examination about the events on the rooftop. "Why don't you know how he got that skull fracture?" "If you didn't cause it, who did? Jake?" "Did Mitchell hit himself in the head?" "Is there anyone on the planet who can explain how this guy was injured?" This day he would also avoid a discussion of newspaper accounts written by reporters who didn't want to be confused by the facts; sensationalism their goal and the advertising dollar their life blood.

Shortly past 11 the same morning, Bobby was awakened to the sound of pounding on the front door of his apartment. At first he thought he was he was dreaming. But after several more pounds, more intense than the first few, he realized someone was actually at his door. "Who is there?" he asked.

"IAD. Open up, Decker," was the firm response.

"Okay, just a minute till I get some pants on," Bobby said.

"Right now, Decker. Open the door and then get your pants on. Otherwise, we will have to kick it in and we don't want to do that," came the reply from the other side of the door.

"All right, all right, there is no need to kick anything in. I'm unlocking it," Bobby shouted through the closed door as he fumbled with the lock in an attempt to unlock the door as quickly as he could.

"What's this all about?" he said, looking at two white males dressed in business suits standing in front of his door that was now unlocked and open.

"Decker, I'm Sergeant Joe Bryant and this is Sergeant Frank Cantrell and we are from the Internal Affairs Division. If you would like to change clothes, Sergeant Cantrell will accompany you, and then we can talk," Bryant said.

"What's going on? Why am I being treated like a criminal? Bobby asked looking confused but fearing this had something to do with Mitchell.

"Let's just take care of one thing at a time. Please change your clothes if that is what you want to do and then we will talk," Bryant responded.

"What if I don't want someone coming into my bedroom? In fact, what if I don't want you in my house and order you out?" Bobby asked, clearly becoming frustrated and upset by this unwelcome intrusion into his personal space.

"Decker, here is a piece of friendly advice. Don't go down this road. It will accomplish nothing and just compound the issues for you and for the Department. Let's go, man; let's get this done. This isn't any piece of cake for us either," Bryant said firmly, but with a slight hint of apology.

"Yeah, right. Okay, you win as usual," Bobby said, as he walked to the bedroom he and Kathy shared, accompanied by a police officer.

As he changed his clothes, Bobby's mind was racing. *What is this about? Did something happen to Mitchell? Did Mitchell die? Are they here to suspend me or worse, arrest me? How will I cope if they are here to arrest me? Should I say anything to them? Can anything I say be used to prosecute me? Should I call a lawyer? If I call a lawyer, will it look like I'm guilty of something? But am I guilty of something? I'm a cop. I should know these things. What the hell is happening to my life?* Bobby's thoughts were interrupted by Cantrell's voice demanding he speed up the clothing change.

When Bobby and Cantrell returned to the living room, Bryant was staring at some of the art that decorated the walls. "I don't know much about art, but this stuff looks like it is worth some bucks," Bryant said with a hint of sarcasm.

Ignoring that comment, Bobby was intent on getting to the reason that these *Goons,* as they are affectionately referred to by the rank and file, the real police officers, were in his house and what they wanted.

"Okay, I changed. Now tell me why you are here and what you want," Bobby demanded.

"Jordon Mitchell died early this morning, and we have some work to do," was Bryant's callous reply.

Those words hit Bobby like a ton of bricks. His mind began to race again, cluttered with more questions than answers, the most predominate: *What is going to happen to me now?*

"So what now?" Bobby asked hesitatingly.

"We have been directed to pick up all of your gear: gun, mace, nightsticks, flashlights, and anything else you use on or off duty," Bryant said.

"Why?" Bobby asked.

"I don't ask the questions; I just do what I'm told. You ought to know that by now, Decker. I assume you have some things here and at the station. So, let's start with collecting what you have here, and then we can take a ride to the station," Bryant said.

"The only thing I have here are my guns, both on duty and off duty weapons."

"I'll need both," Bryant demanded.

"You're going to leave me without a weapon. How am I going to be able to work?" Bobby asked.

"Decker, again, I'm just doing what I was told. Save your questions for downtown."

After retrieving both weapons, again in the company of Cantrell, Bobby surrendered them to Bryant without comment.

"Anything else here?" Bryant inquired, ignoring Bobby's previous statement pertaining to the equipment he had in the house.

"I told you that's all I have here," Bobby responded, clearly annoyed that he had to repeat what he had said before.

"Then let's head to the station. Oh, by the way, Decker, I'm also going to need your badge and department ID," Bryant said just as they started to leave the house.

Startled and confused, Bobby said, "Why do you need those? Am I being suspended?"

"I'm only doing what I was told. Save the questions for someone who can answer them," Bryant repeated.

On the trip to the station, Bobby overheard Bryant contacting someone on the police radio to inform that person they had Decker and his equipment, including his badge and ID, and were headed to the area where he was assigned, to collect the other equipment from his locker.

Still confused and upset, Bobby sat silently in the rear of the unmarked police vehicle. He felt like a criminal.

Chapter Ten

Ronald Rodgers was the Chief of the St. Louis Police Department and not well-respected by the rank and file. Like his circuit attorney counterpart, he, too, was viewed as a political hack who never did a day's worth of real police work. Instead, he spent his days sucking up to politicians who would help him climb the ranks of the Department. He had been the Chief for the ten years Bobby had been on the Department. And while he had nothing to compare, he shared the beliefs of the majority of the officers.

Bobby recalled vividly the Tom Cannon case and what a complete fiasco that was thanks, in part, to the chief. A day after the incident in which this mentally-challenged black man was arrested, the chief appeared on television and any other media outlet that would listen, to announce, *Heads will roll.* At the time, Bobby thought, *why would he say something like that when the investigation is just beginning? Why would he throw the officers under the bus when he doesn't know fact one?* The answer in his mind and those of his fellow officers was simple. He was covering his own ass and the hell with everything and everybody else. After all, he hadn't gotten where he was looking out for everybody else.

But he was still the chief. He ran the Department's day-to-day show from his spacious office on the 5th floor of department headquarters in downtown St. Louis. He called the shots, and the Mitchell matter would be no different.

On this day, he was meeting in his office with the head of Internal Affairs, Lt. Col. Raymond Winston, a 33 year veteran, also African American; both with no real street experience, but politically astute. Each had used his political influence to get out of uniform, off the street and into a *cush* and safe job as quickly as possible. In fact, Winston, senior to Rodgers in years with the Department, made two unsuccessful efforts himself to become chief, but he was defeated by Rodgers and prior to that, he lost the spot to an individual who lasted only three years before deciding the job was not for him.

Many of the officers wondered, sometimes silently and sometimes out loud, what it would be like to work for a guy who was promoted over you and was junior to you in years of service. However, since both were incompetent idiots, it probably didn't matter. The *Peter Principle,* promoting a person to his or her highest level of incompetence, was alive and well in the St. Louis Police Department.

"I just heard from Sergeant Bryant. They just left Decker's house and are on their way in with him. The only equipment he had there were two guns, one duty and one off duty. They are headed to the area station to get the rest of his equipment out of his locker and then down here. They also have his badge and ID. Do you want them to bring him here or to my office?" Winston asked.

The chief, sitting behind his desk looking out one of the many windows in his corner office at the buildings which defined the city, seemed to ignore Winston's question. Finally, he said, "Bring him here; I need to deal with this personally. I can't delegate it."

"What is the game plan, sir, if I might ask?" Winston inquired.

Again, the chief was slow to respond. "Game plan? Hell, I got no goddamn game plan. All I know is, some black kid just died and his death has created a media feeding frenzy with the blacks in this town looking to lynch a white cop. On top of that, we are still dealing with the fallout from Cannon. This just fuels that fire, and I'm front and center on the firing line. All I know is I can't survive another Cannon disaster."

"So what do we do? How do we turn this around so we are not crushed in the stampede?" Winston again asked.

This time without any hesitation the chief said, "We suspend Decker for starters. Put his ass out there on the front line. Put the attention on him and away from us. We need to create an atmosphere to show we are sympathetic to the death of this young man and will see justice done. We need to do all we can to dispel the thought that we are running a racist police department. Perhaps some people who work here are racist, but we are committed to getting rid

35

of those types. In short, we need to put some distance between ourselves and Decker—and Cannon for that matter."

"Well, the Cannon case is simple. We didn't screw that up. It was Cardwell who fucked it up when she didn't file the proper paperwork, which resulted in an all-white jury on the other side of the state deciding a case that should have been tried here. So, I think we do a press conference where we say we hope the prosecutor doesn't repeat the mistakes made in the Cannon case. That way we have killed two birds with one stone. We deflect the Cannon case away from us, and we put this case on the shoulders of Cardwell," Winston suggested.

"But Decker has not been charged with anything," the chief noted.

Winston was quick to respond. "Not yet. But do you really think this politically motivated prosecutor can do anything other than charge Decker with something, particularly in light of Cannon? She is still experiencing the fallout from the black politicians and the mover and shakers on that screw-up. Seems to me this is her chance to redeem herself. Dead black victim at the hands of a white cop. *Déjà vu* all over again. This time she sends the white cop to jail for a long time and is rewarded with a judgeship or whatever the hell else she is angling for. In the meantime, we do our job. Suspend Decker. Investigate the case and send it over to her to do with as she pleases," he said.

Rodgers listened intently to the analysis and offered no rebuttal. "Let me know when they get here. I want you present when I talk to him," he said.

Chapter Eleven

When they arrived at the area station, Decker was immediately taken to his locker and asked to remove the lock protecting its contents. He complied, albeit reluctantly. At the house he had decided he would cooperate for better or worse and not seek the advice of a lawyer, although he realized that decision could come back to haunt him in the long run. But he didn't have a lot of time to make a choice. Besides if he didn't cooperate, they would simply get what they wanted anyhow, and he would eventually pay the price for the inconvenience.

Decker had been down this road before with IAD many years ago, in another case in which he found himself wearing a target on his chest. That experience had opened his eyes to what these people were capable of. For these goons, the end always justified the means, as they really believed they were doing God's work.

The locker contained a lot of accumulated junk, in addition to department-issued equipment, as well as his personal belongings. Once opened, Bryant asked Decker to step aside, as he and Cantrell would remove and inventory the contents.

The first order of business was to photograph the contents before anything was disturbed. Several pictures of this gym type locker, both inside and out, were taken by Cantrell from different angles. Cantrell then began the process of emptying the locker, one piece at a time, lining each up on the floor to be inventoried and photographed. This time there would be no mistakes like Cannon. Each item seized would be placed in an evidence bag with a proper chain of custody to be established in the event the item was needed for trial; should there be a trial. As this process progressed, Bobby looked on with horror and disbelief. *What's next?* he asked himself, hoping for the best, but fearing the worst.

When the locker was completely emptied onto the floor, Bryant and Cantrell examined the contents trying to decide what had evidentiary value and what could be safely left behind. After a few minutes of study and conversation, they decided to package as evidence a night stick, a Taser gun, an ASP baton, a rubber flashlight, a set of handcuffs, a utility belt, ammunition, a notebook, three ballpoint pens, and several items of department-issued clothing that included a blue baseball cap, a dark blue winter jacket, two light blue short-sleeve shirts, a pair of dark blue pants and black tie shoes.

While Cantrell finished placing the last few items in the evidence bags, Bryant asked Bobby, "Is there any other equipment you have, whether department issued or personal, which is not in this locker or your house?"

"Not that I can think of," Bobby said, clearly shaken by the entire ordeal.

"Are you sure?" Bryant asked with a tone of slight aggravation.

"I'm as sure as I can be under these circumstances," Bobby replied, equally aggravated.

Bryant then reached for his cell phone and proceeded to dial a number. Bobby could hear at least Bryant's part of the conversation. He heard him telling the person on the other end, whom he presumed to be an IAD supervisor or perhaps Lt. Col. Winston himself, that he was finished at the area station and needed some direction about what to do next. He ended this brief conversation by indicating he would see the other party in a few minutes.

Finishing his cell phone conversation, Bryant turned to Bobby and said, "Okay. You and I are done here. Sergeant Cantrell can finish up and we need to take a ride downtown to headquarters."

"What for?" Bobby asked.

"A little meeting with the chief," Bryant said with a hint of sarcasm.

Just great. Can this day get any worse, Bobby thought as they left the area station headed to the chief's office in the headquarters building in downtown St. Louis. Although he had been in the Internal Affairs office in the same building several years ago, he never had the need, or the desire, to visit the chief in his office. He didn't expect this first visit to be a pleasurable experience; memorable yes, pleasurable no.

Chapter Twelve

The chief's receptionist greeted Bryant and Decker. From her secure position behind bullet proof glass, she directed the pair to have a seat while she let the chief's aide know they were there. After they had waited for some fifteen minutes without conversation, an aide to the chief finally opened a locked door and invited both Bryant and Decker into the inner office. Once inside, they were led to a large conference room which was decorated with the photographs of officers who had lost their lives in the line of duty. The aide directed them to have a seat, designating specific seats for each while informing them the chief would be with them shortly.

While they waited, Bobby began to look at the photographs: all men, some black but most white and all in their dress uniforms. Some of the names he recognized, but most were before his time. During his short ten years on the Department, three men had been killed in the line of duty; two shot to death and one struck and killed by a drunk driver. Despite his current difficulties, Bobby was honored to be part of a fraternity that included these brave men; unselfish men who paid the ultimate price while protecting others. How different these men were compared to the man he was about to meet.

Suddenly and without warning, a door flew open and in walked the head of the St. Louis Police Department, followed closely by the head of the Internal Affairs Division. Both Bryant and Bobby stood when these executives entered the room. Bobby stood, not because he respected this chief, but because that is the protocol in this quasi-military organization. *Sometimes the form overshadows the substance,* he thought as he slowly left his chair. Both returned to their seats only after the chief sat down and directed them to do likewise. Another reminder of the protocol.

Without introducing himself or any preliminary chit chat, Chief Rodgers, looking directly at Bobby, began what would be a one-sided conversation. "Officer Decker, the man you arrested the other night has died. This department will conduct an investigation into the circumstances of that arrest. Lieutenant Colonel Winston will be in charge of that investigation, which will be conducted by Internal Affairs officers. I can assure you the investigation will be thorough and fair to all concerned. I have no way to predict how long this will take, but I have directed Lieutenant Colonel Winston to expedite the process without compromising thoroughness."

As the chief spoke, Bobby stared, didn't blink, and didn't swallow, while trying to conceal his apprehension, his fear of what would come. He knew a suspension was inevitable and waited anxiously for that shoe to fall. He didn't have to wait long. "In the meantime, I'm going to relieve you of your duties. In other words, you'll be carried on the rolls in a suspended without pay status until this investigation is completed. What this means is, although you are still employed by this department and are required to follow all the rules, you'll have no police authority. You will need to be available to us in the event we need to contact you, so we will need that information before you leave here today. If you plan to leave the area, you'll need the permission of Lieutenant Colonel Winston or his designee to do so. Do you have any questions?"

When any command rank officer asks if you have any questions, they really don't expect a question to be asked. This situation was no different. As such, Bobby simply and politely said, "No, sir," and left it at that, although he had many questions he knew would only be answered with the passage of time. *Would he be charged with murder? Would he be convicted? Would he be locked up? Would he spend the rest of his life behind bars?* A suspension without pay would be a problem, but not the worst Bobby would face.

"Then that is all I have. Lieutenant Colonel Winston will be in touch with you as the investigation progresses. Good luck to you, Officer Decker," Chief Rodgers said, as he stood to leave the room. Bryant and Bobby again stood as they had done when the chief entered.

41

After the departure of both the chief and Lt. Col. Winston, the aide who directed them to the room again appeared and led them to another door that opened into the hallway outside of the chief's suite. Once outside, Bobby asked, "What now?"

Bryant said, "You are free to go. Just remember the chief's admonitions and stay out of trouble and public view while this case is pending. We will be in touch."

"How am I supposed to get home? I don't have a car. Remember? You drove me here, and I didn't bring any money with me," Bobby reminded.

"We're not running a taxi service, Decker. You heard the chief; we have work to do in the mess you created. You are a smart and resourceful guy. I'm sure you'll be able to figure out how to get home," was the cold, impersonal response.

Realizing there would be no benefit in a reply, Bobby simply turned and walked away, while trying to figure out how he would get home.

Kathy's office was in the courthouse a few blocks away. *Should I call her? Sooner or later I'm going to have to tell her I have been suspended and preferably before she reads it in the paper or sees it on television,* he thought. *Or I could call a friend or even my parents or my brother, whose office is downtown. They will also need to know about this before it hits the airwaves, which is likely to occur quickly, given this chief's penchant for press conferences.*

In the end, Bobby opted to contact his brother, Jeff, the lawyer. In addition to the lift home, he could also get some advice on the need for a lawyer and how best to break the news to all who needed to be told. As he dialed Jeff's direct office number, he wondered which would be worse, telling his father or telling Kathy. When Jeff answered, all Bobby said was he needed a ride home.

"Where are you and what's going on?"

"I'm at police headquarters. I'll explain things when you get here."

"This can't be good. I'm on my way," Jeff said.

How right you are, my brother, Bobby thought as he pushed the button to end the conversation, and waited outside of a police department that he might no longer be calling home.

Chapter Thirteen

Joan Cardwell summoned several key staffers to her office for a meeting to discuss the next step in the Jordon Mitchell mess. In attendance were the first assistant, chief trial assistant, public relations director, and most importantly, her political advisor and confidant. Cardwell was serving her third term as the circuit attorney for the city of St. Louis, the chief law enforcement officer. Some jurisdictions refer to this position as the prosecuting or state's attorney. Cardwell didn't try cases. She directed those tasks to others in her office, and she focused instead on running the day-to-day operation that often included public appearances and press conferences. She was truly a politician.

It was no secret that Cardwell had her sights set on greater things; perhaps a run for Mayor or perhaps a seat in the Congress, but more likely her focus was on a judgeship, preferably as an appellate judge. But Joan Cardwell was acutely aware in the state of Missouri, one needed political help and a lot of it in order to be appointed to those coveted positions.

All Supreme and Appellate Court Judges as well as Circuit (trial) Judges in certain counties within the State of Missouri are selected through a process known as the Non Partisan Court Plan. In theory, this plan is designed to remove politics from judicial appointments.

Trial judges in the counties of St. Louis, Jackson, Platte, Clay and Greene, as well as the city of St. Louis, are appointed under the Non Partisan Court Plan. In the city of St. Louis, a panel of two lawyers elected by the Missouri Bar, an organization of licensed lawyers, and two lay people appointed by the governor, along with the chief appellate judge for that circuit, interview and investigate all candidates—ultimately sending three names to the governor. From that list, the governor selects the individual who will fill the vacant judicial seat on the trial bench.

For the selection of appellate judges, the Appellate Judicial Commission consists of three lawyers elected by the Bar, three lay people appointed by the governor, and the chief justice of the Missouri Supreme Court. As with the selection of circuit judges, three names are sent to the governor, from which he must make his selection.

It is painfully obvious to even the most casual observer, the so-called Non Partisan Court Plan is anything but nonpartisan. The governor appoints people to the judicial selection commission which, in turn, reduces the list of candidates to three. The reality of this system is that to attain a judicial appointment, candidates must be willing to invest many hours and dollars currying favor with politicians, both black and white, including a never-ending list of state senators, state representatives, lobbyists, political friends and contributors to the governor and, of course, the governor himself and his staff. Any one individual on this exhaustive list of politicos could derail one's chance of becoming a judge.

As a successful politician herself, Joan Cardwell knew the process. She also knew as an elected prosecutor, she had to be careful with the cases she chose for prosecution. She was further acutely aware of the pressure that can be created by the media as well as special interest groups. She had been reminded of that pressure during the Cannon fiasco. She was still experiencing the fallout from that screw-up.

Cardwell opened the meeting with the obvious; Jordon Mitchell had died. Everyone had been monitoring Mitchell's progress since the *Post* ran the first explosive article. They hoped they would only have to deal with an assault, not a homicide. But that was not to be. Mitchell had died. Now, the only question remaining was who would be prosecuted.

"Mitchell died this morning, and we need to discuss what our next step will be, from a public comment standpoint as well as what type of criminal prosecution, if any, should be pursued," Cardwell announced, knowing full well someone, other than herself, had to take the fall.

Bill Singleton was the chief trial attorney and third in the chain of command. He had been with the circuit attorney's office for twenty three years. Responsible for all trial matters as well as the supervision of the lawyers who spent their days in court, he was a career prosecutor who enjoyed a reputation as a straight shooter. He was not a politician. If Bill Singleton told you he was going to do something, you could take it to the bank. His word was his bond, which served as a nice contrast to Cardwell, who didn't enjoy a similar reputation. But make no mistake, when it came time to do battle in the court room, he was professional, but tenacious. He fought hard but fair, with most defense attorneys respecting him while at the same time fearing him.

Responding to the circuit attorney's inquiry, Singleton said, "Don't we need an investigation before we can do anything?"

"Of course, we will need an investigation before we can make any final decisions. But my question is: What do we do in the meantime before we have that investigation? We have a newspaper that has already tried and convicted Decker, along with the African American community looking for a public lynching. So what do we do before we have a completed investigative report?" Cardwell asked, somewhat exasperated and slightly annoyed by Singleton's question.

Singleton wasted no time responding, "We do nothing and say nothing until we have all the facts," he said.

"It seems to me I have to say something at this point; otherwise, it will appear we are not interested and are doing nothing. What do you think, Myra?" Cardwell asked.

Myra Long was the public relations director for the circuit attorney's office. She'd held that position for the entire time Cardwell had served as the circuit attorney. Her primary role was to make Cardwell and the office look good, no matter how bad the situation. She was a master at spinning stories to benefit Cardwell personally and had no problem threatening reporters who didn't see things her way. If a reporter wrote or aired a story critical of Cardwell and her office or if a derogatory editorial appeared, Long would make sure the offending reporter or media outlet was strategically eliminated from significant future press conferences. The learning curve for these offenders was swift and lasting. In the competitive world of media advertising, you didn't want to be in the back of the bus when a high profile case broke. Conversely, those who wrote only positive articles assisting her boss in future political endeavors would be rewarded with advance notice of a breaking story.

Responding to the circuit attorney's question, Long agreed, "Yes, I think we need to hold a press conference and let the public know we are not trying to sweep this under the rug, but rather taking this case very seriously."

"We take every case seriously and don't need press conferences to say that. How is this case any different?" Singleton shot back.

"It is not necessarily different, but it is getting and will continue to get a lot of media attention and scrutiny. Plus, we have yet another black-white issue with the police department. Also and perhaps most importantly, need I remind you of the Cannon case?" Long said with a hint of irritation because Singleton would question her recommendation.

"No Myra, you don't need to remind me of the Cannon case. We screwed up. No question about that. We were outmaneuvered by the defense, and we allowed that case to be tried outside the city. Fine. That is yesterday's news. What happened, happened. We can't change the facts, and you can't fix them now. But we also can't make our decisions in this case based upon what happened in some other case," Singleton said, determined to continue to question any recommendation he believed was inappropriate.

"Listen Bill, I didn't make the mess in the Cannon case. I'm just trying to clean it up. We can't ignore it, particularly after the media has resurrected that nightmare. I don't doubt for a minute the news accounts will continue to remind people about your screw-up and will continue to compare that case to this one," Long said with increased aggravation, bordering on anger.

"Hold on, Myra. I realize you have a selective memory, but please recall I was not in favor of indicting Tom Cannon. After I was overruled by you and others on that issue, I advocated a dismissal of the charges when our witnesses were destroyed in depositions. Once again overruled. So, if my recommendation had been followed in that matter, we would not be having this discussion and would not be headed down the road to another disaster if we listen to you," Singleton said, making no effort to disguise his anger.

Not only did Myra Long and Bill Singleton disagree on most issues, but they generally disliked each other. From time to time, Singleton would accuse Long of sacrificing the office for the personal benefit of Cardwell.

"That's enough," Cardwell said, determined to put an end to this debate.

"What are your thoughts, Karen?" Cardwell asked, attempting to draw her first assistant into the discussion.

Karen Braxton had served as the circuit attorney's second in command for the entire time Cardwell had held the office. She helped her get elected and this was her reward. Like her boss, she had known nothing about the circuit attorney's office before the election and had no criminal trial experience. She was viewed by the real lawyers in the office as the lap dog of the circuit attorney and seldom was taken seriously. Prior to assuming her current position, she had done probate work for a St. Louis silk stocking firm she solicited for large campaign contributions with unknown promises of future benefits. Along with the public relations director, she, too, was usually at odds with the chief trial assistant. This case would be no different. "I agree with Myra. I think we need to say something," she said.

"No surprise there. For whatever the value, I'll say again what I said when we had this discussion in the Cannon case. This is the life and career of a police officer you are messing with. It is also a department we have to rely upon to be able to do what we do; prosecute criminals," Bill Singleton said in a surprisingly calm voice, given the circumstances. "We ruined the career of one decorated officer and his police family; let's not repeat that mistake here," he added.

"No one is trying to ruin anyone's career, Bill. We are all just trying to do our jobs and protect this community," the circuit attorney snapped, clearly indicating both the conversation and the meeting were at an end.

When everyone had left, Cardwell turned to Carol Masterson who, by design, hadn't said a word during the meeting. Now the real meeting would begin and this one would not resemble what had just taken place.

Carol Masterson was not only the circuit attorney's political advisor, but she was also her best friend and confidant. They'd grown up together and Masterson was the mastermind who'd orchestrated the defeat of the twenty-year incumbent, in Cardwell's first attempt to seek public office. She was a brilliant political strategist and a ruthless human being.

Clearly upset by the remarks of her chief trial assistant, Cardwell turned to Masterson and asked, "What do we do now?"

"We ignore Singleton and everyone else and develop our own game plan, to get you out of this mess with as little damage as possible. First thing we need to do is a press conference in which we make it clear we are taking this matter seriously. Then we throw it to the police department, to make it their problem at least for the time being so we can buy a little time while they investigate."

"How do we handle the Cannon issue? As you know, I'm not exactly revered in the black community," Cardwell asked.

"We ignore it for the time being. The most important thing is to let the black caucus know we are going to do something about this. We need to redeem you with this case." Masterson said as the circuit attorney sat motionless, apparently considering the potential disaster that lay ahead.

After a brief moment of silence, Masterson added, "You do know someone will have to be held criminally accountable for this death." Cardwell didn't respond. But her political advisor was not telling her anything she didn't already know.

"I need to call the medical examiner and see where he is with the autopsy. He promised me he would get right on it and put everything else aside as soon as this guy died. Then we can make some final decisions," Cardwell said.

Chapter Fourteen

Bobby Decker paced in front of police headquarters waiting for his brother to pick him up and drive him home. As he waited, he thought about what he would say to his brother, his parents, and Kathy. But there was not much to tell. For the moment, the facts were pretty simple and straightforward; a suspect he had arrested died, and he was suspended without pay. *That's it. The rest is speculation.* But he knew they would wonder.

When his brother arrived, he wasted no time getting to the point. "What the hell is going on?" Jeff Decker asked.

"There is really not a whole lot to tell. I was suspended."

"What exactly does that mean? Why were you suspended?" Jeff asked.

"It means I don't go to work, and they stripped me of my police powers. They told me they were going to do an investigation into the Mitchell matter and assured me it would be a fair and complete investigation. And if they do that, I should be okay."

"I got that part of it, but what does it mean in the long run? Are they looking to charge you criminally with this guy's death?" Jeff asked, obviously upset and concerned.

"I don't know what it means, Jeff. I don't know what they plan to do. They don't exactly share that with me. All I know is I'm getting some unwanted time off; I'm not getting paid, and I have to deal with it the best I can. Frankly, the way I want to deal with it for the moment is not to deal with it," Bobby said as he stared out the passenger's window, looking at nothing in particular.

"Jeff, I don't think it serves any purpose to dwell and speculate on something over which we have no control, particularly since no one knows what is going to happen down the road. It just adds to the frustration and tension," Bobby added, resigned to accepting whatever would be, at least for the moment.

"Hold on," Jeff, the consummate lawyer, said, about to give his younger brother a lecture. "I can understand you are upset and don't want to talk about it, but we need to prepare for what may come. We need to expect the worst. That way we can never be disappointed if the worst never happens."

"What am I supposed to do when I have no idea where this thing is going?"

"The first order of business is to get a lawyer. The second thing is to keep your mouth shut and let the lawyer do the talking. You need to speak only to the lawyer and no one else, including family and Kathy. The conversation with the lawyer is privileged and protected, the rest is not," Jeff advised, calmly but firmly.

"That is good advice," Bobby said without hesitation.

"Do you have a lawyer in mind?" Jeff asked.

"Yes, yes, I do. I think I may want to talk to the lawyer who represented Tom Cannon. He did a great job in that case. I never met him, but he is supposed to be real aggressive. Doesn't take any shit from the prosecutors or the Department, and I suppose I'm going to need a lawyer for both cases. Plus, he is on the Association's list of lawyers, and I'm hoping the Association will pay for the representation since it was all line of duty. I certainly can't afford to pay for a lawyer."

The Association to which Bobby was referring was the police labor union. Recognizing there was safety in numbers, members of the Department had formed the St. Louis Police Officers' Association in 1973. Surviving legal and internal challenges, the Association emerged and remained a powerful force boasting membership that included the substantial majority of the rank and file commissioned officers. The dues collected were used to defend officers charged with misconduct, as well as for political influence. Bobby Decker, facing potential criminal as well as internal disciplinary charges, expected the Association to cover the legal fees and costs for both cases.

"The money is not a problem. The family can cover that if the Association can't. We just need to make sure we get you the best. I followed the Cannon case and thought the defense outmaneuvered the prosecutor all the way. He may be the guy."

Given his father's attitude about his chosen career, he had his doubts the *family* would be willing to pick up the legal tab. "You really think Dad is going to be willing to finance this little problem?" Bobby asked.

Responding immediately and emphatically, Jeff said, "Yes, I do. Granted, Dad didn't want you to become a police officer and told you so. When you didn't follow his advice, he was pissed, no doubt about that. But at the end of the day, you are his son. He loves you very much and won't abandon you during these troubled times."

"I hope you're right," was the only response Bobby could make.

"But the real question is, how Kathy is going to handle this?" Jeff continued.

"I don't know," Bobby told his brother, while silently believing this would not be good. She would inevitably be forced to make a choice between him and her job. That can never be good.

The remainder of the ride was filled with thoughts of Kathy. He wondered whether he should offer to leave the home they had made together until this matter was concluded. *Would that be best for both of us?* More questions without answers. All Bobby knew was that he loved her very much and would not do anything to hurt her. In these troubled times, he had to think beyond himself. He had to think of the ones he loved; the people who meant the world to him.

Chapter Fifteen

After thanking his brother for the ride home and promising to call him later, he walked slowly to his front door. He knew Kathy would not be home yet, which gave him additional time to think about what he would say. Usually, she arrived after 6, and he didn't expect this day to be any different.

He made himself a cup of coffee, as food didn't appeal to him, and sat on the couch to think about his life. Despite his belief no purpose was served by dwelling on things over which he had no control, he could not help himself. He wondered whether his father was right; police work was a thankless, dangerous job. But it was something he had always wanted to do. He wanted to help people, whether or not they appreciated it. Perhaps in an effort to avoid thinking about the future or perhaps in an effort to convince himself he made the right career choice, he reflected on his early days on the job.

The first day on any job is always challenging. Usually, it is the fear of the unknown, the desire to avoid mistakes. In the case of a police officer, it is the general apprehension that there are those who see the badge as a target. That first day as a real street cop for Bobby was no different. But he planned to be a cop's cop. He set the bar high at the academy and planned to do the same on the street. Idealistic? Maybe. He also knew any climb to the top began at the bottom. Probationary police officers or *probs,* defined that bottom. On this day, Bobby Decker was at the bottom of the learning curve. The academy training was the world of academia. This was the real world. The world of the street. Bobby was anxious to see how those worlds interacted.

Bobby recalled arriving at the 4th District station at 6:45 on that first morning, although he was not scheduled to begin his shift until seven o'clock. To his surprise, no one was there. Eventually, people started to drift in close to starting time. No one was very friendly. Most looked like they either just rolled out of bed or were, in some cases, hung over. The sergeant was the last to arrive. Sgt. Roy Osborn, a white 24 year veteran, had spent a lot of time on the street. He knew what it was like out there. Despite his outstanding record as a street officer, Osborn had been promoted just three short years before. Bobby wondered why.

Bobby hadn't met Sgt. Osborn, but his history with the Department was legendary. He'd heard all of those war stories while at the academy; some fact; some fiction. On this day, the sergeant would conduct roll call. For the first time, the street patrol officers were briefed on what was happening in the city and the district: what the night shift had experienced, pending investigations, and any special assignments. It was also the time when Bobby would be assigned a partner. As he scoped the faces in the room, his head raced with excitement. He wondered who that would be. *Who would show him the ropes? Who would teach him about the rules of the street?* His questions would soon be answered.

"Sit down, shut up, and listen up," the sergeant began. "I've got a couple things to cover before you get your sorry asses out there to earn your paychecks. We had a double homicide up on the north side last night. One or more perps are still at large. It was a drive-by in a dark colored, late model vehicle, perhaps a Lincoln Continental. Got nothing more than that at this time. So, be on the lookout for some assholes driving this type of vehicle and shooting people. Probably, as usual, a drug deal gone bad or gang-related."

The area of north St. Louis, known as the 6th District, was considered a high crime area. It was filled with criminal activity that involved warring groups of gangs battling for control of the drug trade. It also substantially contributed to the FBI statistics annually recognizing the city of St. Louis as one of the most dangerous cities in America. The 6th District was inhabited by a mostly poor, black population.

"The chief and the police board want everyone to be reminded about the COPS program," Osborn continued, with a slight but noticeable shake of his head.

The peanut gallery moaned even before he completed his sentence. COPS was an acronym for *Community Oriented Policing,* a social program to establish a better working relationship between the community and the Department, particularly in the black neighborhoods where that relationship could be tested. The concept was to have the police work closely with the residents of the neighborhood to address solutions to crime problems. In order to accomplish that goal, police officers must develop a network of personal contacts. This was generally accomplished through things such as foot and bike patrols or anything else to get the officers out of the patrol cars and onto the streets.

Routinely, minorities viewed themselves as victims of police harassment. Over the years, these folks had become firmly convinced the police were more interested in brutalizing their neighborhoods than stopping and solving crime. Demonstrations claiming police brutality had become commonplace whenever police related activity resulted in injury or death to a member of the minority community.

The COPS program represented a softer and more gentle approach to law enforcement, a talk first, "can't we just all get along" philosophy. Not unexpectedly, the concept was not embraced by the rank and file, particularly the veteran officers. Most viewed it as another social program developed by a bunch of political hacks, social liberals, masquerading as police commissioners, trying to run a police department. The street cops believed these gubernatorial appointees didn't have a clue about effective law enforcement, in part because they didn't come out of their ivory towers to do anything but socialize with their blue-blood friends. Historically, the state had controlled the police departments in both St. Louis and Kansas City since the days of the Civil War, when tensions erupted between pro-Union and pro Confederate forces. Although state controlled, the cities were required to pick up the tab on this antiquated system and fund their respective departments.

"So, consider yourselves reminded," the sergeant continued, ignoring the groans.

"Now for the business of the Fourth. No real crime running rampant down the streets of our beloved district. For God's sake, if a guy is double parked because he has to run something into an office, don't be an asshole and write a ticket. Move them along, but in a nice way. I'm tired of dealing with bullshit from the captain who gets a call from a board member or some politician, who has a friend you just screwed with," Osborn cautioned.

"Fuck them and the captain," an unidentified voice from the back of the room shouted with laughter from those who didn't have the guts to make such a comment.

"Parker, how funny will it be if I write your ass up?" Osborn responded, not amused by the comment.

Ray Parker didn't respond, he knew better. His 26 years with the Department didn't make him fond of supervisors, politicians, police commissioners, criminals and sometimes, people in general. It was no accident that, after all those years, he was still a patrolman, the lowest rank in the Department. His mouth had gotten him in trouble on more than one occasion. But that same irreverence was admired by the officers, generally, and contributed to his election as the president of the St. Louis Police Officers' Association, a powerful labor organization which boasted a membership of 85 percent of the patrolmen and sergeants. Lieutenants and above were considered supervisory personnel and were ineligible for membership.

"By the way, Parker, you are the senior most member of this platoon and the Captain wants you to ride with the prob until further notice. Don't corrupt him," Osborn said, half kidding, but also quite serious.

"Decker, you are assigned to Parker. Hopefully, you are smart enough to learn the good things he has to teach you and disregard the bullshit," Osborn said.

"It will be mostly bullshit," another unidentified voice injected.

"That's all I have." With that, the sergeant concluded the roll call and dismissed the platoon.

As he poured himself another cup of coffee, Bobby recalled experiencing some apprehension that day when he learned who his new partner/mentor would be for his time as a probationary officer. While at the academy, he'd heard all the stories and the legends about Police Officer Ray Parker. He remembered thinking on that first day, his new partner would at least be interesting, if nothing else. He just hoped he would learn something that would contribute to his goal of being the best cop in the Department.

Chapter Sixteen

For any rookie, the first day on the job is filled with excitement and apprehension. Bobby was no exception. But, on this, his very first day, he figured, or at least hoped, his veteran partner would show him the way. He had some vivid recollections of that first day with his new partner starting with when they met in the parking lot by the marked car assigned to them.

After 26 years on the job, Ray Parker was in no rush to get out onto the street. He was also in no hurry to meet his new, rookie partner. *Idealistic, crime stopper. Another kid fresh out of the academy who has absolutely no idea of how the real world works. How it has to work for law enforcement to win this war on crime. Otherwise, these assholes out here control the world. We can't and won't let that happen.* That was the Parker philosophy. Once upon a time, he was a young police officer. Naïve. Idealistic. Wide-eyed. Stupid. But eventually, with the time spent on the street, in the trenches, dealing with the scum of the earth, he learned and found the right track. It would not take long for Ray Parker to get Robert Decker on the right track.

Bobby recalled the first conversation with his new partner. "What's your name, kid?" Parker asked as he slowly approached the car.

"Bobby. Bobby Decker," was the response.

"Bobby? What are you, ten years old?" Parker responded, sarcasm filtering his words.

"My parents gave me that nickname at a young age. I guess I never really thought about changing it," Bobby replied apologetically.

"Okay, *Bobby*. Why did you want to be a cop? More importantly, why the hell did you choose this Godforsaken department?" Parker asked, sarcasm still in his voice.

"Because I want to fight crime and I thought this would be a good place to do that," Bobby said enthusiastically. "I want to help people and make a difference."

"Oh, shit, another Serpico crime fighter. Listen, Serpico, here's how it's going to work, at least as long as you are with me. We don't go out looking under rocks for shitheads. Believe me, there are enough out there that we don't have to go looking. You got that, Serpico?"

"Yes, sir," Bobby said.

"Another thing," Parker added. "I don't go chasing those shitheads. I'm too old to go running after anybody. I would just as soon shoot them and worry about justifying it in the report later. You can run after them if you want, just stay out of my line of fire."

In his 26 years with the Department, Officer Parker had three kills, all black suspects, all deemed justified and all the subject of controversy. His IAD record, however, was a different story.

The Internal Affairs Division of the St. Louis Police Department is responsible for investigating allegations of police misconduct. Within the Department, IAD investigators are disliked. Publicly, IAD is generally viewed with skepticism, but treated with total disdain, and perhaps even hatred by the black community. Black newspapers, black commentators and black radio stations in the St. Louis metropolitan area routinely criticized this arm of the Department, arguing that police officers would not objectively investigate their own.

The rank and file within the Department shared that criticism, but from a different perspective. They believed the IAD investigators were incompetents who devoted themselves to hanging police officers, in an effort to curry favor and kiss the asses of their supervisors. From its perspective, the Department was mindful of all of its critics, but did the best job it could, always attempting to calm the public storm when allegations of misconduct arise.

After several IAD investigations regarding excessive force complaints, Parker had lost some pay. Two of his brutality complaints were sustained, resulting in a total of a three month suspension without pay. Both cases, like his shootings, involved black suspects who allegedly were resisting arrest at the time of the use of force. Each was justified in the police reports he prepared, which were viewed by IAD as works of fiction. Unfortunately for Parker, in each case several credible eye witnesses refuted various aspects of the accounts Parker provided in his police reports. For his part, Parker, although upset by the loss of pay, was unfazed by the criticism of his behavior.

"Let's get the day started with some breakfast. I had a bad night. I know a place where we can get a police discount. You drive and I'll show you the way," Parker directed.

This was not exactly what Bobby Decker had envisioned for his first day on the job. You can't fight crime while eating bacon and eggs. But he was a prob, the lowest rank in the Department. He could only follow, not lead, at least for the moment. Bobby was determined to change that. Unfortunately, the future, always unpredictable, would not be kind to Bobby Decker. His history with the Department would become legendary. As he enjoyed his free breakfast the first day on the job, the last thing on his mind was any thought that someday, Bobby Decker, would end up on the wrong side of the law.

Chapter Seventeen

Bobby refilled his coffee cup for a third time and continued to recall the events of his first day on the job. After spending an hour in the restaurant, breakfast was finally over and now he could hit the street and do some real police work. This was what he had been waiting for. This was how he'd wanted to spend his life. Unfortunately, he was hooked up with a partner who didn't share his enthusiasm.

Figuring Parker wanted him to continue to drive, he got into the marked police car on the driver's side and waited for his partner, who was still holding court inside the restaurant. When he arrived at the vehicle, Parker stared at Decker for several moments. With the engine running but the vehicle not moving, Parker finally spoke.

"What, you don't like breakfast?"

"I like it just fine, sir," was the response, spoken hesitatingly.

"Well, then what?" Parker pressed. "You left there like you were shot out of a fucking cannon. What's your problem?"

"I don't have a problem, sir" Decker replied.

"Listen, Serpico. Don't bullshit a bullshitter. You have some bug up your ass and we're going to get it out, even if that means I have to send something up there to pull it out. I don't need to deal with some prob pouting for the next seven hours. So, let me ask again, what is your problem?"

"There is no problem. I was just looking forward to doing police work on my first day on the job, not eating breakfast, and a free breakfast at that," was Decker's response, this time with a hint of confidence.

"Let me tell you something, Johnny," Parker said, recognizing the hint of confidence in Decker's voice.

"Bobby," was Decker's immediate response.

"What?" Parker said.

"My name is Bobby, not Johnny," Decker corrected.

"Johnny, Donnie, Bobby, whatever. Listen, kid, you'll have plenty of time to do *police work,* as you call it. As far as the free breakfast is concerned, get used to that, because restaurants will do that frequently."

Looking confused, Bobby commented, "That just doesn't seem right to me. Seems like there is something unethical about it. Restaurants and other businesses pay their taxes and should expect police service without having to pay extra."

"Oh, my God. I can see I have a lot of work to do here. Did you learn that shit in the academy or is that a family thing?" Parker asked.

"Probably both," Bobby replied.

"Well, you would do yourself a favor to forget both," was the sharp but brief reply.

Unfortunately, Bobby recalled, The Parker Lectures, the first in a long series, were just beginning.

"Let's get something straight," Parker began. "We are going to be together for a long time, whether you like it or not. For me, I'm not thrilled. But we need to make the best of it because the situation ain't gonna change. I don't have a lot of formal education. My education came from the street, not books. My education was real, not imaginary. Your real education will also come from the street. If you don't understand anything else, understand there are people out here who don't like you. And there are people out here who will kill you. The first order of business: protect yourself. Assume everyone you meet would just as easily kill you as look at you. That way you can never be disappointed, and you'll always be prepared."

"That's a pretty cynical view of the world, isn't it?" Bobby said.

"Maybe. But I'm a realist. That badge you are wearing, doesn't mean shit to most of the people you'll encounter on this job. For some, it is a target. For those so-called law abiding citizens, you are tolerated when you are helping them. But give them a traffic ticket and watch how that *law abiding attitude* quickly changes."

Bobby listened as Parker continued.

"I don't expect you to shed that idealistic skin overnight," Parker went on. "In fact, you won't get a wakeup call until your ox is being gored. Until one of the so-called *good guys* kicks you in the balls when they file a complaint with IAD after you give them a goddamn traffic ticket. These assholes will try to get you fired because they're pissed that you told them they violated a traffic law. *A traffic law,"* he repeated. "And on top of that, not only do they file the complaint, they lie their asses off about what happened during the stop." Parker was on a roll. "Then the IAD goons investigate this bullshit, and you wind up on the 6th floor answering the complaint. By the way, you are guilty until proven guilty. Your own department throws you under the bus because they have no balls and it is all about their precious image. You learn pretty damn quick that you are expendable. Now let's get goin' and see where we are going to eat lunch."

As he recalled that his first day on the job was not exactly as he imagined, Bobby was now beginning to wonder whether that first day was meant as a wakeup call. Perhaps to let him know this job was not for him, just as his father had told him.

He also recalled his thoughts about his partner on that first day on the street. He was determined to keep an open mind. Surely, a person with that much experience would teach him something. He would not let his partner's cynicism affect his own enthusiasm for police work generally, or this job specifically.

Chapter Eighteen

Still deep in thought, he heard someone trying to unlock the front door. *That can't be Kathy; it's only 4 o'clock,* he thought. He hoped it was not her. He was not ready to deal with the conversation he knew was inevitable. He needed more time to collect his thoughts, to carefully measure his words with the hope those words would persuade her he desperately needed her support for what he anticipated would be his future. He had no confidence her boss would do the right thing and had even less confidence his boss would treat him fairly. His back was up against the wall with no one watching it. When the door opened, he saw Kathy. Her jaw was tight, her lips pursed, and her otherwise beautiful blue eyes signaled anger. His body stiffened. He wanted to run, but had nowhere to go. He had to deal with it at some point. And now was the time, whether he wanted to or not.

"You were suspended?" she began what was about to become an unpleasant conversation.

"Yes," Bobby replied, not knowing what else to say.

"And you didn't call me to tell me that. I had to hear it from the people in my office," she said, releasing the anger in her eyes.

"I thought I would tell you when you got home."

"Tell me when I got home?" she said incredulously. "Did you stop to think word of your suspension might spread like wildfire through the police department and into my office?" she asked.

"Given everything that happened today, I really didn't consider that."

His response did nothing to reduce her anger and frustration and actually only served to exacerbate it.

"Don't you understand, the death of Mitchell is the only thing people are talking about right now, and you are a big part of that discussion?"

"I really didn't have time to think about that, either."
Then, in an effort to change both the tone and the topic of
the conversation, Bobby said, "Why don't we go out and
have a drink and get some dinner?"

"What, so strangers can ask more questions and we
can be subjected to people whispering and staring?" she
asked, obviously not content to change the course of the
conversation.

"Kathy, I realize you are upset and I also realize this
is a hot topic of conversation. However, I seriously doubt
anyone will be whispering or staring at us."

"Bobby, you don't get it. You really don't get it. Whether
they are actually looking at us is not the point. I have that
thought in my head, and I'm having difficulty getting it out.
For me, they are looking and talking about you and, therefore, me because I'm with you," she said unapologetically.

In yet another effort to calm the conversation, Bobby
asked, "What can I do to help you get that idea out of your
head?"

"Once again, you don't get it. You can't do anything to
get it out of my head. Bobby, this is only going to get worse,
and because of you, I'll be in the middle. The police department will do their usual inadequate investigation and then
dump it on my office. Meanwhile, the media and the black
community will be looking for a scalp and encouraging a
criminal prosecution. And you'll be the target of that wrath
and I'll be dragged into it because of our relationship. So,
there is nothing you can do to help. What is it about that
you don't understand?"

Bobby really didn't know how to answer. What Kathy
was saying was true, and he knew it. He would be in the
eye of the storm, and she would be dragged into it with him.
Somehow, some way, he needed to avoid that. He had to
protect the ones he loved. And to do that he was beginning
to realize she would need to distance herself from him, dis-
associate. Regardless of what their relationship was before,
it had to change. She needed some cover, and he knew it.
The pain of that thought was beginning to overwhelm him,
but he knew he had to remain strong. Hoping his assess-
ment was wrong, he asked, "So, what should we do?"

"Before we go there, I need to understand a few other
things. What happened up on the roof that night, Bobby?

Did you cause that massive skull fracture? Was he resisting? Did he have a weapon? Will the force used ultimately be determined to have been reasonable under the circumstances? Talk to me, Bobby. What the hell happened?"

Ignoring his brother's lawyerly advice to keep his mouth shut, he simply said, "I don't know."

"You don't know. You don't know," she repeated in disbelief. "A guy is dead and you don't know how that happened. Who is going to believe that?"

"I don't know that either," he said, his voice trailing off.

"That's not going to fly. That will get you fired and worse, prosecuted and convicted."

Again, Bobby didn't know how to respond. Seemingly, the love of his life, the woman he lived with, the woman he hoped someday to marry, was telling him she didn't believe him. She had him tried and convicted, like so many others. If she didn't believe him, who would? The situation seemed hopeless. His life was crumbling and there was nothing he could do about it.

"I'm sorry you feel that way," was the only thing he could think of to say.

"It's not a matter of feeling that way. I'm a lawyer, a prosecutor, and I have to deal in facts just like you, as a police officer, have to deal with the facts. If you can't provide facts about how a guy dies from a massive skull fracture after he was in your custody, then what can I say? What can anyone say?"

Bobby didn't respond. She was right: What could anyone say?

But Kathy continued looking him directly in his eyes. She asked, "Bobby, did you hit him? Did you kill that kid?"

He had to end this conversation. It was going nowhere and was only going to escalate into a heated argument. The more he said he didn't know, the more she would press for answers he could not provide, and the more upset and stressed each would become. In as calm a voice as he could muster under the circumstances, he said, "Look, Kathy, this conversation is not productive for either of us. I can't explain how this guy's skull was fractured and that is that. I really don't want to talk about this anymore. Can we talk about something else?"

She didn't respond. Instead, she went into their bedroom, closing the door behind her and leaving Bobby in the living room, alone, with only his thoughts. He was numb. He could not imagine life without Kathy. He stared into space, looking for something to distract him and take his mind off of what was happening to his world. Finally, his thoughts returned to his first day on the job; the day he met Kathy.

Chapter Nineteen

The first day ended as it began, uneventful. No bad guys arrested, taken off the street, or even seen, for that matter. Instead, a lot of free meals, glad-handing, driving around the streets, listening to the rants of a disgruntled partner, and general boredom. *This is definitely not what I signed on for,* Bobby thought as he put his gear in his locker at the district station.

Those thoughts were interrupted by an unknown voice coming from behind the open door of the locker next to him. "How was the first day?"

"Not exactly what I had expected," Bobby replied as he continued to store his gear.

"What did you expect?" was the response, the identity of the speaker still concealed.

"Something other than spending my day in restaurants eating and drinking on the house," Bobby said.

"Looking for some action?" The door of the adjacent locker closed, revealing the face of the speaker.

"That would be nice," Bobby replied.

"Don't worry, it will come. Jerry, Jerry Stump," the speaker said, introducing himself and extending his hand.

"Bobby Decker," he said, extending his hand as he replied.

"Some people are heading over to Humphrey's for happy hour, if you would like to join us," Stump said.

"Love to," Bobby said.

"It's over on Spring on the St. Louis University campus," Stump directed.

"Yes, I know where it is. Thanks for the invite. I'll see you there in a few minutes," Bobby said.

When he arrived at the tavern, Bobby was surprised to see most of the officers on his shift were there. This would be a good opportunity to meet his fellow officers. As he made his way through the bar area, Bobby introduced himself to the people he saw along the way, all police officers.

It was no surprise to see his partner, a half-empty beer and an empty shot glass in front of him, standing at the bar complaining to someone about something. It probably wouldn't be long before Parker would be drunk and Bobby was not interested in witnessing that. The last thing he wanted was to listen to another Parker lecture, whether delivered drunk or sober. He'd had enough of that for the last eight plus hours and had more of the same to look forward to in the morning. Fortunately, he saw Jerry sitting at a table with four other individuals just beyond the bar. He headed in that direction, hoping Parker wouldn't spot him. Jerry welcomed him and invited him to pull up a chair.

After the customary introductions, the conversation turned to police work. War stories were shared—most embellished. While in the academy, he had heard all sorts of stories from his instructors, but you never knew what was real and what part of the tale was feel-good fiction. Most of the stories ended with the bad guy arrested. But always with some altercation, usually a physical resistance to avoid the arrest, followed by the customary ass-kicking. Since he had nothing to add, Bobby just listened while taking in the sights and sounds of the bar. He had been to plenty of bars during his college days, but never with cops carrying guns and drinking to forget the horrors of the day and those of the past.

As he surveyed the room, he spotted a female standing at the end of the bar, beer in hand and engaged in conversation with several officers from the 4th District. Although he recognized the officers, he didn't recognize her. He had never seen her before. He knew he would have remembered. She was beautiful. Blond hair, tall and a body that wouldn't quit. *Who is that?* he asked himself.

During his college days, Bobby Decker had made plenty of female friends, but had only one real girlfriend. They'd dated for three of their four college years. They'd been in love and talked of marriage. Eventually, during their senior year, Bobby proposed. But, like his parents, Jennifer Bates, was not excited about life with a cop. She didn't like the salary but, more importantly, didn't want to spend her future wondering whether some day he would not come home to her and the family they hoped to have. Eventually, she gave him an ultimatum, her or the career.

Some days he questioned his decision, but there was never a day he didn't miss her. For the past year and a half, he'd been alone and depressed; no one to talk to, confide in or share life's good and bad times. His thoughts had always turned to her. He'd had a few dates after the relationship with Jennifer ended, but not many. Certainly nothing serious, perhaps because he could not get her out of his head, perhaps because he remembered how it had ended, perhaps because his guilt was more than he could handle. But maybe now was the time to put the past behind him and move on down the road. *I'm starting a new career, a new life,* he thought as he watched the lady at the other end of the bar.

He'd met Jennifer at a mixer during the first week of their freshman year at Villanova University in Philadelphia. They both lived in the dorms on campus, although she was the only child of a prominent, mainline Philadelphia family. They'd spent summers together, working at honeymoon resorts in the Pocono Mountains of Pennsylvania and the Jersey shore to earn some spending money for school. They'd spent spring breaks together traveling to the warm climates of Mexico and Florida to avoid the harsh Philadelphia winters. They were inseparable, that is until the spring of their senior year.

The discussion started early during the fall semester of that year when he announced his desire to return to St. Louis to become a police officer. She liked St. Louis and didn't mind the idea of living there, but did object to his career choice. What started as a calm discussion escalated quickly. Positions became inflexible. For the first time since they'd met, they were no longer inseparable.

Spring break approached and they went their separate ways. They didn't spend that vacation together. She went to Mexico with some girlfriends and he went back to St. Louis to explore a career as a police officer. When they parted on that chilly March day, each hoped the other would see the light. After all those years, after all those good times, neither believed their differences could not be reconciled, somehow, someway. But they were wrong. They'd never seen each other again.

Chapter Twenty

The beer continued to flow at the watering hole along with the war stories, only to be interrupted by a visitor to the table, the beautiful blond at the end of the bar.

"Pull up a chair and join us, Counselor," came an invitation from one of the story tellers, briefly interrupting the latest tale.

"Here, take my seat, I've listened to enough of this bullshit and anyway, I need to get home," the officer sitting next to Bobby said, standing to offer his spot at the table to this very attractive female.

"Did we get all the bad guys off the street today? Or will I be able to take the day off tomorrow, because you won't be bringing me any work?" the newcomer asked, taking her seat.

"We got them all," was the slightly-slurred response from the other end of the table. "Now you need to do your job and make sure these pricks don't see the light of day."

"Don't look at me. We do our job. I can't help it if these city juries keep cutting them loose," was the quick and pointed response.

"That's debatable," was the equally quick reply from yet another part of the table.

Confused by the exchange, Bobby wondered who this person was who had apparently stepped into the lion's den. He didn't have long to wait for his answer. Jerry jumped in and decided to end a debate that could have gotten ugly by steering the conversation in a different direction.

"Kathy, this is Bobby Decker. Bobby just completed his first day on the job. Bobby, this is Kathy Adams, one of our best, if not *the* best prosecutor in the city and perhaps even the state," Jerry said, causing the prosecutor to blush slightly while shaking her head.

"Jerry is one of my biggest fans. Very nice to meet you, Bobby," Kathy said, extending her hand.

"Nice to meet you," Bobby replied, shaking her hand, impressed with the strength of her grip.

Determined to continue and perhaps even escalate the debate, one of the uniforms at the table sarcastically asked, "Don't you get a chance to vote on the jury?"

"Perhaps if you came to see a trial, you would know both the prosecution and the defense are allowed to question the prospective jurors and then strike an equal number, reducing the final number to 12. That's called the *voir dire* part of the trial. That phrase isn't too big for you, is it?"

"Very funny. I don't have time to come to a trial. I'm too busy rounding up these assholes you put back on the street," the uniform added, signaling to the waitress he needed another beer.

"Apparently, from what I can see here, you don't spend all of your time on the street. Are you in here looking for bad guys?" Kathy asked with a hint of a smile.

"I come here to reduce the frustration caused by your office. Seems like every time I bring a case to the warrant office, you folks refuse it, claiming the case isn't any good. I have a bad search. Or the identification is bad. Or there is no corroboration on a one on one. Or bullshit, bullshit, bullshit. I walk out frustrated, because either the lawyers in your office don't know the law, or they are too lazy to apply it. Which do you think it is, Counselor?"

"Neither, but I can appreciate your frustration," was the calm response. Then she continued, "Once again, let me try to explain something to you so you can understand life from my chair. I'll do it slowly this time, so hopefully, you'll get it! The prosecutor in the warrant office first has to evaluate the case from the legal standpoint of whether there is probable cause to issue a criminal charge. Then we decide whether the case can be proven to the satisfaction of the jury beyond a reasonable doubt. In other words, can we win? I suspect you already know all this, but choose to ignore it because you believe every case you bring to us should be prosecuted and won."

"Yes, I'm well aware the case has to be proven to the satisfaction of a jury beyond a reasonable doubt," the officer said, determined to continue the debate with Adams. "I also know we bring your office good cases that wind up with an acquittal or a sweetheart plea bargain deal. I'm surprised your office doesn't issue letters of apologies to these shitheads."

"We do the best we can," Adams said, determined to end the discussion.

"I take it that prosecutors and cops don't always agree on cases," Decker said turning his attention to Adams.

"It is a frustrating business for all who are involved," Adams said. "Juries are very unpredictable. Just when you think your evidence is strong, they walk the guy out the door."

"I can see I have a lot to learn about this job and the people in it," Decker said. "Can I get you a drink?" Decker hoped to spend more time getting to know this lovely lady.

"Sure," Kathy Adams replied without hesitation.

Although he only spent a couple hours with her, Bobby knew he wanted to see Kathy Adams again. He didn't believe in that love at first sight thing. But he did know he wanted to get to know her better. A lot better. He hoped she felt the same. As he drifted off to sleep, thoughts of Kathy replaced those of his partner, Ray Parker, and his uneventful first day on the job.

Chapter Twenty-One

When Kathy got home, her roommate, also a prosecutor, was sitting on the couch and commented, "Home kinda late on a school night, aren't we?"

Kathy Adams and Linda Erhardt had known each other since they had gone to high school together. They had gone to law school together. They worked as prosecutors together and in fact, shared the same office. But they were more than roommates and officemates, they shared their deepest and darkest secrets. They knew everything about each other and together they resolved all the bumps in the road of life.

"Working late," Kathy said, knowing full well her confidant would not believe that.

"Really. Working at the office or in the field?" Linda inquired, continuing the fictional conversation.

"Field," Kathy said.

"Serious or casual crime?" was the next question from her fellow prosecutor.

"Casual at the moment, but could become a serious offense after the investigation is concluded."

"When is the next trip to the field to continue the investigation?" Linda asked.

"Don't know."

Linda pressed on, "Don't know? How can you investigate when you don't know when you are going to investigate?"

"If you knew anything about investigating, you would know you always let the suspect make the first move," Kathy said.

"Judging from the time you got home, I thought the suspect made the first move tonight," was Linda's quick response.

"Mostly surveillance, with some interrogation," Kathy replied, just as quickly.

"What's the pedigree?"

"White, male, about 6-foot-5, 200 or so pounds of solid muscle."

"Is the suspect employed?" Linda asked, pressing for all the information she could get.

"Police officer," Kathy said, hesitatingly, knowing her best friend would eventually be offering some advice on that issue.

"Oh, no. Please tell me the suspect is not a city police officer."

"Okay, I won't tell you that," Kathy said, bracing for the lecture.

Kathy didn't have to wait very long. Shaking her head, Linda said, "Girl, have you lost your mind and your good judgment? The last thing you need is to get involved with a city cop. You know we do battle with those folks every day. We didn't issue a case they think had merit. It is our fault when one of their precious cases is lost because they screwed up on the witness stand. They continuously say we don't know what we are doing and they are perfect. And on and on. And then there is the problem of the office politics. What happens if he winds up as the star witness on one of your cases? Or worse, what happens if he screws up one of your cases? This could only end badly for you."

"I don't disagree with any of that, but there is something different about this guy. He is not typical and for some reason, I'm really attracted to him. I can't explain it. It's a feeling."

Linda's opposition continued when she asked, "And the worst of the worse. What happens if this guy does something stupid and winds up as a real criminal suspect in our office? You know how some of these guys can't stay out of trouble." Although only offering friendly advice to her friend at this moment, Linda had no way of knowing just how prophetic this question would become.

"No guarantees about anything in life. But I don't think this guy is that type. He seems to be smart and caring, and he loves his job. Of course, he is only a prob, so that may change when he gets a taste of the streets and his fellow officers."

"Listen, girlfriend. I can only offer advice. I can't make you follow it," was Linda's final comment, before she rose and left the room to go to bed.

Sitting alone in the living room, Kathy thought about what Linda had said. While she didn't know where a relationship with Bobby Decker would go—if anywhere—she knew she would be taking a chance. If something went wrong, she clearly understood she might be placed in a position where she had to choose between her career and Bobby Decker. Another prophecy which would not be recognized for several years. But she was willing to take that chance.

Chapter Twenty-Two

He waited for several weeks before calling Kathy. He didn't remember why, but recalled that someone, somewhere had given him the advice that you shouldn't appear too anxious when pursuing a potential relationship. Whether that advice was good or bad is anyone's guess. In this case, apparently it worked, because Kathy accepted his dinner invitation and many more.

On this day, his relationship with this woman might be in jeopardy. She was in the bedroom with the door closed, a gesture designed to keep him away, shut him out. While fighting back tears, he tried to remember only the good times and one date in particular. It was a very special evening.

It was Valentine's Day, a day that before he met Kathy, was viewed as a *Hallmark* day designed to improve the net worth of the card company. But this time it was different. This time it was special. He wanted to make it something they both would remember. He was becoming a romantic. He'd made reservations at a bed and breakfast in a small rural town dotted with vineyards and wineries, some 70 miles from the city and the job he wanted to leave behind, at least for this day and night.

They had a candlelight dinner in a little fifteen-table bistro that prepared not only the salad, but also the entrée and dessert tableside. They sipped an expensive Merlot as they watched the chef prepare their special dinner. Cost was not a factor on this day.

After a leisurely dinner, they headed back to the bed and breakfast, since the cold night air made it uncomfortable to walk for any length of time. Once in their room, Bobby built a fire and opened another bottle of wine, which had been placed in their room while they were at dinner, along with freshly cut flowers. While he was building the fire, Kathy went into the bathroom to change clothes.

With the room illuminated only by the light from the fire, Bobby watched as Kathy returned to the bedroom, clothed in a nightgown that highlighted a magnificent body. As she approached, he saw she was wearing nothing underneath. He could plainly see the most private parts of her perfect body. Captivated by her beauty, he rose from his chair, meeting her near the foot of the bed they would eventually share.

His body aching for her, he looked into her eyes and gently kissed her lips. As he did, he slowly untied the only thing that covered her and allowed the garment to fall gently to the floor. Her fragrant body glowed in the foreground of a fire that spread warmth throughout the room on this cold winter night. As he gazed at her naked body he put his finger to her lips, she gently touched it with her tongue.

Bobby could hear her moaning as he moved his finger down her body and he felt the skin react with excited anticipation. He held her in his muscular arms and gazed into her eyes as he guided her into their bed which had been warmed by the heat from the fireplace. He kissed her lips as their naked bodies touched. Slowly at first and then more rapidly, their bodies moved, perfectly synchronized and in harmony as though one, until eventually he exploded to the music of loud, satisfied and fulfilled lust. Feeling completely relaxed and somewhat drained, he looked at her and for the first time said, "I love you."

Instantly, she replied, "I love you, too."

Although this was not the first time they had experienced each other sexually, it was the first time they had made love. This night their relationship soared to another level; one that would be filled with joy and happiness. Other wonderful nights would follow. But none would be the same.

Bobby's pleasant thoughts were interrupted when he heard the bedroom door open. Kathy emerged carrying an overnight bag. He looked at her and said nothing, waiting for her to speak.

"I'm going to stay at Linda's for a few days until I can figure this out," she said with little emotion in her voice.

The look became a stare. He said nothing. There was not much he could say. He knew it was no use attempting to talk her out of leaving. Actually, he was not sure he wanted to. This might be the best thing for her, allowing her time away from him to think, to think about what was best for her.

"I'll call you," she said as she walked quickly to the door.

As he watched the door close, he began to cry. The recollection of that Valentine's Day moment was replaced by the pain of the present. Suddenly, he realized his memories might be all he had left.

Chapter Twenty-Three

The body of Jordon Mitchell had been delivered to the medical examiner's office so an autopsy could be performed. In a death such as this, the law requires an autopsy be performed by the medical examiner, who will decide the cause. The autopsy in the case of the death of Jordon Mitchell would be performed by Phillip Long, M.D., the medical examiner for the city of St. Louis. The St. Louis news media repeatedly reported Mitchell sustained a massive skull fracture and speculated the head injury was the cause of his death. It would be Dr. Long's job not only to verify the cause of death but also to determine the cause of the fracture itself.

Dr. Long had been the city's medical examiner for the past 20 years. A graduate of St. Louis University School of Medicine where he also held a teaching position, Dr. Long had performed autopsies in many high profile cases, but perhaps none more volatile than this one. He had seen, heard and read the publicity, including front page coverage complete with photographs of Mitchell in the intensive care unit of the hospital. Of course, one would have to be living under a rock to know nothing about this case. Having performed autopsies of black males who died at the hands of police officers, Dr. Long was certainly aware of the historical animosity between the police department and the black community. He was also acutely aware of the Cannon case, which had exacerbated that ill will and almost led to street rioting and property damage during a long hot summer several years ago. Fortunately, he hadn't been involved in that case.

When he was notified Mitchell had died, his initial thought was to send the case someplace else. Unfortunately, this was his venue and his responsibility. Like it or not, he had to do the autopsy. Although he was willing to do his duty, Dr. Long was aware of the impact any decision he made could have on the case specifically and the city generally. He also understood he was a white physician performing an autopsy on a black young man who was allegedly injured by a white police officer, and that he was doing so under intense media scrutiny.

He had already received a phone call from the circuit attorney's office asking that he call when the autopsy was completed. More eyes watched him every step of the way. Certainly, it was not a surprise the circuit attorney would have an immediate interest, particularly after the Cannon fiasco. Dr. Long was sympathetic to her and the position in which she found herself in that case. He believed the criticism, escalating to hostility, was neither justified nor fair. However, although sympathetic to her, he didn't want to suffer the same fate in this case.

The autopsy, exclusive of the brain, took over four hours. Ordinarily, an autopsy such as this could be done in half the time, but this was no ordinary case. He wanted to be sure he looked at and identified every body part and every square inch of this body. There could be no mistakes. The report he would eventually prepare must be thorough and complete, as it would become the road map for this entire case. Already, he had received media inquiries and two additional phone calls from an anxious circuit attorney. It was no secret he was performing the autopsy in this case.

During the course of the autopsy, an investigator assigned to the medical examiner's office informed him a demonstration was under way. A group of some 50 people, carrying signs and led by a nationally known civil rights activist, were protesting the death of Jordon Mitchell in front of the police department, a half block from the medical examiner's office. A press conference was scheduled later in the day.

Quentin Jennings was a prominent civil rights activist who lived in New York City and had run unsuccessfully for various political offices, including the Presidency of the United States. He was an associate of the late Dr. Martin Luther King and the Reverend Jessie Jackson. He took responsibility for demonstrations in various cities protesting the treatment of black people, mostly at the hands of white police officers. Quentin Jennings was a name known to Dr. Long. He quickly realized the presence of Jennings would not be a good thing, unless his and other opinions supported the conclusions Jennings and company had already drawn.

Motivated in part by the presence of Quentin Jennings, Dr. Long realized after completing the autopsy that he was going to need some help. He needed someone to share the front line if the guns were pointed in his direction. Other than the brain, the autopsy was really rather routine. It was the autopsy of the brain that would dictate the course of this case. Dr. Long decided he would solicit some help for that autopsy. His choice was Dr. Helen McHenry.

Helen McHenry, M.D., was a medical examiner with more experience than Dr. Long. Dr. McHenry had been the St. Louis county medical examiner for more than 25 years, and had also taught at St. Louis University School of Medicine, from which she graduated with honors. Unlike Dr. Long, Dr. McHenry loved the limelight. She had a reputation among defense lawyers that she was never one to be confused by the facts. She was aggressive, but also persuasive. She didn't shy away from publicity, but actually embraced it. In fact, some of her colleagues had suggested Dr. McHenry had never met a microphone she didn't like. That said, Dr. Long thought she would be perfect for this job. She would aggressively advocate their position and handle the media at the same time. She was the ideal choice, and Dr. Long figured she would not hesitate to become involved.

When he called Dr. McHenry, she was thrilled. But, in typical McHenry fashion, she had questions, lots of questions.

"What do you want me to do?" she asked enthusiastically.

"I would like you to do the autopsy of the brain," he responded with equal enthusiasm.

"Okay, but why do you want me to do that? You are perfectly capable of doing an autopsy of a brain," she noted.

"I know," he said. "But I need another set of eyes on this one. Frankly, Helen, if this thing goes south, I need someone on board with me," he added.

"What do you mean, on board?" she asked with a bit of hesitation.

"Look, Helen, this is a black kid who sustained a massive skull fracture and a subdural hematoma—potentially at the hands of a white police officer, in a city racially charged to begin with. The word from the police department is that the arresting officer has no explanation for the injury, which puts me in a rather precarious position from the start. My quick look at the brain verified his injuries were caused by blunt trauma with a linear object, which means the cop probably whacked this guy with a night stick or a kell light or some other linear object. The brain autopsy will either confirm or refute that preliminary opinion. But if the brain autopsy is inconsistent with the opinions of the media and the protestors, I don't want to be in a position of torpedoing the case. So, frankly, I need someone strong to partner up with," Long candidly explained.

"Interesting. Ordinarily, I don't have a problem with high profile cases. However, this one seems to be a no win for anyone," she replied.

"That's how I see it, and I'm in the middle. I don't have a choice, but you do. So, are you in? Can I count on you to help?" Long asked, attempting to fast forward through the questions and get to the bottom line.

"I'm in, Phillip," she said simply.

"Great. I'll send the brain over to your office today. What does the timetable look like?"

"I would say three to four weeks, but more likely closer to four," Dr. McHenry estimated.

"That's what I thought. Just let me know as soon as you can. As you know, there are many eyes on this one. Thanks, Helen. I appreciate your help," a grateful and relieved Long said.

When he finished his conversation with Dr. McHenry, Dr. Long asked his secretary to see if she could get the circuit attorney on the telephone, so he could return at least one of her six calls.

"Finally, you called me back. I need to know what this looks like," the circuit attorney demanded as soon as Dr. Long picked up the phone.

"I don't know yet. The autopsy is not done."

"What do you mean, you don't know? You did examine him, didn't you? Surely, you have some idea of what killed this kid. I have people climbing all over this and I need some idea of where we are headed, Phillip," Cardwell said, now pleading rather than demanding.

"After a cursory review, it looks like blunt trauma with a linear object. However, Joan, I'm sending the brain out to Doctor McHenry in Saint Louis County to do that part of the autopsy and that will take about four weeks to complete."

"Why so long, Phillip? You know I have everyone breathing down my neck on this thing," Cardwell asked, clearly annoyed by Long's timetable.

"Because we have to let the brain firm up before we can cut it," he said, believing he would not need to provide any additional details at this point.

Pressing for a different answer, she asked, "Is there anything we can do to speed up the process?"

"No, nature has to take its course," the medical examiner said, clearly annoyed by the question.

"Well, let me know as soon as you can," Cardwell said, abruptly ending the conversation, neglecting the customary cordial salutations.

Chapter Twenty-Four

As promised, Quentin Jennings held his press conference in front of police headquarters, the same location where the protest was held and not far from where the lifeless body of Jordon Mitchell was stored. The conference was well attended by both print as well as electronic media from the St. Louis area. Jennings had hoped to attract some national press, but that didn't happen, at least not to date.

With the Mitchell family by his side, Jennings began by telling those in attendance this was a young black man who was brutally murdered by a white police officer. His style was inflammatory, but persuasive. He continued by recounting the various problems that existed between the police department and the black community, suggesting blacks were targeted by overzealous officers who paid little attention to the civil rights of their targets.

The behavior of these officers was condoned and even encouraged by the Chief and other supervisors, he suggested. In support of that statement, he pointed to the Cannon case. He reminded his audience that the white Sgt. Cannon had brutally beaten a mentally-challenged, young black man in his own home and suffered no consequence. Of course, Jennings completely skimmed past the fact that, although acquitted of criminal acts, the officer had been disciplined by the Department with a reduction in rank which ultimately led to his resignation. But Jennings was not holding a press conference to recite facts; he was there to inflame the crowd and encourage a criminal prosecution of Bobby Decker, justified or not.

After additional criticisms of the police department and suggestions they were murdering *our* black babies, the wrath of Jennings turned to the circuit attorney. In recounting her handling, or rather mishandling, of the Cannon case, he said no one could be that inept. He postulated that her behavior in allowing that case to be tried in a venue outside the city where the crime happened was intentional, and not an act of misfeasance. He went on to say this white prosecutor didn't care about black people and didn't care whether police officers were violating the civil rights of blacks on a daily basis.

In support of his accusations, he pointed to the case at hand. "The lack of a prosecution in this case serves to highlight her lack of respect for those black people who are victimized and even murdered by this police agency. A first year law student could prosecute a case where an unarmed black man, like Jordon Mitchell, suffered a massive skull fracture while in the sole custody of a white police officer." The reporters took copious notes. The television cameramen periodically scanned the audience, mostly black faces, but growing by the minute with curious businesspeople stopping to see what the fuss was about.

"Yet, this white prosecutor apparently can't seem to figure out that this is an open and shut case of *murder,* since she has failed to bring any criminal charges against these white-cop murderers," Jennings shouted, as he continued to excoriate the circuit attorney. He was a pro at working a crowd.

"You're right, you're right, you're right," voices in the crowd chanted.

"What is she waiting for?" he continued, enticing the crowd with each word he uttered. "Perhaps she is planning to take this case in front of an all-white Klu Klux Klan jury, like she did the last time one of her white cops unmercifully beat a young, special needs, black man half to death. Or perhaps she is planning to take this to a grand jury where she can make this case go away behind closed doors," Jennings said, his voice rising with each point.

The crowd was now at a fever pitch, screaming, "Justice for Jordon. Justice for Jordon. Justice for Jordon."

The press conference lasted for more than an hour. No one left early. The reporters continued to take detailed notes, some amazed at Jennings' ability to work a crowd. This was a headline for the newspapers the next day and on the television news that night. Also taking notes was an investigator from the circuit attorney's office, sent there to monitor not only what was said, but also who was in attendance.

When the conference ended, the investigator immediately called the circuit attorney. His report was upsetting, but not unexpected. Cardwell knew she would be attacked by Jennings because that was his style; inflame, and ignore factual accuracy. Although she expected this, listening to the investigator describe the specific details was a different story.

How was she going to handle Jennings and the lynch mob he created? She needed to do something and she needed to do it quickly. Her future was on the line. She couldn't afford another Cannon mistake. She needed help. She needed Carol Masterson. Carol would know what to do.

When Masterson arrived at Cardwell' office, she found the circuit attorney sitting behind her desk, staring out the window, shaking her head and mumbling incoherently. "What's going on?" Masterson asked.

Taking a few moments to compose herself, Cardwell briefed Masterson on the Jennings press conference. She also told her about her conversation with Dr. Long.

"What do we do now?" the attorney asked. "This guy Jennings has added a whole new dimension. He is out there stirring the troops. I'm concerned that today we have protests, but tomorrow we may have riots if he is allowed to continue without challenge."

Masterson said in a calm voice, "Joan, you know what you have to do. You can't simply try to put this on the police department and hide behind the fact that their investigation is incomplete like we originally planned. That won't work. This Jennings guy put you on the front line, and I don't think we can spin it away from you."

Yes, Cardwell knew what she had to do. It was obvious. The only way Jennings would be silenced, at least for the moment and a potential riot avoided, was if she prosecuted someone for murder. It was also the only way she was going to avoid incurring the wrath of the black politicians, both state and local. She had already received calls from politicians, both black and white, asking what she was going to do and suggesting the need to do something, and soon.

"But prosecuting at this time is pretty risky without a completed autopsy and no investigation," Cardwell remarked.

"Is that any more risky than if you don't bring criminal charges at this time?" Masterson asked. They both knew the risk they were discussing was personal to Cardwell and had nothing to do with the pursuit of justice.

"I suppose not," Cardwell replied.

"Besides, I doubt that there will be any surprises in whatever investigation the Department conducts. You already know Decker prepared a police report in which he didn't account for any need to strike Mitchell. He just wrote it like a routine arrest where a black kid gets a massive skull fracture. In fact, correct me if I'm wrong, but he didn't even mention the fracture itself," Masterson said.

"That's my understanding."

"So that means he will be hard pressed to deviate from that work of fiction at trial, assuming there is a trial, and you can use that report against him. I think any rational jury will conclude an inability to explain this kind of massive injury when you are the sole custodian of this guy is unbelievable. Plus, this time you'll be trying the case in the city of St. Louis and not Kansas City. The media coverage will work in your favor, particularly when they get wind of the fact that Decker has no explanation for the injury, which I assume we will leak sooner rather than later. Plus, you have that maniac Jennings pounding the drum. The press loves him. Finally, your jury panel will have a lot of black faces. The defense won't have enough strikes to eliminate all the blacks, try as they might. So, you'll have black people sitting in judgment of a white cop who is accused of murdering a black kid," Masterson noted enthusiastically.

"Yes, but we will have some white people on that jury and don't forget this kid, as you call him, was burglarizing a pawn shop in the middle of the night. The defense will hammer that, suggesting police officers have a difficult job. In this case, they had no idea what they were going to find on that roof this dark and rainy night. Yet, they put their lives on the line in the interests of justice and blah, blah, blah," Cardwell said sarcastically.

"All true. But simply because someone is committing a burglary, a property crime, is not a justification for murder.

I think Decker would have been much better off if he had written that report justifying the use of force. Write it in to write it out, as they say over there. Surely, he knew about the skull fracture before he submitted the report, it was all over the news."

"I'm sure he did. I don't know why he didn't do that. Those guys usually don't have any problem writing the reports like that, true or not," Cardwell noted.

Anxious to press on, Masterson said, "Well, it doesn't matter why he didn't write the report that way. That ship sailed. He is stuck with what he wrote and there is no going back, and that benefits you."

"But what if we prosecute and lose, like with Cannon?" she asked.

Masterson was quick to respond. "You lost now, my friend. If you don't prosecute, you better kiss that judgeship goodbye. If you prosecute and lose, same result. But if you prosecute and win, you can make an appointment with the tailor to be measured for that black robe. You will be a hero.

"Most normal people will have no argument with your decision to take on a corrupt police department who takes pride in murdering the suspects in their custody. Oh, sure, there will be some rednecks who will be critical, but they will be in the minority, and their voice will be drowned out by the majority. Our added media spin and manipulation will help. The bottom line is, you have no choice. Let's get going and schedule a press conference for tomorrow."

"Should we do a conference or just a news release?" Cardwell asked.

Without any hesitation whatsoever, Masterson said, "A conference. You need the face time to offset that jackass, Jennings."

Chapter Twenty-Five

The protests and the commentary of the civil rights group didn't go unnoticed in the office of the Chief of Police. He, too, had an aide attending the press conference to monitor the comments and assess the mood. Like the circuit attorney, he was concerned about the future—his own. Also like the circuit attorney, he called a staff meeting designed to protect his public image.

The death of Jordon Mitchell was on a dynamic fast track fueled by an angry section of the community and aided by the news media. The Police Department was squarely in the eye of the storm, and the Chief was drowning. Demands for action needed a response. A response from him. *But what kind of response will calm the masses and redirect the wrath?* A carefully worded public statement was necessary. A long term plan needed. This could only get worse. Another Cannon disaster must be avoided at all costs.

For the second time, the same group of suspects gathered in the Chief's office to plan strategy. *What would the next move be, now that the ever changing landscape escalated from earlier in the day?* They, too, were concerned about that interloper, Jennings, the outsider who came to town to cause trouble.

Although he was an African American, the Chief was subjected to the same criticism as his white counterpart in the circuit attorney's office. During the hour-long press conference, Jennings spared no one. He described Chief Rodgers as an *Uncle Tom* who did nothing to protect his people. Instead, he encouraged racist misconduct among his storm troopers by his inaction.

But what more can I do at this point? the Chief asked himself. He had already suspended Decker, and couldn't fire him unless he gave him a public hearing before the Board of Police Commissioners. And that would be a disaster. He needed some advice. He recognized his limitations in the public relations category. He had been nailed to the cross by his own premature comments in the Cannon case and was not going to let that mistake happen again. After briefing him on the content of the Jennings press conference, he solicited the input of Lt. Col. Raymond Winston, the head of Internal Affairs.

"I don't think there is anything else that we can do at this point. Although we know what Decker put in his report, we don't have a completed investigation. In fact, that investigation is just beginning. We have secured all of Decker's property and have sent some of it to the lab for analysis. Plus, we have requested some of Mitchell's DNA from the medical examiner. What else do we need to do at this time?" Winston said.

"I don't think there *is* anything else from an investigation standpoint. But what about *Johnny Six Pack?* What do we say to the public? Also, what do we do about Jennings? How do we counter him?" the Chief asked.

"I think that we need to do what we talked about earlier today. Call a press conference to dispel the notion that we are doing nothing and explain what we have done thus far in the investigation, including the suspension of Decker. We say that we are taking this matter very seriously and if misconduct has occurred, we will deal with it and allow the criminal justice system to deal with it, as well. We then toss it to the circuit attorney with the hope that she doesn't screw this one up."

"Yes, I think that's what has to be done," the Chief said, adding, "The key point that gets us off the hot seat is the fact that we suspended Decker and took some action, which is more than our prosecutor did. But do you think we should terminate him?"

"No, that would be a bad idea. First, we haven't completed the investigation. We don't have the autopsy results yet and that could be significant. Second, we would have to give him a public hearing before the police board and that has the potential, at least, to be turned into a three ring circus. But it might not be a bad idea to explain the procedural process in a press conference."

"What would you suggest that we say about that?"

"I would say that Decker has been suspended while the investigation continues, with a view toward termination. However, the state legislature, not us, has given St. Louis police officers some rights that most other police officers in the state don't have. This includes a full evidentiary hearing before the Board of Police Commissioners, the governing body of this department. Proof, evidence, concrete evidence would have to be produced to demonstrate that he violated the rules of the Department and should be terminated. When the investigation is concluded, the issue of termination will be revisited."

"I don't know. It sounds like a bunch of complicated legal mumbo jumbo and might look like we are using this legal requirement to dodge the issue," the Chief said, expressing his skepticism with the idea.

"Well, maybe we can explain that the guns should be pointed at the legislature. They are the ones who established this antiquated system, during the days of the Civil War, where the state government controls our police department and the governor appoints his political friends as commissioners to run this department. They are the people who make the decisions, including whether a police officer continues his employment. If you controlled this department without that political interference, Decker's future here would be an easy call. But, unfortunately, you don't and we have to live within a system that we had nothing to do with creating. I'm sure this Jennings character has no idea about that history. I'm also sure that he can spin it to make it sound like this state was an advocate of slavery and still is, whether or not it's factually accurate. He demonstrated his love of the facts in his press conference today."

"I don't know," the Chief said again. "I'll think about it. But I'm thinking that it's too complicated and it won't buy us anything. Our best bet might be to talk about the suspension, our investigation, and then try to throw it to the circuit attorney after our investigation is completed. Maybe we can toss it to her after we get the results of the autopsy. I think that autopsy is going to be important. That may answer a lot of questions."

"Have you had any conversation with her since this mess began?" Winston asked, referring to the circuit attorney.

"Hell, no," came a quick response from the Chief. "That would be a total waste of my time; that lady is all about herself and the hell with everyone else. By the way, didn't Decker have an IAD problem some time ago?"

Surprised that the Chief remembered that, but thinking it was more likely someone else did and brought it to his attention, Winston responded affirmatively, volunteering no details.

"Wasn't that some kind of false reporting issue?" the Chief asked, continuing to press the point.

Again, Winston simply responded in the affirmative with no additional details. He was becoming uncomfortable with this conversation.

"Why wouldn't I mention that during the press conference, or at least leak it at the appropriate time?" he asked continuing the conversation, apparently oblivious to Winston's comfort level.

"I don't think that would be a good idea, chief," Winston said, unable to change the subject. He expected that he would be asked to explain.

As anticipated, the chief wanted to know why.

Winston was silent, a moment. "Several years ago when Decker was a prob," he began, "his partner was Ray Parker, a character who spent more time in IAD than he did on the street."

"I'm familiar with him and at least some of his antics," the Chief said.

"Well, Parker was involved in a shooting in the 6th district. He and Decker were transferred there toward the end of Decker's probationary period. One night while on routine patrol, they interrupted a drug deal on a street corner. Shots were fired by Parker, sending a guy to the hospital for several weeks. A couple of witnesses turned up to say that the guy was unarmed when he was shot and no one fired at the police. We began an investigation. At the time, we thought this would be a good case to get rid of Parker once and for all, but we needed better witnesses than what we had, so we focused on his partner Decker. We figured if we could squeeze him to come in on his partner, that would give some credibility to the other witnesses and we would have Parker by the balls."

As Winston continued to explain, the Chief made no comment, but looked confused. He wondered where this story was going.

"But unfortunately, Decker didn't want to cooperate. When we interviewed him, he supported Parker and said that a shot was fired at them and Parker returned the fire, striking one of the suspects while the other guy took off. He was unclear which suspect fired first. No gun or casings were found."

Interrupting Winston and still confused, the Chief asked, "So how does Decker wind up with a sustained false reporting charge?"

"Well, we thought that if we threatened Decker with a false reporting charge, we could flip him, particularly because he was a prob. We explained to him that as a prob we could fire him immediately and would not have to give him a hearing before the Board of Police Commissioners. But that didn't work and he continued to support Parker and his story. We charged him with false reporting to make good on our threat, but he still refused to throw Parker under the bus. In the meantime, Parker decided that he wanted out and retired. Since Parker was gone, we decided that instead of firing Decker, we would recommend that the board just extended his probationary period, which they ultimately did."

The Chief, confusion turning to anger, asked, "If this guy lied in his IAD statement, why in the hell was he not fired? We have enough problems around here without keeping liars, particularly people who lie to us during their first year on the job. Of course, need I tell you that if you took care of this guy when he was a prob, we would not have our current problem?"

Winston said, "Frankly, we couldn't fire him. After we charged him and before Parker resigned, a witness came forward, some guy who was making a delivery to a grocery store in the area. The newspaper picked up the story and this guy read the article and didn't believe it was an accurate accounting of what actually happened. He confirmed the accounts of both Parker and Decker. We didn't disclose this witness to anyone because the lawyer representing Parker told us that his client was thinking about retiring and we didn't want to do anything to change his mind. After he retired, we extended Decker's probation because we felt we could not dismiss the false reporting charge."

"You are kidding, right?" was the only thing the Chief said.

"No, sir, I'm not," Winston replied.

Shaking his head while looking out one of the many windows in his office, the Chief was clearly angry. The silence was deafening. The tension headache splitting. Without notice, he turned quickly, looked directly at Winston and said, "Holy shit. You are telling me that Decker, the prime suspect in the death of Jordon Mitchell is not a liar although, you, in your infinite wisdom, branded him a liar and didn't fire him. That is just swell. What exactly do you plan to do when the media figures out we didn't fire a liar who is now responsible for the death of a young black kid? Better yet, what are you going to do when Decker figures this out? When he figures out that there was a witness who exonerated him and Parker?"

Winston simply said, "I don't know."

The Chief was quick to respond and made no effort to hide his anger. "You better goddamn figure out something, and you don't have a lot of time. In the meantime, I think we better avoid the media and keep our mouths shut for the time being, hoping that this issue does not surface." He rose and then quickly walked out of his office, leaving the head of the Internal Affairs Division to consider how to avoid yet another Cannon type disaster.

Chapter Twenty-Six

Joan Cardwell spent the morning in her office behind closed doors with her confidant, Carol Masterson, planning her remarks for the press conference that she had scheduled for midday—strategically designed to avoid live coverage on the noon news. She knew what had to be done, but was uncertain as to the specific words she needed to deflect Jennings and his brutal attacks. She also knew that she had to score with the politicos. They held her future in their greedy little hands. She had to deliver. Deliver Decker and calm the outrage. Cardwell had done many press conferences since she was elected as the circuit attorney for the city of St. Louis, but none more important than this one.

So, what do I say, Carol? How do I start the conference? Should I read from a prepared text? were just some of the many questions running through her head.

Carol Masterson was a genius at political spin, a true *Spin Doctor*. She had all the answers. She even had answers to questions that hadn't been asked.

In response to the questions Cardwell rapid-fired at her, Masterson said, "You start with announcing the criminal charges that you intend to bring. That is really all they are interested in anyway, and that will set the tone and be the headline. I assume that you have decided what you want to do in that regard."

"Yes. I'm going to charge both Decker and Corbett with murder second degree."

"Corbett? I'm no lawyer, but what did Corbett do? How are you going to make a murder case against him?" Masterson asked.

"Frankly, I'm not completely sure," Cardwell said, adding, "In fact, I'm not completely sure how I'm going to make the case against Decker, particularly since I don't have a completed autopsy report of the brain, a critical piece of this puzzle."

"I realize there are risks. However, as we discussed yesterday, I'm not sure that we have any choice. That is, unless you want to spend the rest of your professional life in private practice or working for some corporation."

"Not interested in that," Cardwell said.

Masterson said, "You have worked with both of these medical examiners for a long time. You know their personalities. I assume you have had or will have a conversation with both of them to explain the importance of their findings in this case. After all, I assume that this sort of thing is not an exact science. Opinions and conclusions can be formulated based upon some degree of subjectivity."

"It is all subjective. These pathologists are interesting, if nothing else. When you listen to them, you would think they have all the answers to all the questions, based upon scientific fact. They speak with such authority that you would think they have found a cure for cancer and actually, if you ask them, they would probably tell you that they have. And when their conclusions and opinions are challenged, they simply say *we haven't ever seen that before.* I guess that means if they haven't seen it, it's not possible. An arrogant group. Legends in their own minds."

Masterson asked, "So, did you have that conversation with one or both of these guys?"

"Not *that* conversation," Cardwell said. "I spoke to Doctor Long, but I haven't had the conversation you are talking about. Not how this works. I can't just tell them what they have to find.

"Tell me if I'm wrong, but the way I see it, what we have to do is get it out there that we are vigorously prosecuting this case. What happened to this young man was tragic and we won't tolerate that behavior from anyone, including and especially from police officers who are supposed to be serving and protecting people of all races, not killing them." Cardwell was on a roll, perhaps trying to convince herself she was doing the right thing.

Continuing, she said, "Then these so-called experts will understand the position they are in."

To be sure that she understood exactly what Cardwell was saying, Masterson asked her to clarify.

"It's like this. I want to put them in a position where if their opinion is different than the theory I put out there, these two white doctors will be responsible for letting a guilty white cop off the hook for the murder of a black kid, not me. I'll have done all that I could. I took swift action. And I took that action based upon what Long told me. Blunt trauma with a linear object, a flashlight. If he backs up on that, I'll ask the question of why he told me that in the first place. He can answer that question for Jennings and his gang. That is one of the reasons I think we should do the press conference now and not wait until after the brain autopsy is completed some four weeks down the road," Cardwell responded emphatically.

"I agree, let's go. Let's get this done," Masterson said, with equal enthusiasm.

Chapter Twenty-Seven

Dressed in a dark blue conservative business suit, highlighting her stylish blond hair and flawlessly applied makeup to counter the bright television lights, the circuit attorney for the city of St. Louis, Joan Cardwell, entered the courtroom that had been carefully selected by Carol Masterson. In addition to security, the room was also filled with cameras, microphones and reporters anxious to file their stories. This was not her first rodeo. But it was certainly the most important press conference she had ever had. It would shape her career path. It would determine her future.

Shaking hands and acknowledging those present, she slowly made her way to the podium. She was in no hurry to begin. A group of no less than thirty television, radio and print media personalities and their camera crews were gathered in the courtroom. This was the hottest criminal news item in the St. Louis metropolitan area since the Cannon case.

Unlike her other press conferences, this one was open to the public. Masterson felt it necessary for transparency and to offset Jennings' diatribe. When Cardwell scanned the room, she noticed the lawyer the Mitchell family had recently hired. Select representatives of the protest group, led by Quentin Jennings, were also in attendance. Conspicuous by their absence were members of the St. Louis Police Department or anyone representing the interests of Bobby Decker.

As Cardwell glad-handed her way to the podium, one reporter for a local television station remarked to a colleague, "I wonder how she is going to deflect the attention away from her and onto someone else this time."

"She is a master spin doctor," was the quick response from another reporter in the audience.

"Thank all of you for coming, as I know that everyone has an interest in the death of young Jordon Mitchell,"

Cardwell began reading from a carefully crafted script. "Let me first extend my sympathy to the Mitchell family for the tragic loss of their loved one. While I can't bring Jordon Mitchell back to life, I can avenge his tragic and untimely death."

Continuing with the script prepared by Carol Masterson, Joan Cardwell was speaking in the first person singular as though single-handedly, she would see that justice was done in this case. "I'll be filing criminal charges of murder second degree against Police Officer Robert Decker and Police Officer Jake Corbett."

Masterson had also decided it would be best to highlight their position in the community by using police officer titles for each. In that way, the use of the title would serve as a spring board for Cardwell to express her righteous indignation over the behavior of those who had the duty to protect and serve the entire community, not just those of the privileged class. She didn't waste any time developing that theme.

"I certainly hope these criminal charges send a clear message that no one is above the law. It doesn't matter who you are or what position you hold. If you violate the law, you'll be prosecuted. It is truly unfortunate that these two police officers violated their oath of office and caused a tragic and unnecessary death. A wasted young life. I also want to say that the behavior of these two officers is not representative of the entire department or those men and women who serve honorably to protect all who live, work and visit this city. To those men and women we are grateful." She paused. "I'll now take your questions."

The reporters wasted no time asking questions. "Are you taking this case to the grand jury?"

"No. We will have a preliminary hearing."

"Why are you not taking it to the grand jury, like you did in the case of Sergeant Cannon?"

"Because I want total transparency in this case and I don't want anything done behind closed doors, or any suggestion that this prosecution is not completely aboveboard," she said, wondering how many other Cannon questions there would be.

"Do you expect that this case will be tried in Saint Louis?" An obvious subtle reference to Cannon.

"Yes," came the simple response, with the hope of avoiding additional Cannon questions.

"But doesn't a public preliminary hearing increase the publicity and therefore, increase the chances the trial will be moved out of Saint Louis."

"No." Another short response and another effort to deflect direct or indirect Cannon comparisons.

"Can you briefly review the elements of the charge of murder second degree, what you have to prove, and what the range of punishment is?"

"We will prove beyond a reasonable doubt that Officer Robert Decker knowingly caused the death of Jordon Mitchell. Murder second degree is a class A felony which carries a sentence of ten to thirty years, or life imprisonment. The jury will decide the sentence unless the defendant waives jury sentencing."

"Why is Officer Corbett going to be charged? What did he do?"

"He acted with Officer Decker. He aided and abetted Decker, and the law allows one who aids and abets the main perpetrator to be prosecuted and punished as though he acted alone."

"Can you tell us exactly how he did that?"

"I can, but I prefer that question be answered in court."

The truth was that Cardwell couldn't answer that question with any certainty. She actually had no idea how she was going to make the case against Corbett. For that matter, she didn't know how she was going to prove the case against Decker if the autopsy report was not favorable. But if she didn't charge Corbett, he was certain to show up testifying favorably for Decker. By bringing a murder charge, she hoped she could eventually put enough pressure on him to testify for the prosecution with an appropriate plea bargain that avoided substantial penitentiary time. If not, as a defendant, he might or might not be testifying for both Decker and himself. In any criminal case, a defendant cannot be compelled to testify, and his failure can't be used against him. Of course, if he did testify, Cardwell knew his motive to lie to protect himself would be obvious to any jury.

"Can you tell us what the evidence is against Officer Decker?"

"Same answer. All the evidence will be presented in court."

"We spoke to the Medical Examiner and he told us that the autopsy of the brain would be done by Doctor McHenry in Saint Louis County and that it would take four weeks to complete. How can you charge anyone before that autopsy is completed, isn't that critical to this case?"

This was one of the questions that Cardwell feared because it was, in fact, a potentially critical part of the case and she didn't have the results.

Attempting to deflect the question, she said, "I'm aware that the final report won't be completed for a period of time, but I have spoken to Doctor Long, the Medical Examiner for the city of Saint Louis, who told me that on the basis of the autopsy that he conducted, Mister Mitchell's massive skull fracture was caused by blunt trauma with a linear object; namely a flashlight."

Cardwell silently hoped her response not only satisfied the reporter, but also sent a clear message to the Medical Examiner. She quoted Dr. Long correctly. He did tell her that. But she neglected to mention that he said that only after being pressed. She also neglected to mention that he told her that he came to that conclusion after a *cursory review*. Dr. Long was now where she wanted him, squarely in the middle of a very volatile and high profile case.

"Has the Police Department completed its investigation?"

Another question that she had hoped no one would ask.

"The formal report has not been completed," Cardwell said bracing for the obvious follow-up question. *How can murder charges be brought against anyone when the investigation has not been completed?* But fortunately for Cardwell, the question never came.

"Who will be trying the case for the State?"

"Gary Goodrich will be the lead prosecutor and his assistants haven't been selected."

Goodrich was a veteran career prosecutor with some 35 years' experience, and currently headed the homicide unit. An unassuming, distinguished grey-haired, 60-year-old Caucasian, he boasted a 90 percent conviction rate in a venue where the black defendants outnumber the white, and African Americans can be found on most, if not all, criminal juries. That composition can make it difficult to convict black defendants.

When the circuit attorney informed Goodrich he would be prosecuting the case, he initially resisted, suggesting that he didn't want to be under a microscope in this type of high profile case.

He was particularly concerned because of his relationships, both personal and professional, with police officers whom he relied upon for convictions. But more importantly, although unspoken, he didn't want to wind up like his friend and colleague who prosecuted Sgt. Cannon. Goodrich witnessed the grief and aggravation he suffered before, during and after the case, ultimately culminating in his resignation when the situation became completely intolerable. He also knew Cardwell provided no support and instead, contributed to the stress. However, Cardwell remained committed to having him in the first chair and in control of the trial. Goodrich could not persuade her to the contrary and would be the lead prosecutor. That was his job. He really had no choice.

When all the questions were exhausted, Cardwell thanked everyone for coming and promised she would keep the public informed as the case progressed through the court system. Relieved and believing the press conference was a success, she left the courtroom through the rear exit, as Masterson had planned. Her departure was much faster than when she entered through the front door.

Chapter Twenty-Eight

While the circuit attorney was holding her press conference, Bobby Decker was meeting with an attorney. Following his brother's advice, Bobby contacted Jonathan Felbin, known simply as Felbin. He was the lawyer who successfully defended Sgt. Tom Cannon and embarrassed the circuit attorney in the process. He met Felbin on the top floor of the newest high rise office building in downtown St. Louis overlooking the Arch, the city's symbol of the Gateway to the West. The plush offices, complete with a custom marble conference room table that matched the accent marble flooring, occupied the entire floor. His staff of 28 consisted of an office manager, lawyers, paralegals, secretaries, computer operators and investigators.

Felbin built a reputation on providing aggressive representation both in and out of the courtroom. He was not afraid to use the news media to benefit a client. His light brown, long hair and youthful appearance suggested an age less than his 51 years. He would be a stark contrast to the silver-haired prosecutor who would become his opponent. That is, if he took the case. During his 26 years of practice, he was involved in numerous high profile cases and built a reputation, in part, based upon the successful representation of police officers.

Felbin was feared by the IAD investigators and loathed by prosecutors. He was once quoted as telling a female prosecutor in the western part of the state during the course of a high profile criminal trial that she was not his friend when the trial began, and if she was not his friend when the trial ended, he hadn't lost anything. Actually, he had few lawyer friends.

Bobby Decker knew of Felbin's reputation, but also knew that unless he had the support of the St. Louis Police Officers' Association or his family, he could not afford any lawyer, let alone Felbin. He had no money. He was suspended without pay and barely getting by.

With some interruptions, Felbin had represented the Association and its members during his 26 years of practice. However, for a brief period following a disagreement, he parted ways with the organization. Actually, when that happened, the Department hired him to represent the Internal Affairs Division. That relationship, embraced by the command rank officers, was not well received by the rank and file. After several years of facing the man who once defended them, the fences were eventually mended and Felbin returned to the Association. But the time spent representing the Department taught him valuable lessons about law enforcement behavior; lessons he would use in representing Bobby Decker.

Uncertain of whether Felbin would take his case, Bobby began the discussion by addressing the issue of cost. "Mister Felbin, I have been suspended without pay and on a police officer's salary, I obviously don't have much money in savings. And what I do have, I'm using to live. I have asked the Association and my parents for financial backing for the legal fees, but I haven't heard from anyone. At the moment, sir, that is where I'm. I don't have any money to pay you. So, I'll understand if this is a short meeting."

Approximately 85 percent of the commissioned officers with the rank of sergeant or below are dues paying members of the St. Louis Police Officers' Association, each with dues withheld monthly from their paychecks. The dues support both legal fees and political lobbying efforts. Ordinarily, a member accused of misconduct internally only is automatically covered, but criminal charges are handled differently.

If a member is charged with a criminal offense based upon an incident that occurred when the officer was on duty and in the line of duty, the Association would usually agree to pay the legal fees and expenses. Off-duty incidents are handled on a case by case basis, depending on the facts and circumstances. Since the Jordon Mitchell matter clearly occurred while Bobby Decker was not only working, but doing his duty to arrest a burglar, Association representation should not be a problem. Nonetheless, Bobby thought he would mention it to the lawyer at the outset in the interests of full disclosure. He didn't want to waste the man's time.

"First of all, drop the *Mister* thing. People call me Felbin. Sometimes I'm not sure they even know my first name. Second, let's put the issue of money aside for the moment and talk about where this case is, assuming there is a case," Felbin said. "I know you have been a media target and the ever vigilant Chief has suspended you, but what else is going on?" he asked.

"That's really all I know at this time, but based upon all that has happened thus far, I'm expecting the worst," Bobby replied.

"That's probably a good philosophy." Getting right to the point, Felbin said, "Tell me what happened on the roof that night."

"I made an arrest of a guy who was trying to escape on a rooftop after burglarizing a pawn shop. He wound up with a fractured skull," Bobby said.

"Yes, I heard that much on the news, but the real question is how this guy got what the media has described as a *massive skull fracture,*" Felbin corrected.

"I'll tell you what I have told everyone else who asked. I don't know," Bobby replied.

Ignoring the obvious for the moment, Felbin asked, "How did you write the incident report?"

"I just wrote the basics of the arrest."

"How did you handle the skull fracture?" the lawyer pressed.

"I didn't, because I didn't know how that occurred or when it occurred."

Continuing to probe, Felbin said, "But surely you knew by the time you wrote the report that he had a fractured skull. It was an immediate front page headline."

"Sure, I knew he had the injury, but I didn't know how he got it and I can't write about something that I don't know."

Concerned about what he was hearing, Felbin asked, "Who else have you talked to about this?"

"The IAD investigators and my family, but no one else," Bobby said.

Felbin decided to change the subject, as there would be plenty of time to discuss the roof and he could see Bobby was becoming even more stressed.

"Have you had any prior major discipline during your time with the Department?"

"Yes. My probation was extended," Bobby said, offering no additional details.

Unknowingly, Felbin had wandered into another problem area. "Why?" was the obvious question begging for an answer.

"When I was a prob, I was assigned to a partner they were trying to get rid of. He was originally my training officer. In any event, there was a drug deal on a street corner that we broke up. One of the participants decided to try to kill us and fired a shot, which fortunately missed. My partner returned the fire, striking the other guy, who didn't have a gun, while the shooter took off. The IAD investigators found some so-called witness who claimed that no shots were fired at us. When I refuted that account, they threatened me with a false reporting charge. Eventually, they made good on the threat. Apparently, they thought if I corroborated the story that their incredible witness was telling, they would be able to fire my partner, or at least cause him to resign. My partner never did get a trial because, despite my refusal to cooperate, he retired. But my probation was extended after they sustained a false reporting charge. I never had a trial because, as you know, probs don't have any rights and don't get a hearing before the Board of Police Commissioners."

When Decker finished his explanations, Felbin thought, *This guy is screwed.* It was not so much what he said about the events on the rooftop, but what he didn't say. His inability to explain a massive skull fracture would become a real problem. If the prosecutor found out about the sustained false reporting allegation while he was a probationary officer, no less, his credibility would be shot. While the false reporting accusation would probably never become actual evidence in any trial, he knew Cardwell would leak that tidbit and the press would have a field day. But he decided to keep his thoughts to himself, at least for now.

If he was going to take this case, he wanted more information and more detail before he came to any real conclusions about what had happened on the roof that night. In the meantime, there was no reason to contribute to the stress this young man was already experiencing. And despite the preliminary problems he saw, for some reason he believed Bobby Decker didn't honestly know how Mitchell's skull was fractured. Interestingly, for Felbin, believing stories clients told him was a rare occurrence. But for some reason, this case was different.

Felbin concluded the interview with a handshake. He told Decker he would handle his case, still uncertain what that case would be. He told him they would figure out who was going to pay the legal expenses and asked for a copy of the police report. His last piece of advice was to speak to no one about this matter.

Chapter Twenty-Nine

When he arrived home, Bobby opened a beer and sat on the couch to review his conversation with the lawyer. On the one hand, he felt good because he had a lawyer; someone in his corner to fight for him. On the other hand, he needed to give Jonathan Felbin some ammunition; something he could use to defend him on the criminal charges he believed were inevitable. But all in all, this was a fairly good day. At least he had a lawyer. He needed to stay positive.

He thought that he would make another effort to contact his father. Although he had several conversations with his brother Jeff and his mother, he hadn't spoken to his father. Each time he called the house, his mother would tell him the same thing; your father is not available, I'll tell him to call you. But the call never came and today was no different. After a conversation with his mother informing her that he had hired a prominent attorney to advise him, she again said his father was not available, but would call. When the brief conversation with his mother ended, he thought perhaps he made a mistake by making this call and turning a fairly good day into another bad one. So much for staying positive.

While Bobby continued to enjoy his pity party, the phone rang. He rushed to answer it, thinking it might be his much anticipated call from his father. It was not. Instead, it was Lt. Col. Winston, the head of IAD, personally calling to ask him to come to the Internal Affairs office immediately. Considering it was late in the day, Bobby questioned the request. Angered by the question, Winston issued an order directing his appearance. Since it was an order he was obligated to follow even though he was suspended, he told Winston he would be there as soon as he could.

Instead of immediately complying with Winston's order, he called his lawyer on the cell phone number he had been given. When Felbin answered, he explained the situation. Felbin told him he was coaching his young son's baseball game, but would call Winston to see what was going on and why they were ordering him to the IAD office this time of the day.

When Felbin reached Winston, he got the same runaround. The lawyer had exchanged numerous conversations with Winston on behalf of many police officers during Winston's management of IAD. They didn't have a good relationship. Each distrusted the other. Felbin saw Winston as a mindless bureaucrat who had worked his way up the ladder by kissing a lot of political ass. In short, he had absolutely no respect for Winston, whom he regarded as too stupid to make an intelligent decision about anything, including what he was going to have for dinner.

"I'm representing Bobby Decker," he told Winston. "He just called me and told me you asked him to come to your office. What's that about?"

"I didn't ask him to come here, I ordered him to come here right now," Winston corrected.

"Order, ask, beg, plead whatever. Why do you want him in your office at this moment?" Felbin replied in something less than a friendly tone.

"I ordered him to come here because I need to see him and I need to see him now," Winston said, avoiding the question once again.

"Look, Winston, I don't have time to play your stupid little games, so just tell me what you want and we will make a decision as to whether he will appear."

"If he doesn't appear, he will be charged with disobeying a direct order."

"Given your attitude, the time of day and the urgency of this request," Felbin continued, knowing that the use of the word request would aggravate Winston. "I can only assume you have plans to arrest him on some bogus charge issued by that moron Cardwell. How close am I, Winston?"

"If your client is not here within the next thirty minutes, he will be charged with disobeying a direct order and I'll recommend that he be fired," Winston said, unwilling to debate or further discuss the matter.

"That's what I thought. Just another chapter in our book of mutual admiration. Right, Winston?" No response.

"I'll tell you what my friend," Felbin continued, "don't wait up for Decker, and there is no reason to leave the light on."

"That is some real bad advice, Counselor. You're going to get your client fired."

"I don't think so. But I'll take my chances."

When he finished this conversation, he immediately called his client. He related what he had been told, including the threat of termination, adding, "I think he wants you down there right now because they have a warrant for your arrest and they want to lock you up. While you'll eventually have to surrender yourself, the problem with doing it now is that you may possibly spend the night in jail because I don't know what the amount of the bond is. It could be out of sight, given the nature of this case. If it's high and we need it reduced, we're not going to get that done this evening".

Interrupting his lawyer, Bobby asked, "What is a normal bond for police officers? Do we get a break, since there is little risk that we won't show up for court or won't do anything else that is required?"

Responding to the question, Felbin said, "Normally, bonds for defendants who are law enforcement are personal recognizance, meaning that no cash would have to be posted. It would just require your signature promising to appear in court and follow whatever other conditions the court imposes. But this is certainly not a normal case. We don't even know the charge."

Although he didn't say it, Felbin was concerned the charge might be murder, for which there was no police precedent. There had never been a police officer in the history of the city of St. Louis who had been charged with murder. Under those circumstances and given the public attention this case is receiving, it was anyone's guess what the bond would be. But Felbin knew he wanted to negotiate that issue while his client was free, rather than locked up.

"What do you think that I should do?" Bobby asked

"Let's start with what you should not do. I don't think you should go to Winston's office today, unless you don't mind spending the night in jail. If you have been charged with some crime, as I suspect is the case, I don't think Winston can order you to surrender yourself. However, that issue can be resolved later. My position is that all job-related issues become secondary to the criminal case. In the meantime, I think you need to get out of your house, because I suspect that you'll be getting a visit from IAD. I'm in the process of coaching my son's baseball game at the Affton Athletic Association, field four, and I suggest you come here where I can keep an eye on you. Do you know where that is? I'll also make some phone calls to see if I can figure out what is going on."

"Okay, I'll leave now and be there as soon as I can. I know where you are."

As he gathered a few personal items to take with him, his cell phone rang. The caller was identified as anonymous, so he let it go to voicemail. He assumed it was someone from IAD. When he checked the message, it was Jake Corbett asking him to return the call as soon as possible. Panic consumed every syllable. Bobby called him right back and learned Jake had also been summoned to IAD. He was on his way to Winston's office.

"Jonathan Felbin is representing me and he told me not to go. He thinks they want to make an arrest on a criminal warrant that was issued for me," Bobby said.

"I'm heading down there now to meet my lawyer. Do you mind if I have him call Felbin?" Corbett asked.

"That's fine," Bobby responded, neglecting to tell Corbett that he was planning to hide out at a kid's baseball game.

After providing his lawyer's cell phone number, he continued to put some personal items into an overnight bag. He was just grabbing and throwing. He didn't pay a lot of attention to what he was taking. All he knew was that he didn't want to go to jail.

Chapter Thirty

As he drove to the baseball field, he thought about the phone call from Jake Corbett. If his lawyer was right and there was a warrant for his arrest, why would they want Jake Corbett to come to IAD? Was he being charged as well? He hadn't arrested Mitchell or had any contact with him, as he was busy arresting the other burglar. It was all very confusing at the moment but, fortunately or unfortunately, he knew answers would be coming soon.

As he was nearing the baseball park, his cell phone rang again. This time the caller was identified as his brother Jeff, so he answered.

"Bobby, where are you?" Jeff asked, his voice more panic stricken than Corbett's.

"I'm in the car," was his only response, volunteering no other details.

"I just saw the news and the circuit attorney announced that you have been charged in the death of Jordon Mitchell," Jeff said, clearly upset.

"What's the charge?" Bobby asked, trying to remain calm.

"Murder," was Jeff's only response.

The word *murder* rattled around his head like a steel ball in a pin ball machine. He was speechless. Murder? He was in shock. The silence prompted his brother to ask if he was still on the line. "I'm still here," he finally said.

"So, what are you planning to do?" Jeff asked.

"I don't know, Jeff."

"Mom said that you saw Jonathan Felbin and he will be representing you."

"Yes," was Bobby's only response, his head still spinning from the news that he was being charged with murder.

"That's a good choice. He is one of the best and he will take good care of you just like he did for Sergeant Cannon," Jeff said.

"Listen, Jeff, I have to go, but I'll call you later," Bobby said, anxious to end the conversation.

"Are you okay?" Jeff asked.

"Yes, I'm fine. I'll call you later. Hey, Jeff. Thanks for your concern, I appreciate it."

As Bobby was ending the conversation, he pulled into the large parking lot of the Affton Athletic Association located in St. Louis County. He found the field not far from where he parked. He got a kick out of seeing his lawyer wearing a baseball cap identical to those worn by the young players, along with a golf shirt with the embroidered identifier *Saints Baseball,* complete with the team logo. Felbin was standing outside the dugout shouting words of encouragement to his players on the field, while two other adults wearing the same shirts and hats were inside the dugout. It was the only light moment in an otherwise stressful day.

Bobby took his seat in the bleachers next to some people, apparently parents who had kids playing in the game. He soon learned that the game was in the top of the 5th of seven total innings. But one of the parents pointed out that the game might not go the full seven. If the Saints scored two more runs in the bottom of the 5th to take a 10 run lead, the game would end. It was called the mercy rule. This proud parent was confident that the game would be ending before seven innings.

As Bobby watched the game, he thought he would like to have the confidence in his fate that this parent had in this young baseball team. After all, they both had the same coach. But his thoughts quickly turned to the worst case scenario. Murder; he couldn't believe he was accused of murder when he was doing nothing more than his job. A job he loved, but one his family hated. *Perhaps I should have listened to them,* he thought, as he began to second guess his career choice. Perhaps he should have followed in his father's footsteps and become an accountant, or a lawyer like his brother. No, those careers would not have fulfilled him. His mind was racing.

Regardless of what they said he did, he was the same person he had been when he started the job. He was still helping people; many people, of all colors and ethnic origins. Color had never mattered to him like it did to so many of his colleagues. In fact, he recalled times during his career when some of his fellow officers shunned him because he demanded that they stop using that disrespectful and ugly *N* word. But now, none of that seemed to matter. He found himself square in the sights of his own department, the prosecutors, the black community and civil rights activists. Where would all this end?

The parent was right. The Saints scored their two runs in the bottom of the 5th to end the game on the mercy rule. As a matter of fact, they scored their two runs before even making a single out in the inning, much to the disappointment of the players who would not get another turn at bat. The kids won and won big, but they were still disappointed. How funny is human nature? He would be content with any type of win to get him out from under this nightmare.

After giving his players the usual *attaboy* speech in a corner of the outfield away from the parents, Jonathan Felbin and his players walked in the direction of Bobby and the waiting parents.

"Good job, coach," Bobby said, complimenting Felbin on his fine baseball coaching skills.

"Thanks. I called my investigator and asked him to get us some information. I told him I thought you had been charged with something and wanted to know the bond amount. He hasn't called me back yet," Coach Felbin said.

"Well, I got some information. The circuit attorney was on the news announcing that I was charged with murder," Bobby said, looking around to be sure no one was listening to their conversation.

Before Felbin could respond, his cell phone rang. It was the lawyer representing Jake Corbett. Jim Harris was also on the list of lawyers approved by the Association to represent their members.

"Felbin, I'm down at IAD with my client, Jake Corbett, and they just arrested him on a murder second charge with a $250,000 bond that he obviously can't make. I can't find the judge who set the bond to ask him to reduce it. In fact, I can't find any judge to talk to, as they apparently got the word to head for the hills. What are you doing about Decker? He is also supposed to be here," Harris said.

"He is not coming to the party, at least not until I can find a sympathetic judge to reduce that bond to something reasonable," Felbin said, ignoring the fact that Decker was standing next to him.

"Listen, Felbin, help me out here," Harris said, desperation identifiable in his voice.

Confused by that comment, Felbin asked, "What do you mean help you out?"

"I look like an idiot sitting here with my client when your client isn't here. I obviously didn't put it all together and now I'm looking pretty stupid. It would help me if you came down here with your client," Harris said, anxiety still in his voice.

"I'd love to help you, Jim, but I'm not willing to offer up my client to get that done. Sorry. Hey, Jim, I have to run. Will look forward to working with you on this one."

Actually, Felbin and Harris didn't really get along since the Cannon case, when Harris had represented several officers who changed their stories and testified on behalf of the prosecution and against Cannon. Felbin felt that Harris encouraged the recantation, or at least did nothing to prevent it. Without that false, recanted testimony, Sgt. Cannon would never have been charged with felony assault.

As he ended the conversation with Harris, Felbin thought about the irony of the other attorney's request. He was looking for help to avoid personal embarrassment, yet he did nothing to help Sgt. Tom Cannon, an innocent scapegoat caught in a political drama. And now he was willing to offer up another police officer, Bobby Decker, to satisfy his own selfish interests. *I need to keep this guy close to me during the pendency of this case,* he thought.

Over the next several hours, Felbin made several phone calls in an effort to find a judge willing to reduce the bond to a manageable amount. He was really looking for a recognizance bond, because with no current income, Decker could not afford to post cash. Historically, the Police Officers' Association didn't front the money for the bond. Unfortunately, he could find no support this evening and assumed that Harris, likewise, had no success. In fact, one judge he spoke to, although sympathetic to a reduction, said she could not help because as an African American, she feared ramification. Felbin understood.

Chapter Thirty-One

After spending a sleepless night at his lawyer's house, Bobby walked into the kitchen and found a fresh pot of coffee. Lacking sleep, he needed the caffeine to keep his eyes open. A note on the counter indicated that Felbin was at the gym, his daily morning ritual when in St. Louis.

Bobby wondered what was ahead on this day, but figured it could not be worse than yesterday. He knew at some point, he would have to turn himself in, as he could not hide out forever. He knew this day would be filled with media coverage, but the most immediate question was the amount of time he would spend in custody.

When he returned from the gym, Felbin poured himself a cup of coffee and sat at the kitchen table across from Bobby. Neither Felbin nor Bobby had seen any portion of the circuit attorney's news conference on television the night before. The morning paper was in the middle of the table. Bobby saw an article. He tried to ignore it, but he couldn't. It was front page, above the fold, complete with pictures of him and Jake Corbett and a headline that read, "City Police Officers Charged with Murder." He didn't read the article. He didn't have to; he knew what it said and it would not be complimentary.

"Did you read the article?" Felbin asked, pointing to the paper.

"No. I didn't want to start the day like that, but I couldn't help but notice the headline. Of course, I'd have to be blind to miss it."

"I read it before I went to the gym. For the most part, it's a bunch of prosecutorial hype and spin. However, there was one interesting part and that was an interview with the medical examiner. He was quoted as saying the autopsy of the brain was not completed and would not be for another four weeks. He also said the autopsy of the brain would be done by Helen McHenry in St. Louis County."

Bobby was curious about the potential importance of both of these developments and asked, "Why do you think that might be significant?"

"You have been charged with the murder of someone who had a skull fracture. According to the article, you used a flashlight to fracture his skull and I assume the state will claim that death was caused by a brain swell that followed the blow to the head. So, if that is the theory of their case, and I have to believe it is, then the autopsy of the brain is a significant piece of the puzzle that they don't have. Yet, you have been charged with murder," Felbin explained.

"Why would they charge me if they don't know what this evidence will ultimately be and whether it will be favorable to them?" Bobby asked, somewhat perplexed.

"I don't know the answer to that yet, unless the medical examiner is confident the autopsy will support the state's theory and communicated that to the prosecutor who then decided to take a chance. Obviously, she is under some pressure to do something and to do it quickly. But the other thing I find peculiar is Long sending the brain out to McHenry in the county to do the autopsy. Long is certainly capable of doing an autopsy of a brain. He has probably done thousands. So, what is the advantage to Long and the prosecutors to have another medical examiner do this autopsy?"

More questions with no answers, Bobby thought. But there was one question that needed an immediate answer.

"Will I be turning myself in today?" Bobby asked.

Unfortunately, even that question didn't draw a definitive reply.

"That depends on what I can do with the bond today. Obviously, you can't post $250,000. I need to track down the judge who set that ridiculous amount and see if I can't talk him into something fair and reasonable. What do you think you can make?"

"I can't make anything on my own. I doubt that my family will be willing to help out, since my father refuses to speak to me and he controls the checkbook. I don't know about my brother, but I do know he has more law school debt than money saved in the bank, so he probably can't do much either." Listening to his own words and accepting what would most likely be, Bobby added, "If you can't get the bond lowered, I suppose I'll just have to sit in jail until the trial."

"No, that is not an option," Felbin said, hearing the resignation in Bobby's voice.

The last thing Felbin needed was a client who was so depressed that he was of little or no value in preparing the defense and fighting a murder charge.

"Listen, Bobby, I'll find a solution, not only to the bond, but to this entire mess and you'll spend no time locked up, I promise."

But Felbin knew that was a promise he might not be able to keep. This case, if it got that far, would be tried in the city of St. Louis, a venue customarily unfriendly to police officers. The state would not fumble the ball like it had in the Cannon case. Felbin also knew that no judge in the circuit would risk a public scourging by moving the case out of St. Louis, but saw no need to share these thoughts with his client.

Felbin dressed and headed for the office, leaving Bobby alone in the house with strict instructions not to answer the phone or the door. Arriving a little past 7, he knew no judge would be in his chambers at this hour, so there was no sense in even trying. Besides, a personal visit would accomplish more than a phone call; it was harder to say no face to face. In the meantime, Felbin decided to call Jim Harris to try to get an update from him on what happened to his client.

When Harris answered the phone, Felbin said, "What happened last night?"

"Jake spent the night in IAD after they printed and photographed him. I could not find a judge to talk about reducing the bond. But at least they didn't put him in a cell," Harris replied, clearly still upset by the events of the day before.

"They are real humanitarians," Felbin responded, referring to the IAD investigators. "I'm planning to pay Granger a visit around nine when he gets in," Felbin continued, referring to Judge Carl Granger, the judge who set the bond.

Granger also happened to be the presiding judge for all divisions of the court.

Granger had always been pro law enforcement, but he was also pro prosecution, making it difficult to predict what he would do in this situation. Felbin had both good and bad experiences with Granger, who had little personality, ran a very formal courtroom and sometimes let form interfere with substance. But he was the one who had set the bond, and Felbin just hoped he would be fair under all the circumstances.

"I'll meet you over there at nine. Should we invite the prosecutor?" Harris asked.

"According to the morning paper, she assigned Gary Goodrich to try this case. He is not necessarily a bad guy and I have always found him to be a straight shooter. But remember, he is going to do whatever Cardwell tells him, and she is the one who asked for this ridiculous bond in the first place. I have to assume he will resist a reduction."

"Isn't the judge going to require his presence?" Harris asked.

"I'm sure he will, but there is no reason to poison the well until we have to," Felbin said, recognizing that it was inappropriate for one side to have a conversation with the judge when the other side was not present.

Of course, Felbin was able to rationalize that impropriety, since the prosecutor had arranged a private conversation with the judge to get the bond set in the first place. But, right or wrong, he had no intention of inviting the prosecutor until it was absolutely necessary.

"See you there at nine," Harris said, ending the conversation.

Chapter Thirty-Two

Jake Corbett's lawyer arrived at the judge's chambers at 8:50 a.m. The judge was in his chambers, behind closed doors, apparently in a meeting with another judge. Jonathan Felbin arrived a short time later, but before 9:00. The judge was still behind closed doors.

After informing the clerk he needed to see the judge, Felbin asked Harris, "Who is in with him?"

Harris shrugged his shoulders. Felbin hoped the early closed door meeting had nothing to do with the reason he and Harris were there.

The lawyers didn't have to wait long to learn the identity of the visitor. When the door to the Chief Judge's chambers opened, Felbin saw his old friend Judge Steven Godfrey, the presiding judge for the criminal division of the court.

"Little early for you, isn't it, Steve? Had to work out that tee time with Carl for later today?" Felbin said, smiling.

"Listen to who's talking. Felbin, you have had more meetings with Mister Titleist than any lawyer in the state," Judge Godfrey shot back. "But the good news is that this morning Granger has the pleasure of your company and I can escape that aggravation, at least for the moment," he added.

"Given your presence behind a closed door at this early hour, I suspect you and I'll be visiting later this morning to share a common interest," Felbin said, referring to the Decker matter.

"I'll certainly be looking forward to that," Judge Godfrey said, making his way to the door of the waiting room as the lawyers walked quickly toward the open door leading into Granger's chambers.

"Good morning, your Honor." Felbin began the conversation.

"Good morning, gentlemen," was the cordial, yet formal, reply. "What can I do for you?" he asked.

"Judge, we are here to talk about the bonds you set in the cases of Police Officers Bobby Decker and Jake Corbett. I represent Bobby and he represents Jake," pointing to Jim Harris, as they both stood in front of the judge's desk.

"Well, I think we need to talk about this in the courtroom with the prosecutor present. I believe Gary Goodrich is representing the state in this matter. Why don't you round him up and let my clerk know when you are ready to go on the record," Judge Granger said, clearly anxious to have these lawyers leave his office.

"I'll get him right now and be back," Felbin said as he left the judge's chambers with Harris at his side.

Once outside, Harris said, "That didn't take long."

"What the hell, we tried," Felbin said, reaching for his cell phone to call the prosecutor to invite him to a public, on the record conference, with the judge. *The circus is about to begin,* he thought.

As they waited in the empty courtroom, Felbin decided to initiate a conversation with Goodrich to see if they could agree on a reasonable bond. He knew it was a long shot, but he had nothing to lose. As expected, Goodrich was getting his marching orders from the circuit attorney and, apologetically, indicated he could not agree to a reduction.

The court reporter came into the courtroom, followed by the judge. After introducing the lawyers for the record, Judge Granger looked at Felbin, asking him to identify the matter before the court. Felbin explained he was in court seeking a reduction of the $250,000 bond that had been set, pointing out that his client, a police officer, was certainly not a flight risk. Interrupting Felbin's presentation, the prosecutor inquired whether the officers were in custody.

Responding for both, Felbin said, "Officer Corbett is in custody, but Officer Decker is not, at this time."

Turning to address the court, Goodrich said, "Judge, we cannot proceed with any type of bond reduction hearing until both defendants are in custody."

Quick to respond, Harris pointed out that his client was in custody and had been confined since the night before, failing to mention that Corbett spent the night in the IAD office, rather than a cell.

"Additionally, your Honor, there is no formal written motion before you, plus the accused has a right to be present for any bond proceedings," Goodrich pointed out.

Harris's response was interrupted by Judge Granger. "Mister Harris, I'm not going to conduct multiple bond reduction hearings in this case. Plus, Mister Goodrich is correct, the accused has a right to be present and be heard unless otherwise waived and I assume there will be no waiver here. So, if you want a bond reduction, please file a formal motion and let's set it for a hearing at a mutually convenient time. We are adjourned," Granger said. He left the courtroom like he was shot from a cannon.

"What are we going to do now? I'm getting the clear impression this judge is going to do whatever the prosecutor wants on this bond," Harris said to Felbin.

"I don't disagree. Plus having a public bond hearing with the prosecutor attempting to poison every prospective juror in the state, is certainly not in our interests," Felbin added.

"So, what do we do?" Harris asked again.

"I don't know, but for the moment, I'm going to talk to Godfrey to see if I can find out what the hell is going on," Felbin said.

Felbin found Judge Godfrey sitting alone in his office. Watching his friend rush into his chambers, Judge Godfrey remarked, "That didn't take very long."

"No, it didn't. He wants me to file a formal motion and then have a public hearing on something that should have been a recognizance bond in the first place. Every police officer who has ever been charged with a crime has been released on a signature bond without posting a dime. I get the distinct impression after we have a hearing where Mitchell's mother gets to extol his virtues and talks about the butchers in the police department who murder black babies, the result will be no reduction. What the hell is going on?"

"This is no ordinary case. You know that. This town is about ready to erupt and we, on this side of the fence, have to be mindful of that."

"You also have to be mindful of the fact that Decker and Corbett have a right to a fair trial and are innocent until proven guilty. A $250,000 bond is outrageous and you know it, Steve," Felbin said.

"It doesn't matter what I think. This is Granger's call. He set the bond and, as you know, he is the chief judge for all divisions. As much as I might like to, as the presiding over the criminal division, I can't overrule any decision he makes. If it is any consolation to you, during that little meeting I had with him this morning, I shared with him my thoughts about what might be a reasonable solution. I obviously anticipated an issue with the amount he had unilaterally set. But you know Judge Granger, he makes up his own mind."

"Unbelievable," Felbin said, shaking his head as he left Judge Godfrey's office. He needed to figure out something and didn't have much time to do it.

Chapter Thirty-Three

Gary Goodrich wasted no time reporting the events that occurred in Judge Granger's court to the circuit attorney. Cardwell had told him she wanted to be informed of all developments in the case, big or small. She was not pleased when he informed her that Decker was still at large.

"What is that Chief of Police doing to get him off the street?" she asked incredulously.

But when Goodrich had no answer, her frustration turned to anger.

"Well, we need to find out. Go over there right now and ask what they are doing, if anything, to find Decker. They can't find one of their own? Amazing! I'm not going to be put on front street again with another cop case that goes south. I hope you and everyone else understand that."

While Goodrich was heading to police headquarters as fast as his legs could carry him, Felbin called his client to inform him of his meeting with the judge. "Bobby, I just finished a meeting with the judge who set the bond. He is forcing us to file a motion and then have a public hearing where Mitchell's family would be allowed to testify. We can't run the risk of the additional inflammatory publicity a public hearing like that would surely generate. And even if we had a hearing, I doubt this bond would be reduced. We need to find another way to raise the cash or property to post $250,000."

Knowing Decker's brother was a lawyer and his family was well off, Felbin again inquired whether they could be counted on for help in posting the bond. The response was a quick, "No. As I told you before, my brother, although willing to help, does not have that kind of resources. He has a lot of law school debt. My father won't even speak to me, let alone put up money for a bond."

Contrary to Felbin's promise, it was beginning to look like Decker would be spending some time behind bars until a solution could be reached. The lawyer thought that sooner, rather than later, his client needed to surrender because if he didn't, it would begin to look like he was running. The last thing they needed was an already biased media putting that spin out there to *Johnny Six Pack*. Innocent people don't run.

It was obvious Bobby Decker was becoming more and more depressed with each new development. Nothing seemed to be going his way. In an effort to be positive, Felbin entered the conversation with some words of encouragement.

"Look, Bobby, I know things don't look good now, but that is how all of these things go in the beginning. Just sit tight and let me go to work to figure out a solution to this bond issue, which is our most pressing matter at the moment."

But when he ended his conversation, Felbin had no idea how he was going to keep his client out of jail while the case was pending with a bond that high and an inflexible judge.

Felbin headed to his office and gathered the other lawyers to see if they had any ideas. Nothing. He then proceeded to make several phone calls in an effort to pull a rabbit out of the hat. Nothing. After several frustrating hours, it finally dawned on him. Why he hadn't thought of this from the beginning, he didn't know. But he thought of it now. Here it was right in front of him all along.

Jeffrey Fortman was a longtime friend and client. Jeffrey, a trust beneficiary whose family owned 100 percent of the stock in a Fortune 500 corporation, had a personal net worth of millions, perhaps even a billion. Jeffrey would cut off his arm if Felbin asked. The feeling was mutual, and Jeffrey regarded Felbin as not only a close friend, but also a lawyer who had dropped everything, hopped on a plane, and flew to the West Coast to handle a serious situation for him. There are things friends do for each other, and there are other things that extend beyond the bounds of friendship. Jeffrey regarded that serious occasion as one of those times he would never forget.

Felbin had never taken advantage of his friend's financial generosity, but he thought this might be the time. He really didn't know what happened on the rooftop that dark, rainy night. The case was just beginning and the autopsy of the brain hadn't even been completed. But for whatever reason, perhaps it was dealing with police officers for so many years, or perhaps it was the demeanor of his client, or perhaps it was just simply a gut reaction; Felbin believed in the innocence of Bobby Decker.

As he dialed the number of his friend, he was beginning to have some second thoughts. *How would Jeffrey view this? Would this request hurt their longtime friendship? As a very private person, would he be leading his friend into a public spotlight? A nasty public spotlight at that.* But he needed to call him. He needed to act. When Jeffrey answered the phone, Felbin knew then he had to ask the question for a lot of reasons. All Jeffrey could do was say no. That would end the discussion; no explanation necessary.

After some casual chit-chat, Felbin said, "Hey, I have a favor to ask you."

"What's up?"

After a moment of hesitation, Felbin began, "I'm representing the police officer who is charged with murder."

"I saw that in the paper. Looks like another black-white issue, at least the way the protests are going and the way the media is trying to stir the pot. I certainly hope we don't have another Cannon situation." Jeffery was familiar with the Cannon case. He'd had numerous conversations with Felbin about it.

"I think this is going to be worse than Cannon. And that's why I'm calling. Because of the Cannon case, the bond in this case has been set at $250,000."

"Yikes," was Jeffrey's only response.

"I went to see the judge who set the bond earlier today and got nowhere. He wants to have a public bond reduction hearing where the dead guy's family would be able to express an opinion."

"You can't have that. That will just give the prosecution another opportunity to poison the jury pool. I'm sure you are not going to be able to get this one out of town."

"You are right. This one will be tried here, and I can't afford any additional inflammatory media coverage. It will be bad enough with the activists looking for blood and the press encouraging them. But if those comments are made in the courtroom during a bond reduction hearing, and the judge refuses to lower the bond, it will look like he agrees with the comments. And I get the distinct impression in this climate, this judge does not plan on lowering the bond as long as the prosecution is objecting," Felbin said, always mindful of the harm the news media could do to a criminal defendant, particularly one whose duty is to serve and protect.

"So what do we need to do?"

The use of the word *we* didn't go unnoticed by Felbin who quickly said, "This guy is getting screwed and needs a break. I haven't surrendered him yet, because if I do, he will sit in jail until he makes the bond, and they won't even have a hearing to reduce it until he is in custody."

Before Felbin finished making his pitch, Jeffrey interrupted and said, "Why don't I post the bond? I assume you believe in him, and he certainly isn't going anywhere."

The offer really was not shocking. That was how Jeffrey was; generous, sometimes to a fault. But Felbin needed to be sure his friend understood all the issues associated with his kind gesture.

"You do realize this is a very public case, and your name could wind up in the public domain as having put up the money for the bond."

"That would not be a good thing, but not the end of the world."

When Goodrich reached the police department, he wasted no time—bypassing the front desk security—and headed for the Chief's office. He demanded an immediate audience with the Chief. Unfortunately, he was not in. Fearing the wrath of Cardwell if he returned without answers, in a tone that was barely civil, he demanded to see the person in charge of the Mitchell/Decker investigation. He was told that Lt. Col. Winston would be with him as soon as possible.

After what seemed like an eternity, he was finally escorted into the office of the head of IAD. Dispensing with the social chatter, Goodrich got right to the point. "Do you have Decker in custody?" he demanded.

"Not yet," was Winston's simple response.

"When can we expect to get him?"

"I don't know."

"What exactly are you doing to find him?"

Winston had reached his point of saturation with the lawyer's tone and attitude. "Look, Mister Goodrich, Officer Decker is not going anywhere and he will be here in due course."

"That's not good enough. The circuit attorney wants to know when he will be in custody and what you are doing to get that done, and she wants to know now," Goodrich said, his voice loud and demanding.

"This conversation is over. You tell your boss we don't appreciate people coming in here making demands. We will do our jobs, and she needs to do hers. We are all feeling the pressure of this case, but that is not an excuse for un-professional behavior. This will work out best for all of us if we work together. Tell her if she has a problem with that, she knows where to reach me," Winston said, escorting Goodrich to the door.

As he left Winston's office, Goodrich was trying to fig-ure out how he was going to explain this conversation. He had just gotten kicked out of the police department. What-ever he decided, he knew the circuit attorney would not be pleased.

Chapter Thirty-Four

Bobby was grateful to Jeffrey Fortman for agreeing to post his bond. But he didn't look forward to the actual surrender or the demeaning fingerprinting and other parts of the booking process that would follow. He was also concerned about the media circus that would accompany his surrender. He had seen the *perp walk* before, with the reporters jockeying for position to see who could get the best picture and ask the most inflammatory question they knew wouldn't be answered.

"Now that we have the bond set up, what is the next step?" Bobby asked.

"I'll swing by and pick you up in an hour, and we will go to the IAD office, where they will process you. While you are being processed, Jeffrey will be in the clerk's office posting the bond, which will secure your immediate release. As far as the reporters are concerned, we can beat them into the building, because I don't plan to tell IAD we are coming, but I'm not sure we will be that lucky on the way out. Someone will probably tip them that we are there," Felbin said.

"What do we do if they are there when we are leaving?"

"You do nothing but hold your head high. You have done nothing wrong and have nothing to be ashamed of. Do not, under any circumstances, try to hide your face. Look directly into the cameras, or at the reporters. In other words, don't do anything that makes you look guilty. Do you understand?"

Felbin had a lot of experience with the news media. In his years of practice, he'd handled many high profile cases and, in the process, established a very good relationship with the reporters, both electronic and print. They liked him. They knew they could always count on him for a comment on a pending case. On the other hand, Felbin knew he needed the press to level the playing field, particularly since the prosecution put their spin on the case when the criminal charges were filed.

Once when he was surrendering a Police Chief charged with federal civil rights criminal violations, a television reporter asked if he could interview the Chief when the FBI finished the booking process. Felbin agreed to allow his client simply to say that he was looking forward to his day in court when all the facts would be told. But he added the condition that the reporter interview the Chief's wife. After the reporter agreed, Felbin asked the Chief's wife if she would do the interview. Although she agreed, she expressed concern she would not be able to control her emotions and would break down in tears. Felbin instructed her to be herself and explain how the case had impacted the family to the extent she didn't know how she was going to feed her two young children during this process. Her husband would be without a paycheck and she was a stay at home mom. His purpose was to put a human face on his defendant and neutralize the negative publicity that had accompanied the case to that point. Interestingly, when the case finally reached the courtroom, several of the potential jurors recalled that interview.

As anticipated, when Felbin and Decker arrived at the police department to surrender, they went directly to the IAD offices without incident. There, they were shown into the office of Lt. Col. Winston, himself, who made no secret of his dissatisfaction with Decker and his lawyer.

"You disobeyed my direct order to appear here yesterday. Do you have any explanation for your actions?" Winston asked.

Before Bobby had a chance to respond, Felbin jumped in. "There is one thing I can say about you, Winston. You are all about form over substance. Here this officer is charged with murder, and you want to know why he violated some stupid purported order."

"There was nothing purported about it, Counselor," Winston said.

"Is your ego so inflated, Winston, that we have to deal with this nickel and dime issue right now?" Felbin shot back.

Turning to Bobby, Winston continued, "I would like an answer to my question, officer."

Again responding for Bobby, Felbin said, "You're not getting an answer to your question, Winston. Now, if we are not going to get on with this, we are leaving."

"We're going to get on with this all right, Counselor." Turning to Bobby, Winston continued, "You are under arrest for the murder of Jordon Mitchell."

Winston then proceeded to attempt to advise Bobby of his Miranda rights. He was interrupted by Felbin, who told him he didn't need to bother as Bobby understood his rights, had an attorney, and was not about to make a statement. Ignoring the interruption, Winston continued to advise Bobby of his Miranda rights and at the end asked for a confirmation that he understood those rights. Felbin said nothing more during this process, but favored Winston with a look of annoyance and at the end reconfirmed that his client would make no statement.

With the formal arrest out of the way, Winston now turned to internal matters, advising Decker once again that he was suspended without pay. But this time in addition to a suspension for the Mitchell matter, he added a suspension for disobeying his order to appear in the IAD office as directed.

Felbin was quick to react. "Does that make you feel good, Winston?" he asked.

Ignoring that comment, the head of the disciplinary arm of the St. Louis Police Department informed Decker he would have to be booked, fingerprinted, and photographed, a permanent reminder that he had been accused of murder. Seemingly enjoying the moment, Winston next told the officer his bond had been set at $250,000, and he would have to remain in the city jail until such time as the bond was posted or reduced and a court ordered his release.

Felbin decided to delay the pleasure of informing Winston his client would not be spending a minute in jail, not now, not ever. He opted to allow Winston to continue to gloat, believing the moment would be more dramatic later in the day. Instead, he simply inquired as to how long the booking process would take. Sarcastically, Winston looked at Felbin, smiled and said, "I don't know. Why do you ask? Does he have someplace he needs to be?"

Ignoring Winston's ignorant comment, Felbin chuckled to himself, thinking his decision to defer the bond conversation was a good one on multiple levels. He knew Winston would slow the booking process if he knew Decker would be making his bond.

The booking process took less than an hour, in part because Felbin believed Winston was anxious to put Decker in a jail cell with his attorney helplessly looking on. After the booking clerk completed the process, he told Decker to have a seat so he could call IAD to tell them he was finished. In the meantime, Jeffrey was waiting in the lobby of police headquarters, court document ordering the release of Bobby Decker in hand. While Decker remained in the prisoner processing room just a few feet from Jeffrey, Felbin obtained the release order and returned to wait for Winston to arrive and the fun to begin.

Ordinarily, Winston would keep Felbin waiting just to emphasize his importance. But on this occasion, he arrived in record time, no delay in riding the elevator from his spacious 6th floor office to the booking room on the 1st. As he bounced into the room accompanied by one of his investigators, presumably there to put cuffs on Bobby and escort him to the city jail across the street, he looked at the processing clerk and said, "Is he finished?" When the clerk confirmed everything was completed, Winston looked at Felbin instead of his client, probably for the sheer enjoyment of forcing a response, and said, "Is your client ready to go across the street and visit his new residence?"

Prolonging and savoring the moment, Felbin said, "I don't think so."

Smiling, Winston was quick to reply. "Well, Counselor, you don't get to decide that, I do."

Also smiling, Felbin said, "Actually, Winston, as important as you like to think you are, you *don't* get to decide that."

Instead of responding, Winston directed his investigator to place the handcuffs on Decker and walk him across the street to the jail.

As the investigator approached Decker, Felbin, still smiling, looked at Winston and said, "As you are the head of the Internal Affairs Division, I'm going to assume you know how to read, Winston," as he handed him the court document ordering the immediate release of his client. The smile disappeared as Winston read the paper he had just been handed. It was obvious to even the most casual observer that the joy of a few moments before had now turned to anger. Processing clerks began to position themselves to catch the show. The lawyer was putting short pants on a command rank officer. What a treat. Unable to help himself and continuing to bask in the glory of the moment, Felbin turned to the investigator and said, "I guess your boss isn't as important as he thinks he is. He was just overruled."

Winston left abruptly and without any additional conversation, but mindful of the humiliation and those who had witnessed it. Felbin and his client followed Winston out the door of the processing office and into the lobby of police headquarters, only to see television cameras, photographers, and reporters occupying the sidewalk outside. Winston had wasted no time rallying the troops. They expected to see a police officer in handcuffs being escorted to jail. But there would be no show on this day. Instead, they would be able to capture the image of Bobby Decker, leaving for home, a free man. Not exactly how Winston had planned it. As he walked next to his client toward the front door, Felbin wondered where this case was going. His client won round one. A small victory in a long war. Would there be other victories? It wasn't looking good.

Chapter Thirty-Five

As soon as he left the security of police headquarters, the reporters immediately surrounded Felbin and his client like a school of piranha who had just found dinner. As the flashes from the cameras and the television lights blinded them, the reporters fired the questions Felbin had predicted: "Did you kill Jordon Mitchell?" . . . "How did Mitchell die?" . . . "Did you hit him in the head?" . . . "Was Mitchell resisting arrest?" These were just some of the questions Bobby heard until his lawyer was able to take charge and silence the group, making it clear he would respond, but his client would not.

"I'll be happy to answer questions as soon as I can figure out why the circuit attorney has charged this officer with murder. I can honestly say this is a mystery to me at the present time, particularly under circumstances where the investigation and, in particular, the autopsy, haven't been completed."

Felbin had learned earlier that not only had the investigation not been completed, but the autopsy of the brain would take another four weeks and was sent to the medical examiner in St. Louis County.

Felbin continued, "How in the world can you charge anyone, let alone a police officer, with murder, when you don't know all the details of the incident, because your investigation is incomplete? But of course that is the style of this circuit attorney, charge first and ask questions later; a ready—shoot—aim philosophy. A very dangerous practice. But in any event, we need to get this officer out of here. I'll have a statement for you later." With the cameramen and the reporters following as they walked toward Felbin's car, the questions continued despite the lack of response.

Once they reached the car and were safely inside and on their way out of the parking lot, Bobby asked, "Is this how it will always be every time we have to go to court or anyplace else?"

"Pretty much," Felbin said.

"I'm not sure how much of that I can take," Bobby said, clearly drained by the events of the day.

"I can't say you'll ever get used to it, but you have to do the best you can to work through it," Felbin counseled.

"I assume this will be the lead story on the news tonight and a headline in the paper tomorrow, complete with a front page picture and story."

"Yes, it will. But my advice to you is: don't watch television tonight and don't read the paper tomorrow. I'll monitor the news coverage and respond where appropriate. That is my job, not yours. Just go home, have something to eat and get some much needed rest."

"I know that is what I should do but . . ." Bobby said, unable to finish his response.

After dropping Bobby off at his house, Felbin headed home to try to unwind from the stress of the day. On the way, his thoughts were consumed not so much by what the evidence might be, but rather what he knew this young police officer would have to experience before this nightmare would end. He recalled the Cannon case, which was still fresh in his mind and would now be pulled from the archives and thrust back into the headlines. He was not sure whether that would help or hurt Bobby Decker. He could argue it either way. But he knew one thing for certain; his old client, Tom Cannon, would not be happy returning to the spotlight.

His thoughts drifted to where this case would be tried. He knew full well he would be unable to get it out of the city of St. Louis. The prosecutor would not make the same mistake twice by failing to object to the motion for change of venue he would have to file. He also knew that no judge in the city would find all the inhabitants of the city of St. Louis were biased and prejudiced against Bobby, to the extent that the case would have to be moved to another location. That was an impossible burden under ordinary circumstances. Felbin resigned himself to the fact that he would be selecting a jury from a pool that would include a substantial number of African Americans familiar with media accounts, whether accurate or inaccurate.

When Felbin arrived home, he fixed himself something to eat and turned on the television to see how the events of the day would be reported. As anticipated, Bobby was the lead story on all the local channels, with footage of the two of them on the steps of police headquarters and then walking to his car. There was one thing for sure about the television people, they could never get enough video.

Although they'd aired a brief sound bite of the nothing statement he made on the steps, they didn't talk about the $250,000 bond posted, or how a cop would have access to that kind of money. The coverage included the portion of the circuit attorney's press conference where she was asked about the autopsy. To his surprise, Cardwell admitted the autopsy of the brain would be done by someone other than her own medical examiner, and more importantly, would take several weeks.

He listened carefully as Cardwell said Dr. Long had told her the cause of death was blunt trauma with a linear object, a flashlight. How could he know that if the autopsy of the brain hadn't been completed? And why was Long not doing the autopsy? Could the cause of death be determined without an autopsy of the brain? If so, then what was the significance of the autopsy of the brain, why do it at all? Now, not only was the IAD investigation incomplete, but a potentially critical piece of medical information was also missing.

At the moment, this case had more questions than answers. Felbin thought about calling Bobby to tell him what the circuit attorney had said, but decided against it. There would be plenty of time to discuss all the issues and for the moment, it was more important for Bobby to get some rest and put the day's events behind him.

Chapter Thirty-Six

Bobby Decker knew he needed to put this day behind him. He knew he needed to put the last several days of his life behind him, but he couldn't. He thought about the humiliation of the booking process, the television cameras in his face, the flash photography taking his picture, and the obnoxious questions the reporters were shouting at him, each struggling to be heard. He also thought about Kathy, the love of his life, but who was not in his life at the moment. As he sat alone in the home they once shared, he wondered where she was, what she was doing, and how she was coping. He felt her pain and was upset with himself for putting her through this ordeal. He thought about his family and what he was putting them through and what the future would hold for all the people he loved. He was frustrated by an inability to change what was occurring.

Despite the advice from his lawyer, he was drawn to the television and could not resist seeing for himself what they were saying about him. While it was important to avoid allowing this matter to totally consume him, Bobby also knew he had to deal with it. It was not going away. He knew what his lawyer had said, but he didn't know what others had said or how they would spin the day's events. He watched as his image appeared on the screen and he listened carefully to the words that accompanied the images. Like his lawyer, he was shocked to hear the circuit attorney admitting the autopsy of the brain hadn't been completed. Although he didn't know the legal or medical significance, it was obvious, to him at least, that the circuit attorney and perhaps others were very anxious to prosecute him. He knew the IAD investigation was not completed, and now another piece of the puzzle was also incomplete. If he was already being prosecuted, how could the investigation be fair? What would happen if the autopsy exonerated him? Would the murder charge be dismissed? But if that was the case, why didn't the prosecutor wait for the autopsy to be completed before bringing the charge?

He needed another beer. It would be his fourth. He wanted desperately to supplant the many questions that had no answers. Dull the senses. Alcohol would clear his mind. But he needed to supplement his alcohol diet with some food. As he scanned a sparse pantry, he heard someone trying to unlock the door. It was Kathy. She looked more beautiful than ever. *Is she coming back home? Did she have enough time to sort things out? Would things get back to normal, or as normal as they could be in these trying times?* It would not take long for him to get his answers. Kathy was not coming home.

"Bobby, we need to talk," she began. "I saw the television coverage. Your case is all they are talking about in the office and although they don't say anything in front of me, I still hear things and they are not good things. I was called into Cardwell's office today for a *chat.*"

"That must have been very uncomfortable. Kathy. I love you very much and I'll do whatever you want to get you out from under this."

"I know you'll, and I love you very much too, but I really don't know what to do. Cardwell expressed some concerns that our relationship would get in the way with both your case and my ability to do my job."

"That's unfair. You are a professional, and a good one, who can separate the two worlds."

"I know that and you know that, but Cardwell is paranoid. I suppose she is concerned about losing another police case, particularly when the issue of race is involved. In any event, she told me in so many words that I need to make a choice. It seems among other things, she is concerned about the media finding out about us."

"What can we do about that? We can't pretend we were never an item."

"She understands that and is not as concerned about the past. She is concerned about the future."

"Did she have any suggestions?"

"A leave of absence. But I don't know how I can do that. I asked if our living together presented a problem. She said it did. I asked if it would make a difference if I lived somewhere else while this case was pending, but continued to work. She said it might and she would think about it."

With tears forming, Bobby said, "Is that what you want?"

"No, Bobby, it's not what I want. But I can't afford to give up my job. I have no place else to go and I need to support myself," she said, as she walked into the bedroom they once shared.

Bobby sat in silence as he watched her close the door, further separating their worlds. He didn't know what to do or say. He wanted to run to her, hold her and tell her jobs could be replaced, but love could not. He wanted to let her how much he loved and needed her in these troubled times. But he knew he couldn't. That wouldn't be right; it would be selfish and it would cause her to suffer even more than she already had. His thoughts and confusion were interrupted by the door opening and the sight of Kathy leaving the bedroom with clothes in her arms, walking past him toward the front door. Each said nothing. When she reached the front door, she opened it, turned, looked at him through her red and swollen eyes, said nothing, and closed the door behind her. She'd made her choice.

Chapter Thirty-Seven

In the days that followed, the news headlines continued, as did the protests. His court appearance for the arraignment, a simple five minute proceeding where he had to appear in open court to tell the judge he was pleading not guilty, was well-attended, despite its brevity. Getting into and out of the courthouse was a challenge, since protestors were lining the steps. Because of safety concerns, Bobby and his lawyer were surrounded by armed and very large off-duty police officers, who formed a barrier around the two as they navigated the steps. Fortunately, the appearance was without incident, other than another media feeding-frenzy and an opportunity for the protestors to be heard.

With nothing to do but stare at the walls, the days became longer. Bobby was isolated, shut out from the world, left alone to think about an uncertain future. The preliminary hearing had been set in what appeared to be record time.

It was obvious the circuit attorney was anxious to move his case along. He wondered what it would be like. Felbin had explained this was only a hearing to determine whether probable cause existed—to believe that a crime had occurred, and whether he was in some way responsible. It was not a determination of guilt beyond a reasonable doubt, the standard that would be used for the trial.

Particularly given the climate, Felbin had no doubt that probable cause would be found; the murder charge would not be dismissed, and Bobby would stand trial. After the preliminary hearing, the next issue to be decided would be where the trial would occur. Because of the Cannon case, Felbin was less than optimistic the case would be moved out of the city of St. Louis.

Just when Bobby thought things could not get any worse, a newspaper article appeared partially detailing his prior disciplinary history with the Department. Someone, presumably IAD or the circuit attorney, leaked the information. Fortunately, it was part of a larger article and briefly mentioned some false reporting discipline Bobby Decker received during his first year with the Department. Of course, although not specifically stated, the inference was that he was a liar. This was an issue he feared, and discussed briefly with Felbin during his first office visit. Tell the lawyer everything, no secrets, was his brother's advice. Fortunately, this part of the article was brief and was not worthy of Page One coverage, probably because the reporter didn't have time to check all the details. But it was now out there and Bobby figured it was not the last time he would have to deal with the issue.

Soon after the story appeared, Bobby received a call from Felbin, who wanted him to come to the office to discuss this latest problem. Now Felbin would need greater details of the incident. He asked Bobby to prepare a memo explaining, in as much detail as he could recall, what had happened that had led to a false reporting accusation. Since his schedule wasn't exactly overloaded, Bobby went to work recounting those details as soon as the phone call ended.

Chapter Thirty-Eight

The preparation of the memo for Felbin allowed Bobby to reflect on his days as a probationary police officer. Thanks in part to a partner who wanted to retire more than he wanted to do police work, most of his days on the job that first year were uneventful. His partner introduced him to all the restaurant owners in the 4th district, where he was originally assigned; he certainly learned where he could get a free meal. As far as police work was concerned, he'd made a few minor arrests, all without incident, along with routine traffic stops, likewise without incident. In that first year, Bobby hadn't experienced any real action, no real excitement. Actually, the job was rather boring. But that would soon change.

A week before his time as a probationary officer was scheduled to end, Decker and his partner, Ray Parker, were transferred to the 6th district. Known as a high crime area, the 6th district, unlike the 4th, had few viable businesses, and an abundance of derelict, fire damaged and abandoned homes. The predominant neighborhood business was the sale of illegal drugs. Gangs were prevalent and wars commonplace. The sound of gunfire was a nightly occurrence. The people of the community, mostly African American, had tried numerous times to retake their neighborhood, without success. It was, for some, more dangerous than a military conflict with a foreign enemy in a remote part of the world.

Bobby recalled hardly being able to contain his excitement when he was informed of the transfer. His partner, however, was a different story. Ray Parker wanted to end his career quietly, shaking hands, not handcuffing arrestees or fighting with those who avoided the bracelets. But now, life would change. Now Parker had to work. He constantly had to look over his shoulder. If he failed in this war zone, he might pay with the ultimate price, his life. On top of everything else, he also had a rookie partner for whom he was responsible.

Bobby recalled that his first day in the 6th began at 11 p.m. He was scheduled to work the night shift from 11 p.m. to 7 a.m. in the highest criminal district in the St. Louis Police Department. His introduction to the sights and sounds of the district would occur at a time when criminal activity was shielded by the darkness of the night.

It didn't take long for Bobby to see some action. At about 12:30 a.m. on a warm summer night, while on routine patrol, Bobby noticed some activity on a street corner. It was a drug deal, and Bobby knew it. While listening to his partner grumble about the transfer, he slowly approached the corner. One of the individuals noticed the police presence. Without warning, that individual fired a single shot at the police car. The shot missed the mark. Reacting to the gun shot, Bobby slammed on the brakes, causing the vehicle to come to an abrupt stop. Instantly, Parker jumped out, and while standing beside the open door, fired a shot at the two suspects who were now fleeing. That bullet hit its mark, and one of the suspects fell to the ground.

"Call for backup!" Parker shouted, as he left the protection of the police car to approach the fallen suspect. He moved cautiously, with his service revolver pointed at the individual lying motionless and face down on the ground. "Don't move; you're under arrest!" Parker yelled, surveying the immediate area, looking for the other suspect.

"I called for a backup. What do you want me to do?" Decker asked, gun drawn and hand shaking.

"Turn over slowly and show me your hands," Parker ordered. No response or movement from the suspect on the ground.

"We may need an ambulance. I may have hit him." Parker said, gun still pointed at the suspect.

"I'll call for one," Decker said, reaching for his portable radio.

As Parker turned the suspect onto his back, he noticed blood in the area of his stomach. He appeared to be unconscious. "Better tell that ambulance to hurry. This asshole may not be with us much longer," Parker said, as he began to look for a gun and any evidence of criminal behavior.

After calling for the ambulance, Decker assisted in the search. As the sound of the ambulance could be heard in the distance, several backup units arrived. Meanwhile, in the shadow of flashing red emergency lights, a neighborhood crowd began to gather.

Because a police shooting was involved, department policy required that Homicide respond to the scene, as well as the Internal Affairs Division. The scene would be under the control of the ranking Homicide officer. It would be his responsibility to secure the area and coordinate the investigation. The evidence technician unit (ETU) would be responsible for gathering the physical evidence to be processed through the laboratory.

The ambulance arrived before the team of investigators. The paramedics evaluated the condition of the suspect and took preliminary steps to control the bleeding. Once stabilized, the suspect was quickly transported to the hospital. Shortly after the ambulance left, the Homicide detectives arrived, along with ETU.

Sgt. James Boland, a 28 year veteran with nine years of homicide experience, would be in charge of the investigation. Boland reminded Bobby of the television character Colombo, complete with raincoat, and chewing on an unlit cigar. But on this warm night, the traditional raincoat didn't cover the wrinkled suit accented by a stained tie and an equally wrinkled shirt. As usual, his hair was uncombed, complementing a day or two of old facial hair growth. But make no mistake, Boland knew what he was doing, particularly when the case involved a police shooting. He was a cop's cop.

When he arrived, Boland was met by Parker. "What mess did you create now, Parker?" he asked.

"The asshole shot at us and I shot him. That simple. Case closed. You can go home, Boland," was the quick response.

"If only things were that simple," Boland replied.

As the men spoke, an unidentified voice from the crowd yelled, "He shot an unarmed baby."

Looking frustrated and while shaking his head, Boland said to himself, "Here we go again." He knew all too well what was coming. He had been there before. A white police officer shoots a young black man, and the inevitable cry of police brutality would echo throughout the black community, further highlighting the animosity that existed with the St. Louis Police Department. "Will there ever be a time when we can all get along?" he asked rhetorically. "Probably not," was his rhetorical answer.

Chapter Thirty-Nine

Until the investigations were completed, Decker would be riding solo. Department policy required that police officers involved in shootings be placed on administrative leave with pay. Parker would be spending some time at home, and Decker's probationary period would be extended until all investigations were completed. Both Decker and Parker would also be spending some time with the Homicide unit and Internal Affairs, answering questions.

Not unlike the current Jordon Mitchell case, the first order of business was the preparation of the police report recounting the events of the Parker shooting. He and Parker would do that together. The preparation of that report was a relatively simple task, because this was a relatively simple case. Black male, standing on a street corner with another black male and after observing the presence of the police, fired a weapon at the officers, but missed. Parker returned fire, but didn't miss, striking the intended target. But this relatively simple case became complicated after witnesses surfaced claiming the police had shot an unarmed man.

The Homicide Unit investigation was straightforward. The police report prepared by Parker and Decker was satisfactory and would be incorporated in its entirety in the Homicide report. The claims of the neighborhood witnesses would be handled separately. Fortunately, the victim had survived, although he was still in the hospital. No criminal charges had been filed against anyone, despite the efforts of Parker to persuade the prosecutors that the so-called victim was really a criminal who tried to kill police officers.

The Internal Affairs investigation was not as straightforward. Eventually, both Decker and Parker would be ordered to answer questions. In 1967, the United States Supreme Court in the case of *Garrity v. New Jersey* had decided that police officers must answer questions that are directly and narrowly related to the performance of their duties. They had no choice. However, nothing they said could be used in any criminal prosecution brought against them. If they failed to answer the questions, they could be disciplined, to include termination. It was only a matter of time before Decker and Parker would be summoned to the Internal Affairs office.

While the investigations continued, Parker and Decker spoke often. In his memo to Felbin, Bobby explained that Parker warned him the Internal Affairs experience would not be a pleasant one. Parker had been through it before. Parker told him the investigators assigned to that unit were not well-respected by the rank and file police officers who spent their days on the street, dodging bullets. When the time came to be questioned, they would be treated like criminals. The attitude would be: "You are guilty of criminal acts, and we intend to prove it. You will be compelled to help in that process, because you'll answer whatever questions we have, and if you refuse or lie, we will fire you." So, in other words, fuck you. Although he didn't put it in his memo to Felbin, Bobby thought how prophetic the words of Parker were.

The day of the incident, Parker decided he and Decker needed lawyers, who would be furnished by the Police Association. Fortunately, Decker had taken Parkers' advice and joined the Association soon after he hit the street. Therefore he was eligible to be represented by an Association attorney. The Association had a list of lawyers from which the member could choose.

When Decker joined, he was told that for non-criminal, internal disciplinary matters, the Association would pay all the legal fees and expenses incurred by the member. For cases where the member was charged criminally, the Association's legal committee would determine whether to provide legal counsel based upon whether the incident was in connection with the performance of duty. If it was, legal counsel would be provided. Other non-duty related incidents were reviewed on a case by case basis.

With the investigations into their third week, Bobby recalled that neither he nor Parker had been summoned to give an IAD statement. They knew the subject who was shot was out of the hospital, and Homicide detectives were satisfied with the report submitted and had no reason to ask additional questions. But Parker also knew that IAD would not be content to leave it at the police report; they would want more.

Periodically, Bobby would call Parker to inquire whether he had heard anything. Usually, the response was the same. However, one day, Parker had some information he had received from a friend on the inside. That friend had told him IAD was out to screw him and was trying to prove the kid he shot was unarmed. Neither he nor the other individual on the street corner even had a weapon—let alone fired one. Bobby knew there was no love lost between Parker and the *goons* in IAD, as he called them. Their goal was to rid the Department of Parker. They thought they would now succeed where they had failed in the past. Apparently, the strategy would be to squeeze Decker and force him to give up Parker. It was against that background that the case was investigated, Bobby told Felbin.

Several more weeks passed, and finally Bobby was summoned to IAD for a Garrity interview. He was on duty at the time, riding alone in a marked vehicle, since his partner was on administrative leave pending the outcome of the investigation. His sergeant called him on the radio and told him he had to report to IAD immediately. Since Parker had warned him not to go without a lawyer, he called the attorney provided by the Association as he headed for the IAD offices in police headquarters downtown. Unfortunately, his lawyer was not in his office and was in the middle of a jury trial.

When he arrived at IAD, he met Sgt. Graham Jenkins who would be conducting the interview. Jenkins had been on the force for 22 years with all of his time spent behind a desk. He had little or no street experience. But neither did Bobby.

Jenkins told Bobby he would be conducting a Garrity interview regarding the shooting of Garrett Williams in the 6th district. Bobby understood, but explained that his lawyer was in trial and unavailable to attend the interview. That made no difference to Jenkins as he informed Bobby he intended to proceed with the interview, with or without a lawyer. He also was quick to remind Bobby of his probationary status, informing him he could be fired at any time and for any reason without any right to a hearing before the Board of Police Commissioners. That warning would be repeated several times. Bobby viewed it as a threat, if he continued to corroborate Parker's story.

Before the internal interview began, another IAD investigator entered the room. Sgt. James Neeley introduced himself and told Decker he was conducting the criminal phase of the investigation. Because Decker was an inexperienced probationary officer, Sgt. Neeley felt the need to explain his role. He told Decker two IAD investigations were occurring simultaneously, one criminal and one internal. He was assigned the criminal and Sgt. Jenkins had the internal. The rules of the Department, as dictated by the courts, required the construction of what was called a Chinese Wall between the two investigations. While the criminal investigator could share his information with the internal investigator, the reverse could not occur. The contents of the internal investigation had to remain confidential. Neeley went on to explain the reason for the rule. He told Decker the internal investigator had the benefit of compelling a Garrity statement. But the U.S. Supreme Court had ruled that nothing in the statement could be used to prosecute the officer criminally. So, the investigations were separated, with a separate investigator assigned to each.

After reading him his Miranda rights, Neeley asked Bobby if he desired to make a statement. Bobby recalled telling Neeley he really didn't know what to do as he had nothing to hide, but he had previously asked for a lawyer. Neeley then explained since he was requesting a lawyer, he could not question him. He left the room, leaving Jenkins to begin his internal questioning.

Ignoring his repeated requests for a lawyer, Jenkins asked his questions. In his memo to Felbin, Bobby wrote it didn't take long to figure out what they wanted him to say: "No shots were fired at their police vehicle before Parker fired at the suspect." Bobby suggested that because the interview was tape recorded, Felbin could possibly obtain a copy to confirm his suspicions about what they wanted him to say. Bobby was uncertain whether the threats were captured on tape. But, recorded or not, he was positive about the continuous reminders that he was a probationary officer and could be fired immediately for no cause and without a hearing.

As he wrote his memo for Felbin, Bobby was forced to recall some very unpleasant events that had occurred early in his career. Looking back, and particularly recognizing where his life was now, he wondered why he didn't leave the Department after this first demeaning event.

Despite the threats, he continued to say he witnessed shots fired at the police car, although he could not be certain of the number. Eventually, Lt. Col. Winston joined Jenkins in questioning Bobby, presumably because Jenkins was not getting the answers he wanted. When Winston was equally unsuccessful, he tried another tactic. Bobby recollected being told if he cooperated, his prior statements would be forgotten as though he never said the suspect fired the first shot. He would not be charged with false reporting. Of course, if he declined that invitation, a false reporting charge with its attendant consequences would occur. Bobby declined the invitation. He was prepared to suffer whatever the consequences would be.

After the conclusion of his interview, Bobby assumed the investigation would continue. He figured that eventually a false reporting charge would be brought against him and multiple charges against his partner. But without notice, Parker opted to retire. Bobby awaited his termination letter. But that letter never came. Rather, his punishment was an extension of his probation, a consequence Bobby neither anticipated nor understood. But, in any event, he was allowed to continue with his career as a police officer, for which he was particularly grateful at the time.

When he finished the memo, he saved it on the computer, sent it to Felbin, logged off the computer, and reflected on what he had just written. If he had been fired, then he wouldn't have his current problems. His family would have been happy, not so much that he was fired, but that he was no longer a cop. But his relationship with Kathy would not have developed. Of course, that relationship was in jeopardy with more heartache inevitably to follow. It was all so confusing. His life was very complicated.

Chapter Forty

A few days before the preliminary hearing was scheduled to begin, there was another surprise.

Contrary to her public statements, Cardwell decided to let a grand jury, behind closed doors and in a secret proceeding attended only by prosecutors with their witnesses, decide the question of probable cause. Consistent with the old adage that a prosecutor could get a grand jury to indict a ham sandwich, Robert Decker was indicted for murder. Not surprisingly, Cardwell would not subject her witnesses, including the Medical Examiner, to cross examination by the defense during a preliminary. Because prosecutors don't even have to record grand jury testimony, they don't have to call all of their witnesses. It is conceivable the Medical Examiner never testified.

The biggest surprise was Jake Corbett was not indicted. Both Bobby and his lawyer were confused by the move. Clearly, he had been arrested and charged initially, along with Bobby, with the murder of Jordon Mitchell. Although he was never accused of striking Mitchell, he was charged with being an accessory to the murder, acting in concert with Bobby. In the eyes of the law, he was as responsible for that death as his partner. Felbin thought from the outset it would be a difficult case to prove. Convicting a cop of murder simply because he was there was a stretch. Surely, the prosecutors knew that as well.

Was there a tactical consideration in charging Corbett at the beginning? Was he charged along with Bobby to keep him from testifying for Bobby? And now was he not indicted because he would be testifying for the prosecution? Or did the grand jury really decide they had no probable cause to indict him? A grand jury making a fair and impartial decision based upon the evidence rather than what the prosecutor wanted would be a rare occurrence. In fact, it might even be a first. Felbin wondered what Corbett could possibly say that would hurt the defense. Bobby had no answers. They would have to wait and see if Corbett showed up on the State's witness list. Both the prosecution and the defense were required to identify the witnesses they intended to call at trial. The only exception to that rule was a rebuttal witness. Since those witnesses were rebutting evidence heard for the first time during the trial, they could not have been anticipated as witnesses before the trial began.

Some concern about Jake Corbett began to surface even before the indictment was returned by the grand jury. After Bobby was released on $250,000 bond, Corbett was released on his own recognizance, which required the posting of no cash or security. At the time, Felbin thought Cardwell simply didn't want to test the strength of her case against Corbett during a bond reduction hearing. However, some additional concerns surfaced when Corbett refused to return Bobby's phone calls and Corbett's lawyer was evasive in his later conversations with Felbin. But now, all Bobby and his lawyer could do was to wait. See what happened and how things played out, while being cautious in the meantime.

Not unexpectedly, the cancellation of the preliminary hearing and the return of an indictment that didn't include Jake Corbett drew media attention. Felbin's phone was ringing with reporters looking for interviews and answers. He knew he needed to say something to address a variety of issues, not the least of which was the absence of Corbett. Rather than do it one reporter at a time, he decided to gather everyone together and say what he had to say only once.

When they were all assembled in his conference room, he began by addressing the Corbett issue. "All of you have seen the indictment and conspicuous by his absence is Jake Corbett. The question in my mind is not why he is not there, but why was he charged in the first place. Clearly, from the start there was no evidence to support a murder charge. Yet, *Ready Shoot Aim* Cardwell filed it."

Interrupting, one of the reporters asked, "Does that mean there is evidence to support the charge against your client?"

"I was getting to that before I was so rudely interrupted," Felbin said jokingly. "I suspect, contrary to her public pronouncement of transparency when she told you she would not take this case to the secret grand jury, she had a change of heart when she figured out she could not make her case in a public courtroom where there would be cross examination. I also suspect there is an issue with the Medical Examiner."

Felbin had wanted to take advantage of any opportunity to challenge the Medical Examiner ever since he learned the charges were brought before the autopsy of the brain was completed. Continuing, he said, "I can't believe she would bring any charge against anyone before all the medical evidence was reviewed. How do you charge murder when you don't know the cause of death?"

Again, he was interrupted by another question. "Wasn't the skull fracture caused by blunt trauma with a linear object? In other words, didn't Mister Mitchell die because he was struck on the head with a flashlight?"

"I'm told he had a skull fracture. That part is clear. But I haven't seen any report that fixes the cause of death, have you?" Felbin asked rhetorically. When he received no response, Felbin continued, "What was the rush to charge these police officers with a crime, murder no less, before both the autopsy and the investigation generally were completed?" Answering his own question, Felbin said, "I'll tell you what the rush was. She didn't want a repeat of Cannon. She was embarrassed because she charged that case where there was no evidence to support it and then along came this case on the heels of Cannon. Because she was feeling the political pressure, Ms. *Ready Shoot Aim* filed murder charges to silence the protestors before the investigations were completed and before she had any evidence to support the allegation.

"Now she has run behind closed doors to get an indictment against only one officer. So *you'll* think that although she doesn't have evidence against the officer who was dismissed, she must have it against the one remaining. Of course, the true test of that would have been a public preliminary hearing. Then we all could have seen what the evidence is. But now we will have to wait for the trial—unless she also plans to do that behind closed doors."

"Did you get a copy of the completed autopsy report?"

"I haven't seen any completed report," Felbin said.

"Do you know whether the autopsy and the IAD investigative reports have been completed?"

"I have no idea. She has not bothered to share anything with me since this fiasco began."

Of course, Felbin knew the prosecutor was not required to share anything with the defense until after the probable cause determination was made either through a preliminary hearing or by a grand jury. The rules of criminal procedure then require the prosecutor to provide the defense with all the investigative documents, to include police reports and scientific evidence along with witness statements in the state's possession.

After the cameras were turned off and the reporters left, Felbin breathed a sigh of relief that Bobby's prior discipline had never come up. But he also knew it was only a matter of time before he would have to answer questions about the discipline his client received for false reporting.

Felbin sat on a comfortable couch in his spacious corner office and just stared out the window. He had an unobstructed view of the Arch, the Gateway to the West, the iconic symbol of St. Louis. *How could a city, with so much wonderful history be so racially divided,* he asked himself. *How did we get to this point? Will these wounds ever heal? Can black people fairly decide the fate of white people? Conversely, can white people fairly decide the fate of black people?* He answered his own question. *As long as people see skin color when dealing with others, things won't change. Color blindness won't in my lifetime. That won't be good for my client.*

He wondered what he would find in the completed autopsy report when he received it. Despite what he'd just told the reporters, Felbin knew Cardwell would eventually have an autopsy report of the brain that indicated Mitchell died due to blunt trauma with a linear object; a flashlight. And if she didn't, she would dismiss the charges and then proceed to blame the Medical Examiners. With the indictment released to the public, Felbin believed Cardwell had accomplished her goal of putting the Medical Examiners in the cross hairs. If they didn't support her theory of murder, they would be at the forefront of the blame game. And they would be answering the questions, not her. Felbin also knew he would need an expert of his own. He wondered what else the state had, because he knew what he had at the moment: nothing.

Chapter Forty-One

In response to Felbin's press conference, the circuit attorney declined comment, saying only that all the evidence would be presented to a jury in a public court room at the appropriate time. That way, she avoided answering some of the tough questions raised by her opponent. But there was also another benefit from her refusal to make a detailed statement. She knew Felbin would be filing a motion for change of venue based upon the adverse publicity and she didn't want to do anything to assist him in that effort.

The day after he received a copy of the indictment, Felbin sent his investigator, Jack Reilly, to the circuit attorney's office to pick up all the documents in the state's possession pertaining to his case. As he waited anxiously for those documents, he began preparing the expected motion for change of venue. In the motion, he alleged the inhabitants of the city of St. Louis were biased and prejudiced against his client. While it was easy to write that in the motion, it was nearly impossible to prove. He had already hired a statistical expert, a professor at St. Louis University who did polling not dissimilar to what the politicians do when running for office. He would randomly survey a cross section of the St. Louis community on preconceived ideas regarding the guilt or innocence of Bobby Decker. Hopefully, those numbers would show prejudice and support a change, but Felbin was not optimistic.

In the wake of the Cannon debacle, Felbin knew that no judge would be willing to commit judicial suicide by moving the case out of the city. But that would not prevent the filing of the motion. The issue needed to be preserved for an appellate court to review if the case went south and Bobby was convicted. Trial lawyers are forever making a record for appellate purposes, which cannot occur unless the appropriate motions and objections are made during the trial, to give the trial judge an opportunity to make a decision in the first instance. No motion, no objection, no appeal.

After preparing his change of venue motion, he began to think about how he was going to defend a police officer charged with murder, who really was unable to make any substantive contribution to the development of the defense. Although he hadn't seen the particulars in the IAD criminal investigation, he knew it would contain certain basic facts. A young black man, who was burglarizing a pawn shop with another black man in the middle of a rainy night, came into contact with on-duty police officer Bobby Decker; was arrested by Decker; and died of a massive skull fracture. A skull fracture Bobby Decker could not explain.

As far as potential eyewitnesses, there were only two; one for the prosecution and one wildcard. Felbin expected Daniels Jones, Mitchell's accomplice, to ignore the truth and testify for the prosecution. He surmised that when the prosecution finished preparing him, he would swear he saw Decker strike Mitchell in the back of the head with a flashlight. That testimony might be manageable if the police report supplied a reason for the blow. But it didn't.

The wildcard was Corbett, who was no longer a defendant in the case. Although on the roof, Felbin had no idea what he would say. According to Bobby, Corbett's attention was focused on the arrest of Jones at the time he was arresting Mitchell. He didn't think Corbett witnessed anything, particularly because if he had, he would not have had to ask Bobby why he was calling for an ambulance. But at the moment that was just a theory. Felbin well knew, a lot of surprises could occur during a criminal jury trial.

Felbin's thoughts were interrupted by his investigator, who was delivering a copy of the investigative report, or at least that portion which the police department and the prosecutor were willing to release at this time. In criminal cases, the investigation never ends. Even during the trial, investigators are running down leads and checking information. The only difference in this case was that the police department would assign additional detectives to perform whatever tasks were necessary to insure Bobby Decker was convicted of murdering Jordon Mitchell.

As anticipated, the report contained a summary of the statement of Daniels Jones, Mitchell's fellow burglar, who claimed to have seen Bobby strike Mitchell with a flashlight. No surprise there. According to the report, Jones said he saw Decker pull out a flashlight and strike Mitchell several times on the back of the head. Interestingly, the report was sparse on specific details and particulars of how that striking occurred. It was unclear whether the detectives who conducted that interview recorded it. Felbin seriously doubted the interview was preserved on tape as that would supply more fodder for the cross examination of this star witness.

Investigators in criminal cases are never excited about helping defense lawyers screw up their case. As a result, they are careful what is included in reports, since those documents serve as the basis for the development of defense strategies and cross examination. If you put in too much that can be a problem, and if there is too little that can also be a problem. Most experienced investigators err on the side of too little.

Also not unexpectedly, the report made no mention of any interview with Officer Jake Corbett. That was not surprising either. Until recently, Corbett had been a suspect who had 5th amendment rights and also had a lawyer who presumably was not allowing him to talk to the police or prosecutors. But Felbin had some concerns about that, since this lawyer was the same one who represented several police officers in the Cannon case and had them change their statements to the detriment of Sgt. Cannon. Clearly, in that case, Felbin believed those officers and their lawyer succumbed to the pressures associated with the threats of criminal prosecution and incarceration. Perhaps that's just human nature. In any event, human nature or not, Felbin remained concerned.

Chapter Forty-Two

As with any case, once Felbin received the discovery information from the prosecution, he discussed that information with his client. That conversation with Bobby would include a discussion of Jake Corbett. Felbin needed to evaluate the risk of the only other potential rooftop eyewitness appearing at the trial for the prosecution.

"How well do you know Jake Corbett?" Felbin began.

"I really don't know that much about him. We were not friends, if that is what you're asking. I never socialized with him. Never been to his house. Never met his family."

"Did you ever ride with him? Was he ever your partner?" Felbin pressed.

"Never rode with him and he was never my partner. But I have handled calls with him, and I obviously knew him from working in the district."

"Did you ever work with him in preparing a police report?" Felbin asked, mindful that both participated in the preparation of the Mitchell report.

Searching his memory, Bobby finally replied. "I know I have handled calls with him. I can't think of any instance off-hand where we prepared the report together, but I'll continue to give that some thought. And in any event, I know there were no incidents where we would have disagreed or had any conflicts about the contents of any report, assuming that we did prepare one together. That much I'm certain of."

"Was there any disagreement when you and he were preparing the Mitchell report?"

Bobby didn't respond immediately. He was searching his memory. Finally, hesitatingly, he said, "Well, yes. But not really a disagreement."

"Tell me about that," Felbin said, somewhat surprised by Bobby's hesitation and response, since he hadn't previously mentioned any conflicts with Corbett.

"Well, when we were preparing the report he suggested I include something that I disagreed with. But you have to remember we were both under a lot of pressure at that time with all the publicity surrounding this guy who was in intensive care."

"Stop apologizing and get to the point," Felbin said, obviously aggravated that he was hearing this for the first time.

"As I sat staring at the computer obviously frustrated because I was unable to explain how this burglar got a fractured skull, Jake offered some help. His suggestion was to write it in to write it out. In other words, say that I hit him, but justify it."

"Yes, I'm familiar with the practice. I have represented tons of police officers in a variety of situations," Felbin said. "So what did you say?"

"Actually, I hit the ceiling. Not so much at him, but because I was frustrated that I could offer no explanation for this guy's injury. A life-threatening injury. I obviously knew he was in intensive care and could die and that I would be blamed. So, I just said, *That's a great idea. I'm twice his size and the only way I could control him was by whacking him in the head and killing him. That will really pass the straight face test,*" Bobby said apologetically, recognizing that Felbin was aggravated.

"Did the discussion end there?"

"Yes and no. The discussion ended for the moment. But Jake knew I was struggling. So as the day progressed but my progress on preparing the report didn't, he came back to me later in the day and gave me a rough draft he had prepared in which he wrote it in to write it out."

"I'm not following," Felbin said. "He gave you a memo of some kind in which he wrote your portion of the report explaining the fractured skull?"

"Yes."

"How did he do that?" Felbin asked.

Continuing the explanation, Bobby said, "He was on a computer preparing his portion of the report. In a draft he was preparing, he added an explanation of how I needed to subdue Mitchell by striking him with a flashlight."

"Do you remember what he wrote specifically as to how you needed to subdue him with a flashlight?"

"No, because at the time I knew I didn't hit him with a flashlight or anything else. I also knew I was not going to use the draft Corbett had prepared. I thanked him for his concern and threw it away. By that time, I had calmed down a little or at least as much as I could, kinda accepting that this kid was going to die and I was going to be prosecuted. I didn't need a house to fall on me to recognize what was happening on the streets and in the circuit attorney's office. I was there for the Cannon case and the political aspirations of Cardwell have never been a secret to anybody with half a brain."

Accepting his account of the Corbett incident, Felbin went on to provide some counseling to his client. "Listen, Bobby, I know this is very stressful. And I know you can't explain that fracture. But I need to know every little detail, whether or not you think it is important. At this point, I have no idea what the prosecutor will be able to prove. I can speculate, but we won't know until we see all of their evidence. By the same token, I have no idea what our defense will be. You need to assume everything is important and you need to search your recollection for every little detail associated with this mess. For example, I doubt your exchange with Corbett while writing the report will be significant, but I don't know that right now. Do you understand?"

Bobby certainly understood the seriousness of his situation. But at this moment in time, neither understood the importance of the story that Bobby had just recounted.

Chapter Forty-Three

Gradually, the state's evidence trickled in. Felbin was anxious to analyze every sentence. Of particular importance was the autopsy report from both forensic pathologists, Dr. Phillip Long and Dr. Helen McHenry. Felbin knew both well and had been challenged by each in numerous cases over the years. Dr. Long had been the Medical Examiner for the city of St. Louis for many years and had performed autopsies on thousands of bodies who were the victims of foul play. Generally, Felbin found him to be a straightforward guy who was willing to discuss his findings, whether formally or informally, prior to trial. Although soft spoken, he was a formidable opponent when on the witness stand. He knew his trade and did his homework before testifying. As a result, he was ready for whatever the defense lawyers tried to do to him in their efforts to discredit him.

The personality of Dr. Helen McHenry stood in sharp contrast to that of Dr. Long. While Dr. Long was mild mannered and laid back, Dr. McHenry was aggressive and confrontational. While Dr. Long would calmly debate a point and defend his position, Dr. McHenry had little tolerance for those who would dare to disagree with her. She would not hesitate to cut your legs off in the process of that discussion. Dr. McHenry also had the unique ability to completely ignore questions put to her by her opponents and respond with the answers she wanted to give, whether or not related to the question asked. Felbin knew he was going to have his hands full with both of these well-respected members of the St. Louis community. These were hometown docs, and Felbin knew he would have to obtain his experts outside the St. Louis area to counter their testimony. Because St. Louis is such a parochial environment, anyone Felbin brought in from another area would be at a disadvantage from the start.

Dr. Helen McHenry had served as the Medical Examiner in both St. Louis and Jefferson counties for more than 25 years. Like Dr. Long, she was a formidable opponent. While perhaps not as prepared to testify at trial, her personality radiated an air of confidence. As Felbin once told the judge in a high profile, jury waive case, Dr. McHenry had the ability to dazzle juries with her bullshit, not her facts.

The report prepared by Dr. Long was pretty straightforward, containing the results of his examination both internally and externally, as well as toxicology findings from the lab. Each of the vital organs was removed and carefully examined. The heart, the liver, the kidneys and so on. All normal. However, when Felbin got to the section describing the examination of the external parts of the body, his attention was directed to the right rib cage. A contusion was noted in this area which began in the front and extended laterally toward the rear passing over the fifth rib, measuring 12.32 inches in length and 2.175 inches in width. Because Dr. Long sent the brain to Dr. McHenry, his report simply referenced that fact. However, he did examine the skull and document and measure a massive rear skull fracture. Not only would the jury hear this description, but they would also see photographs of the autopsy, over the objections of the defense, which would graphically display Jordon Mitchell's refracted skull and exposed brain. That is never a good moment for any defendant.

Beyond the blood, guts and gore, and notwithstanding the massive skull fracture, the autopsy was that of a normal, 19-year-old African American male. The toxicology report was likewise normal and contained no indication of any drug consumption, whether legal or illegal. As to the cause of death, Dr. Long concluded that Jordon Mitchell died as a result of blunt trauma from a linear object. Not surprisingly, that was the same opinion he had given Cardwell before the entire autopsy was completed.

Although the Long report didn't contain anything unexpected, Felbin could not help but wonder why Long felt it necessary to send the brain to another pathologist to be examined. After all, Phillip Long had performed autopsies on perhaps thousands of brains during his extensive career and this was by no means his first high profile case. Felbin knew there was a reason somewhere for this departure from the norm, but didn't know precisely what it was, just yet. But like many other unanswered questions, Felbin was determined to find the answer to this question as well.

The autopsy report of the brain prepared by Dr. Helen McHenry was also fairly straightforward, documenting brain bleeds and brain swells. Felbin knew before he received either report that he would need an expert; to educate him about the medicine involved, and also to testify. He hoped someplace in this medical morass, there would be some explanation of how Jordon Mitchell died that would have nothing to do with Bobby Decker. But on its face and considering Felbin's limited understanding of the medicine involved, it didn't look good for his client.

Chapter Forty-Four

Felbin was busy trying to figure out how he was going to defend this case. But first he needed a medical expert or two to counter hometowners, Long and McHenry. For that help, he reached out to a nationally-recognized forensic pathologist.

Harry Langdon was a forensic pathologist in New York. In addition to consulting duties with the New York City Police Department and the New York state police, he was also the author of several books on post-death medical crime detection, had a regular television show on HBO on issues relating to autopsies, had appeared on national television talk and other shows too numerous to mention and had consulted with the Congress of the United States on issues relating to the deaths of President John Kennedy and Dr. Martin Luther King. But perhaps Dr. Langdon was best known for his involvement in cases of national interest, such as O. J. Simpson, the professional football player accused of murder; the tragic, untimely death of comic actor John Belushi; and the son of actor, Marlon Brando, accused of criminal conduct. Locally, he had been an expert witness for the prosecution in a case involving a man in southern Illinois, across the river from St. Louis, accused of murdering his wife and two children so that he could be with his paramour.

Without a doubt, Dr. Langdon's reputation and resume were quite extensive and impressive. Through the years, Felbin had consulted with him on several cases, and the two had become friends. When Felbin called him and explained the Mitchell case generally, Dr. Langdon agreed to review the matter. Felbin supplied him with copies of the autopsy reports prepared by both Long and McHenry, Mitchell's medical records, and the police reports prepared by Decker and Corbett, as well as the IAD investigation.

Generally, Dr. Langdon was a prosecution witness. In about 90% of the cases he was asked to review, his opinion supported the prosecution's theory. Felbin hoped that trend would be broken in this case. He would now anxiously await Dr. Langdon's opinion and conclusions, optimistic he could help explain the cause of Jordon Mitchell's death. Of course, there was no guarantee his opinion would be any different from that of the locals. But Felbin really didn't have anything to lose. He had nothing at the moment, and if his opinion concurred with the other pathologists, Dr. Langdon would not be endorsed as a defense witness.

In any criminal case in the state of Missouri, the names of the witnesses each side intends to call must be supplied to opposing counsel. Otherwise, with the exception of rebuttal witnesses, witnesses who were not disclosed prior to trial would not be permitted to testify at trial. The defense hadn't endorsed any witnesses yet. That is not unusual, since the defense needs to fully understand the state's case before a defense theory can be formulated, and witnesses endorsed and disclosed to the prosecutor.

In analyzing the evidence and the circumstances of the arrest, Felbin also thought the flashlight, the alleged murder weapon, would need to be examined. If Decker's flashlight caused the massive skull fracture, what did the flashlight look like now and what should it look like? Washington University in St. Louis enjoys an excellent reputation as an institution of higher learning and has a well-respected school of engineering. Believing they could help, Felbin made a cold call to that department seeking their assistance. He wasn't exactly sure what he was looking for, but he knew Decker's flashlight was going to be the centerpiece of the prosecution. To his knowledge, the prosecutor hadn't had the flashlight examined, or at least hadn't endorsed any witness in connection with such an examination.

The engineering professor he spoke to, Dr. Benjamin Brown, had heard about the case. Of course, given the extensive amount of front page and daily print coverage, editorial commentary, electronic media coverage, radio talk show discussions and courthouse and police department protests, one would have to be visiting from another planet to know nothing about this case. The professor was gracious and willing to help any way he and the members of his department could. In fact, he seemed excited about the prospect of becoming involved. Dr. Brown suggested Felbin bring the flashlight to the engineering department for some tests to see what would happen if this light were to fracture a skull. He also wanted to see a copy of the autopsy reports and Mitchell's medical records.

But there was a problem. The prosecutor had the flashlight and it was neatly tucked away in the protective custody of the evidence locker and inaccessible to the defendant. Felbin would have to improvise. His solution was to purchase an identical flashlight and provide it to the engineers to be used in their examination.

When Felbin met with Dr. Brown to provide the flashlight, he was introduced to a team of engineers, three total including Brown, who would be examining and testing the flashlight. The engineers enthusiastically told him they intended to build some device that they could use to smash flashlights at specific velocities. They would calculate the amount of force necessary to cause the skull damage and see how the flashlights tolerated the impact. Again, each was absolutely thrilled to be a part of this case. The issue of fees and costs was left for another day. Felbin was anxious to see what, if anything, they could discover.

"I suppose you need additional flashlights to do your testing," Felbin said, amazed by the enthusiasm.

"Ten would be a good start, but get as many as you can," Dr. Brown replied as the other two engineers visually examined the flashlight Felbin had brought.

Interrupting the conversation with Dr. Brown, one of the engineers said, "This flashlight is rubber. Is this the flashlight the officer had that night, the one someone is saying caused the skull fracture?"

"Yes. While the prosecutor has the actual flashlight that Officer Decker had that night, the one you are holding is an exact duplicate, identical in every respect," Felbin said.

"Okay. We will get right on it."

"I just want to thank all of you, not only for your willingness to look at this flashlight and hopefully help us out, but also for your enthusiasm," Felbin said.

Dr. Brown responded for the group. "Mister Felbin, we have followed this case in the media and talked together at length. And while we don't know the facts, all of us think there is something very wrong with this prosecution. We read about the Cannon case both when it was occurring and recently when the media revisited it. It was also disconcerting to read that this prosecution commenced before the autopsy was completed. We don't know anything about the law or criminal prosecutions, but it seems to us that unless you can identify the cause of death, your case is pretty weak and you would be on pretty shaky ground. Why would Ms. Cardwell do that to anyone, let alone a police officer?"

Felbin was quick to respond, recognizing this was a window of opportunity to influence his potential experts. As a seasoned trial lawyer, Felbin knew that expert witnesses, regardless of the discipline, were also human. And the more they buy into his client's cause, the harder they work for a result that is favorable to that cause. With that in mind, Felbin said, "Doctor Brown, it is very simple. This elected circuit attorney has other political aspirations."

"What kind of political aspirations?" Brown asked.

"She wants to become a judge and in order to do that she has to curry favor with state politicians."

Confused by Felbin's response, Dr. Brown pressed, "But what does all of that have to do with this case?"

"At the moment, she is not in good graces with the black politicians who can block her efforts to get her judgeship. Politics is a big part of the game at this level. One reason is that she allowed the Cannon case to be tried in Kansas City in front of an all-white jury. You said you remembered the Cannon case, right?"

"That case received a lot of attention when it happened and we recalled it when the paper threw it into this case. But I'm still not sure I follow what you are saying."

"Because of her negligence, the case was moved out of the city of Saint Louis. That upset the black community and in turn, the black politicians. When the Mitchell case came on the heels of Cannon, the black community reacted negatively and aggressively.

"But the cases are different," the professor noted.

"Yes, they are. But for the black community, it was another case of a white cop mistreating a young black man.

Unfortunately, the suspect in this case died and the public protests and pressures on her picked up where they left off. Actually, it was like they never left. She knew she had to do something and she had to do it quickly. As a result, she charged Officer Decker before all the facts were known."

"Will the case then be dismissed if the autopsy does not support the theory of the prosecution that this guy was struck with this flashlight?" one of the other engineers asked.

"Absolutely not," Felbin responded, quickly and emphatically. "Although Cardwell knew she had to bring charges quickly, I believe she also had another more sinister game plan. By charging this officer with murder under the theory that the suspect was struck in the head with a flashlight *before* the completion of the autopsy of the brain, she put the medical examiners in an untenable position. If they didn't support her position, then she is off the hook, because they will torpedo the case, not her. She can then credibly tell those black politicians who hold her political future in the palm of their hands that she did everything she could to get justice for Jordon Mitchell, but could not get any medical support."

"So, what you are saying is that there is still a chance this case could be dismissed if the autopsy report of the brain is not favorable to the prosecution," Dr. Brown said.

"Unfortunately, no. We just received the autopsy report of the brain and as expected, it concludes that Jordon Mitchell's skull fracture and ultimately his death were caused by blunt trauma with a linear object; namely a flashlight. The circuit attorney's plan worked. The Medical Examiners probably didn't want to be left holding the bag, so they supported her murder theory," Felbin replied.

Dr. Brown took a minute to process what Felbin was saying and then said, "Wow, I guess things like this really do happen in the real world. Perhaps I have been living in my academic world too long and I need to get out more."

"The system is not perfect," was Felbin's only response.

Felbin felt good when he left the engineers. He knew that they would work hard to see if they could find anything to help the defense. Of course, Felbin also knew if they came up with nothing or a conclusion that was adverse to Decker, he would not endorse them as witnesses and the prosecution would never know of their existence. But he hoped that would not be the case. He needed something from somewhere because at the moment, he had nothing, absolutely nothing. The prosecutor, on the other hand, had a dead body and a defendant who could not explain a fractured skull, in a city that was erupting racially.

Chapter Forty-Five

The court finally scheduled the motion for change of venue for argument. Felbin would now have an opportunity to present evidence and witnesses that the inhabitants of the city of St. Louis were so biased and prejudiced against Bobby Decker that he could not receive a fair trial. Although Felbin recognized he was not going to persuade the court to move the case out of the St. Louis area, the motion had to be filed in order to preserve the issue for appellate review. The downside was the publicity that would be generated prior to the start of the trial. Felbin, an experienced trial lawyer who had handled numerous high profile cases, knew he ran the risk of insulting people who might ultimately wind up on the jury. Regardless of one's racial makeup, suggesting an entire community is so biased and prejudiced that it cannot be fair, does not generate a lot of sympathy for the defendant.

Since the Grand Jury returned the murder indictment, Felbin's investigator had been monitoring and taping radio talk shows, particularly the Liz Barron show. On a daily basis, she would criticize, try and convict Bobby Decker. Repeatedly and without regard to factual support, she would not simply suggest, but outright say, that Decker murdered Mitchell. If that was not enough to incite people to riot, she would add that police officers generally were terrorizing and targeting black people and killing their *babies*. Barron, who was black, had a large number of listeners who would weigh in on her commentary, which was never favorable to Decker or any St. Louis law enforcement officer, white or black. Those callers would recount one horror story after another involving the police and their black victims, true or not.

In addition to media monitoring, Felbin hoped the professor from St. Louis University he hired to gather some polling data would come up with something to support a change. In a meeting with Professor Bill McFarland, Felbin and he discussed the polling data that had been collected. It was not good. Professor McFarland explained that based upon his poll, most people had heard of the case, but hadn't formed an opinion of the guilt or innocence of the defendant and could participate in a trial of the case. Of those who did form an opinion, the numbers were evenly split with Caucasians concluding the defendant was innocent and African Americans concluding the opposite. That was hardly proof positive the inhabitants of the city of St. Louis were biased against the defendant such that he could not receive a fair trial in the city, and Professor McFarland was not comfortable signing an affidavit indicating otherwise. Obviously, thanks in large part to the media, there certainly was bias. But Felbin knew bias was always present in any high profile case. Unfortunately, the bias in this case was split along racial lines.

In addition to the polling data, Felbin asked McFarland if his opinion would be any different when considering the adverse media coverage to include editorial commentary as well as the radio discussion, not the least of which included the inflammatory Barron show. Unfortunately, his opinion remained the same.

Felbin knew, generally speaking, it was difficult to prove the negative. When talking about disqualifying an entire city, the task was impossible. He also knew any good trial judge would not immediately grant a change of venue. Rather, the judge would see if a fair and impartial jury could be selected. If not, the issue of a new venue would be reconsidered. Recognizing that at least there was a slim chance the case could be moved out of the St. Louis metropolitan area, Felbin was faced with the question of how to handle the pending motion.

Any good trial lawyer never makes a decision like that without involving the client. In his meeting with Bobby, Felbin expressed his skepticism that the motion would be granted. He also expressed his concern that if the motion was pursued in an open courtroom, the risk of alienating potential jurors would increase.

"You understand, Bobby, that telling an entire community it cannot be fair is not a concept embraced by most people. The evidence we have to prove community bias here is weak. Really weak. In fact, we don't have an expert witness to support our position."

In the end, Felbin recommended they submit what they had in the form of the poll data and the media tapes and documents, waive a hearing and allow the judge to decide the issue based upon the information submitted. In that way, Felbin reasoned, the reporters would pick it up, but it would not turn into the three ring circus he speculated would be the case if the parties actually appeared in court to present their respective positions. Under no circumstances did Felbin believe the motion should be withdrawn. Bobby concurred with the strategy.

Felbin contacted the main prosecutor on this case, Gary Goodrich, to explain his plan. Goodrich had no objection as long as he was able to submit his own polling data which, not surprisingly, indicated the entire city was a model for fairness and impartiality when it came to white police officers murdering young black men who were burglarizing pawn shops. Felbin agreed, not with the prosecutor's evidence, but rather with his ability to submit the evidence for the court's consideration.

It didn't take long for the court to rule. Defense's motion for change of venue was denied. That was all that the court order said. No surprises there. The court also issued an additional order scheduling a deadline for witness endorsements and setting a trial date. Now the case was on a fast track, as the judge wanted to put this behind him and the community.

The trial judge was an experienced black man who had been on the bench for eleven years. Prior to his judicial appointment, Judge Harry Bell had been both a state prosecutor in the circuit attorney's office and a federal prosecutor in the United States attorney's office. He enjoyed a reputation of impartiality, although clearly a no-nonsense law and order judge. If your client lost at trial, Judge Bell was not shy about imposing a substantial sentence which could include both incarceration and fines, concepts that were not very comforting to Felbin at a time when he had no defense. Police officers, generally, don't tolerate any period of incarceration very well, let alone a long one. Prison was not a good place for any police officer, for obvious reasons.

When Judge Bell was a prosecutor, he and Felbin squared off numerous times, with each winning their fair share of the contests. More importantly, they represented their clients professionally and aggressively. But most importantly, they respected each other when the lights in the courtroom were turned off.

Harry Bell was a good lawyer who knew the system well, because he played within it. He was an equally good jurist. For criminal defendants, that was not necessarily a good thing. Criminal defense lawyers are generally interested in two things at trial: presenting the evidence in a way that is beneficial to the defendant, and making and preserving the record of trial error for appellate review. It is that second goal that gets in the way with good, experienced trial judges, because they know how to protect the record and justify the rulings the defendant is claiming to be erroneous.

The media was quick to pick up the ruling on the change of venue. Of course, Cardwell immediately found the television cameras to take credit for a decision that had been pre-determined from the start. Listening to her speak, one would think she had worked tirelessly to insure this case remained in the city of St. Louis. Of course, the truth of the matter was she probably hadn't lifted a finger to defend the motion. And probably no one in her office had done much work, other than insuring that an objection to the request for the venue change was filed within 10 days following the filing of the motion, as the rule requires.

Felbin chuckled as he listened to her remarks. Now the change of venue had been decided, she could come out of hiding without fear that she could do anything that would cause the trial to be moved. He suspected the last thing she wanted was to blow the timely filing of the objection in this case like she had in the Cannon case. It would be political death for her if she allowed this case to slip out of town.

When the reporters called Felbin for a comment, he resisted the temptation to mention the daily phone calls he received from Goodrich asking whether he filed a change of venue motion, which would start the clock on the objection time. Instead, he opted for brevity, a position that was foreign to him. He said only that he looked forward to having a jury review the state's flawed theory. Although he didn't believe it, he said he was confident the people of the city of St. Louis would judge this case fairly and impartially. Then, carefully selecting his words, he went on to say the twelve people who would decide this case would also be commenting on the type of law enforcement they wanted in their community. He was equally confident that people burglarizing pawn shops in the middle of the night would be a practice the jury would condemn and would want law enforcement officers to take care of. Intentional or not, his last statement would be the subject of much interest and commentary, both favorable and unfavorable.

The headline in the Post the next day read *Decker Lawyer Encourages Use of Force by Police*. The body of the article quoted Felbin out of context, suggesting he was encouraging other police officers to use force under circumstances similar to the Mitchell case. The accompanying editorial was brutal. Essentially, the author condemned not only Felbin's remarks, but his client as well. The electronic online commentary to the article and the editorial were a different story. For the most part, the responders were sympathetic to the plight of law enforcement officers generally and Decker specifically. The theme was that police officers have a thankless job for little pay and then are rewarded with an indictment when they try to stop criminal acts. Several were also critical of the circuit attorney both for bringing the charges and for doing so before the autopsy was completed, for her own political gain. When Felbin finished reading, he could not help but think that jury selection in this case was going to be an interesting experience. He just didn't know whether it would be positive or negative.

Chapter Forty-Six

While waiting for the findings of both the pathologist and the engineers, Felbin met with Bobby to prepare for the upcoming trial. The first item on the agenda was a frank discussion on what really happened on that roof. Of course, such candid conversations are protected by the attorney client privilege and can never be disclosed to the prosecutor. However, most criminal defense attorneys avoid such discussions for the reason that ethical rules would prohibit the lawyer from putting the client on the witness stand at trial to proclaim innocence where the client has admitted to having committed the crime.

But a *did you do it* discussion was necessary in this case. Felbin's investigator bought up all the flashlights in the St. Louis metropolitan area that were identical to Bobby's and gave them to the engineers, who were hard at work smashing them. Unfortunately, the actual flashlight was in the custody of the prosecutor, and Felbin had to get a look at that light to see if it was damaged in any respect. He needed to know whether it worked. The problem was that it had to be done in the presence of someone from the prosecutor's office. If the batteries had to be replaced, which Felbin assumed they did, given the passage of time, it would also have to be done in the presence of the prosecutor's investigator, who would be watching Felbin's every move while he examined the evidence. Felbin was concerned that changing batteries and focusing on the flashlight would give the prosecution an idea they might not otherwise have had. Or give them an idea of where the defense was going, so they would be prepared to respond.

Felbin had no indication the prosecutor would have the flashlight examined by anyone for any reason. Goodrich was a good trial lawyer in the courtroom, but sometimes overlooked pertinent details in preparing his case. Felbin, on the other hand, had a reputation of not only being prepared, but sometimes being overly-prepared. By the time the case came to the courtroom, Felbin would have exhausted every avenue that had the potential to aid his defense. Unfortunately, at this time, none of those avenues had produced anything of value, which is not uncommon in defending criminal cases. But this case was no ordinary criminal case. This case involved a police officer charged with murder, which could result in a death sentence if penitentiary time resulted. Felbin was no stranger to high stakes criminal cases, but none greater than this one. A young man's fate was in his hands. He couldn't afford to make a mistake or overlook any detail.

Felbin had spent some time trying to figure out how he would frame the question Bobby needed to answer. On the one hand, he had a good relationship with Bobby and didn't want this question to undermine that relationship. But he needed to know, so he could make a decision on whether to pull the plug on the engineers. He needed to know whether Bobby's flashlight worked.

Carefully, Felbin said, "Bobby as you know, the engineers are smashing flashlights to see what should have happened to your flashlight if you had actually struck Mitchell with it. We need to look at your flashlight, which the prosecutor has. I don't know the condition of that light at the moment. I need to know if it is damaged. But, if we look at it in the presence of the prosecutors, we may be putting them onto something they hadn't considered. In other words, if we look at that light and it doesn't work, they may do what we are doing and get some experts to say the condition of the light is consistent with Mitchell's skull fracture and therefore, is the murder weapon. So, here is the question. Do we contact the prosecutor and arrange a time to look at your flashlight?"

Without any hesitation whatsoever, Bobby emphatically said, "You go there and look at that flashlight. If they didn't tamper with it, that flashlight will work. I didn't hit that guy with my flashlight or anything else."

"Done," was Felbin's only reply. This conversation was over, and Felbin felt confident the engineers were going to give him something that would help.

Felbin, Decker, and his investigator, Jack Reilly, appeared unannounced at the circuit attorney's office asking to look at all the evidence in the Robert Decker case. Felbin didn't want to give the prosecutor any advanced notice and time to prepare for this visit. He hoped he would be accompanied to the evidence locker for the viewing by someone unfamiliar with the case. Summoned to the front of the office by the receptionist, Goodrich was clearly unhappy with the impromptu visit.

"You are going to have to make an appointment, Felbin. You can't just drop in on us. We have other things to do around here beyond dancing when you snap your fingers," Goodrich said, making no effort to hide his anger.

"I'm not asking for a dance, Gary, I just want to see what evidence you claim to have against my client. Now if there is no evidence, I can understand that. But if there is, I need to see it and I need to see it now, particularly since the trial is right around the corner."

"Sit down and I'll see if I can find anyone to babysit you while you look. Certainly don't want you to walk off with anything, Felbin," Goodrich said sarcastically.

After they sat down in the waiting area, Felbin commented, "I think he is pissed."

"Do you think?" Reilly said.

"Oh, yeah! Let's talk about how we are going to do this when we get in there. Depending on who is with us; first, I'll ask him to step out of the room so we can discuss the evidence in private. If that doesn't work, I'll distract him. And while I do that, can you then check the flashlight without being noticed?"

"I'll try. I'm guessing I'll have to replace the batteries. Do you want me to leave the new ones in or take them back out?" Reilly asked.

"No, take them out and leave it like we found it. If this flashlight works, I don't want to educate them by putting in new batteries."

"I assume you'll be representing me if I get myself charged with tampering with evidence," Reilly said with a smile.

"Jack, I'll get you out of it if it takes me fifty years," Felbin said, also smiling.

After waiting for close to an hour, presumably for Goodrich to make a point, an investigator who had nothing to do with the case came to the waiting room door. Reilly knew him from the days when he worked for the circuit attorney.

"I guess I'll be babysitting you boys," Jim Barringer said, after awkward pleasantries were exchanged. Reilly and Barringer didn't get along during the time they'd spent together at the circuit attorney's office. The animosity with Barringer reached a peak when Reilly was fired by the circuit attorney because he refused to follow a directive he deemed improper and even unethical. Barringer disagreed with the position taken by Reilly at the time and supported his boss.

This is going to be difficult, Reilly thought, as they entered the large room that served as an evidence locker. All the evidence had been laid out on a table, including: the clothes worn by Mitchell, the items recovered from both Mitchell and Jones, items recovered from the pawn shop that consisted of a sledge hammer and various tools were used to burglarize the shop, a ladder presumably used to gain access to the roof, a bag with various stolen items recovered from the rooftop, items seized from Decker including his jacket, utility belt, service revolver, and, of course, the flashlight.

Once inside, Felbin and Reilly began to casually look at the evidence. After a few minutes, Reilly asked Barringer if they could have a little privacy to discuss the evidence. Barringer refused. As they examined each item on the table, they were in full view of Barringer, who would not allow any item to be removed from the table and taken to another part of the room, making it impossible to change the batteries unnoticed. Recognizing that they would not be able to accomplish what had been planned, Felbin directed Reilly to photograph the items and they left.

Once outside, Felbin asked Reilly if he knew Barringer. Reilly explained his prior relationship. Nonetheless, although they were not able to change the batteries to see if the flashlight worked, they were able to at least make a visual observation and hadn't seen any damage.

The next stop was the rooftop. In any criminal case, Felbin always wanted to visit the scene in order to get a better visual understanding of what the witnesses would be describing orally at trial. Although photographs and sometimes video would be used at trial, there was no substitute for an actual on-site visit. You never know when you might see something the camera missed.

Jack Reilly had arranged to have a ladder at the pawn shop so he and Felbin, along with Bobby, could get up on the roof and have a look. Bobby led the way up the ladder, carefully retracing his steps on that night that now consumed a major metropolitan city. When they arrived, Bobby pointed out the upper roof where the suspects were initially located. He described how both suspects climbed down, and then fled in opposite directions with both Bobby and Corbett giving chase.

When Bobby finished retracing the movements of all present on the roof during the night of April 24, Felbin and Reilly began their own tour of the roof. As they looked around, they observed the skylights for each of the businesses, broken bottles, glass, a few cinder blocks and other debris scattered throughout. Felbin directed Reilly to take photographs of the entire rooftop from all possible angles, hoping they would find something—anything—that would help to successfully defend Bobby Decker in the murder charge he faced. At the moment, with the trial date rapidly approaching, they still had nothing.

Chapter Forty-Seven

When Bobby arrived home, to his surprise, Kathy was waiting. "We need to talk, Bobby," was her only greeting. "I know your trial is coming up and I have been thinking a lot about us," she said, her eyes beginning to fill with tears. "I want you to know that I love you. I need you to believe and understand that."

"Okay," was the only response Bobby could think of at the moment, apprehensive as he was about what was to come.

"I don't know how your trial is going to work out. You never know what a jury will do. My office is doing its best to keep me out of the loop, but I still hear things and what I hear is not good for you. Bobby, I wanted to tell you they plan to endorse me as a witness for the prosecution."

Shocked, Bobby was unable to speak. He just stared at her, trying to process what she had just said. Eventually, still disbelieving what he had just heard, his voice rising, his face red, he unleashed a string of rambling rhetorical questions. "What? Are you kidding? What could you say? What do they want you to say? You were not on that roof and have no firsthand knowledge of anything. I can't believe this."

"I don't know what they expect me to say. They haven't told me. I told them . . ."

"You're an endorsed witness and they haven't told you how you are a witness? What kind of bullshit is that?" Bobby asked, preventing Kathy from finishing her sentence.

". . . I told them I didn't know anything and calling me as a witness would put me in a very bad position. They don't care. Bobby, they want a conviction and they don't care how they get it. I shouldn't say that, but what I mean is they are willing to sacrifice me and anyone else to get that guilty verdict."

"Those slimy bastards. Maybe they think that is a way to intimidate me and get a guilty plea."

"I don't know, but this whole situation has been extremely difficult for both of us. Bobby, I have given this a lot of thought. As a matter of fact, it is practically the only thing I have been thinking about. It is hard for me to say this, but I think we need to go our separate ways."

"What do you mean?" Bobby said, his eyes now beginning to tear.

"Either way this turns out, you'll always be the cop who killed Jordon Mitchell. Even if you are acquitted, you won't be able to escape that. And I won't be able to escape that. Bobby, I want to be a career prosecutor and perhaps even a judge at some point. And this situation will always be there."

Trying to comprehend what this woman who was the center of his universe was telling him, Bobby said, "Are you telling me you are choosing your career over me?"

"No. I'm not choosing my career over you. What I'm saying is I'm concerned that down the road this situation will resurface in one form or another and destroy our relationship, if it has not already done so."

"What I hear you saying is that you are choosing your career over me."

"No, I'm not saying that at all. But we cannot ignore the obvious. We can't pretend this Mitchell thing never happened, and that it will never disrupt our lives together. It is painful now and won't go away."

"But there is also a chance this won't disrupt our lives down the road and we can live a happy and full life together. Why would we not wait? See what happens."

"Because I'm convinced it will just be postponing the inevitable unless we move out of Saint Louis, and I'm not willing to do that. My family is here. My friends are here. My job is here. My life is here. And I think postponing the inevitable will just cause more pain. I have thought about this a lot."

"What about your life with me?" Bobby asked, realizing he was losing this discussion and the woman he loved.

"Bobby, I have made up my mind," she said. She walked to the door, opened it, and never looked back.

Chapter Forty-Eight

The trial was a week away and the media was heating up once again. The protests were intensifying. The front page headlines above the fold returned, along with photographs of Decker and Mitchell. Fortunately, this time the photos of Mitchell were not taken in the intensive care unit, displaying the tubes and other lines attached to his head and mouth and connected to life sustaining machines.

Radio talk shows were unable to find any other subject to discuss. And, of course, the television stations were running sound bites on those who dared predict the outcome of such a potentially explosive case. For Bobby Decker, some of the publicity was good and some not so good. However, for Cardwell, most of the coverage was adverse, presumably because the African American community was weighing in; but the Caucasian population of the St. Louis metropolitan area adopted a wait and see attitude. It was obvious that Cardwell was still experiencing the fallout from the Cannon loss. Unfortunately, Felbin and his team could not predict with any certainty what they would find in the jury pool at the start of the trial.

Beyond the news coverage, Felbin had another more pressing pretrial issue. Gary Goodrich, the chief prosecutor, was complaining Felbin had endorsed his witnesses too late. He claimed a disadvantage because he could not determine what the witnesses had to say in time to effectively respond. He was encouraging the court to strike the endorsement and prohibit the witnesses, all experts, from testifying. Felbin had endorsed meaningless character and other witnesses well in advance, but intentionally delayed disclosing his experts to accomplish precisely what the prosecutor was complaining about, and Goodrich knew it. Felbin also knew that Cardwell would not allow Goodrich to ask for a continuance, because she needed to put this political nightmare behind her and stop the bleeding from the adverse press coverage she was getting.

When Goodrich dragged Felbin before the judge to voice his complaints, the defense attorney suggested the prosecutor take the depositions of the three Washington University engineers and his forensic pathologist, and magnanimously agreed to make the witnesses available. That way, Felbin argued, Goodrich would not only know what these witnesses had to say, but would also have a transcript he could use at trial if their testimony differed. Goodrich's response was everything Felbin expected.

"He knows goddamn well our office can't afford to take expensive depositions. He also knows we can't pay the experts the outrageous fees that they will want for depositions."

Depositions, whether taken in criminal or civil cases, are statements given under oath in a question and answer format, with the lawyer asking the questions and the witness providing the answers. A court reporter is present, taking down all that is said in shorthand form and thereafter transcribing the entire discussion. Most court reporters charge both an attendance fee and by the page. Depending upon the length, depositions can be expensive.

In addition to the fees charged by court reporters, expert witnesses can charge a fee for the time they spend testifying, both at deposition and in trial. Depending upon the discipline of the expert, those fees can also be expensive, ranging anywhere from $50 to $5,000 an hour.

"If he can't afford it now, then he couldn't afford it a month ago. This is nothing more than his effort to deprive this police officer of a fair trial, so the ringmaster of that circus they are running can get her judgeship," Felbin shot back.

"And that is exactly the bullshit he fed the media. I'm tired of hearing that the only reason for this prosecution is because we screwed up Cannon and she needs this conviction for a judgeship. I admit we made a mistake in Cannon when we didn't file a formal objection to his venue motion and he got to try the case to an all-white jury on the other side of the state. But that has nothing to do with this case.

His client is guilty, and Felbin knows it. Decker whacked this guy with his flashlight and killed him. And we have the evidence to prove it. I don't know what kind of a dog-and-pony-show old Felbin is going to put on to escape the truth, but we both know one is coming. That's also why he dragged his feet on disclosing these so-called experts." Goodrich wasn't finished, his face red and his voice at a level easily heard throughout the entire courthouse. "Plus, he says he is going to call Dr. Langdon, a nationally recognized pathologist. And I'm sure he will beat this guy's celebrity status into the ground."

"He's not going to call Langdon. You know Felbin, Gary. He's just screwing with you," Judge Bell said, as though Felbin was not in the room.

Felbin smiled, but said nothing.

Continuing, the judge said, "Gary, I'm not going to strike these witnesses. You can take their depositions if you want and I'll order Felbin to produce them for you. Or you can try to contact them and interview them."

"Can I at least get any reports they prepared in connection with whatever they did?" Goodrich asked.

"I suspect I know the answer, but I'll ask anyway. Felbin, do you have any reports from any of your witnesses?" the judge asked.

"No," was Felbin's quick response as Goodrich shook his head and the judge smiled.

"What a surprise. Can I at least ask what they plan to say?" a frustrated Goodrich asked, his carotid artery beating like a drum.

"Of course you can ask, Gary," Felbin calmly replied.

His frustration now turning to undisguised anger, Goodrich said, "So what bullshit are they going to try to feed the jury."

"See, Gary, if you had asked me nice, I might have told you. But because you came at me with that attitude, I'm under no obligation to tell you, and I won't. If you don't want to ask Cardwell to take some money out of her political slush fund that she has earmarked to buy her judicial appointment and take some depositions, then you'll have to wait for the big show to hear what they have to say."

With that, Goodrich stormed out of the judge's chambers slamming the door, as Judge Bell was reprimanding Felbin for his comment.

Chapter Forty-Nine

Bobby arrived at Felbin's office at 6:30 in the morning, ready to start and finish the trial that had already changed his life. The trial would begin at 9:30, and was scheduled to last the majority of the week, with jury selection as the first order of business. Felbin and his staff were already in the office when Bobby arrived. It looked like they had put in a half day's work—files and papers were spread across a large conference room table, with people running in different directions gathering documents and information. The scene was chaotic.

As with any trial, regardless of how prepared the defense is, there are always last-minute details and unexpected problems that arise. That is particularly true with high profile cases where both the defendant and his representatives are under a microscope.

"Good morning, Bobby," Felbin said enthusiastically, hoping to calm the nerves of a client he knew would be on edge. After all, Bobby Decker was on trial for his life. "Ready to get started?"

"I'm as ready as I'll ever be. I just want to get this over with."

"I understand. Bobby, we are looking good. Not only are we going to win this thing, but we are going to kick some ass in the process. We are going to demonstrate what a despicable human being Cardwell is. We are going to show this case never should have been prosecuted and it was her rush to judgment to satisfy her own personal, selfish interests. When this is done, Bobby, you are going to be a hero and Cardwell is going to be the villain."

Felbin's rah-rah speech was designed to get his client pumped up and ready for action. No pity parties this morning for Felbin or Decker. But in reality, Felbin knew this could be hit or miss. Over the last several weeks, his defense had come together. It made sense. But would it convince a jury Bobby didn't strike that young black man with his flashlight and cause a massive skull fracture, which ultimately led to the man's death? At the end of the trial, questions would still remain. Questions Felbin would not be able to answer with any degree of certainty.

Felbin, his investigator and his staff would ride to the courthouse with Bobby in a fully stocked RV provided by Jeffrey Fortman, the same friend who had volunteered to make Bobby's bond. There would also be security. Armed body guards would ride in the RV, and accompany Bobby and his defense team into the courthouse and into the courtroom. In addition to the guards inside the vehicle, other bodyguards would meet them on the sidewalk in front of the courthouse to accompany them up the 42 steps to the front door. As they had done for other court appearances, guards would surround Bobby and Felbin as they ascended the steps. All who entered the courthouse were always screened with a metal detector, and subjected to additional searches, if necessary. Obviously, guns were not permitted.

For the Decker trial, an additional metal detector was set up just outside the doors of the courtroom where the trial would be held. Without exception, everyone who entered would be subjected to a search. The courtroom could accommodate a total of 125 people. Spectators would be handled on a first come, first served basis, with the media and the respective families of Mitchell and Decker each receiving 10 passes. The media would occupy the first row and the families the second. Armed deputy sheriffs would be positioned throughout the courtroom.

As Felbin was taking care of a few last minute details for jury selection, his investigator interrupted him, carrying a copy of the morning paper. "I think you are going to want to see this before you start picking this jury," Reilly said.

The article detailed the false-reporting discipline Bobby had received as a probationary officer early in his career. This issue had been mentioned in a previous article, but only briefly. This time it was front page and detailed. When Felbin finished the article, he was angry. It was clear to him that Cardwell had planted the story with a friendly reporter to hit on the morning jury selection was to begin. The story pointed out that Decker's probationary period was extended because he participated in a cover-up involving the shooting and death of a young black man. Although Decker was not the shooter, the article indicated he was disciplined for lying to protect the officer who did fire the shots, and who ultimately retired from the Department rather than face termination.

Quentin Jennings, the civil rights activist, was quoted extensively in the article. He suggested if Decker lied once to protect a fellow officer, he would surely lie to keep himself out of the penitentiary. He also criticized the Department for its failure to terminate Decker's employment rather than merely extending his probation. He boldly suggested Jordon Mitchell would be alive today if the police department had done the right thing and fired the white cop.

Interestingly, Bobby's side of the story was not part of the article. Neither Bobby nor Felbin had been contacted for a comment. That didn't surprise Felbin, for a couple of reasons. First, the newspaper was not friendly toward either the Department, generally, or Decker, specifically. Second, if the case went south for Cardwell, she needed someone she could blame, and her target would be the Police Department. Jennings' comments would lay the groundwork for that position. She could hitch her wagon to Jennings and claim if the Police Department had gotten rid of a racist police officer administratively, she would not have to try to meet the heavy burden of proving criminal guilt of a police officer beyond a reasonable doubt.

But now the immediate question Felbin faced was how to handle this issue during jury selection this morning. *Should he bring it up? Should he ignore it? Should he object if the prosecutor brought it up?* Although he didn't believe this prior discipline could be used against Bobby at trial, Felbin thought perhaps he should make sure the judge concurred with his position. The judge's ruling on the issue might ultimately determine whether Felbin would question prospective jurors about the article.

Chapter Fifty

When they arrived at the courthouse, Bobby was met by a throng of reporters, television cameras, and protestors, who lined the steps. Surrounded by armed bodyguards, Bobby and Felbin made their way up the steps, trying to ignore the cat calls and ugly comments, as well as the efforts by the reporters to get a reaction. Once inside, they immediately went to the courtroom and set up at the table assigned to them for the duration of the trial.

As soon as the prosecutors arrived, Felbin told Goodrich he needed a conference with the judge before jury selection began. When they entered the judge's chambers, the judge was reading the paper. After the customary morning greetings, Felbin said, "That's what we need to discuss before we start," pointing to the newspaper.

"I thought that might be the case. But first, I want to talk about how many we will need for the panel and whether we want to do individual or group *voir dire,* or a combination," the judge said.

Voir dire, a Latin phrase that means *to speak the truth,* is the process by which prospective jurors are questioned to determine whether they are qualified to be selected to hear and decide the pending case. In criminal cases, the prosecutor begins the questioning of the group, followed by the defense attorney. Each lawyer is permitted to ask general questions of the group as a whole, in addition to individual questions of each member of the panel. The stated purpose of the questions is to determine whether anyone has any particular preconceived ideas, opinions or prejudices that would prevent them from deciding the case fairly and impartially, based upon the law and the evidence they hear in the courtroom. But the real purpose is to identify those jurors who will be sympathetic to the respective positions of each the parties. The last thing the lawyers want is impartiality.

Once the questioning is completed by both sides, the lawyers can make their challenges to individuals for cause. Those are individuals who have said something that calls into question their ability to be fair and impartial. For example, if someone says that they would give the testimony of a police officer more weight than any other witness or indicates a relationship with one of the parties that compromises their ability to be fair, that person would be eliminated for cause. When this occurs, sometimes the lawyers can agree to remove those individuals from the list. If the lawyers disagree, the judge decides. Occasionally, one of the parties will challenge an individual for cause not necessarily because they said anything specifically, but because their background or their answers generally favor the opposing party.

Once the challenges for cause are decided, the group is reduced to a final number of individuals from which the jury will be selected. The lawyers are then permitted to make peremptory challenges. In a criminal case involving murder second degree, each side is allowed to remove six individuals from the entire list, reducing the number to twelve who will serve as the jury. Jury selection is a process of exclusion rather than inclusion, to the extent that the jury is not comprised of people who have been selected, but rather those who haven't been eliminated.

Court rules require that peremptory challenges be made based upon where the prospective jurors are seated. Seating is done based upon where the name of the prospective juror appears on a random list. As the bailiff calls the names, seats are filled first in the jury box and then in the spectator section from the front to the back of the courtroom. For example, if 70 individuals from the initial pool of 100 are qualified to serve and each side is to strike 6, then the final 12 will be selected from a pool of the first 36 who are seated in the front of the courtroom. The remaining 34 seated behind the first 36 are ineligible for consideration when the lawyers are making their final selection.

The prosecutor makes the first selections from the reduced pool, and then passes those who remain to the defense for their strikes. People can be eliminated for any reason except solely based on race. In 1986, the United States Supreme Court decided the case of *Batson v. Kentucky,* which prohibited the exclusion of potential jurors solely on the basis of race.

In a high profile case such as this, the judge will usually begin with a group of 75 to 100, recognizing many will be excused because they have followed the case in the media and formed opinions they cannot set aside. Simply because a potential juror has followed the case or even formed an opinion about the case does not automatically disqualify that person. The test is whether that opinion can be set aside and the case decided based on the evidence presented in court. In fact, most trial lawyers will avoid selecting a juror who has not heard of a high profile case, figuring if that person is not interested in current news events, he won't be terribly interested in the case that has to be decided.

Judge Bell decided to start with 100 people. He also took into consideration that, given the length of the trial, some alternates would also be needed. The judge considered two alternates sufficient. Alternate jurors listen to the entire case. If all 12 of the jurors originally selected haven't been excused for any reason by the time the case is given to the jury for decision, the alternates won't participate in the deliberations and will be excused.

Once the preliminary jury selection matters were resolved, Felbin addressed the newspaper article. "I assume you read the prejudicial article Ms. Cardwell planted this morning," Felbin began.

"We didn't plant anything," Goodrich quickly replied.

"That's enough. Listen, this is stressful for all of us. Let's get through this without the unnecessary editorial commentary. Now, what is it you wanted to talk about with respect to the article in the paper today?" the judge said, hoping to gain some early control over the two combatants.

"I assume any evidence relating to the defendant's prior disciplinary history with the Department won't come into evidence and be discussed in the presence of the jury," Felbin said.

"What is your position on that, Gary?" the judge asked.

"My position is that it is admissible as evidence of misconduct and a continuing scheme, plan and design. It also goes to the question of Decker's credibility. His own department found him guilty of lying. He prepared a police report in this case, which we also believe is false."

"What he thinks is not important. It is what he can prove and he can't prove the defendant's police report is false in any respect. Additionally, he can't prove Decker previously lied to his department when he said someone fired a gun at a fellow officer. You know as well as I that he just wants to inflame the jury with this nonsense."

"But the police department found him guilty of submitting a false report. How is that not relevant?" Judge Bell asked.

"But he never had a chance to defend himself. He was a probationary officer and unlike veteran officers, he had no right to any due process hearing. He didn't get a trial. No one testified. There was no evidence produced that he was allowed to rebut. Instead, some bureaucrat made a unilateral decision. He was not fired and since then has prepared thousands of police reports without challenge. In fact, he has testified a thousand times for many prosecutors, including Mister Goodrich, who didn't question his credibility. But now, they want to use that against him in a murder trial. Unfair and prejudicial."

"I'm inclined to allow it, particularly if the defendant testifies. But I'll think about it and make a decision after I see how the case unfolds."

"Well, I'll tell you if you allow this inflammatory evidence, you'll be extending this trial by several weeks, because I'll call every prosecutor who put Bobby on the witness stand. But how am I supposed to handle the issue during *voir dire?* That is the immediate question," Felbin said.

"The best you can, I suppose," the judge said sarcastically. "Are we ready to bring the panel in and get started?" Before he got his answer, the court bailiff was directed to go to the jury assembly room and bring 100 St. Louis citizens to the courtroom to begin the process of selecting a jury that would decide the fate of Police Officer Robert Decker.

Chapter Fifty-One

Felbin sat at the defense counsel's table, awaiting the arrival of the panel. One by one, the prospective jurors entered the courtroom and took a random seat in the spectator section. When all had arrived, the bailiff called their juror badge numbers, so each could take their assigned seats, first in the jury box and then in the spectator section from front to back. As Felbin carefully watched each juror take his or her assigned seat, he became concerned at the number of black faces beginning to take their seats in positions that clearly put them within reach of jury service, assuming they were not excused for cause.

Felbin could not ignore the obvious. This was a case that would be divided along racial lines, sad as that was. But the reality, or so Felbin thought, was that black people wanted to see Decker go to the penitentiary for a very long time. The question that remained, but would soon be answered, is how forthright people, white or black, would be in discussing their biases. Or would they hide those beliefs, in the hope of attaining a goal of conviction and incarceration or freedom for Decker?

When all were seated, the bailiff handed each lawyer a list containing the names and some limited information on each of the potential juror. The media was allowed to stand and witness the proceedings, but spectators were not. The television stations recorded the proceedings. However, the judge permitted only one pool camera that all the electronic and print media would share. Photography and audio recording devices were not permitted beyond the single pool camera.

A buzzer interrupted the silence of the room, followed by the bailiff directing all to rise. At precisely 9:30, the judge entered, greeting all with an enthusiastic *Good morning,* and directing everyone to be seated. This trial, as with any trial, began with some preliminary statements by the court. Judge Bell informed the panel this was a criminal case, and then went on to read the indictment, further instructing that an indictment is not evidence. He told the group they were not to use cell phones, electronic recording devices and were not to read or listen to any news reports about the case. They would be permitted to take notes. Finally, he told them they should not discuss the case with anyone until it was given to them for a decision. The clerk was then directed to swear the panel, so their responses to the questions put to them would be under oath.

When judges speak to juries, they do so from prepared texts called jury instructions. Juries decide the facts in every case, but the law governing the case is provided by the court in the form of those instructions. Jurors don't decide the law. In a situation where a person is unwilling to accept the law provided by the court, that person will be excused for cause.

After introducing the lawyers and the defendant, Judge Bell allowed the prosecutor to begin addressing and questioning the panel. As Gary Goodrich began his opening remarks, Felbin was not only analyzing the racial makeup of the panel, but he was also looking at where everyone was seated to try to determine the final group from which the selection would be made. Of course, there was really no conclusive way to tell that at this point, because Felbin had no way to know who would be excused for cause. However, he knew of the 100 panel members, 37 were African American, with the majority seated in positions from which the final 12, together with the alternates, would be selected.

Felbin was concerned. This case was filled with emotion and racial drama. The media coverage, the editorial commentary and the protests only served to fuel the hostility that had historically existed between the African American community and the St. Louis Police Department. And, of course, the Cannon trial and verdict only exacerbated an already bad situation. Felbin was concerned that his client would be the victim of a war he'd had no hand in starting. *This is exactly why this case should not be tried in the city of St. Louis,* he thought, as he continued to look over the panel.

As the questioning progressed, Felbin was surprised. Actually, he was shocked by the responses from both black and white prospective jurors. When specifically asked if they'd formed any opinions about the case and if so, whether they could set those opinions aside and be guided by the evidence presented in the courtroom, several black potential jurors responded in the negative. They clearly admitted a strong belief that Decker murdered a young black man, a belief they were either unwilling or unable to set aside. Goodrich attempted unsuccessfully to rehabilitate each, hoping to seat as many African Americans as he could.

Caucasians, on the other hand, expressed no difficulty sitting in judgment in a case that involved a young black man who'd burglarized a pawn shop in the middle of the night. Trying to eliminate this category of juror, Goodrich also unsuccessfully pressed each to reconsider their responses, delicately encouraging them to engage in greater introspection.

Trial lawyers have to be careful that they don't alienate individuals who might wind up on the jury when asking the questions. Efforts to rehabilitate a person a lawyer wants on the jury and who has admitted bias is a far easier task than attempting to eliminate an individual who steadfastly denies bias and will resist elimination for cause.

As each responded to Goodrich's questions, Felbin, along with his staff seated at the counsel table, took detailed notes. Challenges for cause would be made outside the presence of the entire panel at the end of the questioning by both sides. Usually, judges hesitate to begin excusing people for cause before the questioning is completed, for fear other prospective jurors might adopt responses similar to those who are excused simply to get out of jury service.

At the time the challenge for cause is made, the lawyer seeking to excuse the potential juror must state the specific reasons for the request. Opposition arguments are heard and considered by the court, assuming the parties don't agree on the challenge. Felbin knew Cardwell would not allow Goodrich to consent to the elimination of any black juror, no matter what the response.

Goodrich continued his questioning throughout the entire first day, with short recess for restroom breaks and an hour for lunch. Questions relating to the information learned about the case from news sources would be handled individually with each potential juror in the judge's chambers. The last thing Judge Bell wanted was to have people providing media or potentially inflammatory information to the other members of the panel.

The questioning was rather routine throughout most of the day until Goodrich decided to address the issue of the defendant's prior disciplinary record with the Department and the morning news article that mentioned it. Felbin knew that was coming and was ready. As soon as Goodrich mentioned an article in the morning paper, Felbin was on his feet asking to approach the bench. When trial lawyers want private discussions with the judge, they do so at the side of the bench, out of the hearing of all but the judge and the court reporter, who is recording verbatim everything said during the trial. Fearing questions dealing with the morning newspaper article would taint the pool if discussed in the presence of the entire group, Judge Bell decided to deal with this particular in chambers individually along with other information gleaned from news articles.

Since it was close to five in the afternoon, the court decided to recess for the day. Jury selection would begin again at 9:30 the following morning. The lawyers were directed to return at 9 a.m. to take up any matters needing attention before the panel arrived.

After most of the jury pool had departed, the bailiff approached Felbin, who was in a conversation with the defendant. "The judge would like to see you and Mister Goodrich in chambers before you leave," he said. Directing Bobby to remain in the courtroom until he returned, so they could all leave together with their security, Felbin went to see what the judge wanted.

"The bailiff just told me one of the female jurors wanted to talk to me about an urgent matter. Because I don't know what she wants, I thought it would be best if you both were here when I talk to her," Judge Bell said, directing his bailiff to show the lady into his chambers.

Juror number 346 was a white female, age 54, who had three grown children and had been employed as a corporate secretary for 12 years. She was nervous when she entered the chambers. Recognizing that, the judge invited her to take a seat and encouraged her to relax. Although the court reporter was in the room, she was not recording at least this preliminary part of the conversation. The lawyers said nothing.

"The bailiff said you wanted to talk to me," the judge began.

"Yes. I thought I should mention something I heard at the lunch recess today," Juror 346 said as she hesitated, waiting for the judge to direct her to continue.

"What was that?" Judge Bell said as he directed his reporter to begin recording the conversation for the record.

"I was standing in the hall waiting for the courtroom to be opened after lunch. That's when I heard one of the jurors talking on his cell phone. He said he had jury duty and it was the case of the cop who killed that black kid on the pawn shop roof and he was going to fry the cop," she said.

"Is that all that you heard him say?" the judge asked.

"Yes, because when he saw I was near and was looking at him, he turned his back and walked away from me."

Concerned about what he was hearing and interested in identifying the speaker, Judge Bell asked, "Can you tell us what his name is or what he looked like, or do you know where he was sitting?"

"I don't know his name or where he was sitting but the number on his badge is 189."

Turning first to Goodrich, the judge said, "Do you have any questions?"

"Yes, I do. Ma'am, how close were you to this man?" Goodrich asked.

"Within a couple of feet."

"Other than the conversation you related, did you hear him say anything else?"

"No. As I said, when he saw me looking at him, he turned his back and walked away."

Continuing, Goodrich pressed, "When you heard this conversation, was this gentleman facing you?"

"No. He was not directly facing me. He was kinda on an angle."

"Was anyone else around?"

"There were some other people in the hall, but none as close as I was."

"Now what did he say again?" Goodrich asked, hoping that the juror would stumble.

"He said he had jury duty and it was the case of the cop who killed the black kid on the pawn shop roof and he was going to fry the cop."

"Did he say specifically that he was going to fry the cop?"

"Well, no. Specifically, he said *I'm going to fry him*. But it was obvious he was talking about the police officer."

"Do you have any connection to law enforcement, ma'am?"

"None whatsoever, other than perhaps receiving a ticket," Juror 346 said, her response invoking some laughter from everyone other than Goodrich.

"And you are sure that you have related to us here is what you heard?" Goodrich persisted.

"Mister Goodrich, I'm one hundred percent absolutely positive that is what the man said. You know, I have never been involved in anything like this before. And I heard what you and the judge were talking about today. And I heard all the questions you were asking. And I heard the answers you got. I may not be the smartest person in the world, but I know you are looking for people who can be fair for this case. The comments this gentleman made indicated, at least to me, that he was not going to be fair. So, I became concerned and thought I should report it to someone."

After Goodrich indicated he didn't have any more questions, Judge Bell turned to Felbin to see if he wanted to inquire. In response, Felbin said, "No, judge, I don't have any questions." Turning to the juror and in an obvious effort to curry favor, he added, "I just want to thank you, ma'am, for coming forward with this information. I appreciate that."

"Thank you, ma'am. We will take it from here. We very much appreciate your bringing this to our attention. We will see you tomorrow morning. Have a nice evening," Judge Bell said, concluding the meeting with Juror 346.

While Goodrich was questioning the juror, Felbin found Juror 189 on the sheet that the bailiff had given him. His name is Daniel Montgomery, a black male, age 46, divorced, two young children and employed by an asphalt company for the past five years. Felbin clearly remembered him. He was seated in the jury box, a location that undoubtedly would put him in the final group from which the jury would be selected. Felbin recalled this potential juror gave no response that would justify a challenge for cause. In fact, Felbin's notes reflected the juror appeared to have all the right answers. He had no prior incidents with the police, had no problems with police officers, didn't know any police officers, had some traffic tickets, but never had any problems with the police officers who gave him the tickets. But Felbin recalled having a concern about Juror 189, particularly given his location within the jury pool. There was something about him. Perhaps he was too good, or perhaps he was too anxious in a subtle way to be on this jury. In any event, intuitively, for whatever reason, Felbin clearly had him targeted for future challenge.

After Juror 346 left the chambers and before Judge Bell could ask for comments, Goodrich said, "I find it hard to believe anyone would make those kind of comments when another juror was within spitting distance."

"Of course, you do, Gary, because it is clear you want an all-black jury to try this white cop," Felbin replied.

In an effort to derail another ugly exchange between the lawyers, Judge Bell jumped in, "I don't know. It does seem a little odd this guy would make those statements so close to another juror, particularly one who is white."

Before Goodrich had a chance to respond, Felbin said, "A guy who would make these comments does not impress me as very smart to begin with. So, it comes as no surprise to me that he would not be very careful as to where he would make his racist remarks."

Raising his hand to prevent Goodrich's response, Judge Bell said, "What I'm going to do is bring this juror into chambers before we get started tomorrow and see what he has to say, rather than speculate on what this lady heard or didn't hear."

After filling in his client on the discussion that occurred in chambers, Felbin and company headed for the van and the office amid the same heavy security that accompanied them during their morning arrival. As they made their way out the front door, the television cameras and the protesters were still occupying the front steps. The comments at the end of the day were similar to the ones at the beginning.

But at least Bobby Decker was one day closer to a final decision.

Chapter Fifty-Two

Pushing their way through the protesters and media that lined the courthouse steps again with the help of big men with guns and after clearing the court security metal detectors, Felbin and company began to arrange their files on the counsel table to get ready for the start of day two of the trial. As the prospective jurors began to arrive and take their assigned seats, Felbin anxiously awaited the arrival of Juror 189. One of the last to take his seat, Juror 189 was about 6 feet 4 inches tall, weighed approximately 210 pounds and was wearing dark pants and a blue golf type shirt. His hair was short and his face cleanly shaven. Physically, he looked like an all-American adult male. Someone you would definitely want on a jury, given the right case. But Felbin didn't think this was the right case and he would soon find out if his instincts were correct.

When all the jurors were in place, the bailiff summoned the lawyers to the judge's chambers. "I'm informed that Mister Montgomery, Juror 189, has arrived. Are we ready to talk to him?" Judge Bell asked.

"Yes, I'm ready. But before we bring him back, I would like to ask the prosecutor whether they did any kind of background check on this guy," Felbin said.

Hearing no response from Goodrich, the judge asked, "Did you?"

"I'm not sure I'm required to disclose that," Goodrich replied.

"Gary, I want to know what we are dealing with here. Frankly, I don't give a damn what you are required to do. Did you do some background on him?" Judge Bell asked, clearly agitated.

"Yes. He had a DWI conviction three years ago and a domestic violence arrest, but no prosecution, two years ago. Otherwise, he is clean; no other criminal history."

"Okay, let's get him in here and see what he has to say, so we can get this jury selected," the judge said, directing the bailiff to bring Juror 189 into chambers.

When Juror 189 entered the chambers, the judge directed him to take a seat and said, "Mister Montgomery, an issue has arisen about which we need some clarification." Without warning, Judge Bell looked at Felbin and said, "You may inquire."

Somewhat taken aback, Felbin began, "Mister Montgomery, we received some information that yesterday after lunch while waiting in the hall for the bailiff to unlock the courtroom, you were on your cell phone. During a conversation you were having with someone at that time, it is alleged you made the comment that you had jury duty and it was the case of the cop who killed the black kid on the roof of the pawn shop and you were going to fry that cop. Sir, did you make that comment?"

After a long pause, Juror 189 finally spoke, and his statement was simple. "I don't recall."

"You don't recall? Is that what I just heard you say, Mister Montgomery?" Felbin asked in disbelief.

"Yes. I don't recall," Juror 189 repeated.

"Mister Montgomery, it is alleged that you made that statement, less than twenty-four hours ago and you expect us to believe you don't remember whether you made a statement as serious as that less than twenty-four hours ago?" Felbin pressed Juror 189, clearly unconcerned about whether he alienated this prospective juror. This guy was gone, whether for cause or otherwise.

"Whether or not you believe it is certainly your prerogative, Mister Felbin," Montgomery said, with a hint of arrogance.

"Well, it certainly is, Mister Montgomery," Felbin said, no longer trying to mask his hostility toward this potential juror. Continuing with his questions, Felbin said, "You are not saying you didn't make that statement are you, Mister Montgomery?"

"No. I'm not saying that."

"Let me ask you, sir, do you at least recall talking on your cell phone in the hall just outside the courtroom yesterday after lunch?" Felbin asked.

"Yes. I did talk on my cell phone."

"And do you recall the court telling you not to use that cell phone?" Felbin asked.

"I guess so."

With that response, Felbin announced that his questioning was concluded.

The prosecutor now had the opportunity to see if he could do something to rehabilitate and hopefully save this juror from the challenge for cause that would inevitably come.

"Mister Montgomery, it is also alleged you made this comment in the presence of another potential juror. I must tell you, sir, that I have a difficult time believing you would make this type of comment under any circumstances, but particularly in the presence of another potential juror," Goodrich said, resisting the temptation to call his attention to the race of that other juror. "With that said, do you remember any of the conversation you had on your cell phone yesterday after lunch?"

Before Juror 189 was able to respond, Felbin interrupted and said, "I think in fairness to Mister Montgomery, he should be reminded that he is still under the oath that he took yesterday."

"Thank you, Mister Felbin. I'm sure Mister Montgomery doesn't have to be reminded of how rude you are to interrupt my conversation with him," Goodrich said.

"That's enough," the judge said, ending the banter before it began. "Move on," he directed.

"I had several conversations after lunch with several different people and I'm sure I mentioned that I was on jury duty. But beyond that I don't recall the exact substance of those conversations," Juror 189 said.

"Have you prejudged this case in any respect, Mister Montgomery?" Goodrich asked, continuing in his effort to save the juror.

"No," was the immediate response.

"Are you able to decide this case based upon the law the court gives you and the evidence presented in the court room?"

"Absolutely."

"I'm satisfied, your Honor, and I have no further questions," Goodrich announced.

"I have a few more questions, Judge," Felbin announced.

"No, you don't," Judge Bell said. Turning to Juror 189, he said, "Thank you, Mister Montgomery. You can return to your seat in the court room."

When Juror 189 left the judge's chambers, the judge said, "I'll entertain a challenge for cause on Mister Montgomery."

"I'll so move," Felbin said.

Looking at Goodrich, Judge Bell said, "Do you want to argue this, Gary?"

"Yes, I do. This gentleman said nothing that would disqualify him from jury service. In fact, he said he would be able to decide the case based upon the law and the evidence. How is this any different than the person who has an opinion, but is able to set that opinion aside and base a verdict on what is presented in court?"

"You're kidding, right?" Felbin began. "This guy can't remember what he said less than twenty-four hours ago. He can't remember making a comment as inflammatory as frying a cop. Frying a cop before he has heard any evidence. And suggesting he wanted to get on this jury so he could accomplish that goal. He didn't deny making that comment when I asked him that question. Surely, any reasonable person who didn't remember the particulars of some conversation would deny making a comment as inflammatory as frying a cop. His refusal to deny minimally suggests, giving him the benefit of all doubt, that he knows he is at least capable of making this type of comment. Or that he has made a similar comment at some other time in his life. This guy is a racist and a liar and has no business on this jury. Or, maybe because he can't recall conversations he had less than twenty-four hours ago, he is too stupid to be on this jury."

Responding, Goodrich said, "Perhaps he was afraid to respond because he didn't recall his exact words and didn't want to make a mistake, particularly since he was under oath, as you so quickly pointed out. But, in all events, there is nothing on this record that would support striking him for cause. If we started eliminating people based upon ugly things they have said in their lifetimes, we would have no jurors to hear any case."

"Additionally, this guy violated the court's order to stay off his cell phone. That alone should disqualify him," Felbin added.

"If we started removing jurors for things like that, we would have no one left in the pool," Goodrich replied.

"I listened carefully to his answers, observed his demeanor, and I must admit that I'm concerned about his objectivity. However, I don't believe his answers can justify striking him for cause. You can use one of your peremptory challenges if you like, Mister Felbin," Judge Bell said.

Clearly disturbed by the ruling, Felbin said, "I know I can use one of my peremptory strikes, but I shouldn't have to. This guy is unfit to participate in this case. I want the record to reflect my complete disagreement with your decision and my objection to your ruling. Further, the record should reflect the court's refusal to excuse Juror 189 has and will continue to deprive this defendant of due process and a fair trial."

In all cases, trial lawyers need to protect their appellate record with specific objections. Their failure to specifically object preserves nothing for a higher court to review. Felbin, although perturbed with Judge Bell's decision, was once again making his record in the event that his client was convicted. The court's refusal to strike Juror 189 would undoubtedly be a point he would use to request a new trial, if one was necessary.

Jury selection continued throughout the remainder of the day, with Felbin having his chance to ask questions once Goodrich finished. It was a rather routine process with black jurors continuing to respond one way and white jurors another. Eventually, when the questioning concluded both in the courtroom and in the judge's chambers, the lawyers approached the bench to make their challenges for cause. Most were obvious and individuals were excused by agreement. Many of the obvious challenges were African Americans who freely admitted they could not be impartial. Initially, Goodrich fought those, but later acquiesced when it became clear he was not going to prevail on any. Others were not so obvious and hotly-contested, with the prosecutor seeking to eliminate white jurors and the defense black.

Once the challenges for cause were concluded, the pool from which the jury would be selected was narrowed and defined. The racial makeup was substantially better from the defense perspective than when the selection process began. Of the 24 individuals in the pool from which the jury would be selected, nine were African American and the remainder white. Juror 189 was among the 24 and was one of the nine blacks. Each side would have the opportunity to strike six.

The next six seated behind the first 24 would comprise the alternate pool from which each side would have the opportunity to strike two, leaving the remaining two as the alternate jurors who would serve in the event that something happened to any of the first 12. Of the six in the alternate pool, two were African American.

Both parties would now review the remaining candidates and their notes on each to determine which would fit the jury profile they developed prior to the start of the trial. The lawyers decide the type of juror who would best suit what they are trying to accomplish. Age, sex, race, occupation, family background, education, answers to the questions asked, as well as the questions for which they had no answers, are all taken into consideration.

In this case, the prosecution was looking for a jury of young, black males. Formal education would not be a priority, nor would a long-term employment history. Alternatively, black females and young, liberal whites with adversarial law enforcement experiences would be a welcome substitute. Goodrich would strike six and two alternates first, and pass the remaining candidates to Felbin.

The defense, on the other hand, would look for middle age to older white males. Education was not a high priority but stable, long-term blue collar employment was. The defense would have to be careful, however, that those they selected or their family or friends had no adverse dealings or harbored any animosity toward police officers. Something as simple as a traffic ticket could be significant. Felbin spent a good deal of his time questioning potential jurors on this issue.

As expected, Goodrich eliminated all white individuals, male and female, young and old, educated and uneducated, employed and unemployed. His alternate strikes were also both white. There was little doubt Goodrich made his strikes on the basis of race and race alone. When Felbin was through, there would be little doubt that he had made his choices based upon race and race alone. But in the meantime, Felbin had to make an appellate record. He had to challenge the prosecutor's selections, claiming they were race-based and violated the United States Supreme Court decision in *Batson*. Although in *Batson*, Felbin argued it also applied to any race-based discriminatory practice, blacks and whites alike. Discrimination is discrimination at any level. But as Felbin expected, the judge overruled his objection, allowing all the prosecutor's strikes to stand.

Felbin now was faced with nine African Americans, one of which was Juror 189, out of a remaining pool of 18. Since he had only the ability to eliminate 6 people, there would obviously be an African American presence on the jury. After he completed his selections, three African Americans remained on the jury and none as alternate jurors. Juror 189 was not among that number. The expected *Batson* challenge by Goodrich followed, but like Felbin's, was overruled. The jury was now complete; nine whites, three blacks, eight men, four women. The alternates were both white females. With the selection of the jury, day two of the trial was now complete. The court adjourned for the day and the trial would resume at 10:00 the following morning with opening statements.

After the courtroom emptied, Decker turned to Felbin and asked what he thought. "I think we will be okay," Felbin replied. But his private thoughts contained some doubt and uncertainty. Juries are generally unpredictable. But the notoriety and volatility of this case made this jury even more unpredictable.

Chapter Fifty-Three

Day three of the trial began at 10:30 a.m. The court-room which had previously been filled with potential jurors was now filled with spectators; gadflies, some on the side of the victim, some on the side of the defendant, and some just curious to see this media event firsthand rather than on the nightly news. Reporters occupied the first row on both sides of the room. The second row behind the report-ers on the prosecutor's side of the room was occupied by the family of Jordon Mitchell.

The second row behind the defense table was occu-pied by the family of Bobby Decker; his mother and broth-er. Bobby's father was not in attendance. A few days prior to the start of the trial, Bobby had asked his mother *who* would be attending the trial. She didn't mention his father. Bobby didn't ask the question directly, but hoped his father would be there. He had been optimistic his father would put aside their differences and support him during these stressful times. But it was not to be.

All criminal cases begin with an opening statement. The opening statement is like the forward in a book; de-signed to preview a party's case; an outline of what the evidence will be. The prosecution is required to make one, but the defense has options. He can make one after the prosecutor has finished; reserve until the defense begins; or decline altogether. Usually, if the defense has a viable defense to the charges, he will make an opening statement immediately after the prosecutor concludes his. He does that primarily to give the jury a preview of what the defense will prove and also to let the jurors know the state's theory of the case is not the only one. It also has the effect of tak-ing the wind out of the prosecutor's sails and reducing the impact and any prejudicial effect the statement may have. On the other hand, if he has no legitimate defense and is relegated to challenging the prosecution's theory through cross examination and objections, the defense will either defer or waive his opening.

Gary Goodrich was an excellent and experienced prosecutor. He was animated and aggressive, with a knack for sensationalizing and creating sympathy for the victims of crime. He presented his case simply and talked to jurors, not over them. Juries loved him and his conviction rate was high. He was a formidable opponent in most cases. The case of Bobby Decker was a perfect fit for his style. He could not only create sympathy for a young black victim, but he could also condemn a rogue cop; a cop who tarnished the badge; the type of police officer the city didn't want or need.

His opening statement began with the death of Jordon Mitchell and the massive skull fracture that caused that death. He described Mitchell's young skull, crushed; his brain bruised, bleeding, and swollen. He told the jury Mitchell's brain was so swollen that it had no place to go inside his skull. "A brain so swollen the doctors had to drill holes in this young skull in order to release some of the pressure caused by the swelling, before his head exploded," the prosecutor said, his voice filled with emotion.

Goodrich promised the jurors they would see photographs of that skull and brain. "In fact, you'll see actual photographs of the entire autopsy when the body of this young man was dissected by the medical examiner, in order to conclusively determine the cause of death; a death caused unnecessarily by this defendant, that man sitting right there, who decided to play judge and jury," his voice rising as he pointed at Bobby Decker. "Thanks to this defendant, Jordon Mitchell's last days were spent in the Intensive Care Unit of the hospital, with tubes inserted in every part of his body in an unsuccessful effort to save his life."

When he finished describing the inflammatory details of the injuries and the autopsy, he went on to focus on the testimony he expected from the forensic medical experts. First, he described in detail the credentials of Dr. Phillip Long, M.D., the Medical Examiner for the city of St. Louis. He then recited the resume of Dr. Helen McHenry, M.D., the Medical Examiner for St. Louis County. Goodrich made it sound like the opinions of these forensic pathologists would be the only opinions that would count. After all, they were the hometown representatives of the people and had no economic interests in this case, inferentially suggesting that the opinions of defense experts would be purchased.

"Ladies and gentlemen, the objective opinion of both of these independent experts is the same. Jordon Mitchell died from blunt trauma with a linear object that resulted in a massive skull fracture. The evidence will show the murder weapon was a flashlight owned and possessed by this defendant. That flashlight was seized from the defendant and you'll be able to see it. You will be able to examine for yourselves the object that unnecessarily ended a young life."

Goodrich also informed the jury there was an eyewitness to this murder. He explained there was another young man on the roof with Jordon Mitchell that night. "His name is Daniels Jones," he said.

Knowing that Felbin would make the burglary the focal point of his defense, Goodrich decided to address it first. He didn't want it to appear like he was afraid of the issue. "Mister Jones and Jordon Mitchell together were in that pawn shop. They should not have been there. Mister Jones won't deny that. He is not proud of that, but he won't deny it. He will tell you the truth about that burglary and everything else that happened that night, including when he saw this defendant strike his defenseless friend on the back of his head with a flashlight."

As he addressed the jury, the prosecutor turned briefly toward Felbin to see if there was any reaction. Seeing none, Goodrich continued and said, "Yes, these young men were committing a criminal act, but they were doing nothing for which anyone on the roof that night deserved to die."

With that comment, Felbin was on his feet objecting and complaining that the prosecutor was making a closing argument, rather than an opening statement, in an effort to inflame the jury. His objection was overruled, which allowed Goodrich to continue.

"But one did die. Jordon Mitchell died after this defendant hit him in the back of the head with a flashlight that caused a massive brain injury and ultimately his death," Goodrich said as he raised his voice and again pointed at Decker. Felbin was back on his feet with another objection, but with the same result.

In addition to experts and an eyewitness, there were other witnesses. He told the jury these were witnesses to a cover-up. "Yes, the defendant knew he could not justify the force he used. He knew he couldn't justify the use of lethal force. This defendant was twice the size of Jordon. He weighed twice as much. Neither Jordon nor Mister Jones had a weapon. So, he had to try to figure out a way he could credibly explain his actions."

As Goodrich spoke, Felbin leaned over to Bobby and said, "Where is he going with this?"

"I have no idea," Bobby quickly said, as he tried to make sure he didn't show any emotion the jury could detect.

Felbin then turned to his investigator. "Jack, do you have any idea where this is going?"

"Not a clue," Reilly said.

As those gathered at the defense table conferred, Goodrich continued. "As a police officer, the defendant was required to prepare a police report detailing the events on the roof and detailing the force that was necessary." He told the jury they would see that police report, which he described as a work of fiction. "But you'll hear from a witness who will tell you this defendant wanted to make up a reason why he had to fracture the skull of Jordon Mitchell. But this witness wouldn't go along with the lie. So, the only thing this defendant could do was ignore the injury."

"Incredibly, the police report doesn't mention any injury to Jordon Mitchell. Nothing—you'll see nothing in the police report about any injury or how this young man got a massive skull fracture that ultimately caused his death. Can you imagine? How can this guy cause this type of injury and not know how he did it?" Goodrich asked rhetorically, again pointing at the defendant. "So, when you are unable to write the use of force into the report in order to write it out; when you can't say this young man did something that warranted the use of this type of deadly force, you simply claim you don't know how this injury happened."

Again, Felbin whispered to Bobby, "You have no idea what he is talking about?" Felbin had forgotten he had a conversation with Bobby about Jake Corbett's role in preparing the Mitchell incident police report.

"Remember, I told you I prepared the report with Jake and Jake suggested that we make up some reason I had to hit the guy in the head. But I told him I wouldn't do that," Bobby said.

"Great," was Felbin's only response.

While Bobby and his lawyer were conferring, Goodrich was putting the finishing touches on his opening statement, which was now beginning to sound more like a closing argument. "But by your verdict, you can finish writing the police report in this case. By your verdict of guilty, you can tell Robert Decker you know how Jordon Mitchell sustained a massive skull fracture and a massive brain injury. You can tell this defendant and the world you know he murdered this young black man." With that, Goodrich completed his opening statement while looking directly at one of the three black jurors.

When the judge asked Felbin if he wanted to make an opening statement, he said he would like a short recess. Although he had pretty much decided he would not make an opening statement, he needed to confer with his client about the surprise cover up issues raised in the state's opening.

Once the jury left the courtroom, Felbin said, "Let's talk about this cover up thing Goodrich just mentioned. What is that about?"

"Remember, I told you that Corbett wanted me to write the report in a way that justified the use of force. He wanted me to say something that justified striking him in the head."

"How was he going to justify it?"

"I don't know, because I told him I was not going to do that. But later when I was still struggling to write the report, Jake gave me a rough draft of a report he had prepared."

"What did it say?" Felbin asked.

"I don't know. All I know is that it was his attempt to justify the use of force and the injury. I was not going to go down that road, so I threw it away without reading it. Where do you think the prosecutor was going with this?" Bobby asked, concerned with what he just heard the prosecutor tell the jury he was going to prove: a cover-up.

"Your buddy, Jake Corbett, is listed as a prosecution witness. I suspect we are going to see him during this trial on the witness stand," Felbin said.

"What could he possibly say? Do you think he is going to lie and say he saw me hit Mitchell?" Bobby asked missing the point entirely.

"No, I don't think he is going to say that. But I do think his version of the preparation of the police report is going to be different than yours," Felbin said.

"How?" Bobby asked, again either missing the point or refusing to accept what was sure to come.

"I suspect he is going to say it was your idea to fabricate a justification for the use of force. How well do you know this guy?" Felbin asked. It was the same question that he had asked Bobby previously.

Providing the same response, Bobby said, "I really didn't know him that well. We were never partners. Never rode together and never socialized. I just knew him from the district and always thought he was a standup guy. I can't believe he would lie."

"People do a lot of strange things when they are threatened with criminal prosecution or loss of employment," Felbin said. "Let's prepare for the worst and hope for the best."

Turning to his investigator, Felbin said, "See what you can get us on this police report cover-up thing I suspect is coming our way from our friend Corbett."

Chapter Fifty-Four

Felbin decided against making an opening statement. Although he believed he had an excellent defense and ordinarily would make an opening, he decided against it in this case, because the prosecutor had no idea what the defense experts were going to say. An opening would give him a preview of what was coming and more time to rebut that testimony. The element of surprise is always a trial lawyer's best friend.

After Felbin announced he would not be making an opening statement, Judge Bell decided to take the luncheon recess. When court reconvened, Judge Bell directed Goodrich to call his first witness. To Felbin's surprise, Goodrich called Daniels Jones. Presumably, the prosecutor thought he would start with the burglary and get that out of the way early so the testimony of the experts and other witnesses would overshadow the fact that Mitchell and Jones were committing criminal acts that caused the police to be called to the pawn shop in the first place.

Beginning with some background information in order to make him feel comfortable on the stand, Jones, dressed in a white suit with an open collar, told the jury he was 20 years old, a year older than Jordon Mitchell, with a high school education and currently employed in a fast food restaurant. Goodrich then covered his criminal history. Jones only had one conviction, a misdemeanor stealing. But Goodrich went on to inquire about multiple arrests.

Ordinarily, arrests that don't result in convictions are inadmissible. The jury would never hear about them. However, under these circumstances, Goodrich was trying to convey the impression the police were harassing this young black kid since none of those arrests even resulted in criminal prosecutions, let alone convictions. An interesting strategy, Felbin thought. But one that might backfire. Jones told the jury he had been arrested more than 10 times, mostly for stealing; kept in jail for hours on end and then ultimately released without any criminal charges. He proclaimed his innocence on each.

After covering the background information, Goodrich then got into the heart of the matter. "What were you and Jordon doing at the pawn shop that night?" Goodrich asked, getting right to the burglary, but avoiding the use of words and phrases such as burglary, stealing, breaking and entering.

"We went in to see what was there," was the simple, rehearsed response.

"Why did you go into a pawn shop in the middle of the night?"

"To see if there was anything of value in there," another rehearsed response that avoided the use of the word steal.

"Did you take anything?"

"No. There was nothing to take."

Jones described how he and Mitchell gained entry. He told the jury they went into a welding company first to look around. They didn't find anything. They knew the pawn shop had a skylight. They figured the pawn shop had an alarm system that would be activated if they went in through a window or the door. They needed to get on the roof; get to that skylight. There would be no alarm there. They found a ladder in the welding shop and used that to get on the roof. Once on the roof, they smashed the pawn shop skylight and went in. The jury stared, motionless, mesmerized as if in disbelief over the complexity of this burglary committed by a couple of kids. Once inside, they tried unsuccessfully to access a safe. They located rings and other jewelry in a case and after breaking the glass, they helped themselves to the contents.

When they saw police cars pull up outside, they quickly left the pawn shop through the rooftop skylight. They stayed on the roof until the police officers arrived.

"How many police officers came onto the roof?" Goodrich asked.

"Two."

"Do you see anyone in the courtroom who was on the roof with you and Jordon?"

"Yes," Jones said, pointing to the defendant, Bobby Decker.

"What did the officers do?"

"They arrested us," Jones said.

"Were you able to see what that man you just identified did in the process of arresting Jordon?"

"Yes. Officer Decker threw Jordon to the ground. Slammed his body down. Then he turned him over to handcuff him behind his back. Jordon wasn't doin' nothin'. Not resistin' at all. And then he started beatin' him with a flashlight. Then he put the handcuffs on."

"Which officer did you see striking Jordon?"

"That one right there," Jones said, again pointing to the defendant.

"Did you actually see the blows land?"

"Sure did. He hit Jordon in the back of the head and on his back."

"Did you say anything to the defendant when he was beating your friend?"

"Yeah. But not while he was beatin' him. After he got him handcuffed, Jordon was just lying there on his stomach. He wasn't movin'. I said, *You hurt him. You didn't have to do that. He wasn't doin nothing'.*"

"Did the defendant respond to your comment?"

"Yeah, he said, *Shut the fuck up or you'll get some of the same.*"

"What did you think he meant by that?"

"Objection, your Honor. That question would call for speculation," Felbin said, attempting to interrupt the inflammatory testimony of this witness.

"I'm asking this witness what he thought, not what the defendant was thinking when he made that threat," Goodrich replied, seizing another opportunity to inflame the jury.

"Overruled," was the quick ruling. "You can answer about what you thought the defendant meant by that threat," Goodrich told the witness.

"I thought he was going to hit me over my head with his flashlight if I said anything else."

"And what happened after the defendant told you that you would get some of the same?"

"They took us off the roof and locked me up and took Jordon to the hospital, because he was hurt real bad."

Felbin resisted the temptation to make another objection to the gratuitous comment that Mitchell was *hurt real bad* for fear of highlighting the point.

"That's all the questions I have," Goodrich told the court.

"You may inquire, Mister Felbin," Judge Bell said, directing him to begin his cross examination.

"Mister Jones, you indicated you have been arrested more than 10 times, mostly for stealing, is that correct?" Felbin began.

"That's right. Police harassment. Every time I turn around, they lockin' me up for no reason."

"That would be the city police?"

"City, county, both."

"So, two different departments were harassing you?"

"That's right."

"Mister Jones, on any of those occasions when you were arrested for stealing, were you stealing?"

After another seemingly endless pause, Jones said, "No."

"Mister Jones, less than a month ago were you arrested after you were found in a drug store at 1034 Manchester Road in the city of St. Louis at 3 o'clock in the morning?"

"Yeah. I think so."

"You think so? This was 24 days ago to be precise. You don't remember what you were doing 24 days ago?" Felbin pressed.

"Yeah. I remember. More police harassment."

"Well, were you arrested inside that drug store at a time that it was closed?" Felbin said as he emphasized the words *inside* and *closed.*

"Yeah," Jones said, this time without equivocation.

"So, tell the jury what you were doing inside a drug store that was closed at 3 o'clock in the morning."

With that, Goodrich was on his feet, objecting that the details of the arrest were irrelevant.

"You opened the door to this line of questioning, Mister Goodrich. Your objection is overruled."

Ordinarily, not only are incidents of arrest inadmissible as evidence, but likewise, the details of those arrests are also inadmissible. However, because Goodrich elicited this testimony and additionally suggested his witness was the innocent victim of police harassment, Felbin was allowed to cross examine and test the theory advanced by his opponent.

"Please tell us, Mister Jones, what were you doing in a closed pawn shop at 3 in the morning? Excuse me, I mean a closed drug store at 3 in the morning? Sorry for the mistake," Felbin said, not really feeling any sorrow for the intentional misstatement.

"I don't remember."

"Well, were you lost? Or perhaps you were walking in your sleep," Felbin said sarcastically.

The last comment drew another objection from the prosecutor. But before the court could rule, Jones began to answer the question.

"I remember now. I saw that the back door was open and I went to see why it was open and the next thing I knew, the police were there arresting me."

"Okay. I'm glad we have that straightened out, Mister Jones. By the way, were you ever prosecuted for that good deed?"

"No."

"No surprises there!" Felbin said, waiting for the objection which never came. "But there is no question, is there, Mister Jones, that you and your friend, Mister Mitchell, were, in fact, burglarizing the pawn shop at the time you encountered Officer Decker and Officer Corbett?"

"That's right," was his short answer.

"And has your friend, Mister Goodrich over there, prosecuted you for that offense?"

Again, Goodrich was on his feet. This time, the judge admonished Felbin and warned him about his editorial comments.

"No," Jones said, responding to Felbin's question.

"I have a couple more questions, Mister Jones. You said Officer Decker slammed your friend, Mister Mitchell, to the roof. Was that after both of you tried to run away?"

"Yes."

"The plan was that you would run in one direction and Mister Mitchell would run in another, in the hope that one or both of you could escape if you separated the officers?"

"Yes."

"And Officer Decker had to grab Mister Mitchell to pre-vent that escape and that is when he pushed him to the floor of the roof, isn't that correct?"

"He grabbed Jordon."

"And when Officer Decker pushed him down, Mister Mitchell landed on his back, isn't that also correct?"

"He body slammed him," Jones said.

"But Mister Mitchell landed on his back, isn't that cor-rect?"

"Yeah."

"And then he turned him over to cuff him behind his back?"

"Yeah."

"And that's when you claim to have seen Officer Decker strike him with an object?"

"Yeah. He hit him in the back of his head with his flashlight."

"What were you doing at this time?"

"I was being cuffed by that other cop."

"Were you on your stomach?"

"Yes."

"How far away from Mister Mitchell were you at this time?"

"From about me to you," Jones said pointing at Felbin.

"Would you say that is about fifteen feet?"

"I don't know. I ain't no good at distances."

"And it was dark and raining, is that right?"

"Yeah, but I saw him hit Jordon in the head with that flashlight."

Felbin went to the prosecutor's table and retrieved Decker's flashlight. Goodrich had already marked it and of-fered it into evidence, without objection from the defense.

"Is this the flashlight you are talking about, Mister Jones?" Felbin asked.

"Yes, it is. That's the flashlight he hit Jordon with."

"Thank you, Mister Jones. That's all the questions I have at this time," Felbin announced.

When Goodrich indicated he didn't have any additional questions, Judge Bell told the jury that given the hour, they would recess for the day and begin at 9:30 the next morn-ing.

In any trial, whether criminal or civil, the party call-ing a witness begins the questioning. This is called direct examination. The opposing party then has the opportunity to ask questions, which is referred to as cross examination. When that is completed, the witness can be rehabilitated, if necessary, by the party calling him. That is called re-direct examination. Finally, the opposing party can conduct a re-cross examination. Additional questions by either side are discretionary with the court.

Because his witness had done so poorly during cross examination, Goodrich felt he didn't want to give Felbin the opportunity to ask any additional questions. He asked no follow-up questions and wanted to get Jones off the wit-ness stand. Jones told the jury he saw the defendant strike Jordon Mitchell with a flashlight. That was all he needed. Now, Goodrich would connect that testimony with that of the doctors.

When the court recessed following the testimony of Daniels Jones, it was hard to tell which side had prevailed from the events of the day. Clearly, the prosecutor benefit-ed from his opening statement as well as the absence of a defense opening. But Jones was a mixed bag. Of course, he did say he witnessed the defendant strike Mitchell in the head with a flashlight. But his nose was bloodied on cross examination. The prosecutor made a tactical mistake by opening the door to the arrest history of Daniels Jones, which could impact his credibility. In the end, if the jury didn't believe Jones, then it didn't matter what he said. His testimony was needed to support the conclusions of the experts. But even if his testimony was discounted, Felbin knew the testimony of the experts would be strong.

Chapter Fifty-Five

The *St. Louis Post Dispatch* was not kind to Bobby Deck-er from the outset of this case. The front page photographs of Mitchell in intensive care at the hospital, coverage of the racial issues between the St. Louis Police Department and the black community, damning editorial commentary and articles that sensationalized the various protests, to name a few, were not helpful to Bobby Decker and his effort to defend himself against this murder charge. But the front page, above the fold article in the morning edition of the pa-per recounting the first day of trial after jury selection, had a different tone. Of course, the recitation of what the pros-ecutor expected to prove did nothing to help the defense. However, the remainder of the article was devoted to the testimony of Daniels Jones. It actually made him look like a silly kid, or perhaps a liar. Although his testimony that he witnessed the defendant strike Mitchell with a flashlight was mentioned, it was overshadowed by his testimony re-lating to his various arrests, including his explanation for his most recent arrest at the drug store in the middle of the night. The actual questions propounded by Felbin and the answers given by Jones were quoted at length.

The news coverage was important to Bobby for several reasons. After the trial, he had to live and work in St. Louis. The news coverage would shape public opinion of him for those who hadn't seen and heard the evidence first hand. In order to succeed in the future as a police officer, he had to be respected and credible. He also knew his department made decisions based upon public and political pressure. If he was acquitted of this murder charge, but the news cov-erage made it sound like the jury made a mistake, as with high profile cases like O. J. Simpson, his ability to continue his employment as a police officer whether for the city of St. Louis or some other department, would be compromised.

When Felbin arrived at the office at 6 a.m. to begin preparing for day four of the trial, he was met by Jack Reilly with paper in hand.

"Did you see the *Post* this morning?" the investigator asked.

"No. How was the coverage?" Felbin asked.

"Great, absolutely fantastic. It made Jones look like the liar he is. I can't imagine anyone with an ounce of objectivity would think differently. And I can't imagine this jury thought he was credible. You did a great job on the cross," Reilly said as he handed the paper to Felbin.

"I thought we did okay with him, particularly when we got into that latest burglary arrest at the drug store— thanks to your effort in getting that police report. Because, obviously, Goodrich didn't give it to us, and took a calculated risk that we didn't know about it," Felbin said.

As a retired St. Louis police officer, Reilly knew his way around the Department. He knew where to go to get information and he had a lot of friends who would provide it under the table. In addition, Bobby Decker still had some friends in the police department who were willing to take a risk and help out. The information they were able to gather, unavailable to the ordinary defendant in a criminal case, was invaluable. The police report involving the drug store arrest of Jones was but one of many examples. Undoubtedly, Cardwell and company had already launched an investigation into how Felbin discovered that arrest. In the end, however, that search would bear no fruit, but would certainly aggravate the elected circuit attorney.

Just then Bobby came into the office, and they shared the article with him.

"How do you think we did yesterday?" Bobby asked, since he'd had no opportunity to talk to Felbin after the court adjourned for the day.

"I think that we did all right," Felbin replied, always trying to appear upbeat for his client.

"All right? Are you kidding? I think we did great," Reilly, the consummate cheerleader, injected. "Did you read that *Post* article? Felbin destroyed that witness."

"I suspect that today we will see the forensic pathologists. Goodrich will put them on to connect the dots with the testimony from Jones. He will also put them on following Jones, to take the focus off of the cross and marry the medical with the meat of his testimony that he witnessed you strike Mitchell on the back of his head with a flashlight," Felbin theorized.

"You're probably right. But we will be ready for the doctors and their testimony that will be designed to take them off the hook that Cardwell put them on," Reilly said, an obvious reference to the announcement by Cardwell of a murder charge before the autopsy was completed.

Chapter Fifty-Six

When Bobby entered the courtroom to begin day four, he saw his mother and brother seated in the second row again. He approached both and gave his mother a hug and a kiss, while shaking hands with his brother. After exchanging some pleasantries that had nothing to do with the trial, Bobby took his seat at the defense table, anxious to start. Again, his father was a no show.

As expected, the prosecution would start the day with the medical experts. The first would be Dr. Phillip Long, the Medical Examiner for the city of St. Louis. Goodrich began with his credentials to include his education at St. Louis University Medical School; an internship; a residency; fellowships; Board certifications; teaching experience at his alma mater; publications; awards and honors; and his experience as a forensic pathologist.

Dr. Long explained that forensic pathology is the science concerned with determining the manner and cause of death, through the examination of a corpse and an autopsy examination. He further explained that forensic pathologists carefully examine all parts of the body after death, so they can render an opinion as to how that person died, and what caused that death from a scientific and evidentiary standpoint. Forensic pathologists are then asked to come to court to explain their findings and share with the jury and judge their opinions.

Over the objection of the defendant, Dr. Long then took the jury step by step through a slide show presentation of the autopsy of Jordon Mitchell. The heart, lungs, liver, kidneys, and other vital organs of this young man were normal. The head, brain, right arm and a portion of his chest, however, were not.

He said he found bruises and contusions on Mitchell's right arm that extended onto his chest. These bruises and contusions were in a straight line that began on the outside of Mitchell's right bicep, extending uninterrupted to the middle of his chest and measuring 1.5 inches in width and 12.4 inches in length.

"Do you have an opinion within a reasonable degree of medical certainty what caused these injuries?" Goodrich asked.

"Yes."

"And what is that opinion, doctor?"

"Those injuries were caused by blunt trauma from a linear object."

"Such as a flashlight?"

"Yes."

Observing the human head with the skin and scalp removed and the skull exposed is unsettling under any circumstances. Using the photographs that appeared on a large screen in the courtroom and a laser pointer, Dr. Long pointed out the location of the fracture on Mitchell's skull. It was a large L-shaped crack, clearly visible on the skull.

Dr. Long told the jury he sent the brain of Mr. Mitchell to Dr. Helen McHenry, the Medical Examiner for St. Louis County, and asked her to do that autopsy. As such, he was rendering no opinion on issues associated with the brain.

"Within a reasonable degree of medical certainty, do you have an opinion, Doctor Long, as to the competent producing cause of the skull fracture sustained by Jordon Mitchell?" Goodrich asked.

"Yes."

"What is that opinion?"

"That fracture was the result of blunt trauma with a linear object," Dr. Long replied.

"Could that linear object be a flashlight?"

"Yes."

"A flashlight such as this?" Goodrich asked while handing Decker's flashlight to the pathologist.

"Yes," Dr. Long said.

"And do you have an opinion as to the cause of Mister Mitchell's death within a reasonable degree of medical certainty?"

"Yes."

"And what is that opinion?"

"Mister Mitchell died as the result of blunt trauma with a linear object."

"I have no further questions," Goodrich announced.

"Doctor Long, it is good to see you again," Felbin began. "We have known each other for quite a long time."

"Yes, we have," Dr. Long agreed.

"And during that period of time, I have had the pleasure to ask you questions on a variety of issues."

"Yes, you have and most effectively, I might add," Dr. Long said with a hint of a smile.

"And some of those cases involved autopsies of various brains, did they not?"

"They did."

"And so, you can probably understand why I was shocked when I learned an experienced and excellent forensic pathologist like yourself asked Doctor McHenry to do the autopsy of the brain."

"Is that a question, Mister Felbin?" Dr. Long cautiously asked. As a professional witness, Long knew Felbin was leading him down a path where he probably would not want to be when the dust settled.

"Well, no, that is more of a statement. But my question is why you would have Doctor McHenry do the brain autopsy, when you are certainly capable of doing it yourself? That's a question."

"Because I wanted another pair of eyes to look at the case."

"And why is that, Doctor Long?"

"Because of all the public interest in this case."

"But you have had other high profile cases. How is this different?" Felbin asked, unwilling to let Long off the hook.

"Frankly, Mister Felbin, I'm not unmindful of the ugly discord that has taken place as a result of this case. Unfortunately, it has exacerbated racial hostilities in this town. I didn't want to be in the middle of that, particularly in light of the result in the Cannon case. So I sent that part of the case to Doctor McHenry."

"You said in light of the Cannon case. Are you saying you didn't want to incur the wrath of the elected circuit attorney in the event that findings didn't concur with her theory of the case?"

Goodrich rose to object, but the witness answered the question before the objection was completed.

"I didn't want to incur anyone's wrath."

"To include that of the Joan Cardwell?"

"Yes, I suppose so."

"Doctor Long, let me ask you, sir, after you performed the autopsy, were you contacted by the circuit attorney?"

"Yes."

"How soon after you completed the autopsy did she contact you?"

"The same day."

"And what did she want to know?"

"She asked me what it looked like. I told her after a cursory review, it looked to me like blunt trauma with a linear object."

"Did you tell her anything else?"

"Yes. I told her I was sending the brain to Doctor McHenry to do the autopsy and that it would take three to four weeks to complete that aspect of the case."

"Did you have any other conversations with her?"

"Yes, several. She called to ask me how the case was progressing."

"On those occasions when she would call you, would she repeatedly impress upon you the importance of the case?"

"Yes."

"Did she also impress you with the importance of your testimony and that of Doctor McHenry?"

"I'm not sure how to answer that."

"Well, let me try it this way. Did she ever mention during any of those conversations the importance of the autopsy findings?"

"She said the entire case was important, because she believed the defendant was responsible for the fracture and brain injury."

"And did she tell you or lead you to believe she was relying on you and Doctor McHenry to prove her theory?"

"I knew that."

"Why does it take so long to autopsy the brain?"

"Because the brain has to be sliced into sections to determine whether there is any injury inside that is not visible to the naked eye on the outside. And it takes three to four weeks for the brain to solidify, so that it can be cut into sections for this examination."

Felbin didn't ask the Why question. Why it is important to view the interior of the brain. He knew the answer he wanted, but was not sure that Long would give it to him. But he had another way to get what he was looking for. Another witness would provide it and it should be a game changer.

"Doctor, you said Mister Mitchell died of blunt trauma with a linear object. But since you didn't autopsy the brain, how would you know that? Isn't it necessary to do the autopsy of the brain before you can come to that conclusion?"

"Yes, I suppose it is."

"So, while you might have an opinion about what caused the fractured skull, is it fair to say that you have no opinion about the cause of death, not having performed the brain autopsy?"

"Yes. That is fair, Mister Felbin"

"You also said you found contusions on the right arm that extended to the chest, is that correct?"

"Yes."

"And you said those contusions were caused by a linear object, a flashlight, is that correct?"

"Well, I said that they could be caused by a flashlight."

"Okay. Could those contusions have been caused by any other object?"

"I suppose so, but that would depend on the object."

"Doctor Long, do you know how Mister Mitchell was transported off the roof?"

"I don't know."

"Do you know whether he was secured with any type of device that contained straps?"

Another, "I don't know."

"Do you know whether he was secured on his way to the hospital with any device that had straps?"

"I don't know."

"Could straps pulled tightly and perhaps straps that were too tight, have caused these contusions, Doctor Long?"

"Well, I have never seen contusions that resulted from ambulance transportation."

"I didn't ask you that. Since you seemed quick to tell us a flashlight might have caused these contusions, I'm asking you whether it is possible that straps could have done this. Can you answer that question, Doctor Long?"

"I suppose they could."

"If that is a possibility, did it ever occur to you to determine how Mister Mitchell was transported off of the roof and to the hospital?"

"No," was Long's short answer, recognizing that a debate with Felbin would not work out very well for him.

"You say that a flashlight caused the skull fracture, is that correct? This flashlight?" Felbin asked handing the witness Decker's flashlight.

"Yes," Dr. Long said.

Felbin wondered how Long would know that this particular flashlight caused the injury. However, he didn't challenge the doctor on this point, as he wanted him to take him down a different path with that response.

"Doctor Long, how many foot pounds of pressure does it take to cause a fracture of the type you found on the skull of Jordon Mitchell?" Felbin asked.

"I don't know."

"Well, do you know how many foot pounds of pressure it would take to break this flashlight?" Felbin asked again handing him the defendant's flashlight.

"I don't know the answer to that either."

"Do you know what this flashlight should look like if it caused the fracture as you claim?"

"I don't know."

"Do you even know whether this flashlight that you say is a murder weapon even works?"

"I don't know."

"You never tested it?"

"No."

"Why not?"

"I don't have an answer for that."

"Are you even casually curious whether it works?" Felbin asked, pressing the issue.

"I suppose so," Long said hesitatingly, recognizing he might be embarrassed when Felbin completed this line of questioning.

"Well, let's put some fresh batteries in this flashlight and see whether the object you say caused a massive skull fracture works," Felbin said as he walked to the defense table to retrieve the fresh batteries.

"Will you do me the honor, Doctor?" Felbin asked as he handed the flashlight to Long after replacing the batteries.

With several of the jurors moving to the edge of their seats in the jury box, Dr. Long pushed the on/off switch.

"Well, look at that. The flashlight works," Felbin commented, as he asked the witness to shine the light in the direction of the jury box.

Continuing with this line of questions, Felbin said, "Doctor, as long as you are holding that object that you claim is a murder weapon, since you apparently haven't done so before, will you please examine the flashlight that we now know works, to see if it is damaged in any respect?"

Complying with Felbin's request, Dr. Long examined Decker's flashlight and eventually said, "I don't see any damage."

"You don't see any or there is not any damage? Perhaps you need more time to conduct your examination," Felbin said, unwilling to accept Long's equivocation.

"There is no damage, Mister Felbin," Long said, clearly agitated by the lawyer's questions.

"So, there is no damage and the object you claim to be the murder weapon works, is that the situation, Doctor Long?"

"Yes."

"Oh and just one other question, Doctor. You didn't know any of this until just a few minutes ago?"

"Yes," Dr. Long said, as his agitation seemed to turn to anger.

After staring at the witness for a lengthy amount of time in an effort to allow the jury to absorb the full impact of the flashlight demonstration and Long's testimony, Felbin finally spoke. "Thank you, Doctor. That's all the questions I have."

When Goodrich once again declined an invitation to ask additional questions, the judge took the morning recess.

Huddled in the corner of the courtroom, Felbin and company did a post mortem on the examination of Dr. Long. The first to speak was Cheerleader Reilly.

"Home run," the investigator said.

"I'm pleased," Felbin said, while pointing out that in court live demonstrations in the presence of the jury are always dangerous as they can easily backfire. "We would have been screwed if that light didn't work for whatever reason," Felbin added.

"No doubt about that," Reilly said.

"But now we get McHenry. She is a more formidable opponent than Long. Plus, they are back there now telling her what to expect. I think my cross with her will be very short. I need to make sure I get the answers to my questions, not the ones that she wants to answer. She has a penchant for ignoring the question before her and responding to what she would like the question to be. She is a challenge!" Felbin said.

Chapter Fifty-Seven

Typically for court proceedings generally and trials specifically, the morning recess lasted longer than the 15 minutes the judge announced. But when the judge called everyone back to order, as expected, the state's next witness was Dr. Helen McHenry, a striking blonde haired, blue eyed, 64-year-old woman. As he did with Dr. Long, Goodrich began by acquainting the jury with the professional qualifications of the witness. Dr. McHenry, like her counterpart, received her medical degree from St. Louis University School of Medicine in 1974 and completed an internship and residence at that same institution. She held board certifications in anatomic pathology, neuropathology, and forensic pathology. Dr. McHenry had served as the medical examiner for St. Louis County for the past 28 years. She was a full professor at St. Louis University Medical School where she had taught for 24 years. She was also a frequent lecturer and the author of many publications and a book on adult head trauma, her specialty. In an effort to impress the jury with her relationship with law enforcement, Goodrich established that Dr. McHenry had been honored by numerous law enforcement agencies as well as crime prevention organizations. And best of all, she was homegrown.

Felbin knew Dr. McHenry well. He had faced her in more than 15 cases and considered her a formidable opponent and an excellent witness for the prosecution. In fact, Felbin had consulted with Dr. McHenry on cases in which he was involved and she was not. He considered her a friend. But Joan Cardwell had put these pathologists in an untenable position by announcing a criminal prosecution before they had a chance to complete their work. Most defense attorneys would be concerned this situation might color their positions and opinions, and Felbin was no exception. Dr. Long had already admitted he had asked Dr.

McHenry to autopsy the brain because of the premature action taken by Cardwell.

After describing her professional credentials, Dr. McHenry told the jury she performed the autopsy on the brain of Jordon Mitchell, first weighing and then measuring it. That autopsy could not be done immediately. She reiterated that the brain needed to become firm, a process that takes some three to four weeks. It is then sliced to determine whether there is any internal injury. She used the same photographs as Dr. Long to illustrate her point. In addition to the internal portions of the brain, Dr. McHenry carefully examined the external surface as well.

"When you performed your external examination, did you find the brain to be that of a normal 19-year-old African American male?" Goodrich asked.

"No, I didn't. I found a subdural hematoma, an injury, a cerebral contusion in the right rear quadrant of the brain," Dr. McHenry volunteered, without waiting for the next question.

"What is a subdural hematoma, doctor?"

"A subdural hematoma is really a brain bleed. Technically, blood gathers within the outermost meningeal layer, between the dura mater, which adheres to the skull, and the arachnoid mater, which envelops the brain. Usually resulting from tears in bridging veins which cross the subdural space, subdural hemorrhages, as they are also-called, may cause an increase in intracranial pressure which can cause compression of and damage to delicate brain tissue. Some of the symptoms can include a loss of consciousness, seizures, disorientation, nausea and vomiting."

"In what way is that significant in this case?"

"It is significant because it indicates that the head injury was caused by a traumatic event. In other words, the head of this young man was struck with some object." Continuing without the need for another question, Dr. McHenry added, "At the time, I also knew a skull fracture existed. I lined up that fracture with the brain bleed. And, as I expected, it lined up perfectly."

"What occurs after a person sustains a subdural hematoma?"

"Depending upon the amount of the trauma, the brain will swell. It can swell to such an extent that there is no place for it to go within the cranium wall. In other words, the skull is too small to contain the brain. So, the neuro-surgeons then have to look for a way to relieve that pressure, and what they will do is drill a hole in the skull. They then hope and pray the swell stops. Because if it does not, death results.

"In the case of Jordon Mitchell, did the swelling stop?"

"No."

"Were you present when Doctor Long performed the autopsy on Jordon?"

"No."

"Before you performed your autopsy of the brain, did you familiarize yourself with Doctor Long's autopsy?"

"Yes. I looked at his report and I also looked at and got copies of the photographs he took, which I used here today. In addition, I got copies of his medical records from the hospital and reviewed those. And finally, I looked at a copy of the police report in this case."

"Let me start with the police report. When you reviewed that report, did you see anything unusual?"

"Objection. That question calls for conclusion, specu-lation and conjecture on the part of this witness. Plus, al-though she may claim an expertise in a variety of areas, I doubt that writing police reports is one of them," Felbin said.

"Overruled," Judge Bell quickly responded.

"I thought it was unusual that a significant head injury such as that suffered by this young man was not covered in the police report."

"Why did you think that was unusual?"

"Same objection," Felbin again interjected.

"Same ruling," the judge said.

"I thought it was unusual because I felt a police officer who had custody of and was responsible for the well-being of an individual would surely know an injury this traumatic would have occurred, and it would be addressed in the re-port. I mean this was not like this person had a little cut on his pinky finger. This guy sustained a huge crushed skull. There was a loss of consciousness and vomiting. Surely, that would be an indication something was going on and would warrant a reasonable person to at least try to figure out what the problem was and put it in the report."

This was exactly the type of damaging testimony Felbin expected from this witness. He wanted to lodge another objection because, clearly, this testimony was speculative and certainly prejudicial to the defendant. But he knew this objection would also be overruled, and he didn't want the jury to get the impression the judge was agreeing with what the witness was saying. He thought he had enough of a record preserved for appellate review by the previous objections.

This was the Achilles heel for the defense. Felbin knew from the beginning of the case, this was going to be a huge stumbling block. *How was the defense going to explain the lack of reference to this injury in the report?* Felbin thought he had the answer and a game plan, but was not sure how it would play with the jury.

"Were you able to form any opinion within a reasonable degree of medical certainty as to the competent producing cause of the brain injury you found on the brain of Jordon Mitchell?"

"Yes."

"What is that opinion?"

"That the brain injury sustained by Mister Mitchell was caused by blunt trauma with a linear object."

No surprise there, Felbin thought.

"Could this be that object?" Goodrich asked as he handed the witness the defendant's flashlight.

"Yes, it certainly could."

"Do you have an opinion within a reasonable degree of medical certainty as to the cause of Jordon Mitchell's death?" Goodrich asked.

"Yes."

"What is that opinion?"

"Mister Mitchell's death was caused by a subdural hematoma, which resulted from blunt trauma with a linear object, which certainly could have been this flashlight."

"No further questions, your Honor," Goodrich announced.

Felbin didn't ask for a recess after Goodrich completed his lengthy direct examination. McHenry's testimony hurt, and he wanted to jump right in and neutralize it as much as he could and as quickly as he could. Unfortunately, it was time for the lunch break and Felbin's cross would have to wait.

Chapter Fifty-Eight

During the luncheon recess, Felbin and the defense team discussed how to best handle Dr. McHenry. It was decided brief was best. Felbin knew from past experience he needed to keep Dr. McHenry focused and on topic. Otherwise, she would drag him to a place where his client would not want to go. Felbin knew the points he needed to make with her in order to pave the way for the testimony of his own experts. Then he needed to move on, resisting the temptation to spar with her. She would win that contest.

"Doctor McHenry, how is it that you became involved in this city case?" Felbin began.

"I was asked to do it," was her brief response.

"Well, I figured that. But who asked you to do it?"

"Doctor Long."

"And how did that come about?"

"He called me," another short response.

"As best you can, will you please relate the details of that conversation?"

"He just called me and asked me if I would do the autopsy of the brain of Jordon Mitchell."

"Just that simple?" Felbin pressed looking for more detail.

"Yes."

"And you knew the name Jordon Mitchell?"

"No. I had been out of the country and didn't have the benefit of any local news."

"And you didn't ask him who Jordon Mitchell was and why he was asking you to do this autopsy?"

"I'm not sure. I might have asked him those questions."

"Well, did you or did you not ask him those questions? I'm really not interested in wasting this jury's time by playing twenty questions with you until I hit on the right one to get the answer, Doctor."

Goodrich didn't object to Felbin's gratuitous comment, because he felt that the jury was probably becoming annoyed with the evasive responses.

"Yes, now that I think about it, I think I did."

"And what specifically was Doctor Long's response?"

"I believe he said that this was the case of the African American young man who allegedly died when he was struck in the head with a flashlight by a police officer."

"He made the statement about the flashlight causing the trauma before you even agreed to do the autopsy?"

"I believe so."

"Is it unusual for one expert witness to suggest a finding and a conclusion to another expert in the same case?"

"I don't believe Doctor Long was suggesting anything to me."

"You don't. You seriously don't. He didn't tell you a flashlight caused the skull fracture and the brain injury?"

"No. He said it was alleged."

"Did you ask him why he wanted you to do the autopsy and why he was not doing it himself?"

"He said he wanted another pair of eyes, given the media feeding frenzy and the racial tension associated with the case."

"Did you receive any phone calls from the circuit attorney?"

"Yes. She called to inquire how the case was proceeding."

That is exactly the answer he was hoping to get. "How many times?"

"Several. I wasn't counting," Dr. McHenry said, annoyed at this line of questions which had nothing to do with this case. This defendant was guilty, and she knew it. This lawyer needed to get on with it.

But Felbin didn't get on with it. "How the case was progressing? I don't understand. You were doing an autopsy of the brain which was going to take three to four weeks to complete. Did you tell her that?"

"Yes," McHenry said.

"Did you know Doctor Long also told her it would take three to four weeks to complete?" Felbin asked, intentionally repeating the time frame.

"No, I didn't know that."

"Did you know the circuit attorney charged Officer Decker with murder before your portion of the autopsy was completed?" Felbin asked, with a bit of disgust in his tone while shaking his head.

"Yes, I did know that," Dr. McHenry admitted, to Felbin's surprise.

"Let me see if I understand what you are telling this jury."

"Oh, I can't wait for your summary of what I'm saying, Felbin," McHenry said sarcastically, recognizing her familiarity and relationship with the defense lawyer.

"I'll give you the opportunity to disagree with anything I'm about to say. Not that you ever need an opportunity to disagree," Felbin said, continuing to spar with the witness.

"Thank you," McHenry said.

"As I was saying, if I understand your testimony correctly, Doctor Long injected the flashlight issue before you began your portion of the autopsy. The circuit attorney contacted you several times before you did the autopsy. And you knew the defendant had been charged with murdering Jordon Mitchell with a flashlight, also before you did the autopsy. And finally, you knew your friend, Doctor Long, was gun shy on the case and wanted your help. Is that correct?"

"Objection, your Honor, the question is compound and complex, plus it misstates the prior testimony of this witness," Goodrich injected.

"I think the doctor is smart enough to follow the question. And she is certainly not shy about correcting any misstatements," Felbin replied.

"Overruled. Please answer the question if you understand it, Doctor." the judge said.

"First of all, I never said Doctor Long was *gun shy,* as you say. I said that he wanted another pair of eyes. Second, I did know the other things you mentioned before I performed the autopsy, but those things had no bearing on my findings or my opinion."

"Whether those issues did or didn't influence your opinion is something this jury will ultimately decide. However, you would agree, would you not, that you knew before you did the autopsy that if you didn't conclude that the brain injury and cause of death were the result of blunt trauma with a linear object, you would torpedo the circuit attorney's case, which she started without the benefit of a completed autopsy?"

"I really didn't think of that."

"Well, I would ask you to please think of it now. If you didn't make a blunt trauma with a flashlight finding, this case is over, isn't that correct?"

"I don't know. I'm not a lawyer."

"Oh, come now, Doctor. You have testified in thousands of cases for the prosecution and you know what has to be proven. You know what your job is."

"To the extent the case is exclusively based on that finding, then I suppose the prosecution would not be able to meet its burden," Dr. McHenry said hesitatingly, realizing that for whatever reason, the prosecutor was not going to protect her from this line of questions with an objection.

"Did it strike you as just a little odd that the circuit attorney would decide to prosecute this case before the autopsy was completed when that was the most critical part of the case?"

"Again, Mister Felbin, that is not something I thought about. It is not part of my job. And again, as I said, I'm not a lawyer."

"If your opinion didn't support the theory of Ms. Cardwell, did it occur to you that she would be off the hook and you would be on that hook in an environment drowning with media attention fueled by racial discontent?"

"No, that never occurred to me," McHenry said, as she looked at Goodrich, almost begging for an objection.

Felbin knew he was not going to extract any concessions from McHenry, a professional prosecution witness. She was in it to protect the circuit attorney, not condemn her. But that was not the point. He needed to put his theory before the jury, and asking the question would inject the issue. The jury needed to understand the circuit attorney put this witness and Dr. Long in a no win situation. By charging this defendant with murder under a specific factual scenario, the pathologists were locked in. Felbin knew he would never sell the argument that these well-respected doctors were outright lying. Even he didn't believe that. Instead, he needed to create the impression that these medical experts needed to justify the flashlight, blunt object theory and ignore all else that collided with that theory. Felbin's goal in cross examining McHenry was to set up that collision; a collision that would become apparent when his experts testified. And create reasonable doubt.

Continuing with his cross examination, "Doctor McHenry did you look at all the autopsy photographs taken by Doctor Long?"

"Yes."

"Did you see this one?" Felbin asked handing the witness a photograph of the back of Mitchell's skull.

"Yes. I saw this one."

"The fracture line on the back of the skull is L-shaped. I assume that you noticed that. Is that significant in any respect in this case?"

"I didn't see it as perfectly L-shaped and didn't attach any significance to that configuration, other than it was a massive skull fracture."

McHenry knew where Felbin was going with this line of questioning and gave herself an escape route, anticipating the next question. But Felbin, sensing McHenry was prepared, decided against asking that question. Instead, he would rely on his own experts to describe the significance.

"When you examined the brain, both internally and externally, did you find anything of significance other than what you have already said?"

"Nothing other than what I have already testified to," McHenry confirmed.

"Beyond the brain bleed at the point of impact, did you find any other bruising or cerebral contusion anywhere else on the brain?"

"I did find some additional bruising to the right of the midline," McHenry admitted.

"Where specifically was that?"

"As I said, it was to the right of the midline, I can't be any more specific."

"Why can't you be more specific?" Felbin asked.

"Because I didn't think it was significant."

Unimpressed by her response, Felbin said, "Wait a minute. Isn't one of the purposes of an autopsy to document all observations and findings?"

"Certainly, the purpose is to document all relevant findings."

"Who decides what is relevant and irrelevant, you and you alone?"

"No. Anyone can decide that issue."

"Well, tell me, Doctor, how does anyone other than you decide that if it is not charted in the autopsy findings?"

"In the case of the brain autopsy I did, not only were the photographs available, but the actual brain itself was available for independent examination. In fact, it is my understanding your defense team had the brain itself independently examined."

Indeed, Felbin had his expert independently examine Mitchell's brain. However, the road to obtaining the body part was long and difficult. Initially and incredibly, Felbin's investigator was told the brain had been misplaced. The continued pursuit finally resulted in the production at the Medical Examiner's office in the city. Once the defense's examination of the brain was concluded, it was apparent to Felbin why essential and significant findings were excluded from the autopsy reports prepared by Long and McHenry. The chase to locate the brain for a defense examination became equally obvious.

Felbin had only a few more questions of Dr. McHenry. He laid the foundation he wanted without alerting the prosecutor of the road down which the defense would travel.

"At the location where you found the other bleed, did you find any external injury to the skull?"

"No."

"So you found only one fracture site and that was the one that lined up with the brain bleed on the right rear portion of the skull."

"That's correct."

With that, Felbin announced that he had no additional questions of the witness.

Over Felbin's objections, Goodrich reaffirmed McHenry's findings confirming that the cause of death was the result of a massive skull fracture caused by a flashlight; a flashlight that belonged to the defendant. Goodrich recognized that Felbin had successfully injected an issue, an inflammatory one at that. He needed a specific denial from McHenry. In so doing, he also recognized the danger of highlighting the defense theory. But, in balance, he needed to take the chance.

"Doctor McHenry, it has apparently been suggested by Mister Felbin that your findings and conclusions in this case are contrived to support the state's position that this defendant murdered Jordon by striking him in the head with a flashlight."

But before Goodrich could finish his question, Felbin was on his feet making a speaking objection.

"Objection. While I recognize this witness believes she is an authority on everything, supported by the facts or not, she didn't testify, nor could she testify, that this defendant did anything. Certainly, she can opine about medical findings, the accuracy of which this jury will decide, but she cannot testify who or what caused those injuries. She was asleep in her nice warm, safe bed, not on that roof like this police officer in the middle of a rainy night chasing burglars," Felbin said, interrupted with an objection from Goodrich.

Goodrich had made his point that Decker was a murderer. And Felbin countered again suggesting that this witness was a prosecution prostitute who didn't want to be confused by the facts of this case. The objection didn't matter to either lawyer. Both seized the opportunity to make a prejudicial speech in the presence of the jury. But the experienced trial judge ended the exchange by reprimanding both lawyers, overruling the objection and directing both to move on.

"Doctor McHenry, as I was saying, the defense has suggested your findings are designed to support the state's position that this defendant murdered Jordon with a flashlight. Is that the case?" Goodrich asked.

"Absolutely not. I don't have a horse in this race. I call them as I see them. As Mister Felbin well knows, I have been involved in many controversial cases, some with him, and I have always provided my opinion honestly and objectively, regardless of public opinion. In short, I really don't pay attention to what the media is reporting or what people are saying. The only thing that matters to me is what I see during an autopsy," the witness said, as she delivered her rehearsed response to the question she had known the prosecutor would be asking.

"No further questions, Your Honor," Goodrich announced.

"Doctor McHenry, I just have one question. In all the cases in which you have been involved, have you ever had a murder case where an individual was charged with murder before the autopsy was completed?" Felbin asked, taking a chance on the response from this dangerous witness.

"None come to mind immediately. Although, I cannot say that has never occurred," McHenry said, qualifying her response and always leaving an escape route.

Recognizing that was the best answer he was going to get from this professional prosecution witness, Felbin announced that he had no further questions.

With that announcement, Judge Bell announced the end of day four, with day five to begin at 10:00 a.m.

Chapter Fifty-Nine

Joan Cardwell had intentionally stayed out of the courtroom. She knew she would be a target of the defense and that her decision to charge Decker with murder before the autopsy was completed would be highlighted by the defense. She didn't want to sit in the courtroom only to have Felbin pointing at her in the presence of the jury as he conducted his cross examination of the state's witnesses. She also didn't want to be in a position to refuse comment when the reporters would invariably inquire about issues that arose during the trial. But she was definitely interested in how the day went. She recognized her political future was riding on the forensic pathologists and in particular, on the testimony of Dr. McHenry.

No sooner did Goodrich arrive in his office than Cardwell appeared at his door, seeking his perspective on the day's proceedings. She had been getting updates from her minions, who were monitoring every minute of the trial. But she wanted the viewpoint from the guy in the trenches.

"It went fine. McHenry handled the cross as we had rehearsed. She never lets you down," Goodrich said matter-of-factly.

"What do you mean, fine? Did she carry the day or not?" Cardwell pressed, insisting Goodrich take a position one way or the other.

"Overall, she did fine," he repeated. "But she had her moments," he added.

"What does that mean?" Cardwell asked in her normal demanding tone.

"It means Felbin scored some points on cross," Goodrich replied, clearly aggravated by her tone and attitude after a long and tiring day.

"What kind of points?"

"As we knew he would, he injected the idea that her opinion was designed to support our theory of the case. He also hit her pretty hard on your decision to charge murder before you had all the facts," Goodrich said, looking directly at Cardwell and emphasizing the point that this decision was hers and hers alone; a decision with which he obviously disagreed.

"I had all the facts I needed to charge this guy with murder. He hit that kid with that flashlight and we both know it," she said, her tone changing to anger.

"Joan, while this guy may be guilty of murder, we both know why you charged him at the time you did. We also both know the numerous conversations you had with McHenry before she performed her portion of that autopsy. And we know the nature of those conversations. So, at the end of the day, she performed," Goodrich said, as he turned away from his boss and waited for her response.

The circuit attorney knew what she had done and was smart enough not to debate this point with her prosecutor. After all, she still needed him to carry the day in the courtroom. She offered no rebuttal.

"But I believe he jury will find her credible, despite Felbin's efforts to discredit both you and her," Goodrich added after hearing no response to his previous confrontational commentary.

"That's good. You know how badly we need this conviction. Or I should say, how badly the city of Saint Louis needs this conviction. The city cannot withstand the fallout from another white police officer walking," Cardwell said.

Goodrich thought Cardwell had to be kidding. Did she think he was a total idiot? The only one who needed this conviction was Cardwell, in order to preserve her political ambitions. The city would survive, but she wouldn't. He also knew he could not say that, but he could certainly think it. He had no doubt someday he would be appearing before Judge Cardwell. Unfortunately, he would have played a role in helping her achieve her goal. *And that might very well be at the expense of an innocent man,* he thought. From the start he didn't want to be involved in this prosecution for a variety of reasons.

Since his compelled participation, he was beginning to question the guilt of the defendant. There were a lot of unanswered questions. A substantial number of those questions centered on the issue of whether the pathologists were credible and whether their opinions were genuine. He knew that charging murder before the autopsy was completed was not right. He also knew Dr. McHenry, and to a lesser extent Dr. Long, were evasive when responding to Felbin's questions, particularly in the area of prior conversations between themselves and his boss. But he was a prosecutor and had a job to do. The issue of who was telling the truth was for the jury, not him.

"I'm aware of all that's at stake here, Joan, including a man's life. Now if you'll excuse me, I have to get some things done for tomorrow," Goodrich said, hoping this discussion was over.

"Let us know if you need anything. You are doing a great job and the city is relying on you," Cardwell said as she left his office.

Chapter Sixty

Also closely monitoring the trial was the St. Louis Police Department. The Chief, as much of a politician as the circuit attorney, knew full well he would have to answer to both the Board of Police Commissioners and the public should the case go in the same direction as Cannon's. Internal Affairs investigators Bryant and Cantrell were assigned to monitor the trial. They reported the day's developments to Lt. Col. Winston, the head of Internal Affairs, who in turn reported to Chief Rodgers. But this day was different. The Chief didn't want the report through the typical chain of command, but rather directly from Bryant and Cantrell. When the detectives entered his office, the Chief didn't waste any time exchanging social pleasantries. He got right to the point.

"Are we kicking Felbin's ass over there?" he asked.

"I wouldn't say we are kicking his ass. He is scoring some points, but we are doing okay," Bryant said.

"What do you mean, *we are doing okay?*" the Chief demanded.

"He is making a big deal out of the fact that Cardwell brought the murder charge before the autopsy was completed. Basically, he is telling the jury you can't accuse someone of murder, until you conclusively know the cause of death."

"How is the jury reacting?"

"Hard to tell. No reaction from anyone on anything that is said. They have pretty good poker faces. But personally, I think his argument makes sense. I think she jumped the gun."

"The news coverage seems to be leaning in that direction as well," Winston said, breaking his silence.

"I don't know what Felbin has up his sleeve. But you know he is going to do something. He always does," Bryant added.

"What do you think he is going to do?" Rodgers asked.

"I haven't the slightest idea."

"What does Goodrich think Felbin is going to do?"

"He doesn't know either. He said he had some national big shot expert endorsed as a witness."

"What kind of an expert?" Rodgers asked.

"A pathologist who has testified in some national high profile cases and has a regular television show on HBO dealing with autopsies. Apparently, this guy is well-known and very well-respected."

"You mean Goodrich does not know what this big shot is going to tell this jury?"

"He doesn't have a clue; other than he figures the guy will say something to contradict the testimony of McHenry and Long"

"What the fuck!" the Chief screamed. "You mean to tell me he didn't take the guy's deposition?"

"No, because apparently he was endorsed late and the circuit attorney could not afford to go to New York to take his deposition. And Cardwell couldn't afford to pay his expert witness fee for the deposition. He charges something like $5,000 for a deposition."

"And, of course, I assume she didn't come to us looking for some money," Rodgers said, looking at Winston for a response.

"Not that I know of," Winston replied.

"How did McHenry do?" Rodgers asked, moving away from the issue of whether the prosecution was prepared.

"As she always does. She never lets the facts get in the way of a good story, as they say. But in the end, she dazzles them with her bullshit," Bryant said.

"Are we going to win this thing?" Chief Rodgers asked, looking directly at Bryant.

"I think we are looking good. But you know as well as I do, anything can happen in a jury trial and this one is far from over."

"Should we put a contingency plan in place, just in case this thing goes south?" Rodgers asked Winston.

"What do you have in mind?"

"Well, we know even if this guy is acquitted, we are not going to keep him. Should we prepare and serve the internal charges now? That will give us some separation from

Cardwell. It will also suggest we had no confidence in her from the start. We knew we had to clean up her mistakes with our own internal prosecution, at least to prevent him from working as a police officer ever again. Obviously, if she does her job and gets a conviction, we won't have to pursue internal charges, because convicted felons can't be police officers. Plus, he won't be doing much police work from the penitentiary."

"I can do that. I would think we need a charge of physical abuse, excessive force, violation of the deadly force rule, false reporting, a catch-all of conduct unbecoming and failing to obey a direct order," Winston explained.

"What is the direct order violation?" Rodgers asked.

"That would be the order we gave him to come into the office so we could arrest him. His asshole lawyer told us to pound sand and would not produce him until he could get a bond set and the money in place. Felbin figured out we had an arrest warrant and that's why we wanted him to come in."

"Should we leak the charges to the media?" Rodgers asked.

"No. I don't think we should do anything that might screw this thing up, because then she can blame us for the loss. I'll prepare the charges and send them to Felbin. He said he would accept service," Winston said.

"Okay, but I think we should have a press release ready for the day the verdict comes back. Actually, we need two releases; one if there is a conviction and one if there is not."

"I'll draft some charges and get something to you in the morning for service on Felbin by tomorrow evening."

Chapter Sixty-One

"Call your next witness." The court directed the prosecutor to start day five of the trial. Some of the morning was filled with Internal Affairs investigators identifying evidentiary items such as scene photographs, items seized from the defendant including his flashlight, utility belt and clothing worn that night. The investigators also identified the clothing worn by Mitchell. After the investigators concluded their testimony, the prosecutor announced that Police Officer Jake Corbett would be his next witness.

While maintaining a poker face, Felbin knew this testimony was not going to be helpful; at least not at the beginning. However, Felbin was confident when he completed his cross examination, Corbett would be identified as the liar he was. What he didn't know was how his somewhat naïve client would react. Bobby Decker had been in a state of depression since the start of this case, to such an extent that Felbin thought about having a doctor prescribe some medication. But he decided against that course for fear any drug-induced state would limit Bobby's ability to understand and assist during the trial. Bobby showed no emotion when Corbett's name was called.

After familiarizing the jury with his background, Goodrich walked Corbett through his role on the rooftop. There were no surprises. His testimony was consistent with the story Decker told. He admitted he didn't see Decker strike Mitchell, as he was busy dealing with Daniels Jones. *At least he didn't lie about that*, Felbin thought.

"After the suspects were in custody and while still on the roof, did the defendant request an ambulance?" Goodrich asked.

"Yes."

"Did you know why the defendant requested an ambulance?"

"No."

"Did you ask him why he requested the ambulance?"

"No, I didn't ask him why he requested the ambulance. I asked him what happened."

"And what did he say?"

Ordinarily, that question would require the witness to testify as to what someone else said, which is hearsay and inadmissible as evidence. The jury would never hear the answer if there was a timely objection. But when the statement is attributed to a party, in this case the defendant, it is deemed to be an admission against interest and admissible as an exception to the hearsay rule. Felbin decided not to highlight the response with an objection he knew would be overruled.

"He said he didn't know what happened."

"You're telling us when you asked this defendant while you were on that roof what happened to cause him to request an ambulance, he said he *didn't know what happened?*"

"That's correct."

"Did you think that was odd?"

Felbin's objection was quickly sustained.

"The suspect you arrested didn't need an ambulance, did he?"

"No, sir."

"Did you look at Jordon to see if he was injured?"

"Yes, sir."

"And what did you see?"

"I didn't see any injury. The suspect was lying on his back and it appeared he was unconscious."

"Did you check any further to see if he was injured?"

"No, I didn't. He was not moving, but he was breathing. I knew an ambulance had been called and I thought it would be best if the EMTs assessed the situation. Mister Mitchell didn't appear to me like he needed any immediate assistance."

"Well, if he didn't need any immediate assistance, do you know what would have prompted the defendant to call for an ambulance?"

"No, sir, I don't."

"Did you participate in the preparation of the police report?"

"Yes."

"Did you prepare it together with the defendant?"

"Yes, I did."

"Exactly how did that work?"

"We discussed what happened on the roof in order to be accurate and then we just wrote the report."

"The report, then, is a collaborative effort with both of you providing input?"

"That's correct."

"Let's talk about the conversation that you had with the defendant during the process of preparing this report. In that context, was there any discussion about how the massive fracture on the back of this young man's skull occurred?"

"Yes, I already told you about that conversation," Corbett said.

"No, I'm talking about when you and the defendant were preparing the report, not any conversation on the roof. Do you understand the question?" Goodrich pressed.

"Yes, I understand."

"Then please answer it," Goodrich said, a touch of irritation in his voice. Corbett knew exactly what he was being asked.

"He wanted to write it in to write it out," he said, his voice lowered as he spoke.

"What does that mean? And please keep your voice up, so the jury can hear you."

This is quite a show, Felbin thought in anticipation of the perjured testimony to come. *This guy is pretending he does not want to throw a fellow officer under the bus, but is compelled to tell the truth, the whole truth and nothing but the truth, regardless of who it hurts.* Felbin finished his thought, wondering how this Corbett slept at night.

"Officer Decker wanted to write the report in a way that justified his use of force that resulted in the fractured skull the suspect sustained."

"Did you agree with that approach?"

"No. I objected to it and said I would not be a party to it, because it wasn't the truth," Corbett said, looking directly at the jury when he spoke.

As Corbett was speaking, Felbin glanced at Bobby. Although he was maintaining his poker face, Felbin could see Bobby was feeling the pain of these lies. But all would soon be well, at least as far as the trial was concerned. Bobby was a different story.

"Hang in there," Felbin whispered in Bobby's ear.

"Okay," Decker replied, although clearly upset by what he was hearing. A fellow police officer was on the witness stand lying to save himself at the expense of someone else. It was surreal.

"Let me hand you what has been marked as Exhibit 5 in this case and ask you if you recognize that document." Goodrich continued.

"Yes. This is the police report we prepared."

"Is that a true and accurate copy of that police incident report detailing the events at the pawn shop during the early morning hours of April 24?"

When the witness answered in the affirmative, Goodrich asked the court to receive it as evidence. Without objection from the defense, the document was received into evidence.

"And I notice there is no explanation how Jordon Mitchell sustained his skull fracture, is that correct?" Goodrich said.

"Yes. That is correct. There is nothing in here regarding that issue, because Officer Decker told me he didn't know how that happened," Corbett volunteered.

When the prosecutor announced he had no additional questions, the judge decided this would be a good time to take the luncheon recess.

After the jury left the court room, Bobby, visibly shaken, said, "I can't believe he said that stuff."

His mother and brother sat in the audience, stunned by what they heard. His brother, head in hands, said nothing to his mother, who was staring at the courtroom wall.

"Don't worry, this will be fine. We will discredit him," Felbin said, in an effort to console his client.

Felbin didn't share with Bobby the approach he intended to use in cross examining Corbett. He knew his client was terribly depressed by the entire ordeal. He also knew the most difficult part of the trial would come if Corbett continued to lie. For Bobby Decker, the police department was his home; his fellow officers were his brothers and sisters. It was more than a job; it was his life. Given his relationship with his father, who still hadn't attended the trial, perhaps the Department was more his family than his real family. Felbin recognized the thought of Corbett testifying falsely, outright lying, would be reprehensible to Bobby, and he avoided a discussion of the topic as much as he could in preparing for the trial.

Chapter Sixty-Two

"Is there any doubt in your mind, Officer Corbett, that you didn't see Officer Decker strike Jordon Mitchell with a flashlight?" Felbin said as he began his cross examination of the witness.

"There is no doubt," Corbett quickly replied.

"Did you see Officer Decker strike Jordon Mitchell with any object?"

"No, sir."

"Did you hear anything that sounded like a blow or a striking?" Felbin asked, knowing this question could be dangerous as he didn't know how this liar would respond.

Generally, trial lawyers avoid questions for which they don't already have the answers. But there are exceptions. Felbin thought this was worth taking a chance because, had the witness heard a striking, he would have documented that someplace and certainly would have been asked that question by the prosecutor during his direct examination.

"No, sir," another quick response from the witness.

"Now, you claimed Officer Decker suggested the report be written in a way that would have justified the use of force, *write it in to write it out,* as you say. Is that correct?"

"Yes, that is correct."

"And you are sure it was Officer Decker who suggested that and not yourself?"

"I'm sure," another quick response.

"Let's talk about the mechanics of how police reports are prepared. Are they computer-generated?"

"Yes."

"And as I understand it, you type it into a computer as a rough draft and then only the author can view the document or make the changes. Is that correct? And please forgive me as I'm technologically challenged and I don't know all the technical terms. But is that basically what happens?" Felbin asked.

"Yes, that is what happens. However, I'm sure probably some supervisors can access the documents, if necessary. But I'm really not sure of that one way or another"

"So, in this case, did both you and Officer Decker prepare your respective versions of the report?"

"Yes."

"And that was so you could then compare those drafts and then ultimately combine them into one report. Is that how it worked?"

"Yes, sir."

"Now this suggestion you claim Officer Decker made about justifying a use of force on Mister Mitchell, was that verbal or in writing?"

"No. It was verbal. It was a very short conversation before we began preparing our reports in rough draft."

"You have identified state's Exhibit 5 as the final version of the police report in this case, is that correct?"

"Correct."

"I'm going to show you what has been marked as Defense Exhibit A and ask you if you can identify this document," Felbin said after allowing the prosecutor to view it.

"It appears to be Officer Decker's rough draft."

"And you know that because Officer Decker showed you a copy when you were working on the report. Is that correct?"

"Yes."

"Now please take a moment and compare Exhibit A with Exhibit 5," Felbin directed.

"They look like they are the same."

"Not only do they look like they are the same, but they are identical. Isn't that correct?"

After taking a few minutes to again compare the documents, Corbett said, "Yes."

"Now I want to be sure about one thing. You are positive it was Officer Decker who suggested the report be written in a way that justified the use of force and Mister Mitchell's injury, is that correct? And before you answer, I'll remind you that you are under oath."

"Yes, I'm positive. And I don't have to be reminded I'm under oath, Mister Felbin." Corbett said confidently, appearing annoyed about the reference to his oath and the inference that he was being less than truthful.

"Now, you said you didn't witness anything Officer Decker was doing with his suspect because you were busy taking care of your own suspect, is that correct?"

"Yes. That is correct."

"Well, let me ask you this, sir. If you were focusing on the cuffing and arrest of your suspect and didn't witness what was going on with Officer Decker and his suspect, why would he need your approval to write the report the way you claim he suggested?"

After a long pause, Corbett said, "I don't know. I guess he wanted me to be a witness and corroborate the use of force by saying I saw the resistance."

"But while that would have been nice, I suppose, he really could have written the report the way you say he suggested on that so-called *write it in to write it out* thing without your eye witness corroboration and concurrence, isn't that true?"

"I suppose so."

"Now, let me hand you what I have marked as Defense Exhibit B and ask you if you recognize that," Felbin said, but this time without first allowing the prosecutor to review it.

Goodrich was immediately on his feet demanding to see the document Felbin just handed the witness.

"Mister Felbin, please show Mister Goodrich the document," the judge directed.

After quickly scanning a copy of the same document Felbin had given to the witness, Goodrich asked to approach the bench for a conversation with the judge outside the presence of the jury. "This is a sandbag. I never saw this document before. He didn't provide it in discovery. He should not be allowed to use it. It is inflammatory and prejudicial to the state. We don't even know if it's accurate," Goodrich said, finishing his rambling diatribe, clearly upset and off his game.

"What do you have to say?" the judge asked Felbin.

"First of all, I just got the document. Secondly, I didn't expect this witness to testify the way he did. That was a complete surprise to me. At the moment, I'm merely going to use it to refresh his recollection that he was mistaken about his prior testimony that the defendant was the one who suggested the report contain a justification for the use of force. I don't intend to offer it in evidence, at least not at this time, and therefore, I didn't have to disclose it."

Goodrich knew he had been had. Felbin knew the discovery rules and was now going to use that knowledge as a sword, rather than a shield. There was nothing he could do to stop him.

"I do believe this is a sandbag. But I'm afraid the rules are going to permit you to get away with this, Mister Felbin. Do you have any other surprises for us?" Judge Bell said, clearly annoyed.

Thinking better of arguing with the judge's characterization, Felbin simply replied in the negative.

"Ask your next question," Judge Bell directed.

"Officer Corbett, I believe I asked you if you can identify Exhibit B, the document you have in your hand and presumably had enough time to look at."

"It looks like another rough draft of the report," Corbett said after a long pause. Apparently, he hadn't figured out how he was going to handle the issue he knew was coming, while the lawyers were at the bench with the judge.

"Not just another rough draft. That is the draft that *you* prepared, isn't that correct?" Felbin asked, pointing his finger at the witness, his voice emphasizing the word *you.*

Corbett, his face flushed, sat there just staring at the document.

"Please read the document and take your time," Felbin said, knowing the witness was on the ropes.

As Corbett began to turn the pages, Felbin glanced at the prosecutor, whose eyes were fixed on his witness. This was going to be a disaster, and Goodrich knew it. Clearly, his witness had lied to him. And there was nothing he could do about it now. The witness was on his own.

"Yes, that looks like the draft I prepared," Corbett finally admitted.

"Does that document you prepared contain language justifying the need to use force on Mister Mitchell by Officer Decker; force that resulted in a fractured skull?"

"Yes," Corbett quickly and forcefully responded with an obvious change of demeanor. "I prepared that draft at the direction of Officer Decker," Corbett added without waiting for another question. Always a problem when witnesses try to explain a lie with another lie.

"Well, I thought you just told us your conversation with Officer Decker about the justification for the use of force was only verbal," Felbin challenged.

"I forgot about that report. But now that you showed it to me, I remember."

"Let me see if I understand this, Officer Corbett. Your discussion with Officer Decker on this topic was verbal and in writing, contrary to what you just told us a few minutes ago, with you preparing Exhibit B at the direction of Officer Decker. Is my understanding of your testimony accurate?"

"Yes."

"Before, you made it sound like you were morally outraged when you said Officer Decker made this suggestion to tell a story which would not be true. Were you morally outraged by the suggestion?"

"I didn't want to do that," Corbett said.

"Were you morally outraged?" Felbin repeated.

"Yes."

"But you were not morally outraged to the extent that you refused to prepare Exhibit B, is that correct?"

"I didn't say I would agree to this language as part of the final report," Corbett said, now arguing with Felbin. Another lie to cover up the first two.

Goodrich was now looking for a place to have his eyes land. This was worse than a disaster. This guy had been a defendant. Now, after that murder charge magically disappeared, he shows up as a lying state's witness. He knew exactly where Felbin was headed with this.

"Did your verbal refusal to participate in this fabrication come before or after you prepared Exhibit B?"

"I don't remember."

"Well, if you were not going to incorporate this into the original report, why would you prepare the draft such as you did?"

"Because I was trying to help a fellow officer."

"By preparing a false report?"

After hearing no response, Felbin pressed the witness to answer the question.

"I didn't say that I would have agreed to put it in the final report," Corbett finally said.

"Then why prepare the draft with this language in it at all?"

"As I said, I was helping a fellow officer. It was up to him whether or not he wanted to include that in the report."

"You mean if he wanted to include your language, it would be up to Officer Decker," Felbin said.

"Yes."

"Well, Officer Corbett, if that is the case, can you explain why Officer Decker's rough draft does not contain any explanation whatsoever as to how Mister Mitchell may have sustained his injury?"

Although the question was objectionable because Felbin was asking this witness to speculate on why another person did or didn't do something, Goodrich wanted to distance himself from this witness. Objecting to the question would make it seem to the jury like he was trying to protect the witness. Not only did he have no interest in protecting this guy, but he was praying for a quick end to this slaughter.

"I have no idea," was Corbett's terse response.

"If Officer Decker wanted to make up a reason why he had to strike Mister Mitchell, can you explain why he could not have done that himself? Why would he need you to do that for him?" Felbin asked realizing Goodrich was not about to object to yet another improper question.

"Perhaps because he wanted to see how I would handle the issue."

"Did Officer Decker ever show you a draft he had created in which he justified the use of force and Mister Mitchell's injury?"

"No."

"Did he ever verbally share with you any ideas he had about how the striking of Mitchell could be justified?"

"No."

"So the only one who made up a story about how Officer Decker could justify striking Mister Mitchell in the head, was you. Is that correct?"

"I don't know what Officer Decker did," was Corbett's non-responsive response.

"Mister Corbett . . ."

"That's Officer Corbett," the witness injected.

"For the moment, it's Officer Corbett . . ."

This time Goodrich was on his feet before Felbin could complete his question. His objection was sustained with a stern warning to Felbin from a judge, who was clearly agitated both with the witness and the question.

"Sir, let me ask you this question. Did you know the circuit attorney had originally announced she expected to prosecute you along with Officer Decker for the murder of Jordon Mitchell?"

Here it comes, Goodrich thought as he moved to the edge of his chair, ready to object. He knew he had to protect his boss from the inference that Felbin was about create, particularly because he didn't know how this witness would respond. This guy was a wild card at the moment. No telling what he would say to protect himself.

"No, I didn't know that."

"Wait a minute. You didn't know you were targeted for a murder prosecution?"

"No."

"You were arrested for the murder of Jordon Mitchell, were you not, Officer Corbett?"

"Yes," Corbett said, hoping that this line of questions and for that matter, all questions, would soon end.

"You were arrested for murder, but you didn't think the circuit attorney was going to prosecute you?" the question slightly different from the original.

"I didn't hear her announce that she was going to prosecute me," Corbett said responding to Felbin's original question.

"Regardless of whether you heard her say that, when you were arrested, at that point you thought you were going to be prosecuted for murder, did you not, *Officer* Corbett?"

"Yes."

"Can you explain to this jury, why you are not a defendant? What changed between the time you were arrested for murder and today?"

"I don't know."

"Isn't it true that you made a deal with the circuit attorney that she would not prosecute you in exchange for the incredible testimony you provided here today?"

"No, that is not true."

"Tell us, *Officer* Corbett, what conversation did either you or your lawyer have with the circuit attorney regarding your prosecution for murder?"

This was clearly hearsay and inadmissible. It was an out of court statement by a third person who could not be cross examined. Goodrich needed to make a split second decision whether an objection would do him more harm than good. He decided to object. The judge concurred. The question would not be answered, allowing the jury to speculate as to the response. That was good enough for Felbin.

"Well, I suppose we will have to wait and see whether the honorable circuit attorney pursues criminal perjury charges against you. Can't wait for that," Felbin said.

While Goodrich was flying out of his seat, the judge already began his reprimand, the second in a matter of a few minutes.

"Mister Felbin, I warned you. There won't be another warning. That comment is inappropriate and will be ordered stricken," Judge Bell said.

"That's all the questions I have," Felbin announced.

"Does the State have any redirect?" the judge inquired.

Thinking he could do nothing to clean up this train wreck, Goodrich declined the judge's invitation to ask additional questions, content to get Corbett off the witness stand. With that, the judge declared a recess for the day.

Chapter Sixty-Three

Despite the collapse of a key prosecution witness, the mood in the vehicle on the ride back to the office was somber. Actually, there was no conversation at all. Bobby just stared out the window with a blank look on his face. When he left the courtroom, he spoke to no one and went directly to the car.

On his way out of the courthouse, Felbin was stopped by Bobby's mother. After congratulating him on the cross examination and ultimate destruction of Officer Corbett, she inquired about her son's mental health. Felbin responded by expressing his concern that Bobby's state of mental health was deteriorating. He pointed out that this was the worst day thus far, given the false testimony of Corbett, a fellow officer and friend. He promised to talk to Bobby once they returned to the office to get a more complete picture. Before departing, Felbin suggested a reconciliation with his father would go a long way to improve Bobby's state of mind. Mrs. Decker didn't respond.

The atmosphere in the Circuit Attorney's office was less than congenial. The word about Corbett's performance had arrived before Goodrich. Immediately upon his arrival, he was summoned to the circuit attorney's office where Cardwell, along with her First Assistant, Karen Braxton and her confidant and advisor, Carol Masterson, awaited his arrival.

"What the hell happened over there with Corbett?" Cardwell shouted as soon as Goodrich entered the room.

"Corbett said it was Decker's idea to make up a reason that he had to hit Mitchell in the head. He said this was a verbal conversation he had with Decker and there was nothing in writing. I guess he thought he could not be contradicted with a conversation no one witnessed. If Decker testifies and denies the conversation, then it is his word against Decker's. No big deal. The plan went south when Felbin produced a draft of the police report Corbett had prepared. In it, Corbett tried to justify the use of force after he said the idea was Decker's and that he didn't want to be a party to it. Felbin destroyed him. As he always does, he led him down the path. Locked him into statements he knew he could refute with a written document. He led the lamb to the slaughter," Goodrich said.

"And we didn't know about that? Are you fucking kidding me? And that son of a bitch Felbin not only knew about the report, but he had a copy of it. How did that happen?" Cardwell said again shouting.

"It happened because our witness was dishonest with both you and me. It's that simple. And his client still has friends in the Department who obviously don't like this prosecution."

"We made a deal with this guy that we would not prosecute him for murder in exchange for what, testimony that falls apart because he lied to us?" Cardwell said.

"Not only did he lie about that, but he also lied to the court when he testified that we had no deal with him on the murder charge."

"How the hell did that come up? Felbin?"

"Yes."

"I assume you made no effort to correct that denial," Cardwell said, this time with a lowered voice.

"No, I didn't."

"Good. Keep it that way," Cardwell directed.

Goodrich didn't respond, but simply stared at his boss. He knew he had an ethical duty to bring that false testimony to the attention of the court. He also knew after this case was over, he needed to find another job.

When they arrived at the office, Felbin asked Bobby to come in for a few minutes because he needed to talk to him. Bobby, who had yet to speak, just nodded.

"Bobby, what is on your mind? You haven't spoken a single word since we left the courthouse," Felbin began, once inside the privacy of his office.

Bobby didn't react or respond to the question, but simply stared out the window.

"Bobby, look at me. You need to talk to me," Felbin pressed.

Still no answer.

"Is it Corbett and his testimony?"

"Yes," he finally said.

"Are you upset because you didn't think a friend and a colleague would do that to you?" Felbin asked, attempting to get his client to open up.

"I can't believe any of this is happening," Bobby said as he began to cry.

"Listen. We will get through this," Felbin said, hoping to provide a little comfort.

"And then what happens after the trial, regardless of whether we win or lose? Where do I go from here, if not to the penitentiary?"

"You have to take this one day at a time, Bobby. Today and tomorrow, we are fighting and waging a war in the courtroom; a war that I plan to win. What comes after that, we will deal with it, whatever it might be."

"My Department criminally prosecuted me. The city turned its back on me. I lost the woman I love. My father doesn't speak to me. And now, a fellow police officer has not only testified against me, but he lied to protect his own self-interests. How can I survive that, assuming I'm able to beat the criminal charge?"

"First of all, your Department didn't prosecute you; a circuit attorney did. A circuit attorney with a political agenda who wants to be a judge, with you standing in the way of that goal. Second, I'm sure the same circuit attorney had a hand in shaping the testimony of Corbett. Finally, we are not going to do a pity party here, because you'll survive quite well after this ordeal ends. You are going to be fine and this will be nothing more than a bad dream. In the meantime, you need to focus on what is ahead of us. I need your help and possibly your testimony before this thing ends. Do you understand?"

Bobby nodded.

"No, Bobby. Speak to me and tell me you get it. I don't want just a nod of your head," Felbin said, looking his client squarely in the eyes while holding and squeezing his left arm.

"I understand," Bobby said, without elaboration.

After Bobby left the office, Felbin was concerned enough about his client's state of mental health that he called his mother. He shared with her his concerns and again, encouraged her to reunite father and son.

When Felbin completed his call, his secretary handed him an envelope. It was from the Internal Affairs Division of the St. Louis Police Department. He didn't have to open it. He knew what was inside. Felbin had been down this road many times with other officers he had represented in criminal prosecutions. The Department had served charges and specifications seeking his client's termination, even before the verdict in the criminal case was in. Bastards! As expected, the Department was going to fire Decker, regardless of the outcome of the criminal case.

Obviously, if there was a conviction, it would be easy, as convicted felons cannot be police officers. However, if he was acquitted, there would be another public trial, this time before the Board of Police Commissioners, who would decide whether he kept his job. Felbin had little confidence in the objectivity of this board, particularly given the publicity and racial tension. He had even less confidence in the ability of Bobby Decker to withstand another trial, given his fragile mental state.

Chapter Sixty-Four

The State's next and final witness was not only a surprise, but so unexpected that it had the potential to send Bobby Decker over the mental cliff. When the prosecutor announced the name of this witness to start day 6, Bobby looked as though someone had kicked him in the stomach, knocking the wind out of him. Fighting for a breath and control of his emotions, he didn't even hear Felbin's question, asking him if he knew what this witness might say.

"Please state your name," Goodrich began.

"Kathy Adams."

"What is your business or occupation?"

"I'm an attorney."

"Where are you employed?"

"I'm employed by the circuit attorney's office as an assistant circuit attorney."

"In other words, you are a prosecutor and work in the office bringing this prosecution."

"Yes."

Felbin knew any objection or protest he made to the testimony of this surprise witness would be overruled and it would further serve to highlight the testimony and appear the defendant had something he was afraid of. So, he held his breath and waited for the axe to fall. She was the last witness and usually the prosecutor saved the best for last.

"What is your relationship to the defendant?"

"He is a friend," she said as she lowered her voice.

"Are you involved in an intimate relationship with the defendant?" Goodrich pressed.

"We were at one time, but no longer," Adams said, almost apologetically.

"Do you love him?"

"I did at one time."

"Does that mean you are no longer in love with him?"

"Yes," she said attempting to avoid any eye contact with Bobby.

Certain her statement would be received like a knife thrust into his heart, Felbin looked at Bobby to measure his reaction. Tears might not have necessarily been a bad thing, but the shock was so great that his eyes remained completely dry and fixed on the witness. The inference was obvious and devastating. She was a prosecutor and he was a murderer. She could not love a man who was guilty of the crime of murder; murdering an innocent young black man, no less.

"Did you live together?"

"Yes."

"Do you still live together?"

"No."

Another obvious and devastating inference. She could not live with or stand to be in the company of a murderer.

"Did you move out or did he?"

"I did."

"Was that before or after April 24?"

"It was after April 24," she said, again studying the witness table.

"During the time you were together after April 24, was there any conversation about Jordon Mitchell's massive skull fracture?"

"Yes," she said, this time looking at Goodrich and continuing to avoid all eye contact with her former lover.

"Please tell the jury about that conversation."

Again Felbin decided that an objection would be overruled because, although hearsay, the statement was as an admission against interest by the defendant, an exception to the hearsay rule.

"While Mister Mitchell was in intensive care, I asked Bobby how the skull fracture occurred and he said he didn't know. I then pressed him for an explanation, because I couldn't believe he would not know how an injury of this massive proportion could happen without him knowing," she said, this time looking at the jurors as she spoke.

This time Felbin was on his feet objecting that her beliefs were not relevant and her answer was not responsive to the question of what conversation occurred. His objection was sustained and the jury instructed to disregard her answer, a task similar to unringing a bell or putting smoke back in a bag.

"Please, Ms. Adams, just tell us about the conversation," Goodrich repeated.

"I'm sorry. Let me clarify. I told him I could not believe he would not know how an injury of this proportion occurred while this suspect was in his custody. He just repeated that he didn't know how the injury occurred. I told him no one would believe that and he just said, *I know.*"

With that devastating response, Goodrich announced he had no other questions. Rather than ask for a recess to figure out how he would counter this testimony, Felbin decided to go right at it.

"I noticed, Ms. Adams, that at no time during your testimony did you look at Bobby. Is that because you are ashamed that you chose your job over a man you loved?" Felbin asked while shaking his head and making no secret of his disdain for this witness and her testimony.

Goodrich's objection that the question was argumentative was sustained. Actually, Felbin really wasn't looking for a response which would clearly be self-serving, but rather was content to plant the seed with the jury in the form of the question.

"Well, let me ask it this way, Ms. Adams. Your relationship with Bobby was well-known in your office, isn't that true?"

"Yes."

"And it was known to your boss, Joan Cardwell, isn't that also true?"

"Yes."

"Are you telling us your decision to move out had nothing to do with your concern about displeasing the circuit attorney?"

"No, I'm not saying that. But . . ."

"Thank you. You answered the question," Felbin said interrupting the last part of her answer and attempting to keep the witness on a short leash. Felbin knew this witness, an experienced trial lawyer, could hurt him if the questions were not narrowly tailored to elicit specific responses.

"You were in the circuit attorney's office after the Sergeant Cannon case, were you not?"

"Yes."

Goodrich wasn't sure where Felbin was going with this. He knew that every chance he got, Felbin would spin this prosecution as a payback for the Cannon loss. He also needed to dispel the inference that she didn't want to have a relationship with a murderer. But Goodrich also knew Felbin had to be careful. He didn't want to alienate the black members of the jury. Nor did he want to suggest that a cop got away with the criminal assault of a mentally-challenged black man.

"And so you were aware of the criticism directed at your boss, Ms. Cardwell, by the black community for her handling of that Cannon case, isn't that true?"

"Yes."

"And you were also aware that this case, which was coming on the heels of Cannon, also involved a white police officer and a black suspect."

"Yes."

"And are you telling this jury the Cannon case and, in particular the fallout from that matter, and the embarrassment to your boss, didn't enter your mind when you decided to part company with Bobby?"

"When you ask it that way, I'm really not sure. Perhaps subconsciously it did, but I'm not really sure."

"Let me ask this, Ms. Adams. When you moved out of the place where you and Bobby were living, did you tell the circuit attorney you had moved and no longer were living with Bobby?"

"Yes, I believe I did," Adams replied.

"Did she ask or did you go to her and volunteer that information?"

"I went to her."

"Why did you do that?" Felbin asked. Always dangerous for a lawyer to ask the *why* question without knowing the answer. But with this witness, Felbin thought he had to take a calculated risk.

"Because I thought she would want to know."

"Isn't it true, Ms. Adams, that you went to her because you knew she would be upset if you stayed with Bobby, particularly in light of the criticism in the Cannon case? In other words, did you move out to protect the image of your boss, Ms. Cardwell?"

"I thought she had a right to know," she said, avoiding the question.

"Did you go to her and tell her you were moving in with Bobby?"

"No. that was my personal business."

"Well, if moving in was your personal business, why was moving out also not your personal business?"

"I really don't have an answer for that. Or, at least not one you'll accept, Mister Felbin."

"Oh, I think we both know the answer, Ms. Adams," Felbin said quickly asking the next question to avoid the objection. "You moved out after this incident, correct?"

"Yes."

"You said you told him that no one would believe him when he said he didn't know how this injury occurred."

"Yes, that is what I told him."

"Do you have any personal knowledge as you sit here today of how this injury occurred?"

"No."

"You said you were in love with Bobby at one time," Felbin said, having moved behind his client forcing her to look at Bobby when she answered the question.

"Yes."

"How long were you together?"

"About three years.

"During that time, you were partners who relied upon each other, isn't that true?"

"Yes, it is," she said looking at Felbin, who was still positioned directly behind his client.

"During that time, did you also confide in one another?"

"Yes," Adams said, uncertain of where Felbin was heading with this line of questions.

"After the Cannon trial, did you tell Bobby Cardwell's judgeship was in jeopardy and she would have to kiss the asses of a lot of black politicians to get it back on track?" Felbin said, taking a shot in the dark.

"Objection. That would call for a hearsay response and the question is also argumentative. He needs to ask questions, not argue with the witness," Goodrich said.

"It is not hearsay, because I'm asking this witness what she said, not what someone else said," Felbin replied.

"Regardless of whether it is hearsay, it is argumentative. Restate your question," Judge Bell directed.

"Did you tell Bobby, the man you loved, that Cardwell would have to curry favor with a lot of black politicians to get her judgeship back on track after the Cannon disaster?"

"I don't think I said that," she said leaving the door open for another question.

"Do you deny making that statement or one similar?"

"No. I just don't remember."

"You are not saying you didn't make that statement. You are simply saying that you have no present recollection of making that specific statement."

"That's correct."

"Is that because you have made so many statements critical of her for improperly using her office to curry political favor for her judgeship, that you don't remember this one specifically?"

Another argumentative objection by Goodrich was sustained. But Felbin had made his point. He used this witness to demonstrate how ruthless the circuit attorney was. She would do anything, including destroying a loving relationship, if it served her personal interests.

"Ms. Adams, as a prosecutor, you do believe in the presumption of innocence, don't you?"

"Certainly."

"And you do believe that presumption of innocence applies to Bobby, don't you?"

"Yes, I do," she said emphatically.

"And so you believe he is innocent as we sit here today?"

Before Goodrich could get on his feet to object, Adams said, "Yes."

When Felbin announced he had no further questions, Goodrich announced that the State rested.

Customarily, when the prosecution completes its case, outside the presence of the jury, the defense files a motion for judgment of acquittal, arguing that the state produced insufficient evidence to meet its burden of proving defendant's guilt as a matter of law. The court is then asked to take the case away from the jury and dismiss the criminal charges. Those motions are rarely granted, with most judges allowing the jury the opportunity to decide the case. If the jury ultimately acquits, the case is concluded since the state cannot appeal. On the other hand, if the jury convicts, the trial judge has the opportunity to reevaluate the motion for judgment of acquittal, as well as other legal and evidentiary issues and overturn the decision of the jury.

After overruling Felbin's motion for judgment of acquittal, Judge Bell announced that the luncheon recess would be taken with the defendant's case beginning promptly at 2 p.m.

Chapter Sixty-Five

Dr. Benjamin Brown, a 71-year-old Professor in the School of Engineering at Washington University in St. Louis, was the first witness for the defense. Felbin began by introducing Dr. Brown's extensive credentials, which included a Ph.D., a position as a full Professor at Harvard before joining the faculty at Washington University, numerous books and publications in the field of engineering, in addition to national awards and recognitions.

Dr. Brown explained the task he and his staff of three other Washington University engineers undertook regarding the flashlight which the prosecution claimed was the murder weapon. He explained that his group built a device that would test the durability of that flashlight. They purchased some twenty flashlights identical to the one possessed by the defendant and smashed each on the device that they built. That device approximated the mass of a human skull. The experiment was designed to see how the flashlight reacted to the stress associated with a flashlight coming into contact with a human skull.

"What were the parameters and results of your research?" Felbin asked, recognizing both the questions and the answers could not become mired in scientific technicality.

"We calculated the amount of foot pounds of pressure necessary to cause the type of skull fracture sustained in this case. We then began to test the durability of the flashlights at the pressure which would cause that fracture. Each of the twenty flashlights was totally destroyed," Dr. Brown said, trying to keep his answers short and simple.

"When you say totally destroyed, what do you mean?"

"First, you could not turn any of them on. Second, the reason the lights didn't work was because each was damaged beyond repair. The glass that protected the light was shattered and the light itself was broken."

"What conclusions did you draw within a reasonable degree of engineering and scientific certainty?"

"We drew several conclusions. First, if Officer Decker's flashlight caused the skull fracture in this case, you would not be able to turn it on. It would not be operational. Second, you would be able to clearly see the damage to the flashlight, because the glass would be shattered and the light broken."

"Let me hand you a flashlight the prosecutor has identified as the object responsible for Mister Mitchell's head injury, and ask you to look at that."

After the witness took a few minutes to examine the Exhibit, Felbin continued, "Have you ever seen that flashlight before?"

"No, sir," Dr. Brown said.

"Please compare the flashlight in your hand to the flashlights you and your colleagues tested." After the witness again complied with the directive, Felbin said, "How do they compare?"

"The flashlights we tested were identical to this one," the witness said, referring to the flashlight he was holding.

"The flashlight you are holding, sir, is there any damage to that light?"

"None whatsoever," Dr. Brown said as he turned the light on and pointed it toward the jury box, after conducting a thorough and methodical examination.

"If that flashlight had caused the skull fracture in this case, do you have an opinion within a reasonable degree of scientific certainty, what that flashlight would look like at this moment?"

"I would expect to see a cracked lens at the very least, assuming that the lens was in place at all and not in pieces. Based upon our experiments, I also believe this light would not be functional. In other words, you could not turn it on as I just did," Dr. Brown said confidently. "I don't believe this flashlight injured anyone," the witness additionally volunteered.

Felbin's examination was simple and concise. He extracted what he needed from the witness in language everyone in the courtroom understood. There was no way, according to this expert, that the flashlight the prosecution had tendered as the murder weapon could possibly have caused Mitchell's injuries. When Felbin announced he had no additional questions, Goodrich began his cross examination and wasted no time attacking this witness.

"How much are you being paid for your testimony here today?" Goodrich began.

Perplexed by the question, Dr. Brown asked, "Paid?"

"Yes, how much is Mister Felbin paying you to be here today?"

"Mister Felbin is not paying me anything to be here today."

"Well, who is?" Goodrich pressed.

"No one is paying me anything to be here today. And no one has paid me to do those experiments I described, Mister Goodrich."

"Do you have any understanding or agreement with anyone that you'll be paid?"

"No," the witness replied simply and quickly.

"Then why did you agree to do the experiments and come here today to testify? What is your interest in this case?" Goodrich asked, mindful that lawyers should not ask questions for which they don't know the answers.

"My interest, Mister Goodrich, is the truth. When Mister Felbin came to me with this issue, I told him that . . ."

Before Dr. Brown could complete his statement, Goodrich was on his feet objecting because he realized he had made a mistake and the witness was about to burn him. Felbin was also on his feet, urging the court to allow the witness to complete the answer to the question his opponent had asked. The witness and the jurors sat silently watching the lawyers spar. Felbin was the victor this time, as the judge directed the witness to complete his response.

"Mister Goodrich, we are academicians. We are teachers. We had read about this case, as the media had covered the events extensively. When Mister Felbin contacted us, I felt the issue he was presenting was interesting and could serve as a learning experience for our students. But, although interesting, I needed to insure the university's neutrality and scientific objectivity would not be compromised in this high profile case. I told Mister Felbin when he came to me that we would conduct the experiments, but with the understanding the results would not be confidential and would be released to whoever asked. And he agreed."

"Did you release the results to my office?" Goodrich asked, knowing full well he didn't receive the results of these experiments.

"No, sir."

"Why not?" another dangerous question.

"Because you didn't ask," Brown said, eliciting slight laughter from some of the spectators.

Moving to a different set of questions, Goodrich continued, "You talked about what would happen to the lens area of the flashlight. Did you do any tests on the other end of the light?"

"No."

"So, in testing just the lens area of the flashlight, you made an assumption this was the area that came into contact with Mister Mitchell's skull, is that correct?"

"Yes."

"Do you know, sir, whether there were other flashlights or linear objects on the rooftop that night capable of causing this type of injury?"

"No, sir. I was simply asked to test flashlights identical to the defendant's, and that is what we did."

"You said earlier that you purchased some twenty flashlights that were identical to the one possessed by the defendant on the day in question. How did you know what flashlight the defendant possessed?"

"Mister Felbin provided me with a flashlight and represented that this was the flashlight that his client possessed that night. The light I was just shown is identical to the one Mister Felbin gave me."

"Would you agree, Doctor Brown, that your testimony is based entirely on the assumption this defendant possessed only one flashlight which he used to murder Jordon Mitchell?"

Felbin was immediately on his feet objecting to the characterization of murder. Admonishing the prosecutor, the judge directed Goodrich to rephrase the question.

"You would agree, Doctor Brown, that your testimony is based entirely on the assumption that this defendant possessed only one flashlight on the night of this incident; the one that you were shown?" Goodrich said, complying with the court's directive to rephrase the question.

"Yes, of course, I would agree with that, Mister Goodrich. I cannot have an opinion about any object other than the one we tested," Dr. Brown replied, confused by the question itself.

"That's all the questions I have," Goodrich announced.

"The court will be in recess until ten tomorrow morning," Judge Bell announced.

And with that, day six of the State of *Missouri v. Robert Decker* was completed.

Chapter Sixty-Six

Felbin wasn't confused by the last question Goodrich asked Dr. Brown, but he was concerned. Goodrich had something up his sleeve. Felbin didn't know exactly what it was, but that question was designed to lay a foundation for the prosecutor to present some type of rebuttal evidence. Witnesses who testify in rebuttal don't have to be disclosed prior to trial. *Will the prosecution present evidence that his client had more than one flashlight that night?* But Bobby had already told him the flashlight in evidence was the only one he had. *Could they have evidence that some other object was the murder weapon?* Felbin thought that was a possibility. But it would have to be a linear object in order to be consistent with the opinions of their forensic pathologists.

Felbin had a decision to make. His next witness was going to be another engineer from Dr. Brown's group. This witness was critical to a complete understanding of what happened on the roof that night. However, in light of Goodrich's suggestion that another object was used, Felbin needed to decide whether to save this witness to counter what Felbin anticipated was coming. Of course, if Goodrich's question was merely a smoke screen designed to mislead the jury and there was no rebuttal evidence, the testimony of Felbin's next witness would be lost. The court would not allow the testimony, because the prosecution would have presented no evidence that needed to be rebutted.

When they returned to the office, Felbin asked Bobby again what he was carrying that night.

"I had the flashlight they have in evidence, along with my service revolver and that's it," Bobby said.

"You didn't have any other flashlight or a night stick?" Felbin pressed.

"No other flashlight and I don't even own a night stick. I lost that a couple years ago."

"Get a subpoena out for the IAD investigator who searched Bobby's locker and seized his flashlight," Felbin instructed his investigator, Jack Reilly. "I want to make sure they don't come up with another flashlight or a night stick."

"I'll get that served first thing in the morning," the investigator replied.

"There was no mention of a flashlight or a night stick on the inventory sheet from Bobby's locker, was there?" Felbin asked.

"None that I recall, but I'll double-check that," Reilly said.

Turning to Bobby, Felbin said, "We have a decision to make. I'm concerned Goodrich is going to produce a witness to say that you had another object or flashlight other than the one Doctor Brown tested, which will have the effect of nullifying the tests done by Doctor Brown. We have a witness to counter that. We can put that witness on now or present him after they put their surprise witness on. Strategically, we get the most bang for our buck if our witness testifies last, after the prosecution finishes putting on all of its evidence. But if this is just smoke without substance, we won't be allowed to put this witness on. The jury will never hear what he has to say. What do you think?"

Without even asking Felbin what the witness would say, unhesitatingly, Bobby said, "You do whatever you think is best. I trust and have complete confidence in whatever decision you make, whether it works or doesn't work. No second guessing from me. You have been doing a great job with everything they have thrown at us. I'm eternally grateful to you, regardless of the outcome, Mister Felbin."

Bobby's comments meant a lot to Felbin. Sometimes when you do an extraordinary job and get a great result, clients still complain about something. But Bobby was not that type of client. The tough part for Felbin, as it had been from the beginning, is that he knew he represented an innocent man. Felbin had known from the time he read Bobby's police report that he didn't strike Mitchell with a flashlight. He knew there was no justification for the injury in the report, because Bobby honestly didn't know how the man he had arrested sustained his injury. But that was then. Now, after he uncovered *all the* facts, Jonathan Felbin knew exactly how Jordon Mitchell fractured his skull. The only question was whether this jury would agree. But first, they had to hear the game-changing evidence, which could be in jeopardy depending on the decision the defense made regarding this witness. The moves in this chess game were now becoming critical. One wrong move could put an innocent man in the penitentiary for a very long time.

"For better or worse, Bobby, I'm going to take a chance and hold this witness back. We will either win big or lose big with the decision. But I think the benefits outweigh the risks. I pray to God I'm right. If my decision changes between now and tomorrow morning, I'll let you know. Try to get a good dinner and some sleep, Bobby," Felbin said as he walked his client to the front door.

Chapter Sixty-Seven

"The defense calls Doctor Harry Langdon," Felbin announced to begin day seven of the trial, much to the surprise of Goodrich, who always believed Felbin never intended to call this witness. The mental game Goodrich thought Felbin was playing was now a reality.

The witness entered the courtroom accompanied by Felbin's investigator. Langdon was in his early seventies. His long, silver, uncombed hair and wire-rimmed glasses accented a dark blue wrinkled suit, white shirt and red and blue stripped tie. He had a charm about him. A charm you couldn't quite put your finger on, but one that gave him instant credibility.

The national credentials of this witness were impressive. His resume included many national high profile cases, not the least of which was the O. J. Simpson murder prosecution in California, where Dr. Langdon testified for the defense in a trial that captivated the attention of America and which resulted in the acquittal of the celebrity football player. In addition to his educational training at Harvard, Dr. Langdon appeared on his own television show. He hosted a show on HBO, where he described forensic medical issues while performing an actual autopsy. The show was not for the faint of heart. Dr. Langdon told the jury he was asked by the Congress of the United States to reexamine the autopsies of President John Kennedy and Dr. Martin Luther King. Residing in New York City, he also served as a consultant to the New York State Police Department. He had testified in civil and criminal trials too numerous to mention, mostly for the prosecution in criminal cases. If nothing else, Dr. Langdon was well-known nationally, and Felbin was taking advantage of that celebrity status.

Dr. Langdon told the jury he read the autopsy reports prepared by Dr. Long and Dr. McHenry, as well as Mr. Mitchell's medical records which described his care and treatment for the period of time he was in the hospital. Additionally, he asked for and received some 50 photographs of the brain of Jordon Mitchell taken from various angles once removed from the skull. Those photos depicted the brain after it had been sliced to expose any internal bruising. He repeated that any autopsy of the brain takes some three to four weeks after the brain is removed from the cranium. This period of time allows the brain to become firm, so that it can be sliced and the interior viewed for injury.

His interest in viewing the internal aspects of Mr. Mitchell's brain was to see if he could find any evidence of what he called a *coup contrecoup injury.*

"Please describe what a *coup contrecoup injury* is, Doctor," Felbin requested.

"Coup and contrecoup injury is associated with cerebral contusion, a type of traumatic brain injury in which the brain is bruised. Coup and contrecoup injuries can occur individually or together. When a moving object impacts the stationary head, coup injuries are typical, while contrecoup injuries are produced when the moving head strikes a stationary object. Coup and contrecoup injuries are considered focal brain injuries, meaning that they occur in a particular spot in the brain as opposed to diffuse injuries, which occur over a widespread area," Dr. Langdon explained.

"What does all that mean?"

"What it means is that when a moving object strikes a stationary head, one type of injury will occur. When a moving head strikes a stationary object, a different type of injury is seen inside the brain. In the case of a moving object striking a stationary head, you'll see a fractured skull at the point of impact and below that fracture, you'll see a brain bleed or bruise. Nothing more will be observed. However, in the case of a moving head striking a stationary object, you'll see the fracture and the bleed or bruise underneath the point of impact just like in the other situation. But you'll also see the contrecoup injury, which is a bleed or a bruise in another part of the brain. This happens because when the head is moving and strikes the stationary object, the brain bounces off the cranium wall and strikes another part of the cranium, producing two readily identifiable injuries in the brain itself once it is sliced. However, when a moving object strikes a stationary head, the brain remains stationary and no additional bruising is seen beyond the point of impact."

"How is that significant in this case?"

"Because if Mister Mitchell was struck with a flashlight consistent with the prosecution's theory, only one brain injury will be observed. But if his head was moving and struck something, two internal brain injuries will be observed."

"Doctor, when you studied the photographs of Mister Mitchell's brain, what did you see?"

"I saw two injuries to his brain," Dr. Langdon said as he left the witness chair to show the jurors the photographs which depicted both brain injuries. Positioning himself directly in front of the jury box, he pointed to those two injuries.

"And within a reasonable degree of medical certainty, what significance did you attach to that finding, Doctor Langdon?" Felbin asked.

Still standing in front of the jury box, he looked at each of the jurors and said, "That Mister Mitchell's head was *not* struck with a flashlight or any other moving object."

"Do you have an explanation within a reasonable degree of medical certainty as to the cause of Mister Mitchell's brain injury?"

"Yes. We know that Mister Mitchell had a fractured skull with coup contrecoup injury to the brain. That means that Mister Mitchell's *moving head* struck some type of stationary object," Dr. Langdon said, still standing, looking very professorial and continuing to make eye contact with each juror.

"Doctor, let me show you several photographs of the roof and represent to you that this is the roof where Officer Decker encountered and arrested Jordon Mitchell. I'm going to ask you to look at those photographs and tell the jury whether there is anything you see in those pictures that is capable of explaining how Mister Mitchell sustained his skull fracture and resulting coup contrecoup injuries."

Goodrich was immediately on his feet, objecting that the question was pure speculation on the part of the witness and unsupported by any evidence in the case. Originally, he thought Felbin was blowing smoke about calling this expensive witness. Because Goodrich's office could not afford to take this expert's deposition, he was unable to prepare for what he was hearing for the first time, along with the jury. While medical testimony which contradicted the state's medical examiners was expected, Goodrich never thought Felbin would try to have this nationally-known witness focus the jury's attention on a particular rooftop object capable of causing the massive skull fracture. He needed to make sure this Scud missile didn't land in the middle of his case.

After much discussion at the judge's bench, outside the presence of the jury, Judge Bell overruled the prosecutor's objection, reasoning that this was the opinion of an expert, which the jury was free to accept or reject.

Goodrich was visibly upset and didn't conceal his anger with the judge's ruling. "Are you kidding? This is total bullshit and you know it. This is another Felbin sandbag. Giving this witness a license to encourage the jury to speculate is prejudicial to the state and certainly not fair to those parents of this black victim and the entire city watching the decisions you are making here, and judging the judge." When all else fails, talk about the victim and his family, inject race, and threaten the political future of the judge; routine prosecution tactics.

Calmly, Judge Bell said, "Mister Goodrich, I have made my ruling. I realize you disagree, which you are certainly free to do. But there is no place for profanity on this record. Consider yourself warned. I assume that won't happen again."

"Sorry. It won't happen again," Goodrich said, offering a less than sincere apology.

Felbin said nothing. There was nothing for him to say. The ruling was a huge victory for the defense. It also meant Felbin would not necessarily have to put Bobby on the witness stand. Whether a defendant should or should not testify is a difficult decision in any criminal case, but even more so in this case.

"Doctor, before the objection, I asked you to take a look at the photographs of the roof and to see if there is anything on that roof that could explain how Mister Mitchell sustained his skull fracture and the resulting coup contrecoup injuries. You can now answer that question," Felbin said, reminding the jury of the importance of the question and also reminding them the prosecutor didn't want them to hear the answer.

"Several of these photographs depict cinder blocks. It looks as though there are a total of three cinder blocks on this roof. If Mister Mitchell's head struck any one of these blocks, that impact could have easily caused a skull fracture with the resulting coup contrecoup brain bruising. I say that because you would have a moving head striking a stationary object. These blocks were on the floor of the rooftop and Mister Mitchell's head would have made contact with one of them from a standing position. As such, a moving head would strike a stationary object. Of course, the roof itself could also cause this result, but I can't tell the composition of the roof from the photographs. Other than that, I cannot see any other object in the photos of the roof where this arrest occurred which would explain the injuries I saw."

The last statement that Dr. Langdon made was powerful. After reviewing the medical records, the autopsy reports, the photographs of both the scene and the autopsy, this nationally-known expert told the jury the only explanation for Jordon Mitchell's massive skull fracture was a cinder block or perhaps the roof itself. It was not a flashlight. With that, Felbin announced he had no further questions of the witness.

The testimony of Dr. Langdon was simple and concise. The witness explained in language everyone understood that the prosecutor's flashlight theory was wrong. The medical findings, not one but two injuries to the brain, didn't support that conclusion. But now Goodrich would have his chance to discredit the theory of this witness. *Good luck with that,* Felbin thought as he sat back, anxious to see this war of words between an experienced and talented prosecutor and a professional witness.

"What is the defense paying you for your testimony here today, sir?" Goodrich began.

A weak and desperate start, Felbin thought. *He must not have anything else.*

"Mister Goodrich, my testimony is not for sale and no one is paying for my opinion. Of course, my time, like yours, is important. And just as you are being paid for your time here today, I expect to be paid for mine. Does that answer your question, sir?"

"Not exactly. I suspect your hourly rate is substantially greater than mine," Goodrich shot back, attempting to argue with the witness, a tactic which is generally not very productive with an expert.

"Mister Goodrich, if by your comment you are asking me what my hourly rate is, I cannot answer that. I submit my hours to my office and they send a bill for time and expenses. My interest is in the science and not the finances. But, of course, as with everyone, I do like to be paid," Dr. Langdon said, drawing a little chuckle from a portion of the audience.

"Did you prepare any type of report in connection with your findings and conclusions?" Goodrich asked quickly moving away from the compensation issues.

"No, sir, I didn't."

"Why not?"

"Because no one asked me to prepare a report."

"Is it your practice to prepare written reports in cases where you testify for the defense?"

"Whether I'm called to testify for the defense or the prosecution, I only prepare a report if someone asks me to do that."

"You said you testified in the murder trial involving O. J. Simpson out in California. Did you testify on behalf of the defense or prosecution?"

"In that case, I testified on behalf of the defense. However, most of the time when I testify, I'm called by the prosecution," Dr. Langdon said, anticipating Goodrich's next question.

"Do you keep some type of record of the times you testify for one side or the other?" Goodrich asked.

"No. But I know I'm called more often by the prosecution, because I do autopsies at the request of the New York State Police."

"Have you ever testified before in a case where a police officer was accused of murder?"

"Yes."

Now Goodrich had a decision to make. He had no idea what Langdon was going to say about that case. If he testified for the defense, it would help. But if he testified for the

287

prosecution, it would hurt because the defense would suggest objectivity in his opinions. He came down on the side of the science rather than the party. Goodrich decided not to take the chance.

"Doctor, you said you saw two injuries to Mister Mitchell's brain."

"Yes, that's correct."

"Now, isn't it true that with a contrecoup injury, the head stops abruptly with the brain striking the skull at the point of impact and then bouncing off that site and striking the skull on the opposite side?" Goodrich asked, ignoring the previous answer of the witness.

"Yes."

"Doctor, I'm going to hand you the same photographs of the brain you previously used to explain the coup contrecoup injury that you said you observed and ask you whether the injuries line up. In other words, is the first injury directly opposite from the second?"

"No, it is not."

"Well, how do you then explain that this is the result of one blow as opposed to two, since the injuries don't line up directly opposite one another?"

"Because the brain does not know that the second injury has to line up directly opposite of the first."

"But how can it be any other way if the brain is bouncing from one side to the other?" Goodrich pressed.

"Because the head is moving and the head can move at different angles and push the brain into the cranium wall at a different angle away from the initial point of impact."

"Are you saying, Doctor, that the brain could not possibly move inside the cranium and strike a different area as a result of a single blow with a flashlight?"

"Yes, sir, that is exactly what I'm saying," the witness responded without hesitation.

"No further questions," Goodrich said.

"And redirect, Mister Felbin?" the judge asked.

"No, sir."

"We will take our lunch recess at this time. Please return at 1:30," Judge Bell announced.

Chapter Sixty-Eight

During the recess, Felbin met with his investigator and Bobby in one of the courthouse conference rooms. The purpose of the meeting was to discuss whether Bobby should testify. The prosecution cannot put the defendant on the witness stand. In any criminal case, the defendant need not testify and the jury is told that no adverse inference can be drawn from the failure. The reason for the rule is found in the 5th amendment to the Constitution where people cannot be compelled to incriminate themselves. Whether jurors follow that instruction is a subject of debate among criminal defense lawyers.

The decision of whether or not to testify is exclusively that of the client, not the lawyer. In advising his clients, Felbin generally does a cost/benefit analysis. *Recognizing that the defendant will be subjected to cross examination by the prosecutor, will the defendant be able to add anything,* Felbin rhetorically asks himself. Additionally, in this case, Felbin must take into consideration the fact that his client is a police officer. Juries generally want to hear from police officers who are charged with crimes.

Felbin outlined the positives and the negatives for Bobby. The plus was that the jury would hear directly from Bobby that he didn't strike Jordon Mitchell with a flashlight or anything else. He would also be able to describe Mitchell's efforts to escape and resist arrest, resulting in a struggle that would end his life. But Goodrich would then be able to walk him though the events of that night step by step. The problem there was that just as he was unable to explain the injury in his police report, he would, likewise, be unable to explain it in the presence of the jury. Any testimony would be pure speculation on Bobby's part. He didn't know then and would not, in fact, know now, how Mitchell sustained a massive skull fracture. In short, Felbin knew

Bobby could not factually advance the defense theory and could hurt it by his lack of knowledge.

The defense obviously could not deny that Mitchell sustained a skull fracture. And a massive one at that. But Felbin planned to explain that fracture by using the cinder blocks found on the roof along with a witness who could tie all the loose ends together as the final witness in the trial, hopefully. Mitchell was not hit with a flashlight. Rather, he hit his head on a cinder block when thrown to the ground while trying to escape from the rooftop. The testimony of Dr. Langdon would allow him to advance that theory without Bobby having to explain that he threw him down.

Felbin knew if Bobby testified and admitted that he caused Mitchell to strike the cinder block, he ran the risk of a manslaughter conviction. In criminal cases, juries can be instructed if they don't find the defendant guilty of the crime charged, they could consider whether he is guilty of a lesser crime. In this case, Bobby Decker was charged with murder second degree. If the evidence supported it, the court could instruct the jury that if they concluded the defendant was not guilty of murder, they could consider whether he was guilty of manslaughter, a lesser crime than murder. Clearly, if Bobby, at 6-foot-3, 226 pounds testified he threw Mitchell, a young man half his size, down on the roof, causing him to hit his head on a cinder block, the jury could find he was criminally negligent and convict him of manslaughter.

"What are your thoughts, Bobby?" Felbin asked after explaining the options, both good and bad.

"From the beginning, I have told you and anyone else who would listen I didn't hit this guy with a flashlight or anything else. I have also told you repeatedly that I have no idea how he hurt his head. All I know is I didn't hit him with a flashlight, as the prosecution suggests," Bobby said emphatically. "Frankly, I'm getting tired of saying that," he continued. "There are things in my life I'm not proud of, but this is not one of them. I have been accused of a crime I didn't commit. I have been called a racist and treated like a common criminal. I have been without a paycheck and have no money. I can't remember the last time my father spoke to me or even acknowledged my existence. My employer, like my father, has all but abandoned me. The woman that I love, yes I said, *love* present tense, has not only left me, but on her way out the door has tried to put me in the penitentiary. I have sat through this trial for the past week listening to one lie after another, including a fellow officer who lied to save his own ass. I have had little sleep since this ordeal began."

Felbin and his investigator looked at each other, listening as Bobby continued his rant.

"I'm tired and have pretty much reached the point where I really don't care what happens. I feel like I'm in a prison right now. Going to a different prison will make little difference in the rest of my miserable life. So, you make the call and do whatever you think is best," Bobby said, as he left the conference room while Felbin and Reilly silently watched.

"Wow. What do you think that was all about?" Jack Reilly asked after Bobby left the room.

"He has been under a lot of pressure since this thing began. And now we are almost at the end of the line, he is feeling the most pressure," Felbin replied.

"Clearly, you can't put him on the stand. But do you think we need to have him see a doctor? Get him some medication?"

"No. We need to finish this trial. However, regardless of the outcome, I think he is going to carry a lot of scars. Even if he wins, he doesn't get back the only two things that gave his life any meaning: the woman he loved and apparently still does, and his job. But I think he is strong enough to get through at least the trial. After that I think we should get him some help," Felbin said.

Chapter Sixty-Nine

"Please call your next witness," Judge Bell instructed as the spectators began to fill the courtroom after the luncheon recess.

"The defense rests," Felbin announced.

"Any rebuttal, Mister Goodrich?"

"Yes. The State recalls Doctor Helen McHenry."

As the witness entered the courtroom, Felbin figured she was there to discredit Dr. Langdon's testimony. While she stood before the clerk who would again administer the oath, Felbin wondered how this witness was going to ignore the clear evidence of two brain bleeds and take the jury on a trip through Disney's Fantasyland. Whatever the journey, Helen McHenry, dressed in a flowing purple dress, was ready and anxious to take on her famous colleague. This was her town, and she was not going to let some interloping celebrity take it from her.

"Doctor McHenry, I just have a few questions for you. We just heard testimony that the brain could not possibly bounce off the cranium wall causing multiple internal injuries as a result of a blow from a flashlight. As the Medical Examiner for Saint Louis County do you agree or disagree with that theory?" Goodrich asked, reminding the jury that this was *their* hometown witness.

"I definitely disagree with that theory. The brain of someone who is struck in the head with a flashlight will definitely move inside the cranium, depending on the intensity of the strike. In this case, the fracture was massive, suggesting the blow was administered with a substantial amount of velocity. As such, the brain will unquestionably move and strike a different part of the cranium, resulting in a brain bleed or brain bruise."

"Doctor McHenry, let me show you photographs and ask you whether you can identify more than one brain bleed."

"Yes. I can see two," Dr. McHenry said, agreeing with Dr. Langdon.

"And how do they line up? Is the second directly opposite the first?" Goodrich asked.

"No. The second brain injury is at about a 55 to 60 degree angle to the first."

"Is that what is referred to as a coup contrecoup injury."

"No."

"Will you tell the jury why it is not a coup contrecoup injury?"

"In any coup contrecoup, the initial blow is to a moving head. The force of that blow causes the brain to move from one side of the skull to the other. When the brain keeps moving after it is stopped by the initial impact, it travels to the opposite side of the skull and collides with that side. I have never seen a coup contrecoup injury where the first injury didn't line up directly opposite the second. And that makes sense when you stop to think about it. If I throw a ball against the wall, it will come directly back to me. It won't return on an angle. There is no contrecoup in this case."

"Then how do you explain the second brain injury that you found?"

"A couple different scenarios are possible. First, the blow from the flashlight could have caused that, because it caused the brain to move and strike the cranium at an angle. Second, Mister Mitchell's head could have been struck a second time at the site of the second injury. Third, you can have a brain bleed from a variety of different causes independent of trauma. For example, people who suffer strokes can have a brain bleed."

"Thank you, Doctor. That's all the questions I have."

Before the judge asked, Felbin was on his feet beginning his cross examination.

"When you did the autopsy, did you find any evidence of a stroke?" Felbin began.

"No."

"Then why are you telling this jury that the second brain bleed could be the result of a stroke?" Felbin asked, his voice raised and clearly agitated.

"I didn't say that. What I said, Mister Felbin, was that brain bleeds can have a variety of causes," Dr. McHenry fired back.

"So, you don't really know with any degree of reasonable medical certainty what caused that second brain injury in Mister Mitchell's skull?"

"The second brain injury could have had a variety of causes. But I'm sure of what it wasn't. It was not a coup contrecoup injury."

"And you are certain of that because the brain bleeds don't line up perfectly one behind the other."

"Yes."

"I would like to discuss with you that ball against the wall analogy you used. And thank you for that by the way, as I think it helps make my point. You said when you throw a ball against a wall it comes directly back at you. But would you not concede that a ball can be thrown against a wall at an angle and in such a way that, in fact, it will be returned at an angle to the thrower?"

"I have never seen that," Dr. McHenry said, unwilling to concede the point.

"Well, I guess you haven't played much baseball or played catch with yourself by throwing a ball against a wall. That's all I have," Felbin said without allowing the witness to respond to his statement.

"Do you have another witness?" Judge Bell asked.

"Yes. The state calls George Armstrong," Goodrich announced.

"Who the hell is this?" Felbin asked his investigator.

"I have no idea," Reilly replied.

As a rebuttal witness, the prosecutor didn't have to disclose his identity pretrial. An objection to his testimony at this point would be a waste of time. Felbin had to wait and see whether this guy was truly a rebuttal witness. He thought, based upon the trap Goodrich was trying to set with the engineers and the phantom second flashlight, someone had to put that light in Bobby's hand and this was probably the guy.

After identifying the witness for the jury by name and address, Goodrich asked the witness to state his occupation.

"I'm a Saint Louis firefighter," Armstrong replied.

"Mister Armstrong, were you present during the arrest of Jordon Mitchell on April 24?"

"Yes. I provided the ladder the officers used to get onto the roof."

"Did you watch the officers as they climbed the ladder?"

"Yes. I held the ladder at the bottom as they made the climb."

Armstrong identified Bobby Decker as one of the police officers who climbed the ladder.

"When the defendant was climbing the ladder, did you notice whether he had a flashlight?" Goodrich asked.

"Yes. In fact, I noticed that he had two flashlights. One was in his hand and one was on his utility belt," Armstrong said.

"I'm going to show you a flashlight the court has received in evidence in this case and ask you if you have ever seen that before."

"Yes. That is the flashlight that Officer Decker had in his hand."

Felbin was now on his feet asking the judge if he could approach the bench and have a discussion outside the presence of the jury. When he arrived at the bench, Felbin complained the witness was not offering proper rebuttal evidence and should have been called during the State's case in chief. He also complained the witness was not identified prior to the trial and his testimony was a surprise.

Goodrich responded that the witness had been identified through fire department reports that had been turned over to the defense well prior to the start of the trial. He also took the position that the evidence rebutted the testimony of the engineers that the defendant's flashlight would be damaged if it had caused the fracture. Felbin's objection was overruled. The witness would be allowed to testify. When he returned to the defense table, Felbin asked his investigator to pull the fire department reports.

"The other one he had on his belt, can you describe that flashlight?" Goodrich asked, continuing with his questions.

"Yes. It was a long black metal light. They are called Kel-Lites."

"I'm going to hand you a Kel-Lite I have marked as an exhibit in this case and ask you if the light that you saw looked like this one."

"Yes, it was identical to that one," Armstrong said.

"No further questions," Goodrich announced.

"Mister Felbin, do you have any questions for this witness?" Judge Bell asked.

"Indeed I do," Felbin responded, jumping to his feet, eager to find out how this guy would notice two flashlights in the middle of a dark rainy night so many months ago. "Mister Goodrich, did you prepare a report regarding your involvement while on the scene during this arrest?" Felbin began.

"Yes."

"Did you mention in your report that Officer Decker possessed two flashlights?"

"I don't remember," Armstrong said.

"Well, didn't you review that report before you came in here today?"

"Yes."

"And you don't recall whether you mentioned in that report the very issue about which you are testifying today? Incredible," Felbin said, clearly annoyed with the testimony of this witness.

"Objection, your Honor."

"Sustained," was Judge Bell's immediate response.

"Let me help you out, Mister Armstrong. I'll show you a document and ask you if that is a copy of your report," Felbin continued.

"Yes, it is," Armstrong said, barely looking at the document he had just been handed.

"Do you see any mention in that report of two flashlights?"

"No, I don't."

"But today, you are independently remembering two flashlights," Felbin commented.

"I remember that because I thought it was unusual," Armstrong volunteered.

"But not unusual enough to put in your report?"

"I guess not."

"One final question, Mister Armstrong. Both of the flashlights you claim Officer Decker possessed, were round. Is that correct?"

"Yes," Armstrong replied confused by the question.

When Felbin finished with the cross examination of this witness, Goodrich asked to approach the bench and announced he had one additional rebuttal witness. That witness was from the Internal Affairs Division of the police department who would qualify and introduce documents relating to the internal false reporting charge that resulted in a guilty finding by the Department. Felbin objected immediately.

After listening to the arguments from both lawyers, Judge Bell sustained Felbin's objection. He concluded that the probative value of the evidence would be outweighed by its prejudicial effect. Significant for the judge was the fact that Decker, as a probationary officer at the time, was afforded no due process. Had Decker completed his probationary period, he would have received a full trial before the Board of Police Commissioners. At that internal trial, the Department would have had the burden of proving his guilt by substantial and competent evidence. And Bobby would have had the opportunity to challenge the witnesses and the evidence presented by the Department.

After the judge announced both his ruling and reasoning, Goodrich indicated he had no additional rebuttal evidence. Felbin told the court he had one surrebuttal witness.

"The defendant calls Doctor Anthony Fabrini," Felbin told the court and jury after leaving the bench and returning to the counsel table.

Dr. Fabrini identified himself as an engineer and a Professor at Washington University School of Engineering for the past six years. He received his undergraduate training at Yale, earned a doctorate from Harvard, and taught at a number of universities including Harvard. Among other disciplines, Dr. Fabrini was also a fracture specialist.

"What is a fracture specialist?" Felbin asked.

"It is one who studies the physics of stress and strain, elasticity and plasticity applied to the microscopic crystallographic defects found in materials in order to predict the macroscopic mechanical failure of bodies. In other words, I try to figure out what causes things to crack," Dr. Fabrini said, causing slight laughter among the courtroom spectators.

"Doctor, let me show you a photograph marked as an exhibit in this case and represent to you that this photograph has previously been identified as the fractured skull of Jordon Mitchell. Please take a moment to look over the photograph." Felbin paused for a few moments.

"Have you had enough time to review the photographs?"

"Yes, these are the same photographs that you showed me previously."

"That's correct. Now, Doctor, I want to ask you, within a reasonable degree of engineering certainty, did a flashlight cause the fracture you see depicted in that photograph?" Felbin asked.

"Absolutely not," the witness answered without hesitation.

"How can you be so sure?" Felbin asked.

"Because this is an L-shaped fracture. Flashlights are round objects and you simply cannot make a square with a rounded object."

"What in your opinion would have caused this fracture?" Felbin continued, surprised the testimony hadn't drawn an objection.

"This head would have had to strike the corner of something in order to cause this L or square shape on the skull. A rounded object like a flashlight would not and could not cause this."

"Let me show you some photographs of the roof where Mister Mitchell was arrested and direct your attention to the cinder block in the picture. In your expert opinion, could that have caused Jordon Mitchell's fractured skull?"

"Absolutely," another positive reply from the witness.

"Why do you say that?"

"Because I can see corners on the cinderblock. If Mister Mitchell's head hit the corner of that block, an L-shaped fracture, just like the one you can see in the photograph, would result."

"Thank you, Doctor. That's all the questions I have."

"Mister Goodrich, you may inquire," Judge Bell said.

"Thank you, Judge. Fabrini, your name is Doctor Fabrini?" Goodrich began, suggesting to the jury this witness was a surprise.

"Yes, sir. Tony Fabrini. Please call me Tony," Dr. Fabrini said, taking Goodrich by surprise with his suggestion of informality.

"Doctor Fabrini, when were you first asked to look at this photograph?" Goodrich asked, declining the witness' invitation to call him Tony.

"I don't know, maybe a couple of weeks ago."

"Are you acquainted with Doctor Brown?"

"Yes, I am. He is a colleague."

"Did you have anything to do with the flashlight smashing he was doing for this case?"

"I was involved with the experiments he conducted."

"What was your role?"

"Mainly as an observer with an academic interest."

"Did you discuss his findings with him?"

"Yes. I concurred with his conclusion that if the flashlight which was the focus of the study would have caused the skull fracture in the photo, it would have looked like the flashlights he smashed."

"But if you are a fracture specialist, why was it necessary to do these tests, if it was obvious a flashlight could not have caused the fracture?"

"Well, I'm also an engineer, a teacher, an academician, and a scientist. One of my special interests in the field of engineering, a subspecialty, if you'll, is in the area of fractures. But many things capture my attention in the field of engineering. I don't know specifically what Doctor Brown was asked to do beyond smashing flashlights for comparison to the skull fracture. Actually, I thought it was pretty neat to smash flashlights and compare that to a skull fracture."

"So, you were participating in this flashlight smashing exercise to determine what a flashlight would look like if it fractured a skull and you didn't look at the skull that was fractured?"

"First of all, I simply observed. I had an academic curiosity unrelated to any particular case. I didn't *participate*, in the sense that you suggest. Second, I knew generally that Doctor Brown was conducting the experiment we have been talking about. I'm certain I looked at the fracture. But the narrow issue then was what a light would look like after causing that fracture. You have to understand, Mister Goodrich, we academicians can only do one thing at a time. We are very limited in that regard." Another chuckle from the audience.

"Are you telling this jury Doctor Brown failed to see this L-shaped configuration that you claim to see in this photograph?"

"I don't know what Doctor Brown saw or didn't see. You would have to ask him. But I *did* see an L-shaped fracture. I don't claim to see it. I *did* see it. Here, Mister Goodrich, let me show you," Dr. Fabrini said as he picked up the photograph from the witness' desk in front of him

Ignoring Dr. Fabrini's offer, Goodrich pressed on, "Surely, as a professor of engineering studies, Doctor Brown would also know one cannot make a square with a rounded object."

"Oh yes, I'm quite sure he does know that."

"Then why would he need to be smashing flashlights if he already knew a flashlight could not have possibly caused the fracture?"

"Again, sir, you would have to ask him that question to get his answer. But the issue was what the flashlight would look like if it caused that fracture. In order to know that, the experiments had to be done. In all events, I assure you he knows, as do most people who are not engineers, that you can't make a square with a rounded object."

Recognizing he made his point and additional questions could be dangerous, Goodrich was finished.

When Felbin announced that he had no additional witnesses, Judge Bell recessed for the day and told the jurors to return at 10 am for the closing arguments, after which they would be given the case for their deliberation and verdict.

Chapter Seventy

When Goodrich returned to his office, he was immediately summoned to the circuit attorney's office where she, along with Carol Masterson, her confidant, and Karen Braxton, her first assistant, were waiting. Their greeting was anything but cordial.

"A fracture specialist? Where the hell did that come from? You didn't know he was going to call that witness?" Cardwell asked, her voice an octave short of screaming.

"That would be correct. I didn't know he was going to call that witness. Felbin obviously held him back to get the final word," Goodrich said, a touch of annoyance in his voice.

"And you didn't bother to object," Cardwell pressed, her voice still raised.

"I didn't think it would do any good, since I held back the firefighter and introduced another flashlight. I also thought if I did object and he sustained the objection, it would not withstand an appellate challenge," Goodrich said.

"I don't give a damn about any appellate challenge. I need to win this case now. What is it about that you don't understand?" Cardwell continued.

"There is nothing about that I don't understand. But what you don't understand is that I don't give a shit about your political career or your judgeship. I'm doing the best I can to prosecute this case. I'm making decisions I think are in the interest of my client, the State of Missouri, not what is best for your ambitions. Frankly, I really don't care what you think. I'm sick and tired of your bullshit. You brought this prosecution before the autopsy was even completed and you can bet this jury is going to hear about that again. So, don't blame me for a case you screwed up from the beginning. Now if you'll excuse me, I have a closing argument to prepare," Goodrich said as he made his way to the door.

"Wait a minute. I'm not finished talking to you," Cardwell demanded.

"Oh, yes you are. This conversation is over. And at the conclusion of this case, so is my employment with this office. There is only so much one can take working here and I have reached my point of saturation. I hope you get your judgeship, Joan, no matter how you scratch and claw to get there. All I know is that I'm no longer willing to participate as your pawn in reaching that goal," Goodrich said as he left the room, slamming the door behind him as his final exclamation of insubordination.

"What do we do now?" Cardwell asked Masterson.

"You're assuming the worst at the moment and I'm not sure we are there. I have no idea what this jury is thinking, but I really don't think it is a slam dunk for the defense," Masterson said.

"I'm assuming the worst. Once again we have been out-maneuvered by Felbin. He took chicken shit and turned it into chicken salad. While you're right, the case is not concluded, I think we need to prepare for the worst. I think we need to prepare a press release and make sure the police department is ready to go forward with this guy's termination in the event of an acquittal. At least then, we can put it on a runaway jury and claim they were not interested in the facts," Cardwell said.

"I have already talked to the police department and they claim they are on board with termination," Karen Braxton said.

"Of course, you can't trust them to do the right thing. I'm also concerned they will try to put the blame on us," Cardwell replied.

"We can cover that with a press release that says this office will never put him on the witness stand again in any future criminal prosecution. That should end his police career both in the city and any other place," Masterson suggested.

"Why do you think Felbin didn't put Decker on the stand?" Cardwell asked her first assistant.

"Because he didn't want to run the risk of a compromised manslaughter verdict. If Decker testified, he would have to say he threw Mitchell down on the roof, which is what caused his head to hit the cinder block. The judge would then be forced to give the jury the lesser included offense of manslaughter instruction. That would set up a potential jury compromise if they had disagreement on the murder charge. They could agree instead of murder, they would find him guilty of manslaughter. Apparently, Felbin didn't want to take that chance. He is going for all or nothing. Win big or lose big, that's classic Felbin," Braxton replied.

"Should we ask for a manslaughter instruction?" Cardwell asked.

"Based upon the evidence that was presented, I don't think there is any basis for it, and I don't think the court will give it," Braxton said.

"So, Felbin will get to argue that Mitchell hit his head on a cinder block and get the benefit of that without the risk of a manslaughter conviction," Cardwell said, clearly frustrated.

"That's about it," Braxton said.

"Do the feds have any interest in prosecuting this case under the Civil Rights Act?" Cardwell asked.

"No. I already checked. I'm also sure they would have less interest in cleaning up our mess if there is a not guilty verdict," Braxton said as she shook her head.

"Let's get the press release done and ready for tomorrow. I want to release a written statement as soon as the verdict is in. Under no circumstance do I want to stand in front of those cameras and answer questions if he walks," Cardwell said.

"Do you want me to prepare a statement in the event of a conviction?" Masterson asked.

"No, I'll do that live in front of the cameras. I don't need a script for that," Cardwell remarked. "One more thing. Karen, prepare a termination letter for Goodrich. I want to terminate him as soon as the verdict comes in, regardless of what it is. We can also leak that to the media in the hope it will also have the net effect of taking some of the heat off of us in the event of an acquittal," Cardwell said.

"Will do," Karen said, like the good little obedient soldier she was.

Chapter Seventy-One

After an early instruction conference designed to decide what law to give to the jury in the form of instructions they are required to follow, and after overruling the defense's motion for judgment of acquittal at the conclusion of all the evidence, the court and the parties were ready for the closing arguments. The court decided to allow each side a total of 60 minutes. In all criminal cases, the state, because it has the burden of proof, is allowed to divide its argument into two segments; one before the defense's and one after. However, the second argument cannot be longer than the first. Goodrich decided to split his time 31 minutes for the first half and 29 for the second. The defense is not given an option to divide his argument.

In close cases, closing arguments can be very significant. Most experienced and talented prosecutors save the most inflammatory and damaging part of the closing for the second half. That way, the defense cannot respond other than through objections. Goodrich would do just that. He knew a lot of eyes and ears would be on what he had to say. He also knew Cardwell would put an acquittal squarely on his shoulders. While that didn't trouble him, he didn't like to lose, particularly under circumstances where this would be his last trial as a prosecutor in the circuit attorney's office. He wanted to leave on a high note.

The courtroom was filled to capacity as it had been all week when Goodrich began his argument. He started by thanking the jurors for their service and then went immediately to the written jury instructions the jurors would be allowed to take to their jury room. He spent a good amount of his time discussing the elements necessary to convict for the offense of murder in the second degree, suggesting the state had met its burden for each element.

He explained, as he had during the jury selection process, they had to follow the law given to them by the court, but they and they alone, would decide the facts. They were free to believe or disbelieve any witness. Credibility was something they would determine. He pointed out that merely because a person said something didn't make it so. They were free to believe or disbelieve the statement or opinion. Finally, he told them to use their common sense in deciding what the facts were. Determine who had a stake, financial and otherwise, in the outcome of the case and who didn't, a clear reference to the defense and his experts. As expected, his argument was straightforward and low key. He set the stage for an aggressive and inflammatory finish.

Felbin wasted no time launching his attack, starting with his favorite target, the circuit attorney. He described Joan Cardwell as a political opportunist who wanted to become a judge and would stop at nothing to achieve her goal. Her ambitions were derailed when she lost the Cannon case.

"And that, ladies and gentlemen, is why we are here today," Felbin told the jury.

He went on to explain Joan Cardwell needed the scalp of a police officer to curry the favor of those politicians who were upset with her loss in the Cannon case. Although he didn't specify, Felbin was obviously referring to those black politicians who were upset that a white police officer was acquitted by an all-white Kansas City jury of feloniously assaulting a black, mentally-challenged young man in his own home.

"And that is why the circuit attorney didn't bother to wait for the autopsy of the brain to be completed before charging this police officer with the crime of murder. You will recall the testimony of Doctor Long. He told the circuit attorney he was having Doctor McHenry do the autopsy of the brain, a process that would take several weeks to complete. Three to four weeks, to be exact. But did the circuit attorney wait for that process to be completed so she could get the full picture? No. She charged this officer with murder the very next day. *Unbelievable.*"

"But let me explain to you why she did that. Doctor Long elicited the assistance of Doctor McHenry, not because he was incapable of doing the autopsy of the brain, but because he didn't want to take the heat and public criticism if he could not support the theory of the circuit attorney that this was a murder and the murder weapon was a flashlight. So, the very position in which he didn't want to find himself is the very position in which Cardwell put him when she charged Bobby with murder before the autopsy of the brain was completed. Now, if Doctor Long and Doctor McHenry said anything other than that this skull fracture was caused by blunt trauma with a linear object, the case would be over and they alone would be left to do some explaining. And folks, that is exactly why they refuse to acknowledge the coup contrecoup injury."

Felbin was on a roll. In the first few minutes of his argument, he had eviscerated not only his nemesis, the circuit attorney, but also two local, well-respected forensic pathologists. That was risky, particularly taking on the doctors by suggesting they were at best disingenuous in their opinions and at worst, liars. But Felbin was determined to attach those witnesses to the hip of Cardwell. He was convinced from the start that these pathologists, both of whom he considered his friends, were put in an untenable position by the circuit attorney. And once Felbin became irrevocably convinced of anything, he was not afraid to use it to benefit his client, regardless of who was on the other side of the issue. When he was in a trial, Felbin had no friends.

"Let me tell you what really happened on that rooftop that rainy night. Jordon Mitchell and his friend in crime, Daniels Jones, were caught in the act of burglarizing a pawn shop. Their goal was to avoid going to jail and that is why they split up after jumping from the upper to the lower roof. But Bobby Decker was going to do his job. He was going to arrest these burglars and take them to jail where they belonged. When Mitchell took off, Bobby was able to grab him. In effecting the arrest of Mitchell, who was resisting, his head struck one of the cinder blocks on the roof."

Felbin knew he had to be careful with this argument. Sometimes jurors get crazy ideas and disregard the instruction of law as given by the court that they are required to follow. In this case, the concern was that the jury would find his client guilty of murder, not because he struck Mitchell with a flashlight, but because he threw him into a cinder block. But Felbin knew he had to take that chance. He had to explain the fracture in a way that credibly countered the state's flashlight theory. An injury, even one that was lethal, that occurred when a police officer was trying to do his job, would be forgiven in the eyes of most reasonable people, Felbin thought.

"And that is why, when the autopsy of the brain was finally completed, two injuries were discovered. That is why Doctor Langdon called it a coup contrecoup injury. That occurs when a moving head strikes a stationary object, causing the brain to bounce off the cranium wall. In this case, the head was moving when it struck the cinder block.

"Of course, Doctor McHenry says coup contrecoup injuries only occur if the second injury lines up perfectly across from the first. But Doctor Langdon says that is nonsense because the brain does not know it has to line up perfectly."

"But the coup contrecoup injuries are not the only rebuttal to the state's flashlight theory. There is also another scientific fact that likewise dispels this theory, manufactured by the circuit attorney and supported by her friendly doctors. The fracture found on the skull is L-shaped. What does that mean? It's very simple. Doctor Fabrini explained it. No matter how hard you try, you can't make a square with a rounded object. In the context of this case, that means the L-shaped skull fracture was caused when Mister Mitchell's head struck the corner of something. When you look at the photos of the roof, the only thing that could have caused that L-shaped fracture is the cinder block which was in the area where Officer Decker struggled with the burglar and ultimately arrested him. Of course, the circuit attorney's experts never even considered that issue. Why would they? That would be inconsistent with the script that the circuit attorney gave them."

In addition to explaining the skull fracture, Felbin had to address the testimony of Officer Jake Corbett as well as that of the surprise firefighter witness. He explained that both were discredited. But he didn't stop there. He claimed each had committed perjury.

"Let me start with Officer Corbett. He is representative of this entire prosecution. He is the poster child for the circuit attorney's efforts to fulfill her judicial dream. No one will stand in the way of that dream," Felbin told the jury. "We can only imagine the pressure that was put on this police officer to come in here and lie to you. You will recall he told you Bobby Decker wanted to falsify the police report of this incident by justifying the force needed to arrest Mitchell. Initially, he told you he had a conversation with Bobby, who tried to convince *him* to lie. But when confronted with the document that *Corbett himself* prepared, he had to back off that position. Then he had to explain why he was the author of a false report that he claimed he wanted nothing to do with. His explanation: Officer Decker made me do it. Really? Bobby Decker made you spend the time typing a fictional report that you wanted nothing to do with? He also told you he didn't know he was initially targeted by the circuit attorney for prosecution along with Bobby. If he didn't know that, then he is the only one on the planet who didn't. But he did, in fact, know it and this statement is just another lie. I'm beginning to think you can tell when this guy is lying as soon as his lips move.

"Now let's talk about their rebuttal witness, the firefighter. He is the one who claimed Bobby had two flashlights, which he thought was unusual, but not unusual enough to put in his report. For this incredibly manufactured testimony, I have several comments. Why would anyone burden themselves and be weighed down carrying unnecessary equipment? Why would anyone need more than one light? How is it this guy's attention is attracted to a piece of equipment that has absolutely no significance at the time he claims to have seen it? And finally whether Bobby had one, two, or a hundred flashlights, doesn't matter. They are all round. And you can't make a square with a round object. Once again, in her desperation to win this case through manufactured testimony, the circuit attorney failed. In their rush to convict Bobby Decker, Cardwell and her witnesses either overlooked or ignored the L-shaped skull fracture, which along with the coup contrecoup injury are critical pieces of evidence."

"In the time I have left, I want to address the testimony of one more witness; perhaps the most tragic of all and the most despicable thing Cardwell did in this case," Felbin said looking at the floor and shaking his head. "I want to talk about Kathy Adams."

As soon as Felbin mentioned her name, Bobby Decker covered his face with his hands. It was unclear whether he was fighting back tears and didn't want anyone to see him in an emotional state he could not control. In all events, it was clear to even the most casual observer Bobby Decker was once again feeling the pain of a love he'd lost and would never regain.

"Cardwell used this woman," Felbin said. "She took advantage of a person who worked for her to create the impression that even the woman who loved Bobby thought he was guilty because he was unable to explain how the fractured skull occurred."

As Felbin continued, Bobby's face remained in his hands.

"But the scheme backfired. Bobby Decker was honest when he told the woman he loved, and still loves, that he could not explain the injury. Bobby knew he didn't strike him with a flashlight or anything else. But what he didn't know at the time was that a cinder block caused the injury. How could he? He didn't know about the L-shaped fracture. He didn't know about the coup contrecoup injuries. He didn't know you can't make a square with a rounded object. In short, he truly didn't know how this person he was arresting for burglary became injured. All he knew at that time was that he didn't hit him with a flashlight or anything else.

"Yet, if he wanted to fabricate something, like Officer Corbett wanted him to do, this would have been an ideal time. Certainly the woman he loved would have accepted the explanation that he had to use force in the performance of his duties," Felbin said, carefully selecting his words.

"But he didn't do that. Instead, he told that truth," Felbin said, implicitly suggesting Bobby testified during the trial. "And for that he has been rewarded. The truth will set him free. Because the truth is, Bobby Decker didn't strike Jordon Mitchell with a flashlight. And the truth is Jordon Mitchell's skull was fractured when it hit that cinder block when he was trying to avoid arrest. The truth is the circuit attorney didn't want to know the truth. If she had, she would have done a full, complete and fair investigation including waiting for the results of the autopsy of the brain before she accused Bobby of murder.

"At the end of the day, the bottom line is this: if Jordon Mitchell and his friend, Daniels Jones, hadn't committed a felony by burglarizing that pawn shop, he would still be with us. If Jordon Mitchell hadn't tried to escape, he would be with us today. Unfortunately, he made some bad choices. And unfortunately for him, Bobby Decker was doing his job."

Bobby watched intently, hands no longer covering his face, as Felbin concluded his closing argument.

"I'm confident you'll find Bobby not guilty. First, because the evidence does not allow you to conclude otherwise. The prosecution has the burden of proof. In order to meet that burden, the state must present sufficient evidence to establish guilt beyond a reasonable doubt. They failed to meet that burden in this case. Therefore, it is your sworn duty to give Bobby the benefit of all doubt and return a not guilty verdict.

"Second, the not guilty verdict will send a message to those who are thinking about committing crimes. We in this city support our police officers who are trying to do their jobs," Felbin said, his voice beginning to rise as it filled with emotion. "You will also send a message to the circuit attorney that we don't like this kind of prosecution where the bad guys come in here to testify against the good guys. Daniels Jones committed a crime. You heard him admit that right here in this courtroom. Yet he has not been prosecuted. Instead, he was used by the circuit attorney to prosecute a police officer for her own personal gain. Ladies and gentlemen, you need to send a message to Ms. Joan Cardwell. By your verdict, you need to tell her to put her personal agenda aside and do the right thing," Felbin said, his voice echoing off the walls of the courtroom. "By your verdict, you need to tell her to prosecute Daniels Jones, like she should have done from the start, after you find Bobby Decker not guilty because he was truly protecting and serving all of us."

Felbin concluded, sounding as though he had just finished a sermon at a revival meeting, "Thank you, ladies and gentlemen, for allowing me the privilege of sharing my thoughts with you."

Chapter Seventy-Two

The courtroom fell silent after Felbin completed his closing. He was effective. But the silence didn't last for long as Goodrich jumped to his feet and in a voice that eclipsed Felbin's shouted, "Yes, please send a message. Please send a message to those who live in our community and those who visit our beautiful city. You have nothing to fear from our police officers. The good ones will protect you, but the bad ones will be prosecuted and wind up where they belong in the penitentiary."

Lowering his voice, Goodrich continued, "Officer Decker is a bad police officer who executed Jordon Mitchell."

Felbin began to rise to object to the use of the word *executed,* but thought better of it. If the judge overruled his objection, he didn't want the jury to get the impression the judge agreed that this was truly an execution.

"I'm not condoning what Jordon Mitchell did. Mister Felbin is correct. He was committing a crime. But that is why we built this courthouse and that is why you are here. Justice happens here after a trial, not on the street. This man decided he was judge and jury and killed this young black man," Goodrich said pointing at Bobby while injecting a racial issue.

"Now, let's look at the evidence, starting with this L-shaped fracture nonsense. You look at these photos," Goodrich said, as he showed the pictures of Mitchell's skull to the jury. "That does not look like an L to me. And it really doesn't matter whether it looks like an L to Mister Felbin or his hired witnesses. In the end, the only thing that matters is what it looks like to each of you. I encourage you to examine these photographs carefully."

"Similarly, this coup contrecoup business," Goodrich continued, taking aim at Dr. Langdon's testimony. "They bring in some out of town high priced big shot to contradict the Medical Examiners who live and work among us. This

New York guy tells you the fracture has to be a moving head striking a stationary object because there is another bruise on this young man's brain. But our doctors, who have performed thousands of autopsies on people who live and work in this community say this theory is wrong, because the second bruise does not line up with the fracture."

"Now, ladies and gentlemen, think about that. I'm no doctor, but it seems to me if the bouncing starts at one point, you should be able to draw a straight line to the next. That is all Doctor McHenry was saying. But if you have two separate blows to the head, then you won't see that straight line. Please take a look at the photographs and see for yourselves."

Goodrich left the medical issue there. He knew there was a flaw in his argument, because he could not explain how that second internal brain bruise occurred since there was no external sign of trauma. Any attempt to offer an explanation would ring hollow. So, he decided to move on.

"Next, folks, I want to talk about those guys who get a kick out of smashing flashlights," Goodrich said, causing some of the jurors to smile. "While I respect our engineers from a fine institution like Washington University, there is a flaw in their theory. After smashing all of those flashlights they claim are identical to the defendant's, they concluded the light would be damaged if it caused the skull fracture that we have here. While that theory may or may not be true, it doesn't matter. The problem is they tested the wrong light. They didn't test the light the defendant used to kill Jordon Mitchell."

Felbin was now on his feet objecting. "Your honor, I object to the inflammatory and misleading nature of this argument," he said, obviously referring to the word *kill*, but without highlighting it by repeating the word in his objection.

"I also object to his statement that the engineers used the wrong flashlight," Felbin continued. "They tested the flashlight the prosecutor put into evidence. If that was the wrong light, why did they offer it into evidence?" he asked rhetorically. Felbin knew his objection would be overruled. But since he had only one chance to talk directly to the jury, he had to make his point through a speaking objection.

312

"The jury will be guided by the law and the evidence. Your objection is overruled. Please proceed, Mister Goodrich," Judge Bell announced, without commenting on the specifics of the objection.

"As I was saying, the engineers for whom I have the greatest respect, tested the wrong light. You will recall the testimony of George Armstrong, the firefighter on the scene that night. He does not have any horse in this race. He told you he saw a second flashlight. What reason would he have to say that if it was not true? His testimony was credible. He was credible, an honest firefighter who works with the police all the time. Why would he lie about people he has worked with and will work with in the future? The short answer is, he didn't. He saw a flashlight on this defendant's belt and it was not the light we have here. I could not bring the light he saw into court to show you, because that man didn't want us to find the weapon he used to murder Jordon Mitchell," Goodrich said, pointing to the defendant, his voice rising.

"Before I leave the issue of Firefighter Armstrong, let me briefly address one more thing. The defense says he is not credible, because he didn't put his observation in a report. Of course he didn't. Why would he? I suppose if he knew this was a murder weapon he would have included it in a report. But because he didn't know that at the time, he simply thought it was unusual but not significant enough to include in a report."

"The defense also suggests we used Kathy Adams, the defendant's former girlfriend to create some impression that even the woman he loved thought he was guilty. Ladies and gentlemen, all we can do is present the evidence. You are free to draw whatever conclusions you see fit. For me, I find it incredible that a person can sustain this type of massive skull fracture without a police officer, a trained and experienced police officer at that, knowing how that happened. This was not some little bump on the head. This was a *massive* fracture. And you don't have a clue of how that happened? Incredible."

They want you to believe Jordon hit his head on a cinder block and that is what caused the fracture. But they also want you to believe this experienced officer didn't know that either. That's not believable. Surely, there would be

313

some sign that would suggest the man who is in your custody, sustained a serious injury. But if you caused that massive injury with a flashlight, but wanted to conceal that fact, then you would claim you didn't know how the injury happened.

"Interestingly, Mister Felbin also argues that if the defendant wanted to make something up, his conversation with his then girlfriend would have been the ideal time to do that. Really? The police report didn't contain any explanation for the injury, but later he was going to offer an explanation to his prosecutor's girlfriend. Really?

"The fact of the matter is this defendant knew he could not justify striking this young man, half his size, in the back of his head with a flashlight. Think of it. If the injury was in the front of the skull, then at least he could claim he had to defend himself when Jordon was coming at him. And while that would not necessarily be a believable story, at least it would pass the straight face test. But that's not what he had. Because he hit him in the back of the head, he really was in a box and had no place to go other than to claim he didn't know how this massive skull fracture occurred. It was fortuitous that they found a cinderblock on this roof. Now, they could manufacture a defense. How convenient. Now, they could hire some high priced big shot to create a defense and explain this deadly injury. They knew they had to offer some explanation. They could not come in here and simply tell you they didn't know how this massive fracture occurred."

As he listened intently to the prosecutor's argument, helpless to do anything about it, but poised to object where necessary, Felbin thought this was a powerful point. His client had no choice but to claim he didn't know how the injury occurred because of the location. He just hoped the jury didn't think the same thing.

"Ladies and Gentlemen, the prosecution has met its burden of proof. We have proven beyond a reasonable doubt, in fact, beyond any doubt, that this defendant murdered a young, defenseless, black man. This community, as well as Jordon Mitchell, await your decision. I know you'll do the right thing and return a guilty verdict. There is no other choice."

When the prosecutor concluded his argument, the Sheriff led the jury to a room where they would begin their deliberations. Meanwhile, Bobby and his lawyer left the courthouse, surrounded by security, to await word of the verdict in Felbin's office. Trials were difficult and stressful. But awaiting a jury verdict was the worst part of any trial.

Chapter Seventy-Three

Bobby and his lawyer rode in silence to Felbin's office, each wondering what the jury was thinking. How would the prosecutor's closing argument shape the thought process? How long would they be out? What would happen if there was a guilty verdict?

Once inside the office, Bobby broke the silence by asking his lawyer to speculate on the outcome. He knew when he asked the question that Felbin really had no way to know. However, he just wanted someone to say something. He wanted this to be over. One way or the other, Bobby Decker needed closure. He wondered how he was going to put his life back together if the outcome was favorable. Was that even possible? He'd lost forever the woman he loved. He'd lost a father, perhaps forever, perhaps not. Regardless, he couldn't remember the last time he saw or talked to his father. And his job was hanging by a shoe string. He had been suspended without pay since he was indicted. Whether he could keep the job he loved and that had cost him so much, remained to be seen. Would this life be any different than a life in the penitentiary, he wondered, feeling sorry for himself.

Bobby's thoughts were interrupted by his lawyer's enthusiastic response to the rhetorical question. "I think we are going to be okay," Felbin said, sensing his client was and had been depressed for a while.

"What happens if you are wrong?" Bobby asked, his voice lacking any emotion.

"The jury would then decide the issue of punishment. We would get to put on evidence to minimize that punishment and the state could put on evidence to maximize. After listening to the evidence and arguments from the lawyers, the jury would then retire again to deliberate the sentence," Felbin said, always amazed about how little police officers knew about the criminal justice system in which they worked.

After fully comprehending what Felbin was saying, Bobby finally said, "I again want you to know that, regardless of the outcome, I appreciate everything you have done for me. I think you did a fantastic job. Thanks for being not only my lawyer, but also my friend. You believed in me from the beginning when others left me on that rooftop."

Felbin's assistant interrupted the conversation when she entered the conference room carrying an envelope addressed to Robert Decker. It was from the Department. Bobby took the envelope and stared, first at the envelope and then at his lawyer. He knew what was inside. After what seemed like an eternity, he read the letter. It was as he expected. The Department would seek his termination, regardless of the outcome of the trial. The charges they would use to accomplish that were enclosed. Slowly, Bobby carefully refolded the cover letter and charges and returned both to the envelope. His face was expressionless. He said nothing, but he didn't have to. Felbin knew what it was.

"Listen, Bobby, we can fight this. They have to give you a trial before the Board of Police Commissioners before they can terminate you. We get to cross examine and put on evidence. We can beat this, too," Felbin said, knowing full well that board trials were perfunctory at best. After the dog and pony show, the board would rubber stamp whatever the Chief wanted. And in this case, the Chief's wishes were pretty clear.

Bobby's silence continued. He acted like he didn't even hear his lawyer. Or if he did, it didn't matter. He awaited a jury verdict. But one that might not matter.

During the hours the jury deliberated, Felbin kept an eye on his client who sat in the conference room staring at the St. Louis landscape. There was little conversation and then only polite acknowledgements.

Both Felbin and his investigator had been worried about Bobby since his arrest; a demeaning experience for anyone, but particularly for a cop. If that wasn't enough, he'd been publically humiliated by the media and demonized by the circuit attorney. Although not medically trained, they could recognize depression. For Bobby Decker, that depression seemed to get worse as the trial progressed.

His condition worsened with the testimony of Corbett, but reached its peak when Kathy Bates, the woman he loved, tried to help the prosecution put him behind bars for a long time. Hopefully, a defendant's verdict would come soon and Bobby could get the professional help he needed.

"Why do you think she did it?" Bobby asked, at one point breaking his silence, if only briefly, and obviously referring to Kathy.

"I don't think she had a choice, Bobby. I think her despicable boss made her do it," Felbin said.

Bobby didn't respond, which left Felbin wondering whether his client agreed with his explanation or whether he simply asked a rhetorical question, knowing there really was no explanation why someone you love would do such a thing.

As Felbin studied Bobby's facial expression, his assistant reentered the room. This time she announced there was a verdict.

Bobby said nothing, leaving Felbin to wonder whether he'd heard the announcement.

"Bobby, we have a verdict," Felbin said.

Still no response.

"Bobby," Felbin repeated.

"Yes, I heard you," Bobby finally said.

Chapter Seventy-Four

The security at the courthouse was double what it was during the trial. Armed deputy sheriffs lined the stairs leading to the entrance, holding the crowd back so Bobby and his entourage could enter the building. As he and Felbin climbed the stairs, surrounded by armed, off-duty plain clothes police officers, Bobby could hear the comments from the crowd that lined the steps.

"You're going down, Decker," someone shouted.

"You're gonna get what you deserve, you child murderer," another yelled.

Bobby tried to ignore the unwelcome commentary. But it was impossible. As he went through the first metal detector at the front door, he wondered whether he would be leaving through this same door today. He also wondered how freedom would feel if he was acquitted. Nothing felt good at the moment.

After proceeding through the second metal detector at the front door of the courtroom, he scanned the room filled with spectators, news media and armed deputy sheriffs who lined each of the four walls. His family, excluding his father, sat in the first row directly behind the defense table and across the aisle from the Mitchell family, who sat behind the prosecution table. Goodrich and his staff were already in their seats. Bobby took the seat at the counsel table he'd occupied throughout the trial, next to Jack Reilly, who sat to the right of Felbin. As soon as he sat down, two deputies positioned themselves behind Bobby. Felbin wondered whether they knew something he didn't. Were they poised to take him into custody after the verdict was announced? His questions would soon be answered.

After the courtroom door was closed and secured both inside and out by armed security, the court reporter entered the room and took her seat behind her stenographic machine and in front of the judge's bench. Shortly after the arrival of the court reporter, the jury filed into the room in the order in which they were seated. None looked at the defendant as they took their seats. Some defense attorneys theorize that if the jurors don't look at the defendant as they enter the room after completing their deliberations, the result is a guilty verdict. Felbin hoped this case would be the exception to that theory.

Once the jury was seated, the bailiff asked everyone to rise as the judge took the bench.

Looking at the jury, Judge Bell asked, "Have you reached a verdict?"

A white male in his mid-forties, juror number five, stood to respond to the judge's question. He was selected by the jury to be the foreperson and he was holding the verdict in his right hand. "We have, your honor," he said.

"Please hand the verdict to the bailiff," the judge directed.

After retrieving the verdict from the foreperson, the bailiff carried it across the room and handed it to the judge.

The judge unfolded the paper and looked at the decision. He then counted the signatures to be sure that all 12 jurors had signed the verdict form. In any criminal case, all 12 jurors have to agree on the verdict.

"Will the defendant please rise?" the judge said.

Bobby Decker, along with his attorney, stood to receive the verdict.

Before announcing the result, Judge Bell addressed the audience.

"When I read this verdict, I expect there to be order in this courtroom. The deputies have been instructed to remove anyone who cannot follow that directive. Thereafter, you'll be visiting with me to discuss the consequences of your behavior and the violation of my order."

After surveying the courtroom to be sure the security was in place, Judge Bell began to read the verdict.

"On the charge of murder in the second degree, we the jury find the defendant NOT GUILTY."

Despite the judge's admonition, a mixture of jeers and cheers erupted from the entire audience. The judge immediately reached for and slammed his gavel on the bench, demanding order.

"Does either side wish to have the jury polled?" he asked.

In any jury trial, after the verdict is published, either side can request individual jurors be asked whether the verdict that was just read is, in fact, their verdict. Obviously, Felbin had no desire to request this and Goodrich declined the invitation.

"Robert Decker, the jury having found you NOT GUILTY, you are hereby discharged and are free to go. This court will stand in recess," Judge Bell announced as he stood and left the bench.

The case of *State of Missouri v. Robert Decker* was over. Or at least the trial was over. Bobby felt relieved as he embraced his attorney. The deputies would not allow anyone inside the rail that separated the spectators from the lawyers.

To his surprise, Goodrich came to the defense table and extended his hand to Bobby. "Congratulations," he said, as he turned to Felbin to offer the same congratulatory message.

The circuit attorney was not in the courtroom. Presumably, she didn't want to answer the questions which would surely be asked, given the nature of Felbin's defense.

Still in shock, Bobby walked to the rail and embraced his mother, who was in tears. "Love you, Mom," he whispered in her ear.

Turning to his brother, he said, "Thanks for all of your help and support," as he embraced him.

The reporters were waiting on the steps of the courthouse, anxious to get the defense comments, particularly since the prosecutors declined to be interviewed. The questions began as soon as Bobby and Felbin stepped outside. For the most part, they were routine. How do you feel? Are you glad to be out from under criminal charges? Were you confident you would be found not guilty? Do you have any animosity toward the circuit attorney? Do you think these charges should never have been brought? One question, however, was unexpected.

"Do you think that you'll get back together with Kathy, now that you have been acquitted?" one reporter asked.

Bobby didn't immediately respond. It was obvious the question was like a knife plunged into his heart. For a moment, his eyes began to fill. He took a deep breath, regained his composure and finally answered the question.

"Although the jury has found me not guilty, I have paid an unbelievable price simply because I was doing my job. I have been without pay, abandoned by my own Department and a family member, called a child murderer, listened to people lie—including a fellow officer, have been verbally abused everywhere I went in public, and threatened with bodily harm, including death. But those things pale by comparison to losing the one person in your life that means the most. And to answer your question, no, I don't think Kathy and I'll get back together. That part of my life is over."

"Do you think you'll resume your duties as a police officer?" Another reporter asked.

"I think that is another part of my life that is also over," Bobby said.

"What will you do?" the same reporter asked as follow-up question.

"It's hard to say. It is difficult when everything you have lived for; all the things that meant the most, are gone."

With that answer, Felbin thought it best to end the questioning and get his client out of there. Bobby needed some rest and relaxation.

When they arrived at Felbin's office, Bobby again thanked the lawyer and his staff for all of their hard work. He told Felbin he was going to get away for a little while and would call him in a few days. And with that, Bobby left.

Chapter Seventy-Five

The entire Decker family was present, including Bobby's father. Why wouldn't he be there? After all, there would be no more arguments. There would be no more disagreements about the profession Bobby had chosen and loved. The only question that remained was whether he would feel the pain of remorse for the way he abandoned his son for those many years.

Felbin sat in the front row with the Decker family. Jack Reilly and Felbin's entire office staff sat immediately in the row behind the family. After all, during the past many months, they had become like a second family for Bobby.

The room was filled to capacity, with more people outside who couldn't get in. It was a celebration. People were coming to celebrate the life of Bobby Decker. Included in that group was Gary Goodrich, the man who a week before called Bobby a *child murderer*. When Felbin spotted Goodrich in the crowd, he wasn't surprised. He'd never felt Goodrich's heart was ever really in the prosecution. His departure from the circuit attorney's office a day after the verdict, voluntarily or involuntarily, confirmed Felbin's suspicions. Sitting next to him was a former colleague, Kathy Adams, the love of Bobby's life.

Ronald Rogers, the Chief of the St. Louis Police Department was seated next to Lt. Col. Raymond Winston, the head of Internal Affairs. Their attendance was a bit of a surprise to Felbin, since they had dedicated thousands of department man hours to putting Bobby in the penitentiary. Additionally, on the day of the verdict, the Chief announced he would pursue efforts to terminate Bobby's employment with the Department, having failed in his effort to incarcerate him.

Shortly after Felbin arrived, he was approached by two women, one white and one black. They came together. They were members of Bobby's jury who publicly proclaimed he was not a child murderer. Now they wanted to be part of the celebration. Felbin thanked them for coming, telling them that Bobby would appreciate it.

As expected, Bobby's many friends and fellow officers were in attendance, including Ray Parker, his first gad-fly partner and Roy Osborn, his first sergeant. Also in the crowd was former police sergeant Tom Cannon who was also victimized by a political prosecution initiated by the same vindictive circuit attorney. Tom had been a great source of comfort for Bobby during the days following his indictment.

Jake Corbett stood alone in a corner of the room. In the days following his testimony, he was ostracized by his fellow officers. Perhaps his attendance was a way for him to be seen and, hopefully, regain the support of his colleagues. Or perhaps he just wanted to right a wrong, whether or not fellow officers would accept his effort, so that he could once again sleep at night.

But the biggest shock of the day was the appearance of Joan Cardwell. The devil herself, the face of evil, the poster child for all that is wrong with an absence of term limits for elected prosecutors. When Felbin first saw her, he thought his eyes were playing tricks on him. But when he realized she really had come, her appearance just confirmed his belief that politicians have no souls.

As Felbin approached the podium to begin the celebration, his head was filled with emotion. He wondered whether he would be able to make it through this.

"Ladies and gentleman, I first want to thank each of you for attending a celebration of the life of Bobby Decker, my friend and former client," Felbin began as he looked at Bobby, dressed in his police uniform, flanked by two police officers, one at his head and one at his feet, both standing at attention and dressed in formal, dress blue uniforms. "As I look around this audience, I see the faces of those who supported Bobby and those who opposed him. But regardless of why each of you chose to attend this celebration, I know Bobby is grateful and so am I," Felbin said, completing his introductory remarks.

"As all of you know, the last several months of Bobby's life were difficult. He was tortured and conflicted. But Bobby Decker was a fighter. Bobby was in love. He was in love with a woman and he was in love with his career as a police officer. He would fight to keep both. But in the end, it was too much. It consumed him," Felbin said as he looked at Kathy Adams, tears streaming down her cheeks.

"Bobby Decker was a winner who didn't feel like a winner. Yes, he was acquitted of murder. His innocence was proclaimed by 12 people who didn't know him and had no interest in the case other than to find the truth. And find the truth they did. But that wasn't enough. In his mind, Bobby lost. He lost everything that truly mattered to him. Although innocent, he was convicted by those who mattered to him the most. For Bobby Decker, that was too much to bear. And so he took his life.

"In the days following the phone call I received from the officer who found him in his apartment, I have been conflicted. At first I was very angry with Bobby. How dare you deprive us of you? I thought. But then I thought about all he had endured. I also read again and again the note he left. Ultimately, I forgave him. I want to share with you some parts of that note."

"To Kathy Adams, he wrote: *I know I hurt you and let you down when I could not explain how Jordon Mitchell's injury occurred. For that I'm truly sorry. I also know you had to testify at the trial. You told the truth and for that I'm grateful. I know we will never be together again. But you need to know that I'll always love you,*" Felbin said, observing Kathy with her head in her hands weeping uncontrollably.

"To his mother, Bobby wrote: *Mom, I love you so very much. I appreciate more than you'll ever know the life you have provided me and the support you have shown over these many months. I'm truly sorry it has to end this way, but I believe it is necessary. Please respect that. I'm confident we will meet again.*"

"To his brother: *I very much appreciated all of your counsel and guidance during these turbulent times. Perhaps if I had followed the advice you gave me a long time ago, I would not have had the troubles that I did. I love you very much. I'm confident we will meet again.*"

"To his father: *I'm so terribly sorry I was such a disappointment to you. But I want you to know I was always proud to be your son. I'm grateful for guidance and advice. Unfortunately, I didn't take advantage of your good counsel.*

Please accept my sincere apology for failing to live up to your expectations as a son. I love you, Dad."

"To Jake Corbett: *We both know you didn't tell the truth. But I also understand you had a reason for doing what you did. I accept that and harbor no ill will."*

"To Joan Cardwell: *Everyone has a job to do. I had mine and you had yours. We both loved our jobs and were passionate in the performance of our duties. I respect that. I want you to know at this moment I harbor no ill will against you or your staff."*

"Bobby concluded the message this way: *Finally, I want to thank everyone who stood firmly with me during these last many months. Your commitment was more than anyone could ask for. I love all of you. Please remember me as I was before my troubles began."*

Silence filled the room after Felbin finished reading the letter. What could anybody say? Bobby said it all. But finally, after what seemed like an eternity, Felbin broke the sound of silence. "I ultimately forgave Bobby Decker for depriving me of him because he forgave me. He forgave all of us for taking a part of his life. I knew he was terribly depressed and did nothing about it. I put the warning signs— and yes, there were many—on the shelf so that we could complete the trial. I have to live with that. And for those of you in this room who took a part of Bobby's life, you'll have to live with that. Although he forgave, that was his sentence for us. Bobby decided he could no longer make a difference in this life. In his mind, he wore the scarlet letter. But I suspect Bobby thought he could make a difference in death. And that is why he wrote the note that he did. Please listen to his lesson and don't let Bobby's death be in vain. I sincerely hope we don't convict another innocent man."

When Felbin completed his remarks, he turned, looked at his friend resting peacefully, whispered, "I love you, Bobby," and walked out of the room without looking back.

Author's Note

Whether considered inspired by or based upon a true story, this book is a work of fiction. While real life events generally serve as the foundation for works of fiction, the names, characters, events and incidents in this book are the product of this writer's fertile, fictional imagination and are used fictionally.

During my 40 years as a trial attorney, I have been involved in many interesting cases that have attracted a great deal of public attention. The general story line of this work is one such example. Yes, there was a white St. Louis police officer who was charged with murdering a young black man suspected of burglarizing a pawn shop. While attempting to arrest the suspect on the roof of that pawn shop, the officer was alleged to have hit him with a flashlight in the back of the head, causing a massive skull fracture that he could not explain. And yes, there was a very public trial during which I represented the officer and experts shared their differing opinions as to the cause of death with the jury. And the jury did reach a verdict consistent with that portrayed in the book. But that is where reality ends and my fictionalization of reality begins. All the *behind the scenes* type and other portrayals of defense, prosecution and police department discussions, activities, events and incidents are fictional. Any similarity to actual people, discussions, activities, events and incidents is unintentional.

Actually, two police officers who were on the roof that night were originally charged with murder. However, before a scheduled preliminary hearing, the prosecutor dismissed the charge against the other officer. Unlike the fictional portrayal in the book, the case against that officer was not dismissed in exchange for his agreement to testify for the prosecution. In fact, during the actual trial, this officer appeared and testified on behalf of the defense.

This case also rekindled the hostilities between the black community, however that is technically defined, and St. Louis law enforcement. Prior to the events on the pawn shop roof, another white, St. Louis police officer had been charged with feloniously assaulting a mentally-challenged young black man in his own home. That part of the book is true. When the police responded to a burglar alarm sounding in the home, they found this young man who was unable to explain that he lived there and was not a burglar. A struggle ensued and a police sergeant was ultimately charged with felony assault and preparing a false police report. The black community was not only upset by the incident itself, but also with a change of venue which moved the case from St. Louis to Kansas City. I represented this officer as well. The change of venue occurred because the prosecutor failed to file a timely objection and the court had no choice but to grant the change. Ultimately, the jury acquitted the officer and the elected prosecutor was blamed for the result.

From the outset, I must say that I believed in the innocence of both of the police officers involved in these two unrelated incidents. After 40 years of a trial practice, I'm not naïve enough to believe that all the criminal defendants I represent are innocent. But with respect to the murder accusation in this case, the inability to explain how the skull fracture happened contributed substantially to my belief that my client didn't strike the suspect with a flashlight or any other object. But the beliefs of defense lawyers can't buy you a cold cup of coffee. It is only what you can prove in court to the satisfaction of 12 fair and impartial people that counts. And that was the challenge of this case. If this young man was not struck in the head with a flashlight, how did he sustain this massive skull fracture? After many long sleepless nights, the case finally came together shortly before the trial was to begin. Nationally known forensic pathologist, Michael Baden, M.D., as well as the engineers from Washington University in St. Louis, contributed substantially to the defense theory. I'm grateful to those individuals who searched tirelessly for answers.

Just as defending people accused of criminal acts in highly charged, high profile cases, cannot be done alone, writing a book is likewise not a solo adventure. First, I would like to thank my law partner, Lynette Petruska, for not only encouraging me to write this book but also allowing me to spend the last three winters in Florida working on this project while she was minding the store in St. Louis and dealing with the day-to-day problems of a busy law practice. Because self-criticism can be a difficult process, objective review is necessary in any endeavor. For that, I thank Jeannette Cooperman, Ellen Cusumano and Melinda Mortland who kept me focused and donated many hours of their valuable time, suggesting ways to improve the story and how it should be told. I'm especially thankful to Melinda for her words of encouragement and companionship during the frustrating process of finding a home for this book. Denise Bartlett, my editor and Charlotte Holley of Gypsy Shadow Publishing deserve high praise for giving an unknown writer the chance to tell this story and helping with the process of fine tuning the project. I'm also grateful to Brandy Barth for introducing me to such things as Facebook and Twitter. Also helping with the introduction to the world of social media was my Publicist, Chris Gorrell of Strategy STL. The outstanding photographs were the fine work of Bill Streeter of Hydraulic Pictures. Finally, I want to thank Robert Dodson and Thomas Moran for having the confidence in me to effectively represent them during very stressful times in their lives. I was truly honored.

One last thought remains. Somehow, someway, we need to find a way to resolve the recurring hostility between people of color and law enforcement. More times than I can count during my professional life, I have witnessed that animosity. It is unsettling indeed. While I recognize the problem, I have no solutions. But I hope and pray that people much smarter than I will ultimately find a solution that is acceptable to all.

About the Author

For the past 40 years, Chet Pleban has spent his days in a courtroom talking to juries, trying to convince them that his client was right and the opposition wrong. Many of his clients are police officers who find themselves on the wrong side of the law. In addition to representing people accused of criminal acts, he also represents those who suffered serious injuries and whose employment was wrongfully terminated. For the most part, he has spent his career representing the underdog and fighting big government or large corporations. Many of his cases are high profile. He is embraced by the media and despised by his opponents. Repeatedly, people would tell him, "Your cases are so interesting, you should write a book." So, he did.

Conviction of Innocence was a three year project that he wrote while spending the winter months in Florida away from not only the St. Louis weather but also the demands of a busy law practice. Prior to this work, his writing experience included appellate briefs and court memoranda. There are those, including some judges, who would say that is where he got his start writing fiction.

While continuing to write during the Florida winters, Pleban divides his time during the summer months between his home in St. Louis where he continues in the active practice of law and his summer home at the Lake of the Ozarks. Additionally, he enjoys his three children, Mimi and Jake who live in Chicago, and J.C., the oldest, who also practices law in St. Louis. In particular, an African safari with his daughter and golf trip to St. Andrews in Scotland with his two sons, were some of the most enjoyable and memorable times of his life.

WEBSITE: http://www.convictionofinnocencebook.com
TWITTER: https://twitter.com/ChetPleban
FACEBOOK: https://www.facebook.com/pages/Chet-Pleban/15045593

CPSIA information can be obtained
at www.ICGtesting.com
Printed in the USA
LVOW10s0244230218
567666LV00002B/210/P

9 781619 502369